ADVANCE PRAISE FOR
MOON DUST IN MY HAIRNET

"A powerful exploration of survivor's guilt and trauma. . . Creaden is an exciting new voice in science fiction."

—*Publishers Weekly*

"A poignant, tender sci-fi story with humanity at heart, about overcoming grief and finding hope beyond a ravaged future on Earth."

—Xiran Jay Zhao, #1 *New York Times* bestselling author of *Iron Widow*

"The very definition of hopepunk, *Moon Dust* is the utopian dream of fighting the good fight with kindness, compassion, and community. Inclusive and diverse characters, including the AuDHD-coded Lane, battle corporate evils with hope for positive change. . . *Moon Dust in My Hairnet* should be devoured in one sitting, completely and utterly unputdownable."

—A.J. Super, author of the *Seven Stars Saga*

"*Moon Dust in My Hairnet* brings a charming, passionate voice to its tale of the world-changing power of innocence and imagination. Beautiful and full of heart!"

—Sarah Porter, author of *Never-Contented Things*

"This book helps us dream of a better world, with valuable lessons on grief and community care. Lovable main characters break the mold in all of their neurodiverse, queer, and polyamorous glory."

—Karen Bao, author of *Pangu's Shadow* and *Dove Arising*

MOON DUST IN MY HAIRNET

MOON DUST IN MY HAIRNET

JR CREADEN

MYTHIC ROADS
~ PRESS ~

Cover illustration: Andy Ra (www.silkyflamma.com)
Cover and interior design: Patricia Veldstra

Library and Archives Canada Cataloguing in Publication

Title: Moon dust in my hairnet / JR Creaden.
Names: Creaden, J. R., author.
Identifiers: Canadiana (print) 20240295250 |
Canadiana (ebook) 20240295269 |
ISBN 9781738125401 (softcover) | ISBN 9781738125425 (Kindle) |
ISBN 9781738125432 (EPUB)
Subjects: LCGFT: Science fiction. | LCGFT: Novels.
Classification: LCC PS3603.R43 M66 2024 | DDC 813/.6—dc23

Published by Mythic Roads Press
www.mythicroadspress.com

To the stargazers, storm chasers, cloud watchers, and moon bathers—this is for us.

THE POST THAT STARTED IT ALL

0:00

[Fade in]

[A white auburn-haired girl wearing a stained lab coat smiles at the camera. She stands behind a kitchen counter neatly covered with small components.]

Faraday: Hello, fellow humans! My name is Joan Faraday Tanner, but please remember me as Faraday. Today is my twelfth birthday, and to celebrate, I'm going to demonstrate how to build a device I invented. I believe it can change the whole world, if we let it.

[She lifts a small device. It's a slim cylindrical disc, two inches in diameter.]

0:30

Faraday: I call this the gravdrive. Not only is it portable, stackable, and easy to build, it ALTERS FREAKING GRAVITY. Literally.

[She places the device on the counter.]

Faraday: One by itself can't do much. But kind of like people, if you pair them together, the effects are exponential. Yes, math fans, exponential! I'll include some graphs in the notes, or you can click above, if you want to check out results from our tests so far.

[Hyperlinks appear at the top of the screen.]

1:00

Faraday: Not only can a gravdrive grouping be used for heat or pressure—like, I don't know what you want to do with it yet, but I hope you'll tell me anything cool you figure out—but most importantly, to me, is that it could allow us to plan and build long-term settlements off planet!

[She laughs.]

1:30

Faraday: My parents' university told me I should patent and sell this invention, but I don't want to be a seller. I want to be the one who leads us to live on the moon and beyond! When I learn how to do that, you're all invited.

[A chaotic blur behind her slides into view, crashes into a wall, then ducks into a bathroom and slams the door.]

[LOUD singing sounds from behind the door.]

2:00

Lane: Pee pee in the potty! Poo poo in the potty! I'm doing it, Far'day!

[Faraday turns.]

Faraday: You are! Great job, little dove.

[She faces the camera again, smiling brightly.]

Faraday: That's my baby sister, Lane. Isn't she adorable?

[She adjusts the components on the counter, straightening them more precisely.]

2:30

Faraday: Unless your parents are weird science freak professors like mine, you'll probably have to shop around for some of the components. I'll list them in the post notes, but please share links in the comments if you find any of them for sale? Every time we lift someone else up, we all reach higher.

Faraday: All right, here's how to build it. Step one...

[Transcription skips speech except for several off-hand comments, but it includes hyperlinks to written instructions.]

Faraday: If we don't try, who will?

3:00

Faraday: Step 2...

[Hyperlink to "Updated Instructions including power variations and grouping size" ed.gra.../]

Faraday: There's no such thing as an unimportant job.

3:30

[Toilet flushes.]

4:00

Faraday: Step 3... Maybe it's not the best idea to let white people leave the planet though? I'm undecided on that but also biased because my dream is the moon.

4:30

[Water runs.]

Faraday: Step 4... I think we have a responsibility to try to make all our best ideas come true, don't you? If you have an idea I could maybe help with, I want to hear about it!

[Toilet flushes again.]

5:00

[Faraday makes a concerned look at camera.]

[Wet slapping sounds come from the bathroom, followed by more water running and dripping.]

Faraday: Excuse me for a moment.

[She approaches the bathroom door and knocks.]

Faraday: Lane?

[Inaudible speech]

Faraday: Are you okay in there?

[There's silence as Faraday raises her eyebrows at the camera.]

5:30

Lane: Nothing!!! All good here!

[Faraday crosses her fingers at the camera and returns to the counter.]

Faraday: I hope you find this helpful, and I'd love to hear from you in the comments. I don't know if I'll be making more videos anytime soon, because my next project is designing a model lunar city that's inclusive, peaceful, and self-sustaining, and if I figure out how to do that, I'll probably try to make it real and live there!

6:00

[The bathroom door opens halfway, and a small child with sopping wet curls enters the kitchen wearing a yellow sundress beneath an oversized apron, plus mismatched striped socks. She stands there stimming on her socks until Faraday says "anyway."]

Faraday: So... Happy birthday to me! That dusty white rock in the sky could be humanity's launchpad, the beginning of a shining new era of equality, interdependence, and exploration. That's what I'm aiming for, anyway. Who's with me?

Lane: Bye!

[Both girls wave at the camera, then Faraday's hand covers the screen, presumably to turn off the recording, but audio continues.]

[Faraday laughs musically.]

Faraday: All right, little stinker, what were you doing in there?

Lane: Not me! You're the stinker!

[Audio ends.]

CHAPTER ONE

STEPPING ON IT, THEN IN IT

My new home rested along Peary Crater's northern rim like a sugar balloon nestled into folds of meringue, but I was too numb to enjoy the view. My sister Faraday should have been here to witness her life's work. I plastered on a shadow of her smile as our ship landed without a hiccup.

We were the first to secede from Earth, and not one corporate state managed to stop us.

Only some of us, the very best.

That was how Lunar Trust One began, with twelve hundred nervous people squeezed single file through an insulated tube into a sprawling dome with simulated gravity. When the tube sealed, we shuffled into a gymnasium-sized room in the dome proper. I stripped off my helmet and outer suit, piling it beside the growing tower of others along the front wall. The walls reached two stories high, which was a welcome change from our suffocatingly small ship quarters. There were no windows to hint at the deep black beyond the ceiling. I knew it was there though. It had me stuck to the floor until my parents dragged me to the front where the greeting party waited.

I took position behind my parents, squeezing my boyfriend Andrek's hand. Our arrival wasn't supposed to be like this, all somber like a funeral. Faraday should have been here to lead us, and there should have been twenty-two others my age, my classmates and friends, breathing down my neck or poking me in the back to make me laugh. Instead there were hundreds of strangers, recruits hired at the last minute to fill vital positions.

I shouldn't have resented the newcomers. It wasn't their fault they were filling empty slots in the colony machine. If I were honest with myself, I was jealous of them, because they earned their positions. These people were vital to the trust's success, while I was basically human cargo. I hadn't even graduated high school; I was over a year behind before my sister died. Then it was too late to bother.

My parents hardly looked at me when they turned to check that I was still behind them. Our grief was too fresh, and our promise to make this a day of celebration too hard.

Commander Dae Han, hair cropped and gleaming like a silver helmet, activated a microphone attached to her wheelchair and welcomed us with a watery smile. She had been on the moon with other department heads and staff for over a year to get the domes ready for our arrival. Even she was muted today, despite her full-throated welcome. At her prompting, we all placed hands over hearts and followed her in reciting the Lunar Trust oath.

"I pledge my life to the Moon and the principles of peace and sustainable prosperity. I leave Earth to its suffering history, its warfare and inequality, and commit my will to a new and brighter human future. I am Lunar, and I am free." I squeaked through the vow, choking on memories that swam to the surface, tasting the words which rang as falsely sweet as the mint toothpaste stink of the crowd. So what I said was "sustainabubble property," then I smooshed the "suffering history" bit trying to find my place. Once we reached the "I am Lunar" business, I was caught up, though my voice trembled.

"Fuck you, Earth. I'm Lunar now," I added, louder than I meant to.

"Language, Lane," my mom scolded while laughter rippled behind me.

"It's what *she'd* say," a girl behind Andrek whispered, and I knew she meant Faraday. I glanced back to find that the girl was astonishingly beautiful, with hair that draped like a curtain of black silk over her oak-brown skin. She had the brownest eyes, dark and sharp like thorns.

She caught me looking, and my cheeks flushed lava hot.

I was grateful for the burn. It beat imagining what should have been. If I could make it through the day without crying, I could believe the trust would succeed, and Faraday's dream of a free, peaceful home would be safe.

"You ready for this?" Andrek hugged me so close I had to crane my neck to see his sun-kissed face. His eyes were cool blue lakes beneath wheat-colored bangs, and his smile could melt a glacier. Mensa-smart and cucumber cool, he'd been my parents' first choice for an administrative assistant.

"How can I know?" I asked, and Mom whipped around to give me her I-know-you're-not-still-talking scowl.

Andrek chuckled low. "No, I mean, *here*. This!"

"I'm trying to be." I snuggled into his side. It was still hitting me, our new reality. New prospects and problems. New chances to embarrass myself in front of people who actually belonged.

I shuddered and reset my head toward positive thoughts. No more sirens in the night. No red skies or freak storms, no corporate raids or street riots. Living on Lunar Trust One should be gravy and potatoes, hold the meat.

Dad cleared his throat quietly, telling me to pay attention, so I focused on hearing Han as her amplified voice rattled on with reminders. It was the only sound aside from the rhythmic hum of air pumps and hushed conversations.

Two women pushed forward, arguing as they beelined toward Han. The trust president Aya Marshall and her second Rosamund Barre. Both had been presidential nopefuls who had never stood a chance at leading anything beyond a committee while my sister was alive. Marshall, a sharp-eyed

Black engineer from the Pacific Northwest, was a longtime friend of my parents and one of my sister's early tutors. She and Barre—a willowy political scientist from Free Brazil—stood tall beside Han, appearing far more rested than they had any right to be.

"I realize everyone's tired from the journey and eager to unpack and explore, but I think it's important we reflect on how far we've come against terrible odds," Barre said. "More importantly, we need to take a moment of silence to honor those we've lost on our way to achieving this valiant dream."

"A moment of silence is essential, yes," Marshall interjected, projecting her voice to be as loud as it was warm, despite the critical glance Barre shot her. "But let us speak their names before we assign our loved ones, our leaders, into the past." At that, she brought out a tablet and began to read carefully, adding each person's assigned position with deliberate pauses.

As she read, the fact that I, the least of us, was the only survivor under twenty-five from the original Masdar Collective made each syllable hit like a bullet.

They weren't all my friends, the ones who died with my sister. In truth, I had hated nearly half of them for being pandering fans of hers while being condescending asshats to me, until me and Andrek hooked up. Aside from the twenty-two plus Faraday, there were one hundred forty-seven other adults to be named, many of them the movers and shakers that had made this dream more than a paper wish.

I chewed my cheek into pulp before she reached my sister. *Joan Faraday Tanner, inventor, humanitarian, visionary, and presidential candidate.* Her lovely face—bloody and broken, gasping its final breath—took over my vision. She was the important daughter, the smart and special one, while I, a common lunch lady, was easily replaceable. The star was dead, but the dropout flamed on.

I wondered if everyone in the trust knew how much I sucked and, if they did know, what it would take to make them forget. When Marshall stopped and Barre declared our moment of silence, I felt as small as a bug and less significant.

"Speak with your department head if you have questions, and again, congratulations. It's an honor to support you all through this transition," Han concluded, and her microphone clipped as she shut it off.

Mom looked at me like she was waiting, and I guessed she either couldn't see the pain on my face or simply decided not to comment. My mother had never wiped my tears. That was not her way, but she was the first to take charge of anything else. Years on the coast had darkened her ivory skin to a peachy pink, and her auburn hair was now streaked with gray.

"I hate to leave you now, but we're expected in the lab." She sounded syrupy and wrong, and Dad's hand was sweaty when he patted my back. "I'm sure Andrek won't mind if you need help getting settled in."

"I'll manage. It's not like I can wander off." I pressed my lips together to stop words spilling further, since the more stressed I got, the more likely I was to stick my foot in my mouth. I was an expert word-vomiter, but I was sure there was no career in it aside from being my sister's comic relief. Mom used to say someday my light would shine, as if the only thing between me and my sister's brilliance was other people's attention.

She didn't get me at all.

"We won't work late," Dad promised.

I swallowed a laugh. First night on the moon in their swanky new lab, and they weren't going to work late? They would be puppies in a ball pit for the next year at least. I couldn't blame them. I would be lucky if I liked working in the kitchen half as much as they liked ordering people around.

"Go on. I'll be fine," I said, hoping against history it was true.

Mom gave me a weak hug, and she and Dad disappeared into the crowd. After more than a decade playing with mockup designs, I ought to have known exactly where they were headed, but I didn't have a clue. Reality was so much bigger than my sister's models.

The speed of their step, the hard set of their jaws—they were on a mission already. I was too, to fake it till I made it or whatever. Keep it inside. Distract, deny. Everything would feel better with time. For now, that was the most I dared hope.

After I checked in with the chef to get my work schedule and required uniform, Andrek and I found an empty spot near the western hallway to people watch while waiting for our cases to be delivered to our quarters. I fiddled with the mesh hairnet I'd have to wear, trying to figure out how to position it without cutting off circulation to my brain. It took some doing, but at last I tweaked it into some kind of floppy shape that held my flyaway hairs.

"Masterful," Andrek said, which made me yank the thing off immediately.

I bopped his nose. "I don't need a babysitter. You can go to work too. If you want."

"Oh, I can, huh?" He laughed with his whole face. "You think I'm sticking around for you?"

I crossed my arms. He definitely was, though whether it was to hang out or keep me from having a meltdown, I wasn't sure. I didn't have autistic meltdowns that often any-more, not like when I was little. My sister had promised it'd be easier in the dome, because she kept potential sensory triggers close to mind in her design.

"I'm not staying to play zip-Lane's-mouth. I'm on the hunt. There are dozens of eligible partners to scout, and now's my chance to find out if any are cute as you. So you know, get over yourself."

I grinned at him. We had been an item for over a year, and we talked a lot about growing our circle. I'd always liked girls, even kissed a few, but I hadn't met one I wanted to date. Now hardly seemed like the time, with my sister filling my head like a ghost and all the newness of being on the moon. Still, that shouldn't stop Andrek, who likely needed a break from my family drama.

"Hey, everyone! Line up so Andrek can decide if you're as cute as me," I called out. "Tops preferred, please."

"What do you mean by that?" Andrek demanded, pinching my waist, but I doe-eyed him innocently.

A rich laugh rolled over my head, and we spun in surprise.

"Should we queue here then?" A striking Black guy, dark-skinned and head shaved, breezed toward us with that thorn-eyed girl on his arm. He had an accent I didn't recognize. It was slow and round, leaning on the ends of his words.

"I was joking," I mumbled, feeling my cheeks heat all over again.

"Pity." The guy studied Andrek like he was a museum sculpture. "I'm quite good at queuing."

"I bet. I'm Andrek. She's Lane." He pulled himself so tall he was almost on his toes.

"Joule," he answered. "Joule Sarka. As much as I'd like to stay and change your minds, I'm supposed to report in immediately. Manufacturing waits for no one and such. See you both at dinner, I hope?" He pulled his arm free of the girl and darted away, but not before giving Andrek a not-so-subtle wink.

We watched him go—Andrek visibly pulsing with the unexpected attention, and the gorgeous girl he'd left behind tensing with barely concealed annoyance.

"Viveca Osborne." Her full lips slid out her name as if it were made of velvet. It nearly was, and it was weirdly familiar. She swept her gaze past me like I was invisible and lifted a delicate hand for Andrek to shake. "You're Andrek Evers? The one who accepted the position with Dr. and Mr. Tanner?"

Andrek hesitated, and I came to my senses.

Viveca. The only real contender for the position Andrek

had won. The way my parents had talked about her in breathless wonder, I'd considered petitioning for private quarters.

"Viveca's application was flawless. Flawless!" Mom had mused, and Dad's face had lit, gazing over our heads like the mystery girl approached from the stars.

Dad had muttered something about, "You know who she reminds me of?" because everyone beautiful must resemble my sister somehow. Then they'd consoled themselves about passing her over because "Medical needs minds like hers" and "she'll be running things before long anyway." The fact that she hadn't landed a position in the first round had probably saved her life.

"We may have heard of you," Andrek answered warily and clamped a hand on my shoulder.

"I was hoping to talk to you about a security petition your department rejected. How are we preparing for more attacks from the Royal Corps? Without the war crimes accord, we're far more at risk than our constitution anticipated. Brand Masters isn't the type to give up once he has sights on a goal, and the shipyards are still—"

"Best to leave such things to our leaders." Andrek made a low noise in the back of his throat, like he always did when someone mentioned Brand, the Royal Corps' tyrannical leader.

I went blank, refusing to react.

Here on the moon, the RC was thousands of miles away, like it was supposed to be from my thoughts. They were corporate soldiers, a mercenary group that had outgrown its original design then ate up free states as they fell.

When I was little, the Pacific Northwest faced a viral outbreak during an epic winter, and the RC happened to have a base nearby with supplies and a conveniently worded emergency contract. The PNW's sovereignty got crunched like celery.

Then the United Kingdom suffered a drought leading to an economic collapse, and the RC slurped them up too. State by state, across the planet, everything slipped into the RC's stew.

Brand tried to get his claws into the lunar collective in Masdar, hungry for the ships the trust meant to build on the moon, but my sister had refused to cooperate. That was probably why he had her killed, to break the accord and weaken our resolve before we could launch and fulfill the trust's goals. It had almost worked.

"Especially today," Andrek insisted.

"I think security should be on everyone's mind today, particularly if we intend to be here tomorrow," Viveca snapped. "Particularly the two of you."

His voice flattened. "Admin passed the petition on to operations. Maybe check with them about it?"

It hit me then that operations, a department that used to manage defense and internal affairs, was now in charge. Not my parents or the board, and definitely not my sister, but President Marshall and operations. Aside from the small command crew that traveled with us, a bare dozen survivors, there was only Commander Han's skeleton security detail who were already on the moon.

"Operations… I see. I'll do that. Thank you." She coolly shifted her perfect eyes to me, and just like that, I was visible again. "You're the other Tanner girl?"

"That's me. The leftovers." I shoved out my other hand to take hers then shook it quick, trying not to notice how it was smooth as rose petals. Like, it was painful letting go. How the hell was she so moisturized? My skin had turned to chalk on the ship.

A wistful expression ghosted over her face. "It's so sad about your sister. She was my hero, and she always seemed proud of how I ran her fan club."

I huffed and tried to cover the noise with a cough. Faraday was everyone's hero, but hearing Viveca say it sounded off. Possessive. I should have been used to that, what with the entire world following Faraday on social media and treating her like science royalty my whole life. I thought my sister would have laughed in this girl's face for being so self-centered she deserved an award. I was about to say so, but something warned me she was a lot faster with comebacks than I'd ever be.

"Anyway," she continued. "Your name's on a list for the daily grief groups, and I wanted to invite you to mine."

"Grief groups." I blinked at her. "Did you lose someone too?"

"Not recently, but it's not like grief ever ends exactly. My experience with your sister might help you process her death."

She didn't hide the word "death" like everyone else. It wasn't "her passing" or "our loss." She'd probably call the invasion what it was—a massacre, a murder—instead of a political tragedy. As much as I liked that, preferred it even, I couldn't tell what she was really asking.

"You knew my sister?"

"I see how you might think so, but no." She lowered her lashes to study her shining nails. "We never got to meet in person."

"I don't understand," I said, feeling thick-headed. She didn't speak too fast, but somehow nothing she said fit together. "What experience do you mean unless... Wait, you think being a fangirl should give you access to my pain? That's—that's like—" My voice broke and my insides went slippery as if tears were going to rip through my paper-thin mask.

Andrek's grip tightened on my arm, less protective than preventative in case I started throwing punches, which suddenly seemed like a distinct possibility.

Viveca sniffed prettily. "You misunderstand. See, I was referring to my research experience about your sister. I'm working on my psychiatry degree and apprenticing in counseling. So 'my' group is the one I'm in myself."

I stared hard at her mouth and sipped a slow breath as I pieced her words into sense. She had studied my sister. Studied, like for a science project. My arms went icy and stiff, my tears forgotten.

"You want to counsel me? What am I, your next book report?"

"It's called a thesis, but you're missing what I'm saying."

"Wow." I'd lost all feeling in my fingers, and my heart had started to pound. This girl made me want to crawl out of my skin. "Do you study torture too?"

She shook her beautiful head in confusion like I was the one being horrible. "Torture would be malpractice."

"Oh my god!" I said, nearly screaming.

"Well. When you calm down, I hope you'll think about joining. We'll be in the courtyard before breakfast." She smoothed the hair that fell over her chest and smiled with total confidence. "It was nice meeting you both. Ta!"

Andrek let out a low whistle as she walked off. Even in the stiff, unflattering jumpsuits we wore, Viveca was all curves and legs forever. Beauty and brains and buckets full of obliviousness.

I exhaled less musically through my teeth and worked to unclench my hands. "She's a lot, right? Like, a whole lot."

"That's one way to put it." He lifted my hand and kissed it. "Are you okay?"

"Just wow."

We were both quiet a moment, letting the Viveca storm wash away, then his mouth twisted, fighting a smile. "Do you think you'll go to your new best friend's group? Seems like it might be incredibly helpful. For me. And my very important entertainment research."

"I hate you so much."

"I know." He wrapped arms around my shoulders and tipped his forehead to mine. "I hate you too."

I rested against him, soaking in his warmth and steady heartbeat, inhaling the autumn sweetness that lived in his skin. I wished I could stay cocooned in his arms so my tears might dry up and my lungs refill. I could pretend that Faraday was only a room away, alive and brimming with plans to fix everything that was wrong.

"Andrek?" His name came out muffled because my mouth was buried in his jumpsuit.

"Yeah?"

"I am going to need counseling probably. I mean, not with that snobby fangirl, but..."

He sighed softly, and it buzzed in my ears. "That's probably a good idea."

I kept my eyes closed for as long as I could stand still. If my sister had been here, she'd have been dragging us around to gaze out the viewing windows and explore every room. Her famous smile would've flashed with who-knows-what-comes-next eagerness, followed by her giggles of let's-find-out. I was nothing like her, a decider, a leader, a peacekeeper. I was hardly a whole version of myself since she died and poked through my half-baked identity, leaving me to collapse in the too-cool oven of her lunar scheme.

None of this was what I wanted, but I didn't remember how to want anymore. It used to be so easy, because I had never chased great big things—that was for my sister to do—and I could wish for simple, tiny things like an evening on the town or a new game console. How was I supposed to wish for anything else again, when nothing would change that she was gone and I wasn't?

Fresh tears gathered in the corners of my eyes like dust bunnies under a bed. "Let's find our quarters. I'd rather not cry here."

Attention: ALL

Subject: Evening Menu

Entrees: Golden lentil dal, chickpea enchiladas, beetroot curry

Sides: Cucumber and tomato salad, mashed potatoes, frozen white grapes

Beverages: Apple juice, almond milk, two water tubes

CHAPTER TWO

HER URNSELF AND US

My sister found fame while I was still trying to find my way to the toilet on time. That was in 2042, fifteen years after the United States splintered, and ten years after the United Nations fell too.

Faraday, of the melt generation like me, grew up in a world where whole cities and countries went the way of Atlantis. Coastlines changed, borders shifted, industries imploded or adapted, and nothing, not the sky or the trees or childhood itself, looked like it did in the sitcoms and movies our tightly controlled internet coughed up.

In an era of tragedy and greed, of shredded governments and burning forests, my sister arrived like a glitter bomb. A shiny, splodey, inescapable positive packaged into one unforgettable little girl who only got brighter as she grew. In her comments section, a community took root, branching across language barriers and paradigms until we ended up here. She brought the world hope that the future could be better, that the present wasn't all bad, and it loved her without restraint.

She made me blueberry pancakes, the one meal she never messed up, and I loved her even more.

The world wanted everything from her, but all I wanted was more time.

As Andrek and I walked through the hallways her dream built, the press of the crowd waiting in line to use the washrooms or milling near their quarters lulled me into a fog of sensory overload.

I was listening but not. Aware but not. My thoughts slipped around the crater in my heart as I fought not to fall in. This blurry-brain moment lasted a little too long, and I forgot where I was. Then Andrek and I were in the central room of our family quarters already.

The front door acted more like a hatch on the ship than a regular door; it slid open with an electric whoosh and sealed shut behind us. Inside, there was a couch, two chairs, a table, and a desk, which was all we had to ourselves besides three tiny bedrooms connecting to the back wall. Andrek would take the room originally assigned to my sister. It didn't matter that she would have had her own family quarters if she'd lived. Leaving it empty would have been too much for all of us.

It felt nothing like Faraday's flat with her fiancés—full of sunshine and open flames—where I'd spent most of last year feeding her campaign staff, and it was nothing like our cozy apartment in Masdar either. Where she was happy until she wasn't. Where I was happy until she died.

"Home sweet home," I said and tried to hide my inner cringe.

Four crates blocked the couch. Andrek and I had packed ours a week before the invasion and hadn't seen them in the four very long months since. I snapped alert, suddenly aware of what I'd find within and how perfectly it fit the shape of the hole inside me. An overwhelming need to hold my belongings in my hands and connect to the me I'd been before filled me like hot air in a balloon. The me who'd packed this crate had been a child. Vulnerable, gullible. She'd still thought good things happened to good people, and her big sister would survive to build and launch a hundred ships.

After dropping to the carpet, my fingers tore at the crate. The popping lock was somewhere along the molded indentations around the rim, but I couldn't find it, and the stupid thing had no markings to tell me which one was right. I turned it round and round, growing so annoyed with it and myself that I was mashing every spot I could fit my thumb into. What was wrong with this thing? Why couldn't I make it work?

"Wait. Stop," Andrek said. "Maybe we shouldn't just open them."

I froze, my hands an inch above the cover, jutting forward like weak branches loaded with snow. "Why not?"

My voice was oddly breathy and shrill, and Andrek squinted at me with those clever blues for a long, silent moment. Don't ask if I'm all right, I begged silently. Don't tell me I'll feel better if I talk about it.

"Can we make this special somehow?" he asked finally. "Today's been..." He took a few steps toward his bedroom and winced, stopping to lean against the wall.

"Your leg?" I didn't wait for him to answer. It was my turn to hold him up. I supported him to the stiff couch. The frame was hard printed plastic, but the cushions weren't horrible aside from being a sad beige. "But yeah, today's been so heavy. And the vow," I managed, thinking how rushed it was, seconds from arrival, how hard it was to say any of those words without her there.

Andrek rubbed his jaw like he was sharpening his chin. "She's all I could think about too. How are you holding up?" He hiked up his right pant leg, and I tugged off his boot and the cover that reached his thigh.

I wanted to tell him I was fine, that I was handling it, that being here without Faraday was no big deal. He'd see through me no matter what I said.

"It wasn't supposed to be like this," I admitted. "And it's so much harder than I—You know."

He got the locking pin, and I pulled off his prosthetic, setting it on the couch. When my gaze lingered on the scorch mark along the shin, he turned it the other way. Once he unrolled the sleeve and tossed it aside, he sprawled out and patted his hand over his heart. "Please?"

I went to him, laying my head on his warm chest. I let him stroke my hair and kiss my head and whisper obvious things like "I know" and "I'm here." He held me till my trembling slowed. We shared an easy quiet, and for a second, I forgot the crates.

"Do you think my parents will make it in time for dinner?"

"Not a chance." He drew his finger across my thigh and slid me a smile. "Unpack later?"

I didn't need convincing. When he kissed me, I wasn't missing my sister or worrying about how to exist without her. I wasn't thinking about the empty spaces where the lost voices should live. Plus, Andrek's touch was electric. The perfect distraction.

Apparently, sex pre-melt had been this mega big deal. Like, everyone was obsessed with virginity and monogamy and other stuff that made no sense. I didn't know why they'd been like that, but I did know why they stopped.

The melt hadn't only changed coastlines on maps; it changed minds, especially when whole high school classes started offing themselves en masse, leaving group suicide notes that said things like, "There's nothing to live for and no promise of tomorrow anyway." Pharmacies couldn't keep up with demands for antidepressants and anti-anxiety medicines, and it wasn't like folks could be told the tired old adages about "going outside for recreation" or "saving themselves for marriage" when *outside* had pretty much been an off-limits death trap half our lives, and no one, not even the rich, could ensure there'd be enough water to live another week, let alone until some far-flung marriage date. Contraceptives became more common than candy, and the old rules collapsed along with the climate.

I'd had sex for the first time at fourteen, and it was only that, sex. A natural high of hormones and endorphins. Something to do that didn't cost anything or exhaust resources. My parents knew, and from what I could tell, they were happy I wasn't falling into the same depression others had.

Sex wasn't, and wouldn't be, a cure for the sort of rampant existential malaise that rocked humanity. But it was fun that was easy and harmless and loads better than losing a generation to suicide.

Andrek and I raced each other out of our jumpsuits to join the Moon High Club.

Sometime later, Andrek was fast asleep on the couch, and all I had left to unpack were my parents' crates, which had been filled only days before launch. I used to fall asleep as easily as him, but I couldn't stop the images playing in my head when I laid down anymore.

I scooped out their belongings little by little, doggedly trying to fill our drab quarters with familiar touches. Rare paper memories—hardcover journals, stuffed with letters and keepsakes—I stacked neatly on the desk in my parents' bedroom. Our family photos were stored on a digital frame, which activated as I picked it up, showing flour floating like snow over me and Faraday as we were caught in a moment of laughter during another of her failed baking experiments. The flour shower had been Dad's doing. He always went for the drama shot. I left the frame in their room, collapsed the empty crates, and retreated with a treasure that belonged to us all.

Her urn, a shining ceramic purple sphere.

I settled her onto the couch like she was kicked back on the cushion to cuddle with Andrek's prosthesis while the rest of him napped. Imaginary Faraday was less articulate than real Faraday, and I was only me, but I did my best to put words in her mouth.

Do you know, she'd have said, *your molding and my casing are made of the same molecules? The atomic nature of matter is flexible. So, in fact, the matter that's you might actually be parts of the matter in me.* Here she'd have wiggled closer and whispered, *because when we touch, though we can never completely touch, our molecules are engrossed in an atomic conversation.*

Andrek's prosthesis would tip tap the cushion and dare her to bring her urnself closer and find out. Faraday had been funny like that, always flirting.

But the urn wasn't Faraday, not all of her. Some of her had been donated, to be studied by medical students somewhere on Earth. Her fiancés Khalid and Zara had the rest. I was on the moon, but she was divided like batches of dough. I hoped I had the laughing part and the part that talked in her sleep about pastry crust and spaceships. The part who'd daydream with me about the existence of aliens and always gave good advice.

I set her gingerly on the lone shelf over the built-in table. She looked so small there that I almost packed her back into the crate. She would have wanted to be in a kitchen, trying once again to master anything besides pancakes, but we had no kitchen. Water was precious and controlled, so there wasn't a dispenser or a bathroom in our quarters. I came around the couch and fell into a chair, heavy with too many thoughts and too much newness.

I wished I could skip to the part where being here felt normal.

Andrek woke and rubbed his face. His gaze lingered on Faraday's urn then me. "Want to talk about it?"

An involuntary chuckle rocked my shoulders. Where would I start? "About what?"

"Anything." He collected his jumpsuit and started to dress. "Your job maybe."

"What's there to say? I'm looking forward to being a lunch lady. I mean, it's not glamorous or anything, but..." I struggled for the best words as cozy memories rolled through me—sniffing fragrant steam as I stirred soup on the stove, measuring spices to tip into mixing bowls, taste-testing my sister's latest experiment. I remembered her baking face, the hope shining in her voice as she'd asked me, "What do you think, dove? Good enough to serve?" No matter how busy she'd been pounding out settlement designs or answering her endless fan mail, she'd always found time to cook with me, though nearly all her attempts were inedible compared to mine.

I hadn't been in a kitchen since her death, but I'd missed it. Needed it.

"I think it'll be good. I wouldn't want to do anything else, even if I were qualified. Which I'm not." Except now that I considered it, my favorite part about serving food might not prove as pleasant as it had been during my sister's campaign. I'd always enjoyed talking with people, seeing their faces every day. That would still happen, but now everyone would see me, all of me, with no sister to hide behind.

"Would I sound like an asshole if I said I'm jealous?" He hopped till his foot clicked into place. "Because I am. After meeting Pretty McSnobface, I worry that's going to be my usual gig, listening to people complain about decisions I don't get to make, like an unhappiness secretary."

I heard what he wasn't saying, that slender space he avoided. Everything should have been different. We were supposed to be safe here. Safe and happy. Departments hand in hand like old friends, like family. Instead we were strangers facing unknowns with uncertainty.

"At least you're doing something you like," he said. "And your food's amazing."

I shrugged, but I was grateful he was shifting the subject. "They were all Khalid's mom's recipes."

"Which you cooked and plated. Face it, Lane. You've got a gift."

I didn't answer, but he was talking nonsense, the way smart people liked to do when they thought they under-stood something not-as-smart people dealt with. Faraday possessed gifts, like engineering world-changing inven-tions, inspiring people through charismatic presentations, designing a sustainable independent colony, managing a successful campaign. Even challenging our single-minded parents for autonomy. Following a recipe was nothing. Half the time I ignored the measurements and I was forever winging ingredients because I get in my head, but it was still following directions, even the unwritten ones.

"Pretty McSnobface really got to you, huh?" I asked.

"No! I mean, a little. Not as much as she got to you, I think." He stared at the door to the hallway. "I guess you missed all the rest in there?"

I squinted at the door too, but I didn't sense what he did beyond. "The rest of what?"

He sat on the arm of my chair and rested his chin on my head. "I envy you so much sometimes."

"Why? What did I miss?"

"Okay, so." He settled in with a sigh. "It was like watching rapid mitosis, and not only between the new recruits and old collective but between Marshall's supporters and Barre's, plus those like your family. The *bereft*."

I thought back to the clumps of people knotting together after the moment of silence and wondered how I hadn't parsed what he had. "Was it that bad? And obvious?"

"I won't bore you with the details, but there's a shitstorm of new problems for admin and ops now that we're here. And, socially, the rifts are already showing. I was starting to think none of the recruits would cross the divide until your new best friend came over. As much as she stressed me out with the Brand Masters business, I kind of wanted to hug her for talking to us."

I guessed I had sort of noticed the command crew standing apart stiffly from the other security members, but it hadn't seemed like anything at the time. "The hugging has nothing to do with her boyfriend then, aka I'll-queue-for-you Joule?"

"Ohmigod, he was heart-stopping, right? They've got to be polyamorous, or he does, don't you think?" Andrek fake swooned and fell across my lap like a human noodle.

"Probably," I said. I wanted so badly for big deals to be in our rear view that imagining the opposite clawed at my fragile calm. "Should we be worried, though? About the RC? Viveca wasn't exaggerating about him. Brand won't give up."

"Like I said before, we should let ops handle it. Yes, our security forces are fifty percent less than they're supposed to be, and the ones we've got are strangers. But it's only the first day. We have to trust your sister's designs, our allies on Earth, and the other lunar bases, and let them do their jobs." He cupped my cheek in his palm. "Besides, what difference will worrying make, my sweet lunch lady?"

A soft alert beeped, activating a comm screen that took up most of the front wall by the door. Marshall's greeting clipped through the speakers, swallowing her first words.

Andrek went to adjust the volume, and as her voice became clear, I scanned the links that popped up. One document title read "Faraday Tanner Memorial Plans."

What. The. Hell.

I clicked it and read how the Tanner *family* had answered a petition to "commemorate their daughter's life and outstanding contributions." A list of attached documents with titles like "Her Rise to Fame" and "Early Inventions" mixed in with "Beliefs in Action" and "Changing the World One Policy at a Time" was at the bottom.

Was this why my parents were in such a hurry after the vow? We'd agreed to wait a few more months before discussing anything remotely like this, to let ourselves settle in and grieve as a family, especially since we'd had to share her funeral with millions of people.

They'd promised me more time. It was too soon. I wasn't close to ready.

I snorted in disgust and punched at the screen, but Andrek caught my hand and pulled me toward him. I shuddered in his arms, unable to tear my gaze from my sister's name. Her memory, reduced to miscellaneous documents.

"Dinner will be served for another hour," Marshall was saying, "and third shift workers should report to their departments after. Please note that only five of the ten shower rooms are currently operating, so adherence to the posted schedule is paramount."

The hatch door slid open, and my parents rushed inside.

I twisted free of Andrek so I could point all my anger at them.

Mom's heart-shaped face, so like Faraday's, flushed under my burning stare. She hadn't forgotten to wait before discussing a memorial. She'd *decided* not to wait, promises to her flunky daughter be damned. She opened her mouth to speak, but I gritted my teeth, nearly growling.

Dad reached for me, his chin quivering with regret.

I moved further away and crossed my arms, hating them for leaving me out.

Hating myself for not being someone worth including. For surviving.

I barely registered Marshall's closing words. "Thank you and be well."

The screen went black, but my anger bloomed red hot. I'd make them regret this. "How *dare* you?" Like a volcano, I erupted, spitting vapor vowels and molten consonants.

My parents shriveled under my rage, but not for long.

"We wanted to tell you about the memorial before the announcement," Mom said. Not an apology. Never an apology. "It wasn't supposed to be a surprise."

"The comm obviously works."

She squeezed on a smile. "Andrek, dear, I'm pleased you decided to take our extra room, but this is a family matter. Why don't you go ahead to dinner? We'll catch up soon."

"He stays," I insisted.

Andrek questioned me with a look and laid a hand on my back. "I'm here for Lane."

Mom's eyes darted toward Faraday's urn. "Oh, honey. You didn't need to unpack for us."

"Stop. Changing. The subject," I barked. "You promised to wait."

"That's enough, young lady." She crossed her arms, mirroring me. "The trust has over a thousand people, all with their own opinions and needs. Your sister wasn't only important to us, and you know this. The other trustees need a memorial, for all she represents to everyone who lost a loved one. It's selfish for you to—"

"I'm being *selfish*?" This was such crap. "You're using her again, like you always have. Like she's a symbol and not a person. Your daughter. My sister. She would hate this. You promised we would wait till we settle in!"

"What more settling is there to do? We're here, Lane, and there's no going back."

"You don't understand," my dad said. "The memorial won't happen tomorrow. It'll require planning. Preparation. You're welcome to get involved, in fact, we encourage you to."

"So, a month is all the grieving I'm allowed? I'm supposed to move on now?"

"We all have to!" Mom pointed at the screen. "Weren't you listening to Han? Everything she—we've worked for is at stake now."

I didn't know what she was talking about, but I refused to ask and let her distract me from their betrayal.

Dad nodded vigorously. "We thought we could count on you. You have to understand. Our family has a duty to see the trust work."

"You aren't ready to move on. We get it." She softened her voice. "But your dad and I don't have a choice. We still have a community to run, or your sister's death was for nothing. All those people. This was her dream, their dream. It's still *our* dream. You should want to do your part. People need a message to follow or none of this will last."

Her words bulldozed me back into Andrek. She was right about everything, but that only made me angrier. It wasn't fair that she could bury herself in her work, in her commitment to the trust, while my own pain got bigger every moment. Even my dad managed to push his sorrow into some quiet pocket inside, somewhere invisible.

Andrek, poor guy, stood caught in our grief tornado as my parents' eyes forced a floodlight on me. We each loved Faraday most, and we glared at each other with the words "not her" hanging between us.

"I'm sorry we left you out of the discussions," Dad said.

"We didn't want to hurt you more."

"How long has this been going on?"

"It was out of my hands," Dad added. He meant: *Blame your mom. You know how she gets.*

Mom threw out her palms. "It was for your own good, Lane. You haven't been ready to talk about these things, so there was no reason to loop you in. Besides, we're not the ones who introduced the petition. Collin, tell her."

Dad cleared his throat, letting me know what he said next had been fed to him ready-made. "They're hoping to do a family tribute along with the memorial, you should know. Your mother and I believe it's important for you to participate, as a way to carry your sister's legacy forward and keep her message clear."

"I can't carry her legacy!" I didn't add that having another child in the center of attention was probably what they craved for themselves. Faraday may have sparked to fame like a rocket, but without them pushing and guiding and facilitating her every step of the way, she'd never have gotten so far. "I'm not like her. I'm not—I can't—and I'm just a lunch lady!"

"Lunch *wizard*," Andrek coughed out.

"For now, sure," Mom said. "But you don't have to be some great scientist to fill the void in the trust's heart. You can be you. Quirky, charming, hard-working."

"Do you hear yourselves?" Of course, they didn't. I was to be their funny puppet, a clambering clown with their words spilling out to pick up where their last spawn left off. This was the best they imagined for me, filling in as an extension cord for my sister's legacy.

"You're overreacting, sweetie," Mom said, and she waved at my dad to do something else she'd predetermined. "This is all perfectly harmless. Moreover, it's necessary. If you only understood how the loss of your sister has fractured the trust already. We're barely holding things together."

Dad went to the comm and the next thing I knew my face was on the screen, squinting in the morning sun as I boarded the ship. I had to admit that I didn't look as terrible on camera as I expected. My round cheeks were pinchably cute, and the hesitation in my brown eyes and pursed mouth was more than a little charming. My wild red waves glowed like fire and showed nothing about how shattered I felt inside. As quirky clowns went, I gave myself four out of five stars.

"Adorable, isn't it?" Mom asked brightly. "Once people get to know the real you, things will change. They'll remember what brought them to the collective, what keeps us together. You don't have to be her, just remind them of her. This might be our last chance!"

I saw it clearly then. Maybe they were right about what was at stake, but I couldn't overlook that they saw me as a tool. Quirky, charming, hard-working. Quirky meant weird, so, like, autistic. And by charming, she meant I was accidentally likeable. But, *but*, she threw in hard-working as a prize, because the thing I actually did, on purpose, was try. Try. Me doing my very best, that was the most I could achieve in her opinion. Extra points that I was a fuck-up and wouldn't have ideas of my own to interfere with whatever message they thought the trust needed.

I squared my shoulders. "What you're saying is it's time for me to step in as a sister replacement, no matter what I want. No matter what I think."

Mom's face sagged. I knew this signal. The droop of her jaw. Had seen it first when Faraday moved out of our apartment, never to return, then when the dust from the invasion settled down and the smoke lifted to a world without her wild genius daughter. It meant she felt like she'd failed all over again. She bit her lip. "Please don't refuse to help just because you're mad," she said.

Dad shifted from leg to leg, avoiding my stare. "We only want you to be happy here. And to have a here to be happy in."

"What *would* make you happy?" Mom asked.

"Eating." My stomach rumbled nice and loud, as if to prove my point. "Without you."

They froze like I'd slapped them. We faced off, lonely islands separated by an ocean of shared pain.

"We're coming anyway," Mom said. Her voice was sticky with unspent tears and too high, like a cartoon. I didn't know whether it was real emotion or another ploy. I didn't care anymore.

Andrek and I led the way out the door and down the hall, though, to be completely honest, I didn't have the first clue which way I was going. Per usual.

Attention: ALL

Subject: Request for Volunteers

If you are interested in expanding your work experience, please consider joining the rotation crews! Opportunities are available for first and third shifts in all departments. Training will be provided on site.

—President Marshall

CHAPTER THREE

TAKING BACK CONTROL

I stormed forward, pushing all my feeling through my feet and wishing I were bigger so my stomps made more of an impact. Faraday could stomp like a boss, even on carpet. Or with bare feet. She didn't have to be mad. But here I was, fuse lit and ready to explode, and all I managed was soft flappy noises and some heavy breathing. Andrek kept his distance except for when he redirected me with a tap on my elbow.

The cafeteria turned out to be the same room where we had the vow. It seemed empty without everyone standing shoulder to shoulder and the pile of helmets and space suits. The floor was lined with tables full of diners, and the wall between the east and west hallways was open to a long counter.

Past the counter squatted the kitchen, which I felt weirdly guilty peeking at as we sidestepped along through the serving line, like I ought to be working already. It gleamed with high-tech silver appliances—dozens of ovens and grills and workstations—and kitchen staff gossiped joyfully as they cleaned. Seeing it made me wish I were back there with them.

I took a rainbow-colored tray and surveyed the meal. Mostly dry rations, which would gag me if I weren't used to the stuff from the last month on the ship. But there were also creamy mashed potatoes and a cucumber and tomato salad. Real food.

The bright colors and sharp smell of vinegar washed over me, turning my mood like a key clicking in its lock. Until my mom caught me smiling, which killed the moment at once. I wished we hadn't waited for her and Dad. There might still be enchiladas and curry instead of only rations and sides.

"If we had food like this on the ship, why've we been eating that other crap?" I complained.

"Lane!" Mom fussed, shooting me an exasperated glare as she left with her tray. She headed toward my dad, who sat at the same table as Andrek. Unfortunately.

A white guy on the other side of the counter scooted me an extra container of salad. "I thought the same thing when I saw the menu, but these are lunar, donated from Guanghan then grown right here. I got dizzy chopping them. Hadn't smelled anything so perfect in years." He had kind eyes, soft brown like tumbleweeds, and his skin was linen pale and swimming with freckles. "I'm Stephan Novak, by the way."

"Thanks." I inhaled the scent of the extra salad. Zara made a dish like this, with red vinegar and tiny purple onions. I'd have liked to try adding something different sometime, maybe some heat.

"You don't have to thank him. It's his job." Viveca said, entering the line. "We all work here, so it would be a waste of air and energy to go around thanking every person for every little thing." She chose the next salad, touching it as little as possible, as if it were going to bite her.

"Still busy making friends?" I knew it was the wrong thing to say as soon as it left my mouth, but I couldn't help myself. Stephan seemed nice, and Viveca was so clearly not. "Or do you only do that with people you plan to study?"

"I'm simply stating the obvious," she said. Her back straightened more, and my fingers turned white around my tray. "And hoping to avoid normalizing empty chatter."

"I get it. This is you making conversation." Why was I

still talking? What monster-sized bad idea crawled in my face and decided to pick a fight with Viveca, my parent's favorite recruit?

Stephan made a stricken face. "It's all right. I didn't expect anything—"

"And I wasn't trying to make friends, Lane," she returned, sneering at my name yet looking unbelievably pretty at the same time. Either she practiced that look, or she was completely unaware she was making it. "I'm rather selective with friendship."

"Good," I said as I looked apologetically at Stephan. "I wasn't volunteering."

I hurried away before I escalated to dunking her into my mashed potatoes. Not that I'd ever done anything like that, but she made me want to. My tray clattered on the table by Andrek's, basically across from my parents.

Not far enough.

Dad glanced up from his food. *I'm sorry about earlier,* his face said. A bit of potato was smeared in his mustache. I ignored him.

The table across us held mostly strangers, but down at the end sat a group of parents I knew, whose eyes met mine too fast for comfort, like they were waiting for me to glance their way. Mr. Weissman, a funny dad who used to bring pastries to the schoolroom every Friday, folded his lips into a kind of smile—a new one, not his crow's-feet-crinkle or sniffly chin wiggle.

I didn't recognize it, but I found myself trying to copy the folds, so I knew it felt exactly right. I might wear this expression more often.

"Are you seeing it now?" Andrek asked, leaning in close. "Mitosis."

A quick scan of the surrounding tables confirmed what he said earlier. It was like high school cliques in pre-melt films. The collective folks sat together in tight groups, though I couldn't tell by looking who had supported whom in the election, while the recruits sat apart, whole lengths of table separating the old and new. I didn't see any of the old staff who greeted us.

Only one person moved between. Joule. He saw Andrek and came our way, not noticing or caring how attention trailed him across the room.

"There you two are," he said and stood behind my mom. "Interested in taking a walk after you eat? I was hoping I could pick your brains about Lunar Trust logistics and such. The oral history version. I never expected to end up here, and I don't like not knowing, well, everything. Figured I'd be stuck on Blackstone or some other lunar base making googly eyes at the shipyards for a decade first."

Andrek kicked my foot under the table. "Are you asking us on a date?"

I kicked him back and filled my mouth with tomato. Joule's invitation sounded more like Viveca's than I liked, all learning-about-stuff focused, but at least he was up front about it. My parents were giving us major side-eye.

"Yes, please," Joule answered. "A date with informational benefits."

Andrek smiled so wide his face might break. "I don't see any harm in it."

"Lane?" Joule faced me, maybe for the first time that I noticed. His skin was polished mahogany, lit from within like a jewelry case, and his brown-black eyes were almost too intense to look into directly. Andrek officially had competition in the most beautiful man contest. I liked that he asked us both instead of trying to cowboy my boyfriend away.

I was not ready, though. I hadn't known it until now. It was fine if Andrek was, but I wasn't yet.

"Why don't we see how tonight goes?" I said lightly. Andrek kept kicking me like he was part metronome, but at least one of us should play things cool. "It should be the two of you first anyway. Nothing in my brain to pick."

"One hundred percent fair." Joule settled his elbows on the table and laced his long fingers. His dark eyes sparkled kindly. "But I bet there's plenty."

Then, just as things swerved toward fun, Viveca appeared behind Joule. She stared knives into his head and cleared her throat.

"What is it, V?"

I liked him more for not flinching when her lovely mouth narrowed into a frown. Plus, he called her "V," which I could pretend stood for something less intimidating than Viveca. Like Vicki or Violet. I could get along great with a Vicki or a Violet.

"I've been looking all over for you." She leaned over to kiss his cheek. "Can we talk? In private?" She cut a chilly look at me.

I studied my food and stuffed my mouth. I didn't want to see my parents when they realized this was *The* Viveca or heard the argument between Mr. and Ms. Perfect. But my ears didn't care what I wanted. They worked fine.

"I'm hoping to convince these two to let me take them out," Joule said, oblivious to how mad she was. "We can talk here."

Andrek patted my thigh twice to say "dra-ma," and I peeked at him in time to catch his smirk. I started to think she'd slink away, back to whatever tower her personality escaped from, but then she wrapped arms around Joule's neck and planted herself on his lap. Her hair came dangerously close to my food.

"Joule," she oozed, "You promised you would at least check in with me." I deliberately did not look at her but noticed how the cucumbers smelled like summertime. "Before you lend your considerable intellect to strangers."

"I thought we already discussed tonight. This is my first opportunity to meet the old guard trustees and immerse myself in our new surroundings. You're supposed to start on your project, you said."

Viveca didn't respond right away but also didn't break eye contact with him.

"You've heard about it, right?" Joule asked me and Andrek. He must have had the strength of a bear to pull away

36   JR CREADEN

from Viveca's steady gaze. "The memorial?"

I shook my head involuntarily and kept shaking even after I noticed I was doing it. He couldn't be saying what I thought he was, no sir.

Luckily, Andrek had more head space than I did. Bless him, my guy. "The memorial for Lane's sister?"

"That's it! It's a unique plan, and Viveca's petition should be in a guidebook on how to write petitions," Joule said. "Do you want to tell them about it, V?"

I swallowed the lump of fire that lodged in my throat. Just when I thought I could relax, could adore my boyfriend's crush and despise that crush's girlfriend in peace, my worlds decided to crash into each other. Sure, my parents sucked, but *she* was the one behind this pain parade.

Viveca turned her face our way, but her voice came out distant. "I don't think now's the best time."

"Huh!" A hot laugh forced itself from my mouth. What did she know about "best times?" Did she think of that before writing her petition and barging into my family's mourning process like we were her birthday present? This was probably why she wanted me in her grief group, to mine my tears for her pity circus and put it on permanent display. Come witness the amazing Tanner family as they sold their family member's legacy to a hothead. "Tell us all about it."

"I'd rather—"

"I *insist*."

Joule flapped his hands happily. "Bossy Lane is extra cute! Now you have to, V."

"If you say so." She pulled her long hair to the front and combed through it slowly. The thick waves parted easily, slipping around her fingers like water. "I won't pretend I have it all figured out because nothing's decided. The most popular ideas would take months to prepare, like the sculpture or the annual holiday cycle to celebrate Far—our founder's achievements. This can be the ground from which lunar culture grows, our central symbol."

I exhaled carefully, rounding my mouth like a straw.

Not only for the hothead, folks, but you and you and you, everyone can buy a piece of the action; just ask for the Tanner Family Discount. When the next one dies, we hope you'll buy her too!

Keep it together, temper. "Central symbol."

"Exactly. We could rename the days of the week or the months themselves, since the longer the trust stands, the less it'll have in common with Earth time. Honestly, the renaming may take decades, like, how terrible a name is 'Lunar Trust One?' Why not 'Faraday Settlement' or something that at least says who we are, not just what?" Viveca braided and unbraided her impossibly cooperative hair as she chattered on. "Part of what defines a community are its symbols, the way our values imprint onto language, then our art and philosophy, even the questions we ask about the nature of humanity or existence."

I opened and closed my mouth, searching for words and fighting the urgent need to repeat the worst of what she said. Faraday Settlement. What a terrible name.

Lunar Trust One, that was our name.

The whole point, Faraday's whole point, of the trust's name was that it was only the beginning, a first seed of freedom planted on the moon. Earth's bridge to survival in space. Sure, our four domes weren't self-sufficient—none of the lunar bases were yet—but that was the goal. Guanghan, the Chinese base, had gotten the closest, but they still got material shipments from Earth twice a year. Blackstone, Mirage, and Loris alternated shipments together, sharing what came and what they produced themselves. We would be somewhere in the middle as the only permanent settlements, while the others were truly "bases," crewed by workers and military.

"She—she—but—summertime—" I looked helplessly at Andrek and clamped my lips shut. This sent nervous energy rippling through me, first as a twitch in my shoulder then into my leg, which started shaking uncontrollably.

He squeezed my thigh, holding his hand there for deep

pressure until my leg slowed its bouncing. "I don't know how to respond to that, except to say that sounds like a massive undertaking with a lot of very intense, and very personal, decisions involved."

"Oh, definitely," she said.

"But why you?" I demanded, the screech in my voice more audible than I was proud of.

She leveled those steady browns on me. "Why not me? I've followed her career all my life. Ran her international fan club for six years and wrote two thesis papers about her ideals and impact. I'm uniquely qualified."

"Qualified! Andrek, she's *qualified*." He was still squeezing my thigh but it wasn't tight enough. I wrapped both my hands around his and pressed hard. "Do you have any idea—can you hear yourself?"

"My hearing is excellent. Am I to understand you think I'm not qualified?"

I laugh-cackled again but couldn't word. Then something stung my wrist, like a bug bite, instantly followed by a sting on the back of my neck. I slapped at it and decided it couldn't be a bug, but maybe it was radioactive dust and Faraday would know, she would have known, or it was my brain, spicing things up for funsies like the salad failed to do.

"If you hate my ideas so much, why don't you plan something? Since you think you'll do a better job." She slammed a pretty hand on the table and pushed herself up to stare down at me.

"I will!" I said hotly.

Andrek gasped, and Joule's jaw dropped.

"Lane!" my mom said, and I couldn't for the life of me figure out why. Hadn't she told me to participate? For the good of the trust?

"Have at it," Viveca said. "Don't let me stand in your way."

"I won't."

She actually said, "Splendid."

"I'm still not joining your group, though."

"I don't care in the slightest," she huffed as she got to her feet. "And it's not *mine,* besides. I told you that. I'm only a resident, obviously, at least until my doctoral work's approved. Do realize I'm not going to hand you reins because you shoved in at the last minute. This project, the trust, it matters to me. We'll be partners. Best offer."

"I don't need reins from you," I snapped. "She's my sister."

"I'll send you details about the first planning meeting to make sure it doesn't conflict with your shift in...?"

"The kitchen. And you're welcome, by the way."

"Tha—thank you?" She rolled her hips and stormed off.

"Aaaargh!" I stared at my forgotten food and pulled my leg free of Andrek's hand. Haughty, horrible, manipulative girl. Of all the times for me to let my anger win over reason. I should have stuffed my face and said nothing, let her ramble and be awful then fussed about her later. Why did I always have to be me?

"SCREE-YICK-EEEH!"

My hands flew to cover my ears before I registered why and what I was hearing. It was a noise, feedback screeching from the overhead speakers like a dying animal at maximum volume.

Its scream clawed at me from the top of my head all the way into my toes, vibrating so hard I worried my veins would burst. Even when it finally broke, when there came a moment of quiet, the pain it left behind was like fire.

"Greetings from Earth, lunar colonists," said a voice, too loud, too familiar, plunging me into ice. "I'm Brand Masters, and on behalf of myself and my Royal Corps, I want to congratulate you on taking the first step in your project..."

Attention: ALL

Subject: Water Rations

Per MCO Ruling 23.4, water rations have been raised by twenty percent for all LC1 citizens. Drink up!

—President Marshall

CHAPTER FOUR

REAL TALK

I searched the faces around me for something, some answer to why Brand Masters was being allowed to hijack our loudspeakers, but I saw fear everywhere I looked, panic and silent rage that he wouldn't see, wouldn't care about if he could.

I was of three minds as he spoke, this man, this murderer, who talked as if he were everyone's favorite uncle. One mind heard and replayed each word, chewing on them over and over as they echoed into the cavern of me.

"*Colonists,*" he said, knowing full well that was a dirty word and why we called ourselves trustees. "Your *project,*" he said, like it was a macaroni necklace. "*First* step," as if we hadn't taken a thousand already in order to get this far.

The second me listened in real time, continuing to study faces, trying to interpret every shifting wrinkle.

My third mind screamed and screamed, and it was a miracle that it didn't drown out the others. I wished it would drown him out at least.

"…I hope you'll pardon the interruption. I wanted to send my good wishes to each of you on this momentous occasion," he went on in that oily, pampered voice. "As our goal of sending manned ships into the beyond is equally dear to me, I offer these wise words from one we all revere: 'Success is measured not by the lack of failure but by which steps we take forward after failure blocks one path.' Press forward, brave colonists, and we will surely meet again."

"*Our goal*"—How dare he!—then he quoted, or rather misquoted, my sister?

The volume of my internal screams rose impossibly. I was so angry I couldn't think.

Meanwhile, my parents moved in fast-forward, abandoning their trays, spouting some kind of apology and solemn *we'll-talk-later*s, and rushed toward the closest exit. Straight to business.

My hands still covered my ears like they were cemented in place, and I was not the only one frozen this way. Joule mirrored me with a horrified expression. Viveca, who I'd thought was long gone, stood in the far doorway, her own hands fixed over her ears, her eyes trained on the empty space my parents left behind.

The cafeteria sprang into motion, but I was too dumbstruck to process. Andrek held me, but he felt far away. I didn't know how long I sat there, waiting for the pain to pass or my silent screaming to stop.

"Attention, trustees," President Marshall said over the same speakers, familiar and welcome, though the waver in her voice made it obvious she too was rattled. "Please remain calm as we assess the situation. As a precaution, communications with Earth will be restricted to authorized department heads only and subject to security review in order to prevent more unwelcome intrusions.

"Any messages to Earth should henceforth be sent to your department leaders for review and packaging for delivery through the remaining Masdar Collective. Furthermore, the distribution of personal tablets will be left to the purview of department leaders on a needs only basis. I apologize for any inconvenience and discomfort this will cause and assure you it is a necessary measure for the ongoing safety and well-being of us all. Thank you for your patience and understanding."

"That was unexpectedly entertaining," Joule said, forcing his hands to his lap. "I mean you and V before, not... The rest was a nightmare. Yeah, I—Nope. I can't talk about that yet. Are you two all right? I hope that doesn't kill my chances."

Andrek checked in with me by kicking my foot. He wanted to go, if only to shake Brand's voice from center stage. Sweet Andrek.

A buzzing in my belly sang out an alarm. *Keep it inside, Lane. Distract, deny.*

"Your questionable taste in girlfriends aside," I said, rising and lifting my tray, "I think your chances are still good for tonight." Except I stood too fast, and the buzzing spun to my head, sending me wavering. My breath came out stretched and tight as if my throat was mimicking the tube from the ship. Today had been too long, too much. I grabbed Andrek's shoulder to steady myself. "Without me though, sorry. I need today to be over."

I lay half-conscious for hours, trying to force the ceiling's stipple into faces. The bed didn't feel like mine yet, but the quiet of the rooms beyond, their empty beds, was more familiar than I wanted to admit.

Eventually sleep must have taken me, because I came to, bleary-eyed and not sure how long my parents had been back, except that it was long enough for them to be waist deep into an argument I was definitely not supposed to hear.

"What could she have been thinking, Collin? After fighting us tooth and nail to delay the memorial, she jumps headfirst into planning it herself? She can barely talk about Faraday without bursting into tears, but somehow she's going to be rifling through all her sister's messages and work now?"

Mom's voice scratched at the too-thin walls like sandpaper, her pitch rising higher and higher as she got riled up. "And why in the world did that girl agree to be equal partners? She's so out of Lane's league, we'll have to build a ship to span the distance. It's too much! It's not at all what we wanted for her."

I sank deeper into the bed, covering my face with the heavy blanket which did little to muffle their voices. This was the soundtrack of my life, my parents' doubts beating steadily against my unformed, half-awake thoughts.

How many mornings had begun exactly like this? Too many to number. Too many for it to still hurt as much as it did.

I could have saved myself this headache by posting in a dorm instead of with family, but the idea of living with strangers was even more upsetting than dealing with my parents babying me. I'd rather be hurt in their familiar ways than face too much newness at once alone.

"Shhh," my dad said, and I imagined him putting an arm around my mom. "We don't want to wake her with our worries. She's had so much trouble sleeping, and today was a lot for anyone."

"But I do!" Mom cried. "I want to yank her out of bed right now and shake some sense into her before it's too late!"

"Come now."

"Stop hushing me!" she yelled, then she lowered her voice anyway, and I pulled my blanket down to hear better. "This is serious. Dangerous, Collin. Brand proved it today. His message wasn't a warning. It was an attack all its own. You know it. We have no idea how long we have before he attacks again, and with the accord in pieces, we don't have nearly the support we expected to protect us."

An attack all its own. I decided to ask Andrek what she meant by that as soon as I saw him. I remembered the war crimes accord she was talking about, though. It was one of Faraday's last unfinished projects, which was supposed to redefine war crimes to include corporate attacks like the RC's, and could have, Faraday hoped, resurrected the UN.

"And telling Lane that will do what?" my dad asked. "She's hurting and holding herself together by threads. We can let her choose which threads. We shouldn't worry her about things none of us can control."

"Don't you see that's why she can't take on more now?

Let alone planning a whole memorial? She was only supposed to participate, maybe bake something or introduce family photos. Nothing this big. She didn't even finish high school! She doesn't have what it takes to take on responsibility like this."

Dad grumbled a sound I usually took to mean *So what?* "Neither did I, remember? Graduate. Neither did half our generation after the pandemics. She'll be fine."

"She won't have the support you had. Let alone your luck. You had an entire planet going through everything with you. I tried to make things easier by getting her the kitchen position, but that could be a stretch even without adding this monumental, and very personal, project. I didn't want it this way."

Her words stabbed me—*she doesn't have what it takes*—along with a realization so cold I feared I'd never be warm again. Mom "got" me my assignment? I had figured they must have done something to squeeze me past selections, but I thought, wrongly, that I'd earned the kitchen position on my own merit at least.

Maybe I couldn't do it. Mom was usually right about things. It was her job to be right about such things. And if I couldn't handle it, then what?

"What is it you want to do? Rub that in her face?" Dad was heated now too, and I pictured the red rising in his cheeks. "You're doing it again, Catherine, pushing your fears onto them. That's not our role! Ours is to love them and offer the support they need."

"Her. You mean 'her.'"

"Yes, her. We need to give *her* support and step out of her way."

"What if I can't?" Mom's voice broke, followed by a long moment of silence.

I clamped my hands around my mouth to quiet my breath and stared at the door, willing it not to open. I imagined them close together on the couch, looking into each other's sad eyes.

"Then we talk about it and figure out how to carry each other better. She'll understand," Dad finally answered.

"She doesn't understand anything! She may as well be a toddler—impulsive, rash—she's a tornado and doesn't even... She needs—She needs—I need..."

"Oh, Catherine," Dad said, as Mom sobbed loudly. Maybe she'd been crying all along. "You don't mean that. We both know you don't. And remember you're the one who said Viveca would be an excellent peer role model for Lane. That's still true. Plus, for now this is the only safe place we have."

"But how can we keep it that way? How can we keep pretending it's possible? There's nowhere left to run!"

"First we breathe, my love. Breathe. And I believe you were right to begin with, wanting her to help with the memorial. Even if it's in a different way than you meant. This will help everyone heal, even her."

I imagined another daughter of different parents climbing out of bed and going to the couch to share their tears. That young woman, brimming with feelings and fears, would spill those out on the carpet like a sack full of beans for them to sort through together. She didn't have anything to prove to anyone, and she didn't have to grow up all the way, not yet. Not ever. She trusted her parents to have all the answers. She hadn't bitten off more than she could chew with a project that would likely scour at her fresh wounds while being mocked by someone "leagues" beyond her.

I, however, hid under the covers and prayed the too-thin walls didn't give me away. Goodnight, room that was almost my room. Goodnight, moon.

Attention: ALL

Subject: Colony Safety

Suspicious activities must be reported at once to a department head or command. The safety of one is the safety of all.

Thank you for your cooperation.

—Commander Han

CHAPTER FIVE

MY OWN SHINE

"An attack all its own" became clear without me needing to ask, since the door out of our quarters refused to open the next morning and our comm screen was stuck on a written version of Brand's message and Commander Han's response. If my sister's accord hadn't fallen through, hijacking our comms should be grounds to arrest him, but that was not the reality we got to live in. The locked screens and doors only lasted about an hour, which meant my family missed breakfast, and hundreds of trustees showed up late for their first shifts.

Minor inconveniences, really, glitches in the smooth operations of the trust, but they continued for days until techs rooted out the viral code. The communication ban was far more annoying, even if the reasons for it made sense. Most of us didn't think to send a message to friends or family on Earth before that first dinner, and now it was too late to try.

In the meantime, younger workers like me received a scaled-back schedule, only a couple hours per shift to give us time to regurgitate safety manuals and department-specific protocols while the virus got sorted. I probably wouldn't get assigned a tab, so I'd be stuck using the comm in our quarters. This was my parents' doing, I was sure of it.

On the plus side, I got to ease into trust life. And despite my parents' doubts, I was doing fine so far in the kitchen. Once the review period ended, my normal schedule would be four days on, two days off, always first shift, starting early but ending shortly after lunch service.

For the last day of the forced review, we had testing. I was in a soundproof booth that gave me just enough space to stand up and pace in a small square. I breezed through the general safety checks. All that stuff was drilled into me since before I could read.

Ultimately, they were the same rules we'd had in the Masdar Collective, since that was a closed environment too: don't tamper with equipment without approval, report fevers or breathing difficulties immediately, follow health guidelines to the letter, and so forth. I still got emotional going through it, because there were all kinds of inside jokes my classmates and I'd had about the wording of things that only lived in my head now.

I wasn't exactly sure why I had to go through this, except it was some unilateral decision, and I just got lumped in with the rest of the thirty or so newcomers under twenty-five. I preferred this explanation to the alternate one my brain kept providing, that somebody up top noticed my scores and decided I needed to prove myself all over again. If they were comparing my scores to the high-achieving new recruits, I must look like a disaster. I hadn't even registered as an adult when I should have back on Earth—I'd been too busy to bother—so I was still technically a disabled minor under my parents' care.

I didn't test well, never had. That hadn't mattered so much before when I was surrounded by people who grew up with me. But that was then. Now my "peers," round two, were the best of the best from all of Earth. They were nothing like me, who'd never been picked for anything.

There was a soft knock at the door to my booth, and the proctor stuck her head in. "Standard session has ended," she said, meaning time was up for everyone but those who got extra accommodations. "You have thirty minutes left."

The proctor handed me a water tube and went to tell Joule the time because—turned out—he was also autistic, and being a super genius actually made testing harder for him. I didn't know what tricks he had in his adjoining booth, but he got extra time like me.

His muffled arguments with the testing tablet became full shouts when she cracked open his door. "None of these answers are correct," he yelled. "How can I pick one when they're all technically wrong?"

I stifled a laugh of understanding and turned back to my screen, to the thing that'd been tripping me up all week. Trust organization. The list of fields, arranged by power from command and operations down to food service and sanitation like a feudal pecking order, felt like a slap in the face, a broken promise. This wasn't the way we learned it in the collective, and not a bit like Faraday envisioned the social utopia.

I'd seen trust diagrams, perfectly true to her designs. Interlocking webs of systems—too intricate for me to fully process, but clear enough to get the gist that each department depended on the others. Without sanitation or maintenance, there was no breathable air. Without the gardens and food service to prepare the food, we would all starve. On and on the web went. No power schemes, just interwoven systems.

The test didn't care. The hierarchy glared in black and white on the screen. If Faraday were here, she'd burst in and talk some sweet sense into someone. I didn't have a scientist's spirit to explain, nor my sister's magical way of bending words to inspire. It just looked so wrong this way, so I kept blanking on answers I ought to have known about who to report to and which department was in charge of which critical system.

I felt like I'd been stuck in this booth for weeks. Sweat dripped down my face as I went through the questions once again, and I had to stop often to mop my face and slurp more water. My stomach was in knots and my muscles ached like I'd been running. And all the while, there was this pressure in my chest as if my sister herself was inside me and beating against my ribs, trying to break free.

"I'm doing the best I can," I assured her, not meaning to speak aloud. The whine in my voice scraped against my ears, and I straightened my back. "But I'll try harder."

One answer after another, I squeaked through the questions until time ran out.

Apparently I passed, because the proctor approved my official schedule, and I started my first regular shift the next morning, marking two weeks since we'd arrived.

I served crunchy grains and dried fruits for breakfast alongside Stephan and the other staff. If it weren't for the barrage of unfamiliar faces and names coming through the line, plus the odd trio in space suits or lugging around helmets, this could have been the cafeteria in the collective beneath its smoggy sky outside, with a planet full of people living their perfectly normal lives.

Voices flew past me like a wordless wind as I soaked up how strange it still was to be here. As far back as I remembered, getting to the moon was the goal. Escaping Earth, creating a utopia.

Reaching the end game at twenty was sort of anticlimactic. Shockingly normal.

After the breakfast shift, Chef Maria Acevedo, whose coal-black eyes gleamed against her sepia brown skin, directed us into two and four-person teams. I ended up cutting vegetables with Stephan at the prep station until Chef pulled me in front of her open office. A sign on the hatch door said, "Panic Room. Knock before entering." Lilting string music floated out, and I caught a glimpse of squashy bean bags piled atop a sofa.

"I ate at your sister's fiancés' place once or twice while you were cooking for her presidential campaign, did you know?" Her voice was scratchy like a well-loved blanket, and her calloused hand found my shoulder when I didn't answer right off. "I'm terribly sorry about Faraday and your friends. There are no words for your loss. All our loss. It's the sort that will only continue to ripple and never smooth over."

"Yeah," I choked, wishing I could put things into words that well. Maybe she should have been helping Viveca plan the memorial instead.

Chef pinned me with a steely expression. "It's a lot to process, I'm sure. Do use my office if you ever need a break. In the meantime, I hope the kitchen brings you some comfort. I don't trust just anyone to add to my menu."

"Add to your—huh?" I stammered.

"To the menu. Today," she said with a smile. "Would you make dessert tonight? Your choice, but I suggest something soft. People's palates are still adjusting."

I waited for a "but," except there wasn't one, and my nervousness cracked like an egg. Chef's expression wasn't one of guilt or duty, no matter whether Mom had put her up to this or not. She wanted me to pick something.

More, she wanted this to be my happy place on the moon—the chattering voices and sizzling dishes and easy reward of filling bellies—and if it was too much sometimes, the noise and energy of the kitchen, there was her office to relax in.

It couldn't have been more ideal if it tried. I felt genuinely good for the first time in months.

"Thanks, Chef, I will," I heard myself say then added, more deliberately, "Maybe a simple pudding? I'm better friends with cake, but I haven't met our ovens yet."

"Understood." Her ruby lips split into a full-faced smile. "Pudding first then. Excellent decision. Holler if you need any help." As she walked away, my stomach did a few cartwheels of joy like it had never forgotten how.

Time was so weird. Our digestive clocks were the only ones that made sense anymore. There was breakfast, but no morning, and lunch came without a midday. The one thing that made sense to me was the cooking itself.

I started with a huge pot, six gallons of full fat coconut milk and nearly that much almond milk, whisking in arrowroot starch and coconut sugar until it was perfectly blended. Then I used obscene amounts of vanilla with a generous helping of lime extract to give it a special kick. It would need more sweetening later, but I wanted to get it boiling first.

After I got the pudding simmering, I played at being a lunch lady until teams were sent to clear tables.

Stephan followed me into the cafeteria, dragging a trash cart behind him. It had compartments for compost and recyclables and a sterilizing light we were supposed to wave our hands under for washing. I grumbled under my breath at the mess the diners left us and searched for a broom, but two small vacuum bots detached themselves from the cart and scooted by, tidying the floor.

"I'll get trays," I said and immediately tripped over one of the bots, which earned me snide looks from the few remaining diners at the nearest table. Then the first tray I lifted slipped out of my hands and landed with a clang, splashing something cold across my chest.

Laughter rang in my ears, but I didn't look up. Instead, I squatted low to get the tray and kind of hovered there and hid. I was used to stuff like this, skirting around fans who thought it was hilarious to gawk at their hero's bumbling sister. I bet *they'd* be happy with a statue.

"Don't mind them." Stephan took the tray and stowed it on the cart. "They're just bored."

"Are they still watching?" I peeked through the chairs, waiting for the laughter to turn into the mocking I was used to. Only the brightest minds belonged in the trust, no matter their economic background or physical disability. Only the best, plus me. "Not good enough" might as well have been tattooed on my forehead.

Stephan leaned over me, smelling warm like the vanilla extract I'd spilled earlier. "It. Doesn't. Matter." He said it like it was the easiest thing in the world to ignore getting laughed at.

He set to cleaning around me, and after a few deep breaths I rose to work beside him. His focus was contagious. So much so we were pushing the cart toward the kitchen before I noticed my attention lingering on the flat gray walls. They sucked the light inside them, and I was uncomfortably aware of how close I was to the edge of the dome, with the vacuum of space just beyond. The cafeteria's relentless gray made that dangerous reality impossible to ignore.

"These walls need something," I whined. "They're killing me."

Stephan glanced over my shoulder. "They are pretty awful. Warehouse like."

"Exactly." I shuddered. "What would you pick instead, if it were up to you?"

"Trees," he said without stopping to think. "I miss them already. And birds. You?"

"I don't know. Something bright, like sunsets. Anything but this."

"A sunset through the trees then," he agreed. "That would be perfect."

The idea reminded me of Faraday and her fiancés' flat, which had had color on every inch of space not open to the street. Even when they'd pulled the shutters tight over the metal grating, there were murals of the street outside painted within, frozen into acrylic joy. The only gray left after she moved in had been a silver spoon Khalid's mother loved, and my sister had hung it beside the red pots in a place of honor.

She'd known how to do that, to offer respect without shrinking or glorifying the person, but I didn't know whether she was born knowing or if it was something else I missed in school somehow.

"Are you all right?" Stephan's eyes softened. I mentally

filed his expression away under *this is what Worried Stephan looks like.*

"Gotta be." I moved around him to deliver the cart. The automixers had kept my pudding from burning, but there was something not quite right about the smell. And it didn't have the consistency I wanted yet.

Faraday had taught me whatever she was trying to learn to cook, but I'd have to learn a lot more to keep up with the rest of the staff. I could make nearly anything without meat, which was good because we didn't have any. Stephan was really upset about that. Apparently, he was quite a hunter or something before.

Our ingredients were different, but they were supposed to work the same. Like, instead of white sugar, we had a full pantry of sweeteners. And instead of dairy, there were nut milks and oil-based spreads. I was going to miss cheese the most, but maybe all the fresh fruits and vegetables would fill the void. We did have a whole selection of honey, a gift from Loris, where Chef worked before.

I was no genius like my lost friends and sister, nor a rock star academic who catapulted into college during puberty. But this, this magic of taste and texture and subtle aromas, was the shine that was mine.

My parents were so wrong about me, and they didn't even know. They'd never bothered to visit when I cooked for Faraday's campaign.

I added some dried honey to the pot and waited for the scent to shift and sweeten. This was the crucial moment. All I needed was instinct and attention, and I had plenty of both.

The honey gave the pudding a pale caramel color, like the sun rising over dunes. That rush, that moment when the night's cool whispered away and the promise of heat screamed from the horizon. Its smooth texture glided around my spoon with exactly the right pull.

Chef tapped my shoulder. "Looking good over here!" She pulled a tasting stick from her apron and dipped it into the pot before touching it to her lips. "Just a hint of lime?"

The rest of us didn't wear aprons since our jumpsuits didn't require much protection. I had my hairnet on though, and it squeezed my temples and kept my red locks from falling.

"I heard you had trouble on the floor," she said, and I assumed she referred to me fumbling the tray and crawling around the table. I was stunned she noticed, but maybe Worried Stephan was also a blabber.

"Just some new recruits picking on the help."

She tsked. "No good to think like that. New and old. *The help.* Gotta think different now. We're all Lunar. There's no us and them here."

I bit my lip to hold back the argument that sprang to mind. There was still an Us and Them. *Us,* who'd been part of the collective all our lives, which was basically only me now, because adults had had lives before my sister. And *them* meant everyone else. New people.

I guess there were some folks in the middle like Andrek, who hadn't grown up in the collective *or* been added at the last minute, but whatever. He didn't count. Us and Them was how everything would always be.

Chef moved to the prep station, still tsking, then returned to the cooler with her arms full of chopped vegetables. She couldn't understand the way it felt. Maybe she was forgetting what it was like to not be "Chef," the way I was afraid of forgetting what it meant to be a sister. If I didn't hold on tight, it would slip away under the steady rush of newness and change.

As I turned off the heat and spooned the pudding into tiny dishes to cool, I repeated Chef's words in my head like a mantra, trying to wish them true for her sake, at least. Maybe my parents had gotten me this assignment, but I was here now, so I belonged. We were all Lunar.

But were we? Like, was that something that had happened the moment we arrived, or was it still happening? I couldn't shake the sense that I wasn't as Lunar as, say, Chef, who'd lived on the moon way longer, and those who had made it here on merit.

With these thoughts swimming through my mind, I headed to our designated family washroom after work, the one closest to our quarters, making it to the door as my family's allotted hour began. The navy walls shined with disinfecting mist, and I was careful to put on the nubby-bottomed slippers so I didn't slip over the floor.

A selection of soaps, lotions, conditioners, oils, and mineral toners squatted on shelves surrounding the double vanity; the conditioner and oils already needed refilling. Fresh towels, neatly rolled, stacked atop each other on another shelf, behind a clear sliding panel. Condensation beaded over the panel surface, turning into snaking rivers as I washed my face and hands.

I'd been using the group washrooms, mostly to avoid my mother's appraising looks. Those had assigned cosmetology staff to do hair and makeup and such, plus bright walls and music designed to keep the crowd moving through. Today though, all I wanted was quiet and to soak my tired muscles, even if it was only a sitz bath. My feet ached from standing and bending, and pain arced into the back of my knees and lanced across my shoulders. I lingered in the sitting tub until the water went cold and I had more goosebumps than freckles.

I heard a soft whir, and Dad came in, whistling.

"That you, sweetheart?" he asked.

I groaned under my breath and hit the button to drain the water. "Yeah, finishing."

"Good, good. Don't mind me. Just taking advantage of a private space to stretch these old bones." His voice got swallowed by the stall's door then returned clearly. "I'm glad I caught you. How was your first full day?"

I hated questions like this, so open. Did he want the whole itinerary or only the highlights? Was I supposed to say how each part felt or the entire day, and how would I start tallying my feelings to answer? Plus two for getting to make pudding. Minus five for being laughed at then scolded for the way I talked about it. I yanked down a robe and wrapped it tightly, even though the soaker shower's door fully shielded me from view.

"Lane?"

"I don't know!" I finally said, because *fuck*. "Is Mom coming too?" If she was, then I wanted to dress and scoot out of here fast before she realized how right she was to doubt my whatever-ness at getting through the day.

Dad stayed quiet too long, so I went ahead and put on my tank top and shorts. Just in case.

"Dad?"

"If I say yes, you'll leave, won't you?"

"Probably, but, like, is she?"

"Doubtful. Busy at work."

"Oh." I stepped out of the soaker and saw him leaning over the vanity, studying his eyebrows in the mirror. Our eyes met, and he smiled.

"How long are you going to avoid her this time?" he asked, pulling his gaze back to his reflection. "We miss you."

I pumped lotion into my palms, emptying out the unscented bottle. "Till she stops hating me."

"She doesn't." He frowned at the spurting bottle, then at me. "Why would you think that?"

"'Cause it's true." I smeared lotion over my bare arms, using the pretense of rubbing it in to massage my sore muscles. If he noticed, he didn't let on. "She thinks I'm useless."

"Lane, no, that's not true."

"She thinks I don't belong here and that I can't handle anything, like real work or responsibility. That I'm—that I don't have what it takes!"

He looked at me hard. I felt it, burning into the side of my face. I'd said too much.

"You heard us," Dad said softly. "That first night."

I didn't answer him. I rubbed and rubbed, though the

lotion was long gone.

"That's why you've been skipping dinners and hiding yourself away."

"It doesn't matter. She hates me, and she's right. All I'm good at is goofing off."

"Lane, no," he said, turning me toward him then dropping his hands as quickly. "Your mother... That's not what she meant, even if it's what came out of her mouth. You understand how that can be. She's hurting too, and I promise—I promise you, sweetheart—she doesn't hate you. She's simply scared."

"I know! She's scared everyone will see what a failure I am and how it'll look for her and the trust."

"That's not it. You can't possibly believe that." He pulled me to him and put his arms around me. I stood there stiffly, at first, his hug sour with lies. Mom may have been scared about more than me messing things up for everyone, but she'd never tell me what really scared her. The RC. I bet she'd tell Viveca though. Mom would expect she'd be able to manage what I couldn't.

I was not crying, but my voice came out blubbery anyway. "Did she pull strings with Chef to let me make dessert?" My breath pulled tight in my chest, and I was afraid of his answer, that he'd say yes and steal the one good thing I had to myself. Still, I had to know.

"Dessert?" He stepped back, though his hands maintained their hold on my shoulders. I snuck a glance at his face, at his furrowed eyebrows and his mouth an off-center knot, and relief rushed through me. He had no idea what I was talking about. "Chef let you pick dessert?"

"And make it," I added hotly.

"That's wonderful!" He squeezed me and pulled me in for another hug. I let him. "Now I'm *really* looking forward to dinner. Will you join us tonight?"

I barked a laugh at how quickly he'd turned this around. "Maybe."

"I hope you do," he said then he laughed too. "I also hope

they get to restocking the lotions, because you're still dry as a twig and you didn't leave me any."

Attention: ALL

Subject: Evening Menu

Entrees: Steam rolls, butternut squash burritos, green curry

Sides: Papaya salad, sugar snap peas w/dressing, pommes frites

*****Dessert***** Fruit tarts

CHAPTER SIX

IDEA BURPS

A week or so after my dessert debut, Andrek and I finagled some couple time in his room before my first meeting with Viveca. Our schedules didn't align often since I was on first shift and he was second, so we had to balance our time between meal breaks, late nights, and the one off-day we got in common. Music swallowed the hum of his projector and the ratcheting noise of my Playbox 6.

I tugged a brush through my copper tangles while he slammed past my high score at Web Warz Risk. "It's not fair how good you are at this."

"Fair has nothing to do with my skills." He blew a lock of hair away as his fingers flew over the controller. "Yes! Sixes! Eat that, Anonbritches_019! And, anyway, you haven't convinced me about your girlfriend yet."

"You have to quit with that. Viveca's not my girlfriend. I don't rib you about Joule."

"But you wish she was."

"Maybe *you* wish that, so you'd have something to think about while I'm sweating in the kitchen and you're lounging in bed with Joule." He could tease about girlfriends all he wanted. I didn't care. As reluctant as I'd been to get involved with the memorial, this was sister business. No more putting it off.

My parents had finally stopped whispering about me at night, and Mom had commented how I "seemed ready now" last night at dinner. And I was determined not to let some random fangirl decide how Faraday got remembered.

My brush slung to the carpet and smacked the wall in the middle of the projected Risk map. I scrambled after it, but Andrek dived over me and got there first.

"Let me try?" he asked, frowning at my disheveled hair. "It's only fair after I messed it up."

We repositioned on the bed, and he pulled me close and began to work on my knots. "But the way she sprang that security petition on me was weird, right?" he mused. "And she's submitted two more since. She's obsessed, I swear. She must write petitions in her sleep."

"I mean, yeah, that's weird, but not outrageous weird," I said, confused by my urge to defend her when all I wanted to do was smash her face into things when she was in front of me. "As far as goals go, she could've chosen worse. At least she's trying to do something useful."

"I don't like it, Lane. Her interest isn't natural. Ops may have reduced personnel, but they've also got pulse guns and electric net cannons. And if it comes down to it, the whole trust could hunker down for months in the subbasement. It's like she wants people to stay scared forever." He sighed, his breath hot and fragrant on my cheek. "You know, if you wanted, I could do the memorial planning with you. I don't mind making enemies if it means keeping you safe from her personal circus."

"After you crawl into bed at midnight?" It was cruel how people did that. Convinced you of a problem you were happily ignoring, then offered solutions they knew were unrealistic. Of course I'd rather do the memorial with him, especially if that meant working from bed. But he wasn't in any position to wrestle the project from her, and my parents certainly wouldn't lighten his current workload to free up his time.

"I could try to get up earlier. Or, *or*, I could spy on Viveca to learn her sleep-writing skills, and, so long as you're in my bed, I could soak up your ideas by osmosis."

"You're not going to wake up earlier," I said. "The rest is silly."

"I could try!"

I winced as he caught a knot on the back of my head. "Don't punish my hair for the truth."

He worked quietly for a few minutes, taking more care. The projector's screen saver kicked on, flooding the small room with warm desert light, a photograph from some of his travels.

Regret stung the back of my throat, but I couldn't look away. I should have traveled more while I'd had the chance. Maybe someday I could go back to Earth when the trust worked out travel visas and whatever else it took for a non-planetary citizen to visit. A cramp like hunger stirred in my gut.

"Switch with me?" He handed me the brush and I crawled over the bed to sit behind him.

His hair was doing that impossibly cute messy thing it did after sex, so I hesitated to touch it. "Your hair's perfect."

"I figured." He wiggled his shoulders, and I rolled the brush handle near his neck. "But ditch the brush? Do me like dough."

I dug my fingers into the knots across his sloped shoulders, avoiding his stress breakout. He let out a moan as my hands moved over the faded scars on his back. They criss-crossed, pink over white, hatched like tic-tac-toe boards all the way down to his waist. Sometimes it was easy to forget they were there.

He pulled free from my fingers and faced me, a worried wrinkle between his eyes. For a long moment, he didn't speak, but he cupped my chin in his hand and gazed at me intensely. This was his scheming look, but I couldn't imagine what was behind it.

"Counting freckles?" I asked, breaking the spell.

He released my chin. "I miss you. And I'm worried. I don't

think you can trust that girl. She's trouble in a pretty suit."

"Andrek!"

"Fine, a stunning suit. Seriously, Lane, I've got a bad feeling. She's scary smart. What if she starts digging into the RC's possible connections in the trust? I don't want to tell you what to do, but... I wish you'd stay away from her."

I leaned my forehead against his, and we shared a heavy breath of things unsaid.

There were two important things to know about my sweet Andrek, and he was stingy about who got to learn either. First, he was *always* sweet. Fact. Second, his sweetness had never stopped him from doing whatever he had to do to survive.

He'd been through a lot of whatevers before we met.

He'd grown up roaming the sprawling townships of Incorporated South Africa. His festival musician mom had died when he was really young, like barely talking, and her bandmates never managed to hunt down his soldier dad. So Andrek spent his early years on the streets, until he got conscripted into a gang of thieves. Then another and another.

I gathered he was kind of a hot asset, clever and cute as he was. White as he was. He didn't like to talk about those years, but he wore the reminders.

At some point, it was hard for him to say when since street kids didn't generally go about with calendars or have birthday parties, he'd escaped his last handler and found his way into a shelter. It was there he learned to read, then some weekend Samaritan sponsored him for an elite academy in Free London.

After he'd graduated, at maybe fifteen-ish, he got drafted into the local army.

Specifically, the RC.

It wasn't as if Andrek was loyal to the RC or anything. He hated Brand Masters as much as I did, and he'd confessed this truth to me as soon as we went from dating to being partners. But growing up the way he had, Andrek couldn't run away from a legally required draft that meant guaranteed food, shelter, and opportunity.

He'd worked for the RC a few years, then he applied for the collective and joined my sister's campaign as soon as he came of age at nineteen. He left all the RC stuff off his selection paperwork, of course. His transcripts showed him as a ward of Johannesburg, so when the RC started attacking the collective, he'd decided it was best no one else learn about his forced military experience.

I didn't want to imagine what someone like Viveca would think of Andrek if she knew about his link to the RC. She didn't seem like she'd ever let that go. I could, because I knew him, his heart, but it was too risky to let others find out. Besides, he wasn't at fault for the attack that killed my sister and the others. He was with me through the worst of it, and if he hadn't pulled me out of the rubble afterward, I'd be dead like the rest of my generation.

I'd never tell his secret. Certainly not to Viveca. I knew how to keep silent about what mattered. Somehow I'd have to keep the two of them far away from each other.

"I'll be careful," I promised him. "Trust me."

The Minor Cult, as the incorporated press sometimes called it, or the Hope Movement, according to the free media, hadn't started with my sister. Mom said humans had always worshipped the young, the savants in short pants, prodigies winning medals and ribbons and peace prizes while still pimpled with pre-adolescence.

After Faraday's first message went viral, she was compared to the other great children of history—Amadeus Mozart and Bobby Fischer, Amariyanna Copeny and Greta Thunberg—as people played and replayed her later videos on gravitational dynamics, which had also veered into ethics, entropy, and her hope for the "continuation of *homo sapiens sapiens* as a space-faring species."

I'd never understand all she said in her videos, nor could

I explain the gravdrive invention she presented so cleverly, but I knew the effects of both like I knew sugar was sweet. Her comments section birthed a community of like-minded people sharing information and ideas until it grew far beyond responses to her actual video.

She shook the pre-melt generation from its slumber and made space colonization a tangible possibility, maybe an inevitable certainty. That she did so sporting an oh-so-serious smile and bursts of uncanny wisdom made her easy to adore. But that she'd come onto the scene all Joan of Arc the week cell phone factories stopped production and Yellowstone blew made her warnings impossible to forget.

It wasn't only that she was charismatic, and she was definitely that, or that she was warm and smart or pretty and palatably white, all of which definitely factored in. It was that her message of hope arrived when people had none, and her invention had reminded people what it meant to look forward to something, to believe. And she'd followed all that up by spitting into the face of power every chance she got, no matter who'd been watching.

The lunar collective, which was an extension of Faraday's first fan club, loved to keep her front and center, and as it exploded into something that required a board of trustees and a five-floor R&D operation, it found other prodigies flocking to join. Like minds and such, plus their families.

Dad told me I'd also had a short-lived fan club for a while. Autistic families celebrated the brief appearance of me sock-slipping across the kitchen floor to the hall bathroom behind Faraday while I sang the pee pee in the potty song. I was the poster child for the "in their own time" parenting community for a whole two weeks. I was glad I didn't remember any of that.

As I trudged through the gray hallways of the trust for my first meetup with Viveca, I traced my fingers over the door numbers to make sure I didn't knock on the wrong hatch. I wondered when exactly in her life Viveca became infatuated with Faraday. If it had been right after the first video, why didn't she join the collective sooner? She acted so proud about running the fan club, but, like, the fan club post-collective hadn't been anything special.

I thought. I'd stopped following her fan groups after the collective formed and set up in Masdar, so maybe some of them being special news missed me. Paying attention to boring things would never be part of my skill set.

I noticed the open hatch before I realized it was number 906. Her quarters. My fingers wound round and round the zero, appreciating the symmetry, the rightness of it, as I tried to convince myself to walk inside. Should I knock? I mean, the door was open.

But I heard voices.

Viveca's made my stomach go squirmy, how it sat in that unexpected place like a sound I didn't know I wasn't hearing before. It brought back the softness of her hands and those challenging eyes, and a current of heat rose in my core.

I gulped that nonsense back because it didn't matter. It was a silly hormonal crush. A nothing. Besides, she was horrible, and she hated me.

I had meant to plan my approach, so when she went all bossy-pants and slammed vocabulary down on me like a gavel, I wouldn't clam up and choke. For days I'd lain awake, convinced an idea one thousand times better than her Fara-days-of-the-week would strike me before breakfast. Not because I was such a fountain of ideas, but because that idea was so *so* bad, anything else must be better.

I'd had no ideas at all. Then pudding happened. Then mousse and cookies and pie. Making nice with the ovens had stolen my whole brain, and time had run on ahead of me.

Another hatch opened a few doors further down the hall. Music spilled out, some pre-melt symphonic mix, and out danced a middle-aged couple with their hands lost inside each other's home clothes. Drapey things, colorful. Fabric for no reason.

I recognized the song playing. "Work It." It had been on Faraday's victory playlist.

An idea burped up like an air bubble in bread. Finally. I stepped over the threshold.

Viveca's quarters were worlds apart from what I'd been imagining. Maybe it was the way she talked, or how she presented herself as royalty with a capital "R," I'd assumed she was some rich kid from the heartland of the Incorporated American States. A New2Yorker. A blue blood, born of two continents, with every advantage beauty and intelligence could win.

But instead of old-world treasures, crushed velvet, and family portraits, the back wall was papered with drawings and essays, most of them lauding my sister's gravdrive and her original dome designs. Faraday's face was doodled in the margins over and over.

From the story the photographs painted, Viveca and her gaggle of friends—Joule and others I didn't recognize—had gone to some posh brick and ivy school when they were tweens, but after that she branched off into private studies and travel, where she smiled identical smiles for the camera in brightly-lit apartments, straw huts, and gleaming hotel lobbies.

It was beautiful, in a peculiar way. I'd met superfans before, but this was different somehow. She must have used her entire weight allotment to transport these keepsakes.

That was commitment or something.

The only creation of mine that earned keepsake status had been a macaroni sculpture made during my extended time in the collective's kindergarten where we had small, tutored courses in the spare rooms of the research department.

My gaze hitched on a photo of Viveca, Joule, and another young Black person, presumably before a formal. They looked magnificent, Joule in a tux and Viveca in a strapless hunter-green gown that swung loose around her forever legs. Their other partner wore a purple suit. They were shorter than Viveca, with round cheeks and a bright smile.

The most recent picture was of Viveca and an older white woman I guessed was her mom, except the pasty woman looked nothing like her statuesque, dark-skinned daughter. Different noses, chins, eyes, hair, figures—nothing in common. I looked for a picture of her dad to round out the image in my head, or anything from her early childhood, but there weren't any. Not even one.

Maybe her dad was a donor. Or she was adopted. Or maybe he was the greatest guy in the world, and that was who her grief never ended for, so they kept his pictures somewhere else. Seemed weird to me though. I'd die without pictures of Faraday. Even now, my eyes kept flicking to Viveca's doodles of her.

Voices rose from the bedroom, and I froze, listening.

"Please be serious," Viveca was saying. "You're the only one I can talk to about this."

"Now though?" someone asked, their voice muffled. It couldn't be Joule. It was too high, and the accent was old Carolina drawl, not European.

"Yes now! I can't wait around for their next move," Viveca answered, but not in the snap turtle way she said most things. Huh. "It's only a matter of time—" there was some ruckus from the mattress that swallowed the rest of her sentence. "I need your help getting an open channel. Your mom's the only way I can think of."

"You could lose your residency, V. You're finally safe. I just—"

"I don't have a choice! You know what they're like. I've wasted too much time already trying other ways."

"I hate this so much."

"Will you help me?" Viveca asked.

The squeal of my boot on the floor brought a sudden silence from the bedroom, while I was still wondering who the mysterious "they" could be. Viveca had said "what they're like" as though it made her sick. An ex maybe? A rival? Did psychologists even have rivals? I suppose if any did, she probably would.

"Hello?" I called innocently like I'd just arrived. "I guess I'm early. The door was open."

"One second!" Viveca bellowed back.

I plopped onto the couch and a few moments later she appeared in her doorway. She led me to her bedroom where makeup and other wildly expensive cosmetic products sat neatly on a shelf. It occurred to me that none of these things were supposed to be in her quarters, since the washroom attendants were in charge of stuff like that. But given the pranks involving disappearing lotion that now extended to towels, stocked water tubes, and who-knew-what else, it made sense to keep precious things out of view. Still, I couldn't reconcile the luxuries with the worshipful wallpaper.

"Lane, this is my girlfriend Halle," Viveca said.

"Lane freaking Tanner, oh my god!" Halle squealed. She rushed me, wrapping me in a tight hug that stole my breath. "I'm so excited to finally meet you! You're even cuter in person."

She was Black and beautiful, and chubby like me, but rounder and softer in all the best ways. Her dark chestnut skin had coral undertones, and she had springy black curls twisted with ocean blue strands that framed her oval face.

It hit me all of a sudden that I recognized her from that formal photo where she'd worn a purple suit. That must have been before she fully transitioned like Chef and Zara.

Before I could respond, Halle pulled back and sprawled on the freshly made bed in her wrinkled uniform. In less than a second, she was playing a game on a tablet and humming happily beneath a headshot of Viveca.

I looked for signs of tension on her face but saw nothing there to prompt me to ask what they'd been talking about. Besides, if I didn't want Viveca digging too hard through my secrets, I should leave hers alone. At least for now.

"Make room for Lane," Viveca ordered, and Halle rolled over.

I perched on the edge of the mattress and chewed my lip. Why hadn't I made her come to my quarters instead? We could have sat in my austere living room and not been bombarded by a lifetime of memories.

Viveca studied me, from my super-brushed hair to my over-sized feet. I wore a clean uniform, but I had the shirt part loosely tied around my waist so only my navy tank top showed. She sighed.

"What?" I fidgeted with my bra strap which had worked its way into view. "What are you thinking?"

She crossed her arms. "You look nothing like her."

Really, ice queen? All my years of looking into mirrors, and I never realized. "Neither do you."

Halle giggled but kept her focus on her tab. She was so easy to read it made Viveca seem much more accessible.

Viveca cleared her throat. "But you're smarter than you act."

"I hope you have a point."

"I'm getting there." She cocked her head, still staring. "Did you know you're the youngest person here? Out of twelve hundred, you're the baby."

"Oh." I had no idea, but I couldn't be the youngest by much, months or days at most. There must be other twenty-year-olds. And I'd seen Viveca's file. She had only just turned twenty-one herself. What a ridiculous thing to hang up on. "Does that matter?"

"It might be useful to mention when we present our final plan."

"I don't want special treatment."

"I'm only exploring options. I don't—I don't always come across the best in person. Maybe you noticed. Did you do sports?"

I laughed. "I'm awkward and slow, but I played soccer some."

"Me too!" Halle chimed in. "They're building a field in the next dome."

Viveca shushed her with a finger and asked me, "Were you any good?"

"Hardly." I wasn't terrible, but I wasn't good either. "Better at yard games." I mimed a frisbee toss.

"At least you had some training. Math, history, or science. Which was your best subject?"

I groaned, disliking this conversation more every second. "None of them, okay? I scraped by at everything."

"Art?" She was relentless. I could almost see her mental spreadsheet shrinking with each answer I gave.

"I like to *look* at art." Was she going to make me list everything I sucked at? All at once? I didn't need her help for that.

"Favorite music?" she asked.

"Depends on my mood."

"What did you want to grow up to be when you were eight?"

"A mermaid."

"Aww, so cute!" Halle cut in, raising her eyes. "Wait, not one of those creepy lake mermaids, right? 'Cause... ew."

"Seriously, Lane. What realistic life goal did you have?"

"Look, I never got high marks for anything except cooperation, and I never thought about my future outside of coming to the moon, but my sister was supposed to be—and I was supposed to have more time too. To figure out me. I don't see what this quiz of yours is supposed to accomplish or what it could possibly have to do with my sister's memorial." I was on my feet somehow. "And I don't have to be a genius to notice you're picking me apart for fun. What the hell are you on about?"

I waited for her to lose the cool mask and banshee-claw me with her gorgeous fingers. Why hadn't I taken the lead and suggested a dance right away? At least then we'd be arguing on topic.

Halle frowned at her game.

"I'm trying to get to know you is all, to know who I'm working with. You don't have a college transcript for me to study, or I'd have just done that. I honestly am not trying to fight with you. This is how I talk!" Viveca's voice cracked with exasperation and her lower lip trembled.

Just once, but my anger withered.

I couldn't count the times I'd had to say those same words

to my parents and tutors, to strangers and classmates. Even friends. People said I rambled or didn't make any sense, that I talked too loud or too quiet, too fast or too slow. That I sounded mean or angry when I was trying to be friendly. Rude when I was sure I was being polite.

It's how I talk.

"I don't want to fight either," I said. "This is personal is all." My gaze wandered to the door. I should leave before this got worse. Try again another day. Another month even.

She sat beside Halle and patted the bed. "Come here." Her voice was soft but not sugary like it was for Joule. It was amazing to me how she had so much control over her tone while her words seemed to be fighting for control as they came out. "Take a breath."

I exhaled noisily. It didn't help. I sat anyway.

"That never helps me either, but it was worth a try. Halle?"

"Tapping in!" Halle bopped my shoulder with a pillow. "So, what do you do for fun?"

I glanced at her game device, a modified mobile tab, abandoned on the bedspread. I wished I had one of my own, but apparently kitchen staff didn't warrant personal tech assignments.

"The usual stuff," I said. "I play games, watch movies, read books. I used to cook for fun lots, but now it's my work. I like baking though."

Halle lit up. "You game *and* make pie? V, please don't scare her away. I love her so, so much."

"I'm trying not to. Shh." Viveca settled into a lotus pose. "We should start with some ground rules, because you're right. This is personal. We're going to be delving into your sister's life and legacy. I don't need a degree to tell me you've got some major resistance to collaborating with me on the memorial. Maybe the memorial in general."

"Sounds about right," I said.

The more she talked, the harder it was for me to keep up. She was like a speeding train that went all directions at once and anything I said aside from agreeing or not might derail her entirely. Then it would have been on me to pick up the pieces and direct the conversation, but I wasn't that fast or clear about where I was going, so this whole talking-to-each other experiment would completely explode.

"We'll meet three times a week," she said. "Twice after first shift to review your sister's history, and half the day on Fridays to go over proposals. We're on the same schedule, so it should be easy to coordinate our time off."

"Wait." My brain rattled through reasons that wouldn't work for me, how I *couldn't*. Why I shouldn't. Pressure built like steam in my chest, and words spilled out of me as "I'm a Little Teapot" played at full volume over my voice. "Couldn't we just—what if we—I mean, maybe none of that's necessary. I had an idea on the way here, and we could do that and be done. A dance. We plan a dance. Fara—she *loved* to dance. We do that and boom boom, no more meetings."

"Lane..." Viveca sighed again. Halle cringed and buried her face in her game. I'd said it wrong and ruined it.

"What? Really, it's perfect."

"No," Viveca said, quieter but flat as a pancake. "Isaac Newton got a tomb and a gate. Marie Curie has dozens of statues. Moses got a mountain."

"That's my vote!" Halle chirped. "Give Faraday a mountain."

Viveca snorted a laugh, surprising me. "A dance is too small. Too fleeting. Plus, think about the people who it mattered most to your sister to include in the trust, disabled and neurodiverse people. Would a dance memorial work for deaf people or wheelchair users? And that's only people who are physically here on the moon. What about those still on Earth who want to participate? We have to think about next year and the next. Hundreds of years from now."

"If you knew any deaf people or wheelchair users, you'd know they like dances too," I countered, mostly under my breath because I knew it only defused half her argument.

If humans did manage to survive more than another hundred years, they ought to know Faraday's name. Her story. She'd be the reason we made it that far.

What had I been thinking throwing up a dance? I slumped, deflated.

"It'll be all right," she pressed. "We'll figure it out. And if there's something we can do to make this all easier for you, tell me."

Think fast, I told myself. This might be my only chance to make demands she agreed to without a verbal avalanche. Despite my best effort to block out her pillow talk with Halle, it swam to the front of my mind. Whoever *they* were, they were more important to Viveca than Faraday somehow, more important than staying on the moon even. But Halle was a gamer, so maybe I'd misheard the whole thing. They could have been role playing or something.

I wished I could relay their whole bit to Andrek, because he was a master problem solver and could have set it all straight, but considering how suspicious of Viveca he already was, that could make things worse. He might not want me working with her at all.

I didn't want that, though I didn't know *why* I didn't want that. Me being involved was a fluke. An accidental collision of my temper with her mouth.

It was just... people like Viveca didn't usually talk to me. Not nicely. And they certainly didn't listen to me. We might as well have been different species. She was a Can, and I was a Cannot. Graceful versus awkward. I was cute enough, especially on a good hair day, but I was not "pretty" the way she was.

Plus, she was scary smart, like, it was probably hard for her to talk to people like me. My sister was like that too, and I could tell how difficult it was for her to try to explain things sometimes. But Viveca, for better or worse, was doing what she could to give me a say.

I needed to keep Andrek away from her, and her away from him. And I had to stop thinking about how pretty she was and smelling the aftereffects of her and Halle. It was far too distracting.

"For starters, we should meet somewhere else." I said. "And three times a week won't work for me, at least not to start with, but maybe we can build up to it."

She shrugged one shoulder and gestured to the door. "I only wanted to meet in my quarters this time to get better acquainted. You can pick the next place."

As I walked out of her bedroom, I added, "And I don't want you spoon-feeding me your ideas one at a time. I'm not a baby bird. Send your whole petition to me along with all your notes so I can catch up. I might need a month or so to get through it all. And some topics are going to be off-limits."

We settled onto opposite sides of the couch beneath her memorabilia wall. Halle dragged her feet and flopped onto a chair, still engrossed in her game.

"Fine. Now are you done looking for a way out of this? Because this can't be some half-assed project."

I stared at my feet, considering. Goodbye, leisurely naps and after dinner games with Andrek. Goodbye, free time to zone out or date or anything fun. Hello, stopwatch morning quickies and micromanaging my waking hours to the minute. I imagined my too-packed schedule wavering, off-balance.

Don't let me fall, my sister whispered, and the purple globe, her home of ashes, teetered atop my stack of toy commitments. Of course I couldn't hear her, but some part of me could and there she was, plain as day, her hand outstretched, reaching.

Then my mom was in my head too, saying how little I could handle, that I didn't have what it takes. But she was wrong. I would make it work somehow.

I told Viveca, "All in," and relished the genuine smile that lit her face.

Then a groaning sound filled my ears, and the air rippled strangely.

Halle toppled forward out of her chair with a yelp.

I thought I screamed, but an ear-splitting growl drowned me out. The endless pages overhead fluttered as the wall shivered. Popping noises jolted beneath me, as though assorted sizes of bubble wrap were getting steam rolled.

An alarm blared a raucous, repetitive whine that set my ears ringing in response.

The rational part of my brain relayed that something had happened to the gravdrives. I didn't know what exactly, but it must have been bad.

Loud and clear as that rational part was, it got swallowed up by the rest of me, that was too busy freaking out and screaming, "DANGER! DANGER!" to listen to reason.

My breath came in rapid spurts, and my skin went ice cold, tense as stretched rubber. Halle was crying and crawling across the floor, but her body kept lifting and dropping, her eyes wide as cereal bowls.

Everything shook and shook. Coal-colored dust spit out of the ceiling's air recyclers and swirled like smoke clouds. The lights flickered. Emergency power blinked blue across the wall trim, turning day to dusk.

Papers floated through the air.

Viveca shrieked over the din, "Quake! Get to the walls!"

Attention: ALL

Subject: Missing Supplies

Whoever is hoarding towels and toiletries, stop it! Return these items to any restroom storage area immediately!

—Dr. Tanner, Planning

CHAPTER SEVEN

LOSING GROUND

I must have learned about moon quakes during conditioning. It seemed the sort of thing that must have been covered alongside radiation poisoning, freezing temperatures, and bone density issues. I knew Guanghan and Blackstone had struggled with quakes their first couple of years, but by the time Mirage and the one whose name I always forgot got built, they'd worked out most of the kinks. I tried to remember what to do, but I couldn't think straight. It was happening too fast.

Dust stuck in my throat, and I gagged and clutched at my neck when all I wanted to do was cover my ears. I dropped to the floor, mostly on purpose, and clambered toward the walls.

Somehow, miraculously, Viveca maintained her composure. In short order, she gathered safety harnesses to slip around our waists and clip to the wall. She produced masks from somewhere, and she tightened one over her face before tossing the others to me and Halle. My eyes were so clogged with dust, I couldn't tell where she found any of these contraptions. Halle's screams soured into something like squawks as she buried her head under her arms.

The alarm wailed on and on, seeming louder every second. A cool blue light sparkled on the swirling carbon dust, like it danced along to that metallic clatter and deafening drone. I felt numbed by it all, too barraged to feel properly scared.

It was entirely possible my brain had no idea how to process real danger. Not because I was autistic, but because Earth was bananas and nuts, day after day.

Once, I had slept through a hurricane that stole our garage clean off the house, the same storm that had swallowed California. I'd been all, "Oh wow, the sky is green and purple, what?" at bedtime, then it was snooze town the whole night through until I woke, ready for breakfast and curious why the air smelled like tree sap.

Every moment on Earth was either one minute past or before the next terrible emergency. No reason the moon should be different.

I crawled closer to Viveca, and as she fit the harness over me, her face was no longer hers. Instead, I saw Faraday, her face fierce and full of plans.

My chest splintered, missing her, and something inside me broke.

"Faraday?"

"Hold still. I'm trying to help you," Viveca ordered, but I couldn't answer. The lights flickered off and I was plunged into darkness, into the one space in my head I tried so hard to avoid. With a pinched breath, I plummeted to the center, and it wasn't now but then.

Then.

The night she'd died.

Faraday's eyes shone my way, their light yet undimmed, and her crimson skirt swung in orbit around her legs. This was Masdar, just outside of the collective's compound. Drums boomed and rattled past as the band circled her campaign crowd.

A transformer blew in the distance. Then another.

Her smile curdled. Darkness descended, and sirens drowned out the drums.

"Fuck!" I screamed. I reached for her, but she was too far, and the street had shifted. Faraday's face twisted with anger. Panic. Smoke and dust stung my throat. I forced my feet over broken pavement and shards of glass as Royal Corps squads zipped down from the sky like falling stars.

An explosion rocked the world as sirens and alarms rolled together into thunder.

"This way," Faraday hollered, and I followed when she ducked into an alley, trying not to look at the familiar faces on the bodies littering the ground as I hurdled over them. Her hand broke free from mine, and she lit a torch to rummage through her duffel bag, withdrawing sturdier clothes and boots. "Take the cut through ahead. It's a shortcut to the collective. I'll meet you there as soon as I can." She slipped off her dress and stuffed it into the bag, redressing quickly.

"I'm not leaving you!" I screamed.

She pushed the duffel at me. The zipper didn't close all the way, and the sleeve of her dress stuck out from the hole. It wasn't even folded. "Our meeting place isn't far. I'll be fast."

She hugged me, but I couldn't feel it. She kicked an oven-sized grate to the alley floor, then she crawled through the hole, dropping into the darkness.

I started toward her, but I was too slow, too far away. An angry roar shook the alley, and I jumped out of the way just as the ceiling cracked and caved in, pouring sandy rubble over me.

Something was burning. The broken ceiling had blocked the hole.

"My leg. I can't move!" Faraday cried, and I wasn't strong enough to lift the rest of the wreckage out of the way. Trickles of fire snapped and spread toward me, but I ignored them, clawing at the blockade, clearing enough away to see her face crisscrossed by beams of light.

The Royal Corps were in the tunnel too, and my sister was trapped in their path.

"Lane! Go!"

"Enemy soldier!" a man yelled. I couldn't see him, but his voice told me he was awfully close. "Come forward with your hands in the air!"

"I can't move!" she yelled back, her voice pitched in desperation. "I'm unarmed. Not a soldier."

Gunfire popped in the distance. Too close. So many voices shouting.

Dust caked my throat. "Don't hurt her!" I braced my legs against the burning rubble, tugging with everything I had.

"Comply or I will—" The wreckage gave, enough so chunks of ceiling fell through the opening to land beside her. "There's more coming through. Fire!"

Gunshots pierced through the screaming.

My throat was raw.

"One down. Find another way!"

I couldn't move or think. I saw Faraday below in the firelight, her torch rocking back and forth at her side.

One down. *One* down. One *down*.

Gunshots and someone went down.

Someone. My sister.

Black liquid poured from her chest, her face cloud white, but she was not dead. She wasn't. She couldn't be. She *wouldn't*.

Her eyes were open and clear as ever, weren't they?

The alleyway buckled, burying me, unable to know.

In the dark, always.

The harness clicked into place, buckling me back into reality, into the trust. The lion's roar of the air recycler sucked specks of dust into its circular maw. Tears rolled down my cheeks unbidden. I blinked through them, and my sister's ghost vanished from Viveca's features. She squinted at me like I'd started belting showtunes.

I thanked her quickly and squeezed her hand. For some reason I was afraid to let go. When she turned, I wiped the memories away and made myself small, tucking my head down.

We hugged the walls, gripping our lifelines, while the dome trembled like an unsteady snow globe. I gripped my harness cord and waited with hitched breath for the quake to end. My body ached all over, and I expected bruises would

JR CREADEN

bloom beneath my clothes.

The vision of my sister was a fog that wouldn't lift. The rush of relief I'd felt at seeing her, or thinking I saw her, terrified me, as if her face alone could erase the guilt I felt or all that had gone wrong since death took her away.

"Minor quake," Joule explained, his breath hot in my ear. I didn't remember him arriving, but he was strapped in between me and Halle, with Viveca on my right. The tremors had stopped, and the alarm had too, but the recyclers droned on. "Wrong time for a deep quake. This has to be from an impact. Likely a meteor hit somewhere in our atmosphere. Dampeners would have absorbed most of the impact, but our dome can withstand—Oh. I think it's settling."

The air recyclers powered down, and our ragged breaths grated in the sudden silence. We chimed in, one after another, with *I'm okays*, before Viveca basically catapulted out of her harness to glare down at me.

"What just happened?" she demanded.

"I suppose you couldn't hear me," Joule said. "I was explaining—"

"Not that, Joule. Lane!" Viveca's stare bored into me. Brown, not green. Not my sister. Andrek's words swam back to me, *She's scary smart. What if she starts digging?*

"I." I couldn't decide how to answer, so I struggled to unclip my harness and got to my feet, settling on evasion. "It's nothing. Sensory overload or whatever."

"That was *not* nothing," she pressed. Her gaze roamed over me as if she was clocking my pulse and breathing, cataloging every way my body betrayed me.

"Sensory stuff, oh yes," Joule agreed. "We all get that, don't we?"

"Spectrum squad, yay," Halle sang, but her voice was weak and wobbly.

"That's not what I'm talking about, and Lane knows it." Viveca crossed her arms and studied my hair. "You called me Faraday. Did you hit your head?"

"Maybe? I don't think so, but it's fine now, okay? I'm fine."

She couldn't know where my mind had gone. She wasn't psychic. It wasn't like this happened to me a lot, usually only when there wasn't enough light as I fell asleep. I was good at avoiding it the rest of the time. "I should go and, like, check on my parents and Andrek. Send me the schedule or whatever. Bye, all."

Halle waved with a shrug, and Joule flashed his beautiful smile.

I stuffed my hands into my pockets and made for the exit.

"Lane, wait!" Viveca put herself between me and the door.

"Why?"

"There's no uncomplicated way to say this." Her pitch rose sharply. "I apologize that the memorial got sprung on you the way it did. I should have considered how this would affect your family. How it would affect you. As young and inexperienced as you are, of course you'll need time and help. After what you've been through, that's got to come first."

I shook my head. She was going to go on about those grief groups again. I felt silly for being so against it, especially knowing Faraday wanted all the trustees participating, since we'd have left a planet and who knows what else behind. And that was before we'd lost more.

But I didn't like being told to do things by people who didn't know me. "I don't need—"

"Don't be ridiculous." She laid a hand on my upper arm, her thumb sliding into a tender spot above my elbow where the harness had rubbed.

I could feel her staring, but I didn't raise my head. I watched a little vein on her neck throb as she spoke softer. Only to me.

"Of course you need therapy, Lane. You've lost your sister and the friends you grew up with, left your home planet, and now here you are volunteering to make enormous decisions about honoring the very sister who sent you here in the first place. I know what I saw. You were gone."

"Why does it matter so much to you?" It wasn't what I mean to say, which was something closer to "mind your business," except now that it was out, I decided it was a much better question. Especially since it made her stutter-step and let me pass.

But before the hatch closed behind me, she added, "Like it or not, I'm signing you up for a group before we start meeting officially, because it should matter more to *you*."

Attention: ALL

Subject: Quake Report

Our heartfelt gratitude goes out to our lunar neighbors at the IAS, UC, and EAC bases, whose foresight and hard work into moon quake stabilization allowed us to prevent catastrophic losses during today's impact event.

Though two dozen of our own suffered injuries, we are pleased to share Medical's report that they were minor and easily treated.

—President Marshall

CHAPTER EIGHT

TO BE SEEN

As soon as I left my quarters for work the next morning, I got stopped in the hallway. A maintenance crew had a number of wall panels stacked on the floor as they worked on something with the mess of wiring beneath. Surrounding the crew and their tools was another chattering group, security. There was no way around them, so all I could do is wait for them to let me pass.

"Fixing the door controls, I hope?" Mom asked, stepping up beside me. "That was scheduled a month ago, but I'm glad it's finally become a priority."

She surveyed the crew with a wary gaze, probably reviewing each worker's stats in her head. Her hair was neatly styled into a bun, though deep circles ringed her eyes and the pallor of her skin told its own story.

I preferred tired Mom to normal Mom most days, but not while trapped with her in the hall. Maybe I could slip into our quarters and squeeze in more sleep.

"A few more minutes, ma'am," a security guard told us. She had platinum blonde hair fixed into a long, sturdy braid.

"Apologies for the wait, er, twice over."

Mom waved her hand dismissively and turned to go back to our rooms.

"Yeah, that's going to be locked for a bit now," the guard added. "Sorry again."

Mom rose one shoulder in a sort of shrug then leaned against the wall.

I slid to sit on the floor beside her, trying to think of something distracting to talk about so she didn't start in on me.

"At least it's getting fixed," I said brightly. "Though it's weird they need a security team to help."

"All the active work crews have security assigned now." Mom rubbed her temples and shifted her feet as if she were considering sitting too.

"Oh," I said, suddenly interested. "I haven't heard anything about that."

She shook her head and appeared to settle on not sitting though she glanced at the floor forlornly. "No reason to broadcast issues. Only stirs rumors. I shouldn't have brought it up."

"What else has gone missing?" I asked, grateful to have landed on a topic that didn't center me. "Will there be security in the kitchen too?" I hadn't noticed any extra security at work. They were always around, I supposed, but why wouldn't they be? Everyone had to eat.

"Odds and ends." She cleared her throat and caught me looking at her. "Minor issues. Don't worry about it."

"At least they're minor."

"Right," she said, lowering her voice. "Anyway. Focus on the memorial. That's where your attention should be." She went quiet a moment, and I expected her lecture to start any minute, so I rushed to find something else to say.

"Can I get a tab? Like, are there extra in your department?" For once I was pleased with what jumped out of my mouth. It'd be awesome to have my own, so I could game wherever I wanted like Halle did.

"What for?"

Gaming, obviously, but I couldn't tell her that. I meant to say, "So I can pay better attention to the announcements," which she'd have liked and agreed to, but instead I said, "Because Viveca's sending me her memorial files, and I'll have a ton of reading to do."

Mom's face hardened. "I don't think that's wise," but she didn't tell me what part wasn't wise—the sending or the reading or me having my own tablet.

"I'm trying to do a good job, Mom, like you wanted. For Faraday." I knew better. I did. But I'd lost control of my lips. "And I'm taking it slow, aren't I? Viveca would have had us building some stupid statue days ago probably."

"You'd do well to follow her lead. She's got a good head on her shoulders." She leveled me with an inscrutable look. "But try to keep things professional? You don't want to exhaust your dating pool in less than a year."

Her opinions about Viveca flooded back to me all mixed together. Flawless. Out of my league. Running things before long. So of course she must have thought I'd screw things up with Viveca if I ever managed to start something.

"I won't do well to follow, actually. I hate her ideas."

Mom's gaze drifted to the ceiling as she asked, "Then what are yours?"

"I don't know yet," I said, basically growling. "That's why I need a tab."

"If her ideas are so awful, why do you want her research?"

"I don't know what else you want from me!"

"None of this is what I wanted, Lane. Please lower your voice." Mom gestured vaguely at the blonde guard, whose sideways looks at me were full of sympathetic cringe. She'd rolled up the sleeves of her uniform, revealing hot pink scars lacing her forearms.

I didn't care if we had an audience. Sure, I'd been dodging this talk for weeks on end, but Mom had been letting me. What kind of mom did that?

"First you were all 'A memorial is important for the trust, Lane, so screw your feelings,' but as soon as I got involved, you're saying 'She can't handle it.' Why can't you give me, like, the tiniest bit of faith?" I was on my feet somehow, and the half an inch of height she had on me didn't seem so much anymore.

"You're completely out of line right now, and I don't think you have any idea what you're saying. Where is all this anger coming from? The memorial *is* important, more than I can possibly explain. And I do think you should be involved, we all should, just not in the capacity of—"

"Of contributing more than a goofy smile and a thumbs-up?" I pasted on my fakest smile and thrust my thumbs out. "Quick," I said, using only the corner of my mouth, "take a picture for the propaganda."

"That's not what I mean. You keep twisting my words!" Bright spots of mottled pink flared over her cheeks. "If you would calm down, we can sort this out."

"I am calm!" I yelled and immediately recoiled from the way her eyes flared.

"All you ever want to do is fight with me," she said, almost too softly to hear. "But I'm not the enemy."

"Then why do you always act like one?"

She groaned and scratched violently at her hair until the bun collapsed. "I don't think I do."

She sounded so sad that I hated her more for it, how her feelings made me dance circles around her while mine changed nothing. "What about a tab? Can you get me one?"

Mom was silent as she forced her hair into a semblance of a ponytail, grizzled hairs floating free over her forehead. Finally she said, "I'll look into it," which meant *The answer's still no.*

I sighed and sank to the floor.

The blonde guard cleared her throat and waited a painful moment for Mom to react. "Sorry again, about the wait. We'll get this cleaned up right away."

"Yes, that's fine. Thank you all." Mom took a loud breath and turned back to me. "I—I hope you have a good rest of the day. I love you."

She wove around the workers, and the guards stepped quickly out of her path. I caught the blonde one's eye and grimaced, provoking a sad laugh from her.

"Not that it's my business, but I think she means well," the guard said. "And not that you asked, but I'd give anything to fight with my mom again. She and my brother worked security for your sister's campaign before... you know. Maybe you knew them? Iris and Jonah Hetzel. I'm Danielle. Danny."

I tried to remember an Iris or Jonah from security but came up blank. "I don't think I met them. Were they—I mean—Did they...?"

Danny busied her hands twisting the end of her braid. "They were there, yeah, but only my mom's body was found." She squared her shoulders and set her jaw. "Anyway. Maybe cut yours some slack. You never know what'll happen."

I didn't know what to say, so I gave her a tight smile. "Thanks, Danny. I'll try."

Two hours into the worst shift yet on the moon, I was holed up in Chef's office nursing a bloody finger and a splitting headache. I couldn't get myself together.

Chef had this sign on her wall that very colorfully explained how time worked on the moon. Like, a lunar day was actually 655.72 Earth hours long, so a "bad day" on the moon was really only a bad few seconds. I didn't totally get it, but I appreciated the sentiment as I rocked on her couch and tried not to scream about how ill I felt all over.

My body was basically one big bruise, and I didn't bruise pretty and purple. I went straight to a mottled blue-black before it faded into puke green and jaundice yellow like the grossest tie-dye ever. According to my bruising timeline, I'd be looking exactly my worst when Joule took me and Andrek out for our rain-checked date that night. Or roughly half a lunar second from then.

I kept thinking about how desperate Viveca had sounded

with Halle. Then that lip quiver and an apology. A real person was under the mask she wore—her being with people as awesome as Halle and Joule was proof—so I'd be an asshole to hold it against her when she was the only one of us to keep her cool in the quake, the only one able to act with more than shock.

She hadn't been unsettled during the quake because she was already unsettled. Already afraid. Of *them*, whoever that was. Somewhere between her Faraday-obsessed childhood and her triumphant admission into the trust, something had spooked her enough to carry that fear here to the moon.

Knowing she hid something so important prickled curiosity across my skin. I'd always loved a good mystery, but it felt crispy and strange in real life, with real people. I'd focus on the memorial with her for now, hoping the truth would come out.

Anyways, in the meantime I'd have my hands full trying to make her treat Faraday like an actual person instead of only a glorified hero. My sister was both, and Viveca's ideas would be intolerable until she understood that.

"Knock, knock," Stephan called, peeking through the curtain Chef had fixed over the door opening. "You done bleeding out yet? Chef needs us on the serving line."

I uncurled from the couch and brandished my throbbing finger. "Second bandage did the trick. I'll be out in a few." I didn't add "minutes," because that lunar time sign had my head all screwed up.

"Not like that," he scolded and made me scoot to make room for him. Before I could form the words to argue that I was fine, that I didn't need help, he removed the clunky dressing, cleaned, treated, and redressed my wound. "There. Smooth edges and not too much pressure. You shouldn't even feel it under your gloves now."

"You could be a nurse," I said, impressed at how much better my finger felt when I hadn't even realized it was still bothering me. "You make that look easy."

Stephan blushed at my compliment. "Anything you do

often enough starts to look easy from the outside."

"Still. Thanks."

"Besides, there's better company in the kitchen," he said with a wink. "Don't forget your hairnet."

"I would never!" I scooped up the tangled thing and stretched it over my head. Flecks of dry dough from this morning's pie-making crumbled onto the couch, and I scraped them into my hands before I left. I wasn't sure if the trust had rodents, but the collective sure had, so I'd rather not take chances.

The serving line was extra complicated today because we were serving mango and black bean wraps, and Chef thought making them ahead of time would be disgusting. "Hot beans and cold fruit turn into inedible lukewarm mush if they sit too long," she told us.

So, twenty of us stood elbow to elbow, serving each plate fresh alongside a pile of rice pilaf, seaweed salad, and a handful of grapes.

My mouth watered at the blend of aromas, even as my headache throbbed at the clamor of kitchen staff and caf- eteria chatter. On my left was Stephan, laying the warmed tortillas flat between the rice and salad, then scooting each plate to me for spiced beans.

"One helping or two?" I asked over and over, until the words became their own meaningless mush, the swarm of faces a slideshow of the same. I sprinkled a dash of dried mint or parsley over each plate, just to add that one special touch. Every few minutes though, we got backed up wait- ing for more tortillas—Chef preferred we serve right off the grill—and those in line ended up pulling us into their conversations.

Most trustees who got stalled chatted about the quake, comparing their bruises and shock, and how well they had or hadn't reacted when the alarms sounded. Stephan, who sported an eggplant purple eye, told vivid tales of being caught in the group showers.

"I'd just come from a gym class, so I was still clothed,"

he said for the fifth time, now to Danny and a group of her fellow guards. "But the others weren't so lucky. Soon as the lights went out after that first rumble, you'd have thought we were on a sinking ship. Limbs tangled like ropes, water sloshing everywhere. We were all too slippery to get our safety harnesses on right. Total mess!"

"I heard about that," Danny said, grinning at me as I heaped beans directly onto her fresh tortilla. "Seems like the most embarrassing way to meet new people."

"You're not wrong."

I tried to join in too, after a while, and rolled up my sleeves to show how strange the colors looked next to my constellations of freckles. But Stephan's story was more interesting, while mine still felt personal and private.

By the time folks made it back for seconds, there was a steady back-and-forth across the line about other topics, like the recent storms on Earth and which nation states were most vulnerable to the RC because of it, the ships we'd soon build, and all sorts of self-care talk.

And, of course, Faraday. If they'd met her, where, and when. What they'd been doing when they saw her first video. How her first, second, and third books made them feel or led them to discovering what they wanted to do with their lives. The whole cafeteria hummed her name as stories poured out. It was good.

Really good.

I started to think this was what Viveca and I should be doing before making any big decisions—listening to people, letting them tell us how they wanted to honor her.

Once my shift ended, I was high with so much energy I practically floated to my quarters. My bruises still sang with pain, but that was yesterday's news, yesterday's problem, because, tonight, Andrek and I had a date with Joule. An actual, somebody-made-special-plans, not-just-a-hangout-or-hookup Date. A real, I-had-better-not-fuck-this-up-for-us Date.

"Ohmigod, will you get in here please? I'm losing my mind!" Andrek screamed the moment I stepped into our wrecked living room. Every surface but the table had clothes piled on top, and a cursory glance told me he'd gathered options from every decade since humans first made it to the moon, maybe further. Dark skirts and pants of all lengths covered the chair, jewel-toned dresses hung from the shelf, precariously close to Faraday's urn, and a veritable rainbow mountain of pinks, butter yellows, sandy beige, and mint greens engulfed the couch.

The visual effect was super overwhelming and made my head spin.

"What kind of unholy deal did you make with entertainment?" I poked at something lacy pink and shuddered at the coarse texture. "And why is there so much pastel? You know it washes you out."

He whimpered. Pitifully. "Will you puh-*lease* come here?"

"I thought you were wearing Bentley," I said, referring to his favorite suit, the one outfit his RC money paid for that he didn't shun.

I headed toward his room, stopping to run a finger down the hem of a hunter-green dress. If I wore this, would Joule think of his dance with Viveca? A shiver wiggled through me, and I retracted my hand.

Andrek stumbled out, groaning loudly and struggling with who-knew-what behind him. "Lane, help me!"

He spun and leaned against the wall to steady himself, his hands lost inside some laced contraption that ran the length of his back. I guessed it was a corseted vest.

Along with that, he had on his tailored pants, the lower half of "Bentley"—slim-fit, navy with silver pinstripes, and damn sexy. His breath whistled out of him, and his face was splotchy with red spots.

I untangled his fingers and went to town undoing the lacing, working hard not to giggle.

I'd seen him nervous before. Plenty. His nerves had been so high when we met, the day of his first interview with the collective in Masdar, it had seemed like the wind could shatter him like glass.

This was different though, a whole new level of excitement and anxiety, which sent a flurry of thoughts scampering through my head.

What did it mean that Joule had him all worked up this way? What did it mean that I'd hardly thought about it? Joule had made a point of asking us both out, but maybe he was only being respectful of what Andrek and I have. He hadn't included Viveca or Halle, which was best, whatever. I still needed to keep as much distance between Andrek and Viveca as possible.

But was it a big deal that I didn't stir Andrek up this much, this way? It had always been so easy with us. Comfortable, relaxed. I couldn't decide if I should be worried or not, and the indecision alone knotted my stomach like a pretzel.

This date had to go well. Andrek did so much for us, and he'd been so careful with me. He needed Joule or someone like him to lighten the load he carried inside. Otherwise our own "good thing" wouldn't last nearly as long as either of us needed it to. And that would be tragic.

Once he was free, Andrek let out a colossal breath and wrapped me in a hug. "Oh, thank you, thank you. I don't know what I was thinking. Terrible idea. I wanted to fancy things up somehow."

I tried not to feed the bear that was my internal back-and-forth by gauging the hug's intensity or length. Just because he wanted Joule didn't mean he wanted or needed me any less. "Bentley isn't fancy enough?"

"No!" He released me and draped himself over the pastel mountain that was now the couch. "Have you *seen* Joule? That jawline, ahhh! His voice! What are you wearing?"

I clamped down my runaway thought train. "Did he tell you what he planned? Maybe I should wear a jump—"

"No the fuck you *shouldn't*," he said, and I stifled a laugh at the squeak in his voice, because he was obviously in a whole mood. "Which is why I laid some things out for you on your bed. I like the cream best, but I'm not sure if it matches Bentley. Hence the, uh, all this."

He patted the fabric mountain tenderly. So tenderly, in fact, that my swirling gut sank with the responsibility he'd put on me. *Please don't mess this up*, he was saying without words.

I went to my room and shut the door behind me, ignoring Andrek's indignant sigh when it closed. It was probably best if he didn't see me spiraling when he was already on edge. I knew he loved me, that what we had was special. I needed to get my game face on and support him. Support *us*.

On my bed were three outfits, all with pants, thank goodness. I'd never been comfortable in the open air of skirts and dresses, though I liked to imagine myself wearing them. I couldn't ever figure out how to move or sit, and I ended up so in my head that I couldn't have any fun.

The cream thing was, ironically, still a jumpsuit, albeit a silky blend with wide palazzo-style bottoms. The top half had a loose-fit bodice with a low-hanging drape neck and long sleeves that cinched at the wrist. No tags, covered seams, nothing to irritate my skin, and it would cover my worst bruises. There were tiny, barely noticeable, midnight blue specks that shimmered like tinsel and gave the cream an illusion of depth.

Like the negative of a starry sky. Or a super elegant cupcake.

"Do you love them?" Andrek asked through the door. "If you don't, you can pick something else."

"Hang on." I smoothed the outfit over my clothes, admiring the subtle way it held its shape. It was perfect. Impossibly perfect.

My core unclenched, and the fog in my head cleared. Andrek really was thinking of me, who I was, what I liked, what I needed to feel comfortable. Whatever he—or we might have with Joule wouldn't change "us."

I cracked open the door and saw him waiting for me, a hopeful smile below his worried eyes. A new thought struck like a lightning bolt. It was good that I didn't make him nervous, that he didn't need to break into hives or obsess over his appearance. With me, he was free to be all parts of himself.

And so was I.

"What do you think?" I asked.

He leaned down and kissed me thoroughly, sandwiching the creamy silk between us. "Tasteful and fun. Like you."

Attention: West Gym Users

Subject: Basic Hygiene

Whoever is leaving used towels on the floor, STOP IT. The laundry bins are next to the door for this exact purpose. Not only does it make the gym inaccessible for low mobility and wheelchair-using trustees, it's plain disgusting. We don't need our floors to be a petri dish for your germs.

—Sanitation

CHAPTER NINE

LIKE A TOP

By the time Joule arrived, I'd showered and dressed, and Andrek had decided not to wear a top aside from his Bentley vest. At some point, thespians came and hauled the extra clothes away, but I missed that chaos while I washed up, luckily.

Even still, between the three of us, emotions ran so high I phased out more than I'd like. I managed to process that Joule looked super-hot, said something about surprises and his plan to take us on a proper tour of the trust, since, according to him, we hadn't explored enough. Or I hadn't, at least, since all I did was go to work, the washroom-slash-gym, and back to my quarters. My one visit to Viveca's quarters didn't count because that was only yesterday.

The first fifteen minutes of our date were a blur of the hallway's flat gray panels and speckled molding under lemony lights. Andrek and Joule kept me between them, and Joule explained his favorite facts, pointing out different departments as we walked.

They made like they were talking to me, but really they were nerd-gushing over my head while I concentrated on keeping up with their long legs. I was already fucking things up, I could tell. The best I could do was stay out of the way as much as possible to let them focus on each other.

"Each dome's diameter is precisely three-point-one-four miles," Andrek said, "which makes Lunar Trust One—"

"Pi miles wide," Joule spouted, and when I looked at them in confusion, they were both waggling their eyebrows. "Lane, do you get it?"

Together they repeated, "Pi miles wide!"

"That's a lot of pie?" I asked.

They erupted into laughter, and I forced a chuckle too, so I wasn't the odd one out. It sounded weak, but it seemed to convince Joule.

Andrek, who knew better, half shrugged and changed the subject, letting me slip into my head, except now I was thinking about pie.

Faraday had made a pitiful looking pie for her first date with Zara and Khalid. Chocolate cherry pecan. It had tasted great, because I helped, but it looked a complete mess. I remembered how she'd burst into our flat after, smelling like all things good and warm, her cheeks pinked, and her lips swollen from kissing. She'd been on a lot of other dates, mostly with couples or trios, because her time had been so precious. "I finally found them, dove," she'd told me that night. "The ones who fill me."

It had struck me as cruel then, what she'd said, when she knew she was my whole world. As though I was nothing, as though I gave her nothing. I hadn't met Andrek yet though, so I couldn't understand what she meant, how there was a part of her that would always be outside of me, where I didn't belong.

Now I wondered how she knew for sure, how she could tell that they were the ones for her, whether it was just a choice she'd made or if it was more like a truth she happened upon.

With me and Andrek, it was different, a choice and a truth at once. But we were the couple now, entertaining a third. I didn't know how to do this dating thing at all, I realized.

"First stop!" Joule announced as we reached a closed hatch labeled "Courtyard."

The guys swung the hatch door wide for me as if they'd practiced the move their whole lives, or at least the last few weeks while they'd been seeing each other alone. They were so in sync already, and I felt clumsy and out of place, despite their careful attention.

I stepped inside, thinking only of their *them*ness and my *other*ness, but what I saw shocked all thought away and sent me backward.

Space was right the fuck above me, and it went on forever.

My brain assured me there was a dome, meters thick, and that the view must be an illusion meant to give trustees a sense of "outside," but my eyes argued otherwise, and panic set in. A meltdown was on my horizon; it was only a question of when.

"Awesome, right? The dome's not even a mile high, as many have asserted," Joule said.

That didn't seem true. I couldn't see the dome surface at all. It was just dark nothingness. I gulped my breaths, unable to pull my gaze from the black sky.

"If you look closely, you can see the seams in the video screen," he went on, like this was the most interesting topic and not trivia to ward off the nothing overhead.

"Guys?" I whispered. It was the most I could manage. "Are you sure we should be out here?"

"It's safe." Joule laughed deeply. "If we walked out onto the open moon dressed like this, our lungs would freeze before they could collapse."

That helped. Weirdly.

I forced my chin to my chest and noticed we were standing on grass. Real squishy green grass that stretched across the whole courtyard. There were even bona fide weeds. Dandelions.

My shoes were off seconds later and I dug my toes in. I couldn't help myself. I dropped to the ground and sprawled, letting the grass tickle and poke my skin. It made me think of a blooming cactus I'd had in the collective. It had never flowered. Mom said it was too young. We both were.

The guys stood over me talking, but I'd completely lost track of their colony manual conversation. Something, something else boring, and atmosphere and maximum occupancy, but did you know blah blah and ice asteroid miracles, social welfare, and ethical transparency. They chattered about the other bases, especially Blackstone and Guanghan, and how resources flowed back and forth across the moon. Andrek was in science heaven.

I hitched up my sleeves to expose more skin to the ground. The view wasn't so scary from down here. I could see Earth's curve, glowing. If this was a video projection, it was expertly crafted. Maybe it was a real-time image? There was a breeze, and I almost convinced myself it wasn't forced air hissing through the recyclers.

It could be wind if I didn't look. When I did, warmth bathed my face, and I shielded my eyes. Not the desert bake or the glare of sunset spraying over the treetops, but bright and warm all the same.

Here I could breathe.

Here I could relax.

"This is the best place ever," I said.

Their shadows fell over me, overlapping.

Joule laughed again. "Word is you've seen only the corridors of one-quarter of one dome. I hear the garden has seeds that haven't grown on Earth in thirty years."

"I don't care," I said. "This is my place, and I shall call it Lane Land and defend it with my life."

"Hard to defend anything from the ground," Andrek pointed out.

"Shut up, you. I do plenty from the ground."

To my surprise, they stopped talking and dropped next to me in the grass. After a comfortable silence, Joule told us how he'd left Czechia for Masdar just in time. A lot of folks from the free states had fled to the collective once the Royal Corps had come calling.

It seemed too personal to ask which environmental or political tragedy led his family to Czechia in the first place, so I waited for him to explain if he wanted.

Instead he talked about his work. Apparently, he was a problem-solving whiz, so rather than assigning him to a single task, he sort of belonged to the whole manufacturing department, flitting between other peoples' projects, somehow able to pick up on whatever others had missed.

I was amazed when Andrek talked, because he was usually so cagey about his past. He told Joule about his stint in military service and growing up unhoused. He stopped there, not naming Brand or the RC, but even though he avoided those subjects, his voice held notes of vulnerability I hadn't heard from him since the attack. He wasn't performing for Joule at all.

Neither said a word about the RC's final attack or what it had done to the war crimes accord or why the launch date had to be moved so soon after, which was thoughtful of them. They didn't mention the looming memorial either, thankfully.

I didn't say much. It wasn't like I stayed silent, more like I didn't have anything important I wanted to add. My life story was well known, and my own work projects were public fare on full display every day.

I wiggled to my belly and stared hard into the blades of grass. Delicate roots gripped the imported soil, and it was so perfectly random and asymmetrical I got dizzy.

"I don't know what's taking so long with my surprise. It should be here by now," Joule said, and I perked to attention because I'd forgotten all about surprises. "You may not have as much time to play with yours as I'd hoped, Lane, not before we leave."

"We have to leave?" Groaning, I planted my face onto the dirt. "Can't we stay all night?"

He pushed himself up. "No, there's a group meeting here in—" he checked his tab "—ten minutes, actually."

"For real?"

Andrek's hand found mine and squeezed. "We can come some other time. If you want."

"I'm glad you like it," Joule said, flashing me a warm smile before launching into another technical lecture, this time about the trust's designated green spaces.

I chewed my lips and tried to hush my brain, which was busy working to convince me that I wasn't really on this date. I was some kind of chaperone. A kind gesture to Andrek, the one Joule actually wanted to connect with.

I'd managed to forget about his promised surprises a second time when Viveca showed up in the courtyard with a cart loaded high with space suits, mag boots, and helmets.

I winced when I saw her, because this was the exact opposite of keeping her and Andrek apart. That was going to prove harder than I'd thought, especially with our boyfriends falling so hard for each other.

Viveca handed out suit sets and dragged me aside to help me into mine. After she gave my outfit a cursory glance, she issued a quiet "hmm."

"What's that mean?" I demanded. As usual, it came out more harshly than I intended. Not that I heard it myself so much as I saw her face tighten, her eyes sharpening. "It's borrowed."

"Fits you, is all," she answered. "I was expecting something with spikes or spurs, I guess."

That was rich. Like I was the prickly one. "I wasn't expecting you at all. I thought you two were fighting." In fact, I knew they were fighting, because every time I saw them together in the cafeteria they'd been arguing.

Her laugh startled me with its warmth, even as she shook the suit for me impatiently. "We're always fighting, and that's our business, not yours. Step in now. I don't have all night."

I complied, forcing one leg then the other into the protective boots and pants. "That doesn't sound like..."

I wasn't sure how to finish. Love? Fun? Healthy, maybe.

"Oh, because we're not snuggly cuddle bears like you and Andrek, we must be badly paired?" She shoved the sleeves onto my arms and set into the locking seals that wrapped the front of my chest. "If you're curious about what makes 'us' work, ask Joule. I don't need to prove anything to you."

"Of course not! It's just—" I stammered for the right words, the ones that wouldn't work the opposite of what I meant. "I've never dated, aside from Andrek, so I don't know how other people do it. I'm not sure I'm ready." I snuck a glance at her face as she worked her way up the seals over my chest. "I didn't mean to sound... To pry, I mean."

She met my eyes, and it was like an electrical surge before her thick lashes fluttered to cover the charge. "Oh."

For a moment I wanted her to say more. There was this hesitation in her voice that made me wait, but right then the boys laughed.

Our boys. Having the best time so easily.

It wasn't fair.

"Did you manage to get it?" Joule called, and Viveca straightened abruptly, which sent her shiny hair flying behind her. It smelled like candy. She eyed Andrek's vest with an intense look.

"I wouldn't have been late otherwise." She snapped at my seals with a finger flick that I felt through my spine then nodded approval of her work. "Check the cart. Under the helmets."

I bet she'd been on thousands of dates. Fancy ones, unlike me and my "Let's eat something and have sex before we play video games." With those eyes of hers and those unstoppable lashes so thick they were like three pairs per eye. Her candy hair.

I bet she could dance too. Sexy dances like the tango or salsa, not like me who sort of stomped and flapped to the backbeat. No one would have ever invited her to be the third wheel on her boyfriend's date.

"I need to talk to Lane a minute, okay?" she said. "Girl stuff."

I froze so fast my knees locked and I nearly tipped over onto her. "What, why—"

She pulled me a few steps further away, then whispered conspiratorially, "Be gentle with him, all right? He's nervous. Like, obsessively nervous. It's his first time dating a guy seriously, which is huge on its own, plus you were his imaginary friend when he was little. So just... If he seems aloof or whatever, don't believe it, that's only his autopilot mode. Tonight is important to him."

I couldn't follow her because it didn't make sense. I was his imaginary friend. "Really?"

"I know it might seem like it's all about Andrek," she said, and I was definitely *not* imagining the shadow that fell over her face when she spoke his name. "But that's not it. He has a challenging time talking in groups, but he couldn't keep seeing only one of you without sending the wrong signals. It's fine if you're not ready, or if you don't want to be involved romantically. He'll understand." She ran her hands through her hair and peeked over my shoulder at the guys, worry playing over her features. "You'll be gentle, won't you, and allow time for him to open up? Don't let them pair up without you."

I heard her. I did. But I was doubly convinced then that she saw someone different than I did when she looked at Andrek, and it recolored everything she'd said.

I shook my head, then nodded to mean yes, which I expected made me look like a bobblehead doll and probably didn't communicate anything.

"I will." I squared my shoulders, more certain than ever that it was Andrek who needed protection, not Joule. "He's safe with us. Don't worry."

She stepped back, smiling with something like relief, and patted my shoulder awkwardly. "Good. Thank you. Just—thank you. And go to group tomorrow. We've already wasted too much time."

Viveca whirled away with another burst of candy scent, answering some question of Joule's, and I was left with my back to the boys trying to figure out what to do with my face before I turned around. My body was not answering me fast enough when I told it how to behave.

I didn't know that I was ready for another boyfriend, or if I even wanted one, but Joule was actually a genuine fan of me. Me! Her Joule, with his giant brain and thousand-lumens-bright smile. And Viveca had to make sure that I was gentle? That *I* wouldn't hurt *him*?

Or Andrek wouldn't. I could have been totally wrong, but it seemed like she didn't want me to leave Joule alone with Andrek.

I already knew that would be impossible.

"Lane? I'd like to show you something," Joule called.

My head was still shaking. How long had I been doing that? Back and forth. Up and down. I might have been rubbing my face too, though I couldn't feel it. Or maybe I could, but the heavily padded gloves didn't feel like me.

My senses spun out, away from center.

Dust but rippling like water.

I didn't get her. I didn't get her. I didn't get her. Each time I thought I had a pin into what she was after, what made her up, she went and scrambled the recipe.

No, no, it was like she changed the cookbook entirely.

It was maddening. Distracting.

Was I always this wrong about people? Perhaps I'd always been wrong about people but never knew. Maybe no one wanted to tell me. Maybe I only picked people to be around who wouldn't tell me I was wrong. Who wouldn't dare. What if I was also the one I was wrong about?

That wasn't it. Couldn't be.

I couldn't be only wrong. I'd worshipped my sister, and that was the one person everyone agreed was unmistakably "good": Joan Faraday Tanner was a Whole Good. And I was *also* right about her being the greatest ever first.

And no matter how suspicious Viveca acted around Andrek, I was right about him too. So, one might argue that meant I was excellent at reading people, sorting out their ingredients and understanding how they'd taste. One could totally argue that.

I could. Right now.

Viveca must have been an outlier then. The one person I read backwards. Except also Joule. Maybe. I'd pinned him as a "good guy" but not as someone who'd wanted to be my friend since he was little.

I'm smelling strawberry, not just candy.

Strawberry candy.

What an absolute mindfuck.

"Lane?" Andrek moved into my peripheral vision and held still.

"She... Wait?" I slowed the pace of my head shaking and found my way back from dust. I was not totally ready to come back to my body yet, but I didn't want to keep going in circles. My breath wouldn't pick a pace.

Turn now, I thought, and this time my legs obeyed with only a slight delay.

Andrek gave me a small smile. See? I was right, and he was the sweetest, and Viveca needed to keep her nose out of his business.

Joule had a silver briefcase in front of him. And two helmets. Because we were putting on space suits, duh. I was barely listening, but I was sure I didn't remember anyone mentioning going outside.

How had I missed the strawberry scent? It was right there in the front.

"Andrek, let me check your suit before I go," Viveca said.

I shrugged at Andrek that I was all right now, but it was only almost true. I was making my way toward all right. If I were fully there, I'd be finding a way to stop Viveca from going near him.

Joule came closer to me, helmets and the briefcase held easily in his hands. We sat on the grass side by side.

"Maybe now isn't a great time," Joule paused to straighten the grass where I'd been lying before. He didn't smooth it to set the blades of grass erect, rather he patted it down to make the space remember my shape. As if to say, *Stay. She was happy here, not too long ago.* His dark gaze darted toward me.

"It's cool," I managed as I heard Andrek thanking Viveca. My breath was still this uneven staccato stumble, lurching then lagging. I was afraid I'd croak if I spoke more.

"This was supposed to arrive when we did, except, never mind that. I should have warned you both, I suppose, about going outside. Not the sort of thing to spring on someone. I'm sorry. I don't know if you're in the mood for all that, but anyway. I'm rambling. This is the thing I planned for you. It's a gift." Joule slid the briefcase between us and clicked the latch open.

I reached to lift the case's top, not smiling yet, because my face was still between decisions and attention. Viveca was at the door, leaving, but I waited for her to be all the way gone.

Then I looked at my gift. Inside the briefcase, row after row of numbered plastic vials glinted under the artificial sunlight. There was one larger vial without a number, filled with clear liquid, and some kind of 3D printed device too, which Joule plucked from the molded foam.

"It's an edible bubble machine," he said, putting the device in my hands. It was cold and remarkably light. "All these vials are concentrated flavors, for mixing however you want. You know, to try out recipe ideas without any waste."

Andrek sat beside me and *oohed* quietly.

Joule selected three vials and pulled out his tab to read something over. "Like this," he said, opening the screw-tops and releasing one miniscule droplet from each into the largest vial's solution. "Coconut custard, vanilla, and almond, with the tiniest bit of lime. Recognize it?"

"My pudding!" I gasped.

He plugged the solution into the device and pointed to the button. "That's what I was going for, but you'll have to tell me if it's right."

I turned on the device and pressed a trigger for it to start. At once, bubbles exploded from its front. There was no odor, but when Joule waved the air, it sent a few of the spheres at my face, and the taste was immediate when the bubbles popped.

"You made this for me? It's amazing!" I could feel my smile stretching my cheeks wide. Bubbles streamed around us until I turned it off.

"I sent you the flavor list, but I can label the bottles if that's easier. There's not much smell, so it might be hard to identify what's what unless you have the list. And there's plenty more solution, but I can always get more made for you, or different flavors. I probably shouldn't have added anything before explaining all that, because it's so full now, but maybe you could add different things and mix it how you—"

I interrupted his ramble with a tight hug.

"Thank you," I said. "This is the best gift I've ever had."

He was stiff as a wall at first, but after a second, he softened and put one arm around me carefully. Like he was afraid I'd break.

I squeezed him even harder. Maybe we didn't have to date each other for him and Andrek to. We could still be friends.

Andrek grabbed the device and aimed it at us at full blast. Joule and I broke apart and chased him around the courtyard until we were laughing so hard we collapsed onto the grass again.

When I caught my breath at last, I asked, "Why are we wearing space suits anyway?"

Andrek's surprise, turned out, was more of an adventure than a gift like mine was. While helping build the shipyard scaffolding, Joule had discovered what he called "G-jumping" by adapting Faraday's gravdrives for individual use. It was like bungee jumping in reverse.

I didn't completely understand it, but Andrek must have because he couldn't stop grinning and muttering about flying.

We linked arms and headed through the hallway to the northern arc then descended into the subbasement. It was a vast storage space full of cargo crates, material tanks, and extra equipment, plus the entrance to the trams that led to the secondary domes. After securing our helmets, we squeezed onto slender benches as three-foot tall bots loaded cargo meant for the shipyard into the hold.

"Strap in tightly," Joule reminded us. "It picks up speed more than you'd expect."

Then the yawning whine of the engine swallowed sound. The tram set off, whisking us away from the dome. Amber light swept overhead in a slow strobe, and we sped into the shadowy lunar tunnel.

It was strange moving fast after weeks of walking. The persistent forward tug, like my insides were off-center, thrilled me. Our speed pulled at my arms, and I wanted to raise them and yell "Faster!" But nothing would ever match the speed of the launch. I'd already reached peak velocity.

Joule's helmet tipped against mine with a click. "Do you think you'll jump? It's fine if you don't want to after..." He meant my meltdown, or rather, my almost meltdown but way-too-obvious shutdown. "Are you sure you're all right?"

I chewed my lower lip, sure that I wasn't sure about anything. Nope. Not now, not ever. Not for me. "Probably not."

"I get it. Truly. I melted earlier too. I almost needed to reschedule after lunch with V and one of her mind-meltingly bad pep talks." He belted a laugh that I felt in my bones. "She thinks she's so great at them when, really, she's the worst. The absolute worst."

His eyes narrowed, but the strobing golden light obscured the rest of his features beneath the helmet's glare.

"Is that what happened with you?" he asked. "It was, wasn't it? And I invited her there. I'm so sorry, Lane. She has the best intentions, I swear it. She always does, but she's terrible at gauging her effect on people."

I made out the hint of a frown, and I wanted to scrub it off him. "It wasn't her."

"You don't have to pretend for my sake. I'll make it up to you, I promise. We'll do something low-key together soon. Just us."

I gripped his hand. "I'd like that."

"Between you and me, my stomach's still a queasy mess. I don't *want* to jump either. Maybe I'll just do it once or twice to show him how."

A loud clank sang, and the tram stopped. That was when I decided I was most definitely not going outside. Not today, not for date purposes, not even for Andrek.

I watched the guys play from the comfort of the tram station with no regrets except that Faraday couldn't see how her gravdrives had become more than paradigm shifting. They'd become fun.

The station window was thinner than the dome, offering an unfiltered view of the shipyard. Unlike the courtyard, it was easy to tell what I saw was real, not a projection.

Earth didn't loom huge amid the stars; it hung quietly over the white horizon like a delicate crescent earring. Politely visible.

Missable. Like me.

I could have covered it with my pinkie finger if I wanted. Or I could have turned on my helmet's adaptive features and zoomed in to see cities as globs of white light, where the planet sat in our shadow. How many of those cities belonged to the RC now? The communication lockdown made it impossible to get news that ops didn't want us to know about.

I dragged my gloved hand over the window, wondering if I could bring myself to cover the planet just for a moment. It should be harder to erase eight billion people, a whole planet, millions of years of human history, billions of years of plates shifting, plants growing, evolution to extinction.

I didn't do it either. It would have been so easy, but I didn't try.

Andrek soared, a mere speck high above the steel beams that reached like shining arms into the velveteen sky. He screamed so loud, whoops of joy and *holy shit*s, I had to turn the volume down in my helmet. I could barely see the cord connecting his suit to the tallest beam, but every so often it caught the light, appearing like a white snake slithering toward the stars.

"That's it, you've got it," Joule guided him, his voice a purring whisper through the speaker. "Hit it now!"

There came a brief flash of neon green light as the gravdrive array sparked to life across Andrek's core, and he dropped, sinking toward the shipyard proper and into Joule's open arms.

"Did you see me, Lane?" he hollered, breathless with wonder. "Did you see?"

"I saw," I said, but I could hardly form the words through how numb I felt.

Faraday would've loved this so much. How was I supposed to memorialize her when things kept changing and moving?

If I could hold things still somehow, for even a moment, then maybe I could see the way.

CHAPTER TEN

NOTHING NEEDED

Sleep came slow and skittish, like it was afraid of taking me too deep. I woke every hour or so, straining my dry eyes for the shape of Andrek beside me, but he wasn't there. I'd known he'd be wound up after g-jumping, but I thought he'd still come home at some point.

Sometime halfway through the night, I dragged pillows and blankets to the living room couch, where at least the steady blink of the screen kept me company and distracted me from the memories that replayed in my head.

I ended up checking the comm, hoping to see the files from Viveca. Instead I found a surprisingly cold message from Chef, telling me not to come in tomorrow because my hours were being cut "due to my poor performance" and that "further training may be necessary before resuming normal shifts."

I read it three times in a row before deleting it, looking for some clue to tell me what I'd done wrong, my heart sinking further each time.

Why hadn't Chef said something in person if I was fucking up so much? Wouldn't Stephan have told me? That hurt more because I thought he and I were getting close. Not best friends close or anything, but coworker close, at least.

I felt tired all the way into my bones, and my thoughts were still fuzzy around the edges from over-exertion. Usually my meltdowns were better spaced out, not back-to-back without a proper refueling. It left me numb, like after-dentist-appointment-numb, when I knew there was scorching pain creeping closer every second below the cottony relief.

My parents' alarm bristled me into wakefulness again, but rather than retreat into my bedroom or Andrek's, I burrowed deeper under the blankets and waited for them to hustle past on their way to work.

No such luck.

"Exciting night?" Dad asked. He landed hard on the chair and made old man noises while he tugged on socks and shoes. "You got in so late."

I peeked blearily into the room and accidentally caught Mom's eye as she sauntered in.

"Oh no, honey," she said, as if by some mothering magic or whatever she saw the sleeplessness and emotional exhaustion seeping through the bare inch of exposed skin. She was beside me at once, pushing a water tube into my hands. "Aren't you supposed to be at work? I hope you let Chef know you aren't feeling well."

The last thing I wanted to tell her was that my hours had been cut. It would only confirm her doubts about how little I could deal with. I sat up and downed the tube in seconds.

Mom gave me another. "Let's get you to bed. You obviously need more rest."

"No, I—" I gulped the water and uncurled my legs. It was like they saw into my brain, into the numb, barely-there of me. Maybe they could, but I wasn't their little girl anymore, desperate for reassuring head pats. If they had only walked by, I would have been perfectly happy in my blanket nest for several more hours, wallowing in my misery. But they hadn't, and I didn't want to be nursed, at least not by them. I could manage myself. "I need to get up. Big plans today."

They watched warily as I untangled the blankets and wrangled them and the pillows into some kind of shape I could carry. Their silent conversation was so noisy it followed me into my room. "Poor little Lane, she's pushing herself so hard," and "We should talk to Chef about her hours."

Nope, nope. Didn't want them talking to Chef and hearing how bad I was at the assignment they got me. I couldn't understand it myself yet. I hurried out to show how fine I actually was and wished them a great day while pulling my curls into a tight, and super-adulty, bun. "I'm good."

I really did have plans, after all, because today was the day I was to endure my first grief group so I could finally get Viveca off my back about it. And then, *then*, I was taking charge of my sister's memorial for real. No more tongue-tied baby business or letting Viveca string me along one emotion at a time, not now that I knew she thought I was someone worth fearing. Or capable of protecting Joule somehow.

Faraday was my sister. *Is.* Always would be. And right now, it was she who needed the most protection.

Dad stopped me at the door. "If you have time, come along with us to the washroom before breakfast. We've got a hairdresser booked for the next hour, and your mom promised no work talk." He brandished their tabs to show them turned off and stashed them in his shoulder bag.

Mom froze for a moment before adjusting her face. Having me along for their appointment was clearly not part of her plan, but she tried not to let it show.

"That's a great idea. Come," she said. "We hardly see you anymore."

I agreed, reluctantly, because I did need a trim and kept forgetting to schedule it. Plus, I had hours to kill before my therapy group.

Our hairdresser was a middle-aged white woman with massive calves and tiny hands. She swooped into the washroom, chittering to herself in an almost non-stop commentary. "More repair traffic in the halls, sorry, see, I meant to be here early to set up and make pretty." She clucked her tongue and regarded each of us and the supplies appraisingly. "Missing towels in here too, I gather. And conditioner, soap, extra slippers, water tubes? Cheese and rice, this is unacceptable. Whoever's behind these pranks needs to cut it out."

She dragged a cart in from the hall and worked methodically, weaving between us like we were pieces of furniture as she stuffed supplies into the cabinets and spun lids off the bottles, refilling each.

Mom and Dad shared a look I read as *she's a lot*.

"I'll start with you, Dr. Tanner. Can I call you Catherine? That was my granny's name, bless her soul, and titles seem so pre-melt to me, no offense. Of course, you earned yours. I'm Beth." She took Mom's hair into her tiny hands, leaning in close to study her scalp. "Do you want color? I can match or you can go wild with it. I brought the rainbow, just in case. I expect you want to keep it long?"

Mom grimaced as Beth tugged hanks of her hair this way and that. "No color, no. All I want is a trim to touch up the layers and thin out the back."

Beth snorted in disapproval and dropped Mom's hair. "And a deep condition for all of you. I insist." She lathered a cream onto Mom's crown without preamble and started raking it through. "Rub it in. It won't hurt you. Now you, Collin, yes? A whole family of redheads! Quite unusual these days, with everyone ending up a little from everywhere. All Lunar now."

Those words again. She worked the cream onto my head last, her tiny hands moving as fast as her mouth. "Such fine hair if you take care of it. But your skin! What have you been doing with yourself, child? The log says you've lost weight. Are you eating enough?" She spritzed my face with who-knows-what and fixed a mask over my forehead and nose.

I wanted to protest, and I actually tried to get the words out, but she was already back to Mom, pulling her now-damp locks straight with a comb. The mask stung for another second, but then it cooled and wasn't that bad, so I left it on.

"Lane?" Mom asked, interrupting Beth mid-spiel about color treatments again. "Are you eating enough?"

Beth looked affronted but continued snipping at Mom's layers.

"Yeah," I said automatically. Then I thought about it, seeing if I could count the skipped or half-eaten meals. I couldn't. "I think I am. I'm always around food, it feels like."

"It's easy to get dysregulated with so many unexpected shenanigans going on. Glitching doors, missing supplies, prank messages. I'll send a note to the kitchen if you like. They can help track it," Beth offered.

I shrugged and said okay.

"Whiz of a system our trust has going, tracking every-thing." Beth's laugh was like a steel drum. "Except for this morning, am I right? Nobody where they're supposed to be, departments half empty! Everybody thinking they got fired. What a disaster!"

Beth laughed all the way through her words like it was the funniest joke in the world, but Mom and Dad had come alert. Dad hastily turned on his tab since Mom was pinned under Beth's scissors, making a face that I swore meant *I told you I needed to go in on time today*.

"Catherine," he wheezed.

Mom squared her shoulders. "Beth, I'm so sorry. We're going to need to cut this short."

"I was hoping you'd say that!" Beth squealed, gripping her scissors tighter. "I know exactly the look for your face shape."

"No," Mom said and stood. "I mean we have to leave."

Beth's smile faded. "I can still get to your daughter, if you two need to go."

Mom leveled me with a glare. "I expect she's missed at work too, along with the rest of the staff sent fake... What shall we call them?"

Dad cleared his throat. "Performance reviews."

"It wasn't real?" I ripped off my mask. "Chef didn't change my schedule?"

"I knew you didn't have the day off," Mom muttered, as if this was somehow all my fault. She threw a thank you at Beth and bounced Dad and I into the hall.

By the time we reached the cafeteria, Dad had explained that, yes, my schedule was the same as ever. Somebody had sent fake messages to half the staff, stripping the work force this morning and sending the trust into disarray and confusion.

"This may take some sorting out," Mom warned me as she hugged me quick, more of a lean-against than a hug. "But I hope we can have dinner together. Maybe bring a picnic to our office if we're running late?"

I bit back the if-I-had-a-tab-of-my-own retort since she was looking at me warmly, and office picnics hadn't happened in a while. But, seriously, if I'd had one, they could have told me they were going to be late without me waiting around.

"It was just a prank, right?"

"Probably. Too silly not to be," Dad said, chuckling. "Don't you worry about it, dear."

He kissed my head, and they turned to leave. Mom glanced over her shoulder though, her small mouth pressed tightly. Her face said she was worried plenty, and that maybe the rest of us weren't worried enough.

I stayed late to help Chef recover the kitchen from the prank, which meant breakfast for dinner and a short batter-flinging contest between me and Stephan. I won.

The grief group met somewhere different every other day, and today they were in the cafeteria, which made it extra easy for me to make it there myself afterward. Low pressure even.

I didn't imagine any grand healing moments in my near future. My only expectation was to be bored and maybe a little annoyed, but none of that mattered if it meant I'd satisfied Viveca's unreasonable demand and could get back to the business of saving my sister's legacy.

Someone named Milo waited by the counter for me to

finish filling my tray with grits, scrambled tofu, peppery potato mash, and a cup of mandarin orange slices. They said they met Faraday a bunch of times when she did conference rounds, back before trust construction began, and that I had her smile.

They had hard-core grandparent energy, if said grandparent happened to be covered in fading tattoos and speckled with piercings. I especially liked the row of glittering gems that dotted their eyebrows like twin rainbows.

I wasn't sure how to name what was so endearing about Milo, except that their voice was warm and something about their words skipped right over pleasantries into familiarity, as if we'd always known each other. The way they talked about group made it seem like fun, not all hyper intense like Viveca said.

They tugged me across the cafeteria, chattering into my ear. "Come on, baby red. You'll like this crowd—Ha!—because we're all ornery and complicated." We stopped at the far corner table so Milo could make introductions. "Y'all, this is Lane, maker of pies, server of lunch. Lane, meet Ty, Greg, Cheese, Ira, Danny, and our maestro, the good Dr. Fromme."

I scanned the others, recognizing their faces if not their names. Ty I knew, since she worked the grill on my shift, and Greg I'd met a couple times. He was a liaison for operations and occasionally walked Andrek to our quarters while they talked shop. He used a text-to-speech device and was always modifying the voice with different accents. Then there was Danny, whose friendly smile shook some more of my nerves loose.

"Howdy," said the one called Cheese. She was a little person, like Commander Han, and had the most incredible spiky gray hair. Next to her was Ira, I guessed, or Extra-Whatever, as I'd been thinking of him so far.

"I'm glad you could join us," Dr. Fromme, I assumed, said. I'd named her Cookie-Monster in my head because she actually growled in line once, and I'd laughed so hard I gave her my own portion. "If you have a seat, we can get started.

How's everyone doing? Bit of an adventure this morning, I bet, but here we are, on the other side of things again."

A rustle of shrugs answered her. I wasn't sure how to respond yet, so I squeezed between Milo and Danny and stuffed my mouth with a spoonful of grits.

Dr. Fromme smiled broadly and cleared her throat. "To catch you up, Lane, we've been talking about the stages of grief."

"Bunch of hooey horseshit," Cheese interrupted.

"—and how they may not directly apply to every individual's personal grieving process," Fromme continued smoothly. "Have you heard of Kubler Ross's stages? Denial, bargaining, anger, depression, acceptance?"

I swallowed hard, wishing she'd stop focusing on me so much. I thought I could simply come and listen, absorbing by presence without heavy participation. That was what I wanted, anyway.

"The idea is that we visit these stages along our path to healing, though the path isn't linear or static. We may circle back through any of those stages at any time, whether for a second or a month, but by actively processing these states, we can direct our own healing forward."

"Which is why I call horseshit," Cheese put in. She speared a potato with a fork and used it like a baton to emphasize every word. "In a hundred years, you'd think we could've come up with something more universally accurate. Even better, we could've come up with something to speed this shit-business along, or a way to not have to feel it somehow."

I inhaled sharply at that last part, drawing everyone's notice toward me. Immediately I shoveled more food in my mouth, not caring what it was, so nobody asked me to explain. Luckily, no one did, and Greg took the moment by clearing his throat loudly and tapping furiously at his tablet.

"You would prefer to feel nothing then? To swallow a pill and turn off your grief?" Greg's tab read aloud in a rich Scottish brogue. "I wouldn't wish that on my worst enemy."

Cheese bobbed her potatoed fork emphatically. "Yes,

unequivocally yes."

Dr. Fromme leaned away from the table and surveyed us. "Interesting! Anyone else want to weigh in? Would you want to take a pill to turn off your grief? Why or why not?"

"I'll tell you why," Cheese started. "It fucking hurts. I've hurt enough."

"I would too," Danny said, her voice gravelly-low and ponderous, as if she'd thought about this a lot. "Just to see what it's like not to feel like this."

It occurred to me that I didn't know who anyone but Danny was grieving, and nobody'd asked me either. For some reason I imagined we'd all start with that somehow, the naming of the dead, like "I'm Lane, and I'm grieving my sister and my classmates" or something. Some part of me was disappointed by this, especially since I didn't know the context for the others' losses. My mind offered up possibilities for Cheese and Ira, but I smacked that thinking down. It was disrespectful to assume, wasn't it?

I heard Milo sniffling quietly beside me, their eyes shining and watery. "I don't know," they said, and Cheese took their hand. "I don't know if I'd be brave enough to try something like that. I lost my parents so young, and grief kept me focused, kept me moving forward. And when I lost my first wife and our son—" their voice wavered, and they breathed like the air had gone thick "—I couldn't bear feeling—Running from the pain led me to a whole new life, one I wouldn't trade for anything. If I'd been able to turn it off then, I would have. So I'm glad that wasn't a choice."

"Mmm," Dr. Fromme hummed, which could have meant anything. "How about you, Ty? Lane?"

Ty grumbled a "Nope" in response but didn't elaborate.

I knew my answer was no too, because of how awful it felt when Cheese mentioned the idea. Thinking about why was extremely uncomfortable, like having a spotlight directed at me. It was probably for the same reason I hadn't wanted to come to one of these groups in the first place, and why it felt so wrong for Viveca to keep pushing me.

I opened my mouth to mumble a simple *no* like Ty, but the past few days had loosened something in me, because I didn't have the energy to filter what came out.

"I don't know if I want to heal," I found myself saying, and all at once I was standing on the edge of that cramp in my heart, looking straight at it. "Maybe not, like, ever? I mean, what is grief anyway except pain and memories, and that's all I've got left of... of her. It's not like I can wave that away without losing something else important, so no, I wouldn't take anything to turn it off, even if I could, because it wouldn't be fair or right to feel nothing, even if the alternative is feeling like... Like this."

The others went quiet and still. I stared at my tray, at my food going cold, at my fingers gripping my utensils, and I hoped nobody was looking at me, but I didn't dare check. I'd said what I meant, even if I wished I'd kept it locked in my head.

"Exactly that," Greg agreed, though Cheese harrumphed and shook her head. Danny met my eyes and patted my shoulder, so it felt like she understood what I meant at least.

Dr. Fromme started talking again, something about how all our feelings were valid and there was no right or wrong answer when it came to these things.

I only half listened as I forced myself to keep eating, chewing each bite precisely so nothing stuck in my throat. This wasn't my plan, saying any of that, and now it was too late to stuff the words back where they came from. And maybe, since I'd admitted it, I could find a way to use that for something good.

Because that was the problem with Viveca's hero-worship, at the heart. It was all glory and goodness and celebration-of-excellence horseshit. A memorial that mattered, that meant something forever, couldn't only be positives and fluff, not when the person it was about died before they got to see what they'd built, not when they were *murdered* right at the beginning of their dreams coming true.

So Viveca was right on some level, that Faraday needed to be remembered for her inventions, for how amazing she was at inspiring people to make huge changes and try previously impossible things. If my sister had lived to the ripe age of eighty, or sixty, then that might have been enough.

But she hadn't. It didn't matter how much she managed in her shortened life, because she could have, would have, done so much more.

The memorial needed to hurt, at least a little. Maybe a lot. Like that fake performance review, disrupting my insides and my day.

When people remembered my sister, they should be disrupted too. Angry that she was stopped from doing more, furious at those who were so in love with their own power that they'd stolen her from us when she was only getting started. And because I couldn't let that go, because I wouldn't dare try, I was exactly the right person to plan her memorial.

Attention: ALL

Subject: Evening Menu

Entrees: Vegan lasagna, spicy greens and brown rice, shepherd's pie

Sides: Sweet corn muffins, salted asparagus, tomato salad

*****Dessert***** Moon pies and berry sorbet

CHAPTER ELEVEN

MISUNDERSTOOD

I tried to keep my resolve hot until my next session with Viveca. I had hoped I'd catch Andrek in our quarters, since no one knew how to hate on the RC like he did, but he never showed, so I passed time relabeling the vials from Joule and imagining new flavor combinations. Eventually, I took my restless bones to the gym, sending a message to Viveca to meet me there.

All the washrooms had adjacent gyms, though I found I preferred the ones designated for disabled people only. They smelled different, less sour, and the machines tended to get wiped down more completely than the others.

At this time of day, it was usually pretty quiet, and I had the whole gym to myself. I sped through the recommended weight training—we were all supposed to do at least twenty minutes per day—then selected a stationary bike, because I liked the feel of speed without the stress of impact from running on the treadmills.

I rode hard, my hands tight on the handlebars. A couple of people came and went, including Danny, but after a short greeting to me, they only talked to each other, and I was free to think my own thoughts. The faster I pumped, the further I got from the cramp in my heart that kept begging me to "do something" already.

Sweat soaked into my jumpsuit, and I hopped off long enough to zip myself free, then climbed back onto the seat. My freckled legs turned pink from exertion, mottled and blotchy like paint spatters, and my waves frizzed like I'd been run through with electricity.

I would tell Viveca exactly what I'd realized the memorial needed to be. A dance was an epically bad idea, like, I might as well have suggested we prance through the courtyard wearing flower halos. It was a ridiculous, childish idea.

Her ideas weren't great either, but we could tweak them together and figure out something darker and more meaningful. A statue wasn't such a terrible plan, maybe, if that showed Faraday reaching toward the stars but cut short, never to arrive.

But how? Show the gunshot wounds, the black pool of blood spilling from her chest?

I gagged at the image, hot tears springing to my eyes, and my feet slipped from the pedals. No statues then, but something else. Once I convinced Viveca what we needed to do, she'd use her giant brain to come up with a hundred new answers.

Probably.

I'd have to get her as angry as I was first, which shouldn't be too hard.

Especially since Viveca already seemed sparky enough to set fires with her fingertips when she burst into the gym. She looked like she always did—shiny hair, glossy lips, unnaturally-tidy jumpsuit—but something about the set of her jaw or the shine in her eyes was like a storm cloud rolling out in front of her like a red carpet. Even her elbows looked extra pointy as she stood in a power pose.

"I thought we had an understanding," she said, each word sliced razor thin.

"Huh?" I wiped my face on a towel and pushed myself up straight on the bike. It was annoying how she managed to knock me off guard so effortlessly, but part of me was relieved I hadn't been wrong about her mood.

"I told you to give Joule time."

"What do you think I did?"

"Then where is he?"

I climbed down and wrapped the towel around my head. "At work, probably. Same as Andrek. It's not their day off."

"You haven't seen Andrek either, then?" Her voice was thin, almost shrill, soaked with desperation, and it filled me with icy worry.

"I left before they did, but—"

"You left them there alone?" She grabbed my shoulders, digging her nails into my skin. I didn't think she was trying to hurt me, or knew she was doing it, but I didn't like it. She was shaking. "What if something happened while they were g-jumping? I can't believe you just left them!"

"Viveca, try to calm down, okay? Have you messaged Joule?" I dragged her hands from my shoulders and held them. Hers were large, and still so soft, but mine were strong from working resistant dough. "We can sort this out, I'm sure."

"He was supposed to meet me, and I waited, but he..." She pulled away and scrambled for her tablet. "I should have thought of that first. I don't know what I was thinking. Stupid, stupid, stupid."

I rocked on my feet, unsure how to help. Joule had implied that she was autistic too, but I'd never seen someone like her, as put together and self-assured as she was, crack so fast. I was always halfway there, so I got it, and I knew this was the real her, who she was beneath the perfect masks she kept. My masks weren't like hers, painted with ambition and genius, and I tended to wear mine slippery and loose, making sure I had nothing to prove.

This wasn't a meltdown. I didn't think, anyway. She was un-masking.

Did she want my help? If she was letting me see this on purpose, then I felt honored. But if she wasn't, would she be embarrassed about it later, or act meaner when she realized all I'd seen?

Others could come into the gym at any moment.

"Come with me," I said, circling an arm around her waist but not quite touching her. "Let's talk in the sauna." And I thought it was more a testament to how off she felt than how convincing I was that she followed me into the closed cedar room, letting me seal us inside alone without taking her attention from her tab.

There was a public comm on the sauna wall, the screen thicker than the one at home, I guessed to protect it from the humidity in here. I went to it and messaged Andrek, telling Viveca what I was doing as I fumbled through the commands.

The guys were fine. They had to be.

Right?

To Andrek, I sent, "You okay? Haven't heard from you all day," and because I'd caught Viveca's worry like a contagion, I sent another to my dad asking if he'd seen or heard from Andrek.

My message to Andrek went unread, but I heard from Dad immediately.

"He asked for the day off, but he's been in the office anyway. Hope all is well with you kids! Love you, bean."

I showed it to Viveca, but it only aggravated her. When she heard from Joule, though—a puffy-eyed video message apologizing and promising to meet her for dinner—she listened silently, slumped for only a second, then jumped to her feet and began stripping down to her underwear.

Whatever was going on in her beautiful head, I took it as a sign she was on her way to recovery and the crisis was averted.

Or so I thought *until* she started muttering and pacing, and I could only catch a third of what she said because it was so fast. What I pieced together sounded like something out of a spell book, plus cuss words in at least six different languages. Suffice to say she was madder now than she was worried before.

I didn't understand, but I also didn't want to change

subjects to the memorial until she was in a better mood, or at least not upset about a boy. Our boys. And more fully clothed, because every cell in my body screamed for help, and I couldn't not look at her unless I closed my eyes. There was no room in my head to get mad at Andrek and Joule too. She took up all the emotional space and air, so the only thing I could do was sit and witness.

It felt wrong somehow, seeing her this exposed without an explanation, literally and otherwise, but also it was possibly the most enchanting I'd ever seen a human be.

Her hands, which I'd been not-so-secretly obsessing over since we first met, the ones she used like expert props most of the time—they were loose at her sides and doing this fluttery thing every few seconds, which looked extra amazing because her nails were painted a metallic rose, and they caught the warm light like falling glitter. And her walk, usually so precise, either ship-commander stiff or dancer-lovely, it was neither of those but both of them too. Like there were all these different versions of her walks, but they'd been pinned to a wall, separately labeled, and now she was unhitched, set free, and she was all herself at once.

I'd never seen her knees before, and I was astonished to see they were a little ashy, as were her elbows. Not cracked, but drier, a few inches of perfectly human skin.

She was so heart-stoppingly beautiful. Now more than ever.

I didn't turn the sauna on. That turned out to be a good decision, because Viveca and I stayed for nearly an hour. Sometime between me admiring her knees and her finally sitting down, I found the translator key in my brain to interpret what she'd been muttering about.

She was, really truly, upset with Joule, but he'd only been the tip of what was bothering her.

"He's supposed to come by to see me, every morning if he didn't stay the night. That's our agreement, and it's been our routine going on three years. He knows. He knows." Viveca lifted her long legs onto the cedar bench and squeezed her arms around them.

I got what she was on about. Routines were important. And agreements between partners equally so. Joule was her rock the way Andrek was mine. More than a rock, they were the spikes blocking the dam, keeping the right things safe inside. Three years was a long time to lean on someone.

"Do you think, maybe, we could cut them slack? New relationship energy can be so heady." I glanced sideways to see what her face was doing. It was blank, though. Unreadable. "They'll come around once we talk to them about it."

She rested her head on my shoulder, and I swallowed hard. "It's not that. And if it is, talking won't change anything. They'll be lost in each other for weeks, right when I need Joule the most."

I didn't ask her to explain, because it sounded personal and complicated, and the taste of danger sat inside her words the way it had when she'd begged for Halle's help. Maybe, like me, she wished she could leave the past in the past, but it wouldn't let her.

Plus, it was impossible to concentrate when her warm face touched my bare shoulder, her silky hair sliding over my back and chest. Hormones were so annoying sometimes.

"Maybe we can help each other through it," I said. It was a risk, since any moment her masks might pop on and eviscerate me, but I took a chance that they wouldn't and slipped my arm around her.

She let me!

She even scooted closer, tucking herself against my side. "It's not fair how easy it is for guys. They do things and say whatever they want, and if they like someone, they put it right out there like it doesn't matter. Like we won't be stuck with the consequences for years if things don't work out."

I couldn't argue because it was exactly what had gone through my head last night. Somehow though, I had expected it wouldn't be the same for someone as pretty and accomplished as she was. So continued my week of being wrong.

"What about Halle?" I asked. I knew it was more blunt

than polite right now, but I didn't see how she fit in. I didn't get how I was supposed to figure out this whole third-person business either, and I bet she'd designed a system or something. "I mean, I'd like to hear how you and Joule met, and Halle. How did that work?"

She was quiet for a long time. I couldn't tell if she was choosing not to answer or deciding how to. My fingers wound through her hair of their own accord, and I couldn't make them stop.

"How we met doesn't matter," she started. "We were basically babies in a playgroup. Not babies, really, tweens. We didn't get serious right away after we hooked up, either. That took time. Halle though, she and I just work, you know? She's monogamous, so it's different. Not less complicated, but different than me and Joule."

Even though I never knew what to expect her to say next, the tension humming between her neck and shoulders buzzed through me. Her lashes tickled my jaw, and the cedar planks seemed to swell with the breath I held.

"You know by now, right? That I don't hate you? Everyone always thinks that. It doesn't matter what I say, people hear what they want to hear, but I only hate one person, and it's not you. Whatever happens, I want you to know."

Viveca caught my hand, the one tangled in her hair, and brushed her thumb over my knuckles. She tilted her chin as I turned my head, and her face was close, so close that I tasted espresso on her exhalation. Her full lips pushed forward as if her tongue played nervously over her bottom teeth.

Condensation droplets bled into each other as they traveled down the rectangle pane of glass on the sauna door. I was convinced I heard them colliding.

Was "I don't hate you" her way of saying "I like you?"

I thought I did know she didn't hate me, or I'd started to suspect it at least. She was nothing like I thought she was underneath. I wanted to know more about her, all the whys of her and what drove her so hard.

I could have kissed her right then and started to learn.

I leaned closer and whispered, "I only hate one person too."

No! Why did I say that? Why was I not saying, *I don't hate you, either. In fact, all I can think about is kissing you, and I'll lose my mind if I don't?*

But the words were out, and I was not in control, because my mind was stuck on today's mission which had nothing to do with her silky hair or her hand in mine.

Her hand in mine! What was I doing?

"That's what I was hoping we could talk about, actually, for the memorial," my traitorous, unromantic self said, spoiling the mood like a bucket of mud. "How to make everyone remember my sister but also make sure they hate Brand Masters for taking her from us. To hate everything he stands for and to stop people like him from doing that to someone else."

She made a noise, something between a gasp and a grunt, and I had no idea what it meant. I only knew that kissing was completely off the table.

Her hand fell to her lap with a soft thud. Then, in front of my eyes, she slipped her masks on. I watched the change, despairing at my horrible non-kissing mouth and what it had done. Her back straightened, brow hardened, jaw stiffened, and, in one fluid motion, she was a mile away, though all she'd done was stand.

I shivered involuntarily as air rushed in to replace her warmth. It was too late to take back what I'd said, and she was unreadable again. It had me queasy trying to figure out how to recover.

Autism alone couldn't account for the many facets of Viveca, though that was definitely one part of her too. She contained multitudes, and her masks were armor for things I had no way of knowing yet.

I scrambled for a towel because I was suddenly feeling all my skin. "Do you get what I mean? I don't want to lose sight of Faraday, who she was and all she's done, but we have to take that farther, because she can't anymore."

She zipped her jumpsuit so quickly I was surprised she didn't catch her hair in the tracks. With her back to me, she asked in a voice tight enough to snap, "What made you think of this? Did Andrek say something? Are you sure you can trust him?"

"What? No, what?" I wrapped the towel around my middle. It was impossible to believe we were holding hands a minute ago, because I couldn't bring myself within a foot of her now. "It's something that occurred to me during therapy. That we can't lose focus on why she's gone."

"How do we do that?" Our reflections met eyes on the dewy glass.

I looked down. "I don't know yet."

"Then we can't stop it from happening again."

I felt like she'd punched me in the ribs. Of course we couldn't, like, literally stop greedy assholes from existing, but we could at least try to keep them in the frame so history recognized them. Right?

"I had another thought too. Like, we could gather stories about her. Not only from trustees. Maybe it wouldn't matter so much for our final plan, but you never know."

"Are you talking target audience research?" She spun to face me, her expression shining with intensity. "Or are you hoping to go through her correspondence?"

This may have been the most stressful conversation of my whole life. I swore I'd had a full year's worth of emotions in minutes. "Yes?"

She measured her breath, sharp in, long out. "Fine, okay, right. We can do that. And I can send it to you if you really want it. If you're ready."

I shook my head, lost again. "Send me what?"

"Her correspondence."

Ice and fire chased through me. "You have that? That's…" I shouldn't read it, even if she did. Faraday was always messaging people, me, her fiancés, her fans. That was too much. Like reading a diary. I wrung my hands helplessly.

Viveca cocked her head, seeing me spiral. "I need you

to know something first."

"I'm not ready," I blurted.

"But I have to tell you—"

The comm, which had been swirling a screensaver but was still open to my messages, beeped an alert. On came a video message request from my mom. Weird.

"Hang on," I said, moving around her to open the channel. "What's up, Mom?"

My mom's face was huge on the screen until she leaned back, giving me a glimpse of Dad and Andrek past her shoulder. All of them zeroed in on me, then Mom's eyes narrowed, flicking pointedly toward Viveca.

"Are you busy?" Mom asked. Extra weird.

Andrek covered his mouth, but I could tell from the angle of his eyebrows. Something was wrong. Very wrong.

"Kinda? We're—"

"Reschedule," Mom said, and I saw her hand reaching to end the call. She was in a real hurry. "You need to come to Planning. Straight away, please."

The screen went black, and I logged out. As soon as I did, Viveca put a hand on my shoulder.

Her touch was light and feathery, gone before I fully registered it. "Can we talk after dinner?"

"Meet me in the courtyard." It was all I could think to say.

My heart, my mind, my skin, every part of me felt pulled in opposite directions, and I'd already felt off-balance from days of poor sleep. I couldn't imagine what was going on with my family or why they suddenly needed me, of all people, in their super-exclusive planning department, but it had better be for something fluffy.

I couldn't handle any more emotional surprises.

I walked through the halls while trying to keep a lid on my bubbling worries. Whatever was happening, my parents would tell me soon enough, so all I needed to do was move forward, breathe, and let my spiking hormones shift out of focus.

When I'd been overwhelmed with classes, family drama,

and the antics of my own brain, but there was some collective event to attend, Faraday used to tell me, "You don't have to clean the whole house. Just make a little room."

I gulped back the sting of her voice in my head, enduring the added blow that the room I needed to make was packed to the ceiling with missing her.

But I tried. I made a little room.

CHAPTER TWELVE

STONE STRUCK SIDEWAYS

My parents greeted me formally and steered me into their shared office. Remnants of our life in Masdar filled every shelf and surface. They sat behind a long desk covered by stacks of reports. It was strangely warm, homey even, despite the grim set of their faces.

Andrek swiveled in a chair on the other side of the desk and held out a hand. He still wore the Bentley vest, though he'd found a shirt and layered it with a white lab coat like my parents had.

I didn't take his hand. I may not have been spitting mad like Viveca had been earlier, but I was rather annoyed now that I was looking at him. He never came home, he ignored my messages, and he hadn't met me in the hallway to prepare me for whatever drama my parents were on about. It was all forgivable, but not without discussion first.

"What's going on?" I asked, taking the empty chair and pointedly looking only at my parents.

Mom rubbed her temples with both hands, but it didn't hide the questioning arch of her eyebrow. Dad pressed his fingertips together and gave me a wan smile.

I waited for one of them to speak, sitting on my hands so

I didn't fidget too much. Experience dictated that whoever talked first would determine the course of the conversation. If Mom went first, then Dad was there to soften the blow. That meant bad news, but not so bad Dad couldn't make me feel better.

If Dad went first, then Mom would still be there with the facts, but only after Dad had determined I could "take it."

Dad cleared his throat, and my own went dry. "Thank you for coming to see us, Lane. Did your big plans pan out?"

Not good. Extra bad. He was feeling out my mood and it was extremely obvious. I snuck a glance at Andrek. He was staring at the floor.

Dad's voice was smooth as mirror glaze icing. "I'm sorry we had to interrupt. You were with Viveca?"

They knew I was, so I was sure he was stalling. Or fishing for something. I didn't like it.

I added an "uh huh" to match his obvious with my own.

Mom lowered her hands to her lap. I didn't look at her directly, but I felt her studying me—my frizzy hair, blotchy skin, damp jumpsuit—and frowning at what she saw. Words filled the air around her like steam, building pressure.

"That's comforting to hear," Dad remarked blandly, though I'd said almost nothing and him just as little. "We hoped we could chat a little about your friends."

My hands wiggled free from beneath my thighs at that. I squeezed one thumb then another as I waited for him to explain, but the words around Mom got thicker, and Dad now watched Andrek, not me.

"Why?" I asked him, when the quiet went on too long to tolerate. "You probably know them better than I do."

"Why would you say that?" Dad returned.

I rolled my eyes. "You read everyone's applications and did their interviews. I only know what people tell me."

Mom made a nothing noise, something between a snort and a sniffle, and Dad put a hand on her back. Holding the words still, maybe.

"What do you want to know?" I tried instead, because

they were exhausting me with this pageant of theirs, and my mind had started spinning through possible reasons for their questions but none of them made sense.

"Well," Dad started, and I knew it was coming now.

"Have you noticed anything unusual," Mom finished, "with your friends?"

Define unusual, I thought, but that wasn't helpful. I couldn't decide which tack to take, or who they were asking about or why, and I couldn't answer anything unless they were clearer. "Besides Andrek sitting here like he's a puppy who peed inside?"

Andrek laughed and covered his mouth, and just that fast things were okay between us again. I knew he'd apologize properly whenever this business was over.

"No," Dad said, massaging Mom's back to coax her into taking the lead. "With your new friend. Viveca."

Before I responded to that surprise, Mom slid a tab across the desk. It was open to a document with way too many names on it to be quickly legible.

"Look at this list and tell us if anything stands out to you."

I spared a couple seconds to skim, but that was all. "What's going on? Why are you asking about Viveca? You're the ones who were obsessed with her all the way here."

Andrek went rigid in his chair, not looking at me, so I knew he was behind whatever this was. My annoyance flared at him, kicking up so hard and fast I made a spinny noise in the back of my mouth.

Okay, sure, I'd noticed "unusual" things about Viveca since I met her. She was pushy and blunt, and she teetered between emotionally clueless and too in-tune for comfort. And I thought I'd read her wrong in every interaction except, maybe, the last hour, but that was probably me and my crush, or my jealousy and stubbornness, and not understanding her masks yet.

There was also her talk with Halle that I had no business listening to, and which I'd blown way out of proportion in my not-sleeping fits, but how could any of that possibly have an iota of significance for my parents and Andrek?

And that was when I remembered my parents didn't know about Andrek's work in the RC.

But Viveca had asked if Andrek could be trusted. She'd made that weird face at his Bentley vest, and I'd wondered what she thought she knew about him. Worse, what if she actually knew about his time in the RC? If I said anything sketchy about her, could that bounce back to hurt Andrek? I wished he'd just tell the truth already.

The noise I was making stretched into a screech with the volume on low.

My parents' eyes became pendulums, wide and swinging, and I slapped the desk with my palm.

Then once more, to be sure I did it right. "What. Is. Going. ON?"

Mom rose to her feet like a helium balloon. "I'd like you to look again when you're ready. This is a list of names that have been indicated in a recent security check, and your input might be valuable."

I was looking, all right, but I wasn't reading. I'd made my eyes into stones that held all the frustration they were handing me.

Andrek shifted again, and I could tell he was shaking his head, though stones couldn't see. "You know the security restrictions for communication with Earth?"

"Yeah," I said, enjoying my stone eyes now because they hid the little ping in my brain that said, *Hmm. Viveca?* I muttered something about not being able to message Zara and Khalid or update my video games.

"This list—" Stones may not see, but they felt Andrek pushing the air nearby, gesturing at my parents to hush. "—shows the accounts that received or sent messages when those restrictions were compromised. That's not to imply all these people were involved, or any of them for that matter, but they're the ones the system flagged when communication glitched."

"Am I on there?"

"No," Mom and Dad said.

"Was Viveca?"

"No," Andrek repeated, "but Joule was. Twice. Both within the first few seconds of the breach. On our first night here, then again right before the hatch doors glitched."

"Then why are you asking about Viveca?"

"Because I vouched for Joule," he replied firmly. Too firm, until he added, "He's being questioned by operations now, but she's the only one who would have also had his tablet's passcode."

"Oh." I scooted back in the chair to think.

Andrek vouched for Joule—some sleepover they must have had—but not Viveca.

I bet Joule would vouch for Viveca if he weren't already suspected. I was tempted to myself, even knowing that she definitely had something going on with the communications breach, something potentially risky, simply because it felt like they were attacking her without cause.

I wouldn't risk Andrek though, no matter what, so I decided not to cooperate. "Why would she have anything to do with this mess? You don't even know for sure she's the only other person with his passcode. He lives in a dorm with like eight other people, and I bet they don't all have their own tabs, just like I don't. And did you even stop to think how racist it is to round on a young Black man and his mixed girlfriend while you sit us down and try to get dirt on them? That is fucked up. Faraday would be spitting right now."

"Racist?" Mom's voice teetered toward a squeal. "You're calling us racists?"

"Your mother used her own body to shield protesters before you were even born," Dad said, but all I heard was *How dare you.* "Who do you think taught your sister the politics she—"

I didn't wait to hear the rest. "I don't care what you did then or about your politics. It doesn't excuse what you're doing *now*. Look at what's actually happening."

Dad opened his mouth, but Mom hushed him. "Collin,

stop. Lane's right. We didn't consider that."

Dad eye-checked Andrek for permission to talk again, which was one hundred percent not okay and would definitely be part of our argument later. He wasn't my service animal. "We aren't blaming you or your friends for anything. If operations conclude that any of you are involved, we'll assume it's because someone else is manipulating matters. We're only asking to rule things out, so we can help keep you and the trust safe."

I scratched my head.

I chewed my lip.

I wondered if there was any room left inside me for another thought.

"I can't think of anything—I wouldn't know—What do you mean *safe*? What do you think whoever it is is involved with?"

Dad slid the tablet to Mom. They believed me. "That's classified, honey. I'm sorry."

"After all this, really?" I glared at Andrek, and he winced. "You too?"

"I," he started, then shook his head at my parents. "You might as well tell her. She'll find out in a couple days anyway, if she doesn't figure it out on her own." Then, to me, he said, "I'm sorry."

"Please keep this to yourself. We can't give in to panic," Mom said, her back to us. She picked up a ceramic knick-knack, something globular and indeterminate that little Faraday made. The words around her had grown too heavy to keep spinning, too thick for her to turn and face us.

Bread's mixed, dove, Faraday might have whispered. *Let's give it time to rise.*

My dad locked onto the whatever in her hands, his frown deepening into his mustache. Andrek stared away. If I could trust my internal compass, he was staring away from Earth.

A nameless dread grew like a pimple in my middle, and I didn't think my ribs were strong enough, or my skin relaxed enough, to hide it.

"Mom."

"The RC launched a fleet several hours ago," she finally said. "They're headed here, to the moon."

Attention: ALL

Subject: Reservations of Common Areas

Don't forget to register when using common areas for private events to prevent overcrowding.

—Dr. Tanner, Planning

CHAPTER THIRTEEN

BYE BYE NOW

I needed to get out of here, now, before his secret slipped out of me. It was something I'd known, that I knew, but it hadn't clicked into place in regards to an invasion until right now, because the idea of ships invading—Mom said a *fleet*! How many was that?—hadn't become real yet.

I didn't want it to. Because when it did, I'd have to consider the looks on their faces, the utter hopelessness, and that I already knew too many things through family osmosis, things like the trust's main defenses were its relationships with the other security bases and its strained relationship with the free states. That an invasion could mean the end of Faraday's dream.

How close this must feel to Andrek. No wonder he was so far away. I knew he wasn't throwing out a welcome mat for the RC, but who else would believe him? If my parents knew, would he be in operations getting questioned instead? Would I?

Should I? Since I was bald-faced lying to my parents' faces about Viveca, when—*this* got packed in my head somehow too—she was all, "Brand Masters isn't the type to give up," and "If I don't do something to stop him now, it'll be too late?"

Oh.

She knew this was coming. She'd always known.

Ohhhhh.

I'd heard her right, but I'd listened wrong, all wrong,

and I didn't know her reasons, but I knew I was on her side. Brand Masters had to be stopped.

I crossed my heart solemnly. "I vouch for Viveca then. The only unusual thing is how much I think I like her. And that she might like me back."

Nobody reacted, at least that I could tell. Which made sense, because the rest of them were pinned securely to the reality that had ships were headed to us—*invasion* ships, with soldiers that zip down from the sky and kill sisters. But I was thoroughly loosened from the entire reality board, not going to breathe again until I planted my face into a pillow and screamed everyone's secrets before they swallowed me whole or squeezed me out.

I had to leave. Now.

"Let me know if you want our last meal delivered from the kitchen, you know, because end of the world, wooooh." I wheezed a laugh as I climbed from the void to my legs and out of the chair. "Or whatever. Bye bye now."

"Lane," Mom said, and Andrek was still not back to the moon. "We can't take her off the suspect list. That's out of our hands."

"But we can suggest she be moved to the end of that list," Dad offered. "So long as you understand you'll need to keep your distance for a while, until she's cleared too."

"No," was all I could make myself say.

Attention: ALL

Subject: Evening Menu

Entrees: Sweet potato casserole, roast casava

Sides: Cinnamon apples, ginger carrots

Dessert Honey cake

CHAPTER FOURTEEN

FREE FALL

It was only lunch time, but I found my way to sleep.

I slept in a ball, buried under my pillows.

I slept in my parents' room, on top of their covers, with my mom's robe as a blanket.

I stole everyone's pillows, then the Bentley jacket, and slept with them piled onto the floor next to the couch.

And I didn't know if any of it was "good" sleep, but I was thirsty enough for it that I called it "good," and my brain went cemetery-quiet and cotton ball soft. Dreams slithered toward me each time I repositioned, though I chased them away, preferring the dark, silent nothing.

When I finally woke, I discovered someone had carried me to my bed and tucked me in. The Bentley jacket was buttoned around a pillow under my head.

"Your parents are worried sick about you," Andrek said. He sat guard at my open door, and the dim light from the living room puddled in his lap.

I groaned and yanked the covers over my face, not remotely ready to process anything he had to say.

Not about my parents. Not about Viveca.

And never ever about his old army's invading fleet and the end of the world.

"Lane." He came closer and through some silent boyfriend magic managed to slip under the blanket.

I rolled away. Pretended to snore.

His arm snaked around my waist. "I'll tell them, if you want me to," he offered. "So you don't have to hold it anymore. It can't make that much of a difference now, honestly."

Sometimes he got me so well but expecting me to say I "want him to" do something risky for my sake only was peak awfulness and a terrible responsibility to put on me. I pretend-snored louder.

He wanted me to say it was okay not to tell my parents. That I'd be fine holding his secret till he was ready.

I didn't know if I could promise that either.

I wanted him to tell me not to worry, that the RC didn't usually blow through with weapons hot, because Brand was more of a businessman than a general. That it was probably not the end of the world or the trust. That we were safe to worry about other, smaller things, and how about some yummy dinner.

He didn't say any of that, and neither did I. He molded himself around me till I felt the rapid thump of his heartbeat against my back, the gentle kiss he placed on my hair.

He smelled like fear.

We laid there for what felt like centuries, curled like seashells around his racing heart. At some point, my parents came through, and they closed my door. I wished time would stop now, here, before anything else bad had a chance to happen.

He sighed onto my neck, likely thinking the same thought. "I'm so sorry."

And though it wasn't the conversation we needed to have, not even the beginning, I twisted in his arms and found his mouth with mine, pulling his heat into me. Our tongues met instead of words, and we shed our clothes like they were made of paper, not zippers and fabric and snappy elastics.

His skin on mine was liquid smooth, and the friction between us a familiar soup of feelings. When we broke apart, spent, I was smiling despite my mood and the hurricane of worry waiting impatiently for me to acknowledge it.

We talked then, trading whispers that were practically kisses, with the blankets draping over us like a tent. He was so, so sorry. For not coming home or answering messages.

It wasn't what Viveca thought, that our boys were holed up in some romance bubble. They were stranded in Dome 3 because security shut down the tram after getting the news of the launch. Maybe there was some romance while they waited, but due in no small part to being scared out of their minds.

And he was sorry he threw Viveca's name forward without good enough reason, especially considering how important she was to Joule. And maybe me. "It was heartless and thoughtless, and I'm an asshole for that. I panicked."

But he was terrified, and cornered, and he didn't know what else to do. I punished him with tickles until we both felt better.

"Assuming we survive," I said, once I was able to speak above a whisper and ready to leave our nest, "we need to work out our schedule with Joule. And such."

"And such?"

"I mean, I think I should get extra sleepovers because of seniority," I teased.

Andrek tackled me and kissed a circle around my belly button, punctuating with, "Is. That. What. You. Think."

"Maybe," I said, relishing the heat of his hands and wondering if it was worth it to get dressed again. We could decide to spend the rest of our lives in this tiny room. There were definitely worse ways to go.

"This isn't about Viveca?"

"Why? Do you plan on turning her in for something else?" I fetched clean clothes from my single drawer and stretched them over me. He cleared his throat, and I tossed him his own, which had found their way in front of the door and under the bed.

"I guess I don't get it," Andrek said, his voice layered with tension. He dressed slowly, and I wondered how long it'd been since he slept. "I mean, yes, she's banging hot, but I thought you hated her for being snobby."

"I thought so too," I admitted carefully, because there was still so much in the air, things I didn't know. Things I wanted to learn if there was enough time. "But that's not who she is."

Don't think about why, don't think about why.

Walls went up. Reality stepped back.

He started lacing his boots. "Can I ask what changed? Last night she seemed to knock you off kilter."

"You've officially spent too much time with my parents." I gurgled a laugh, grateful that I could. It wasn't like us to lie or hide stuff from each other, but I didn't know what to say yet, or what was mine yet to say. "I'm not sure what's changed, except that it is. Changing."

"But breakfast is ours, right?" He stood and tested his foot. "Barring unforeseen security emergencies?"

"Ours," I said, pretending any of us could ever know anything for certain while there were monsters coming from the sky. "Always."

Andrek and I took dinner in Chef's office rather than the cafeteria. A simple meal of casserole, spiced apples, and bright orange carrot sticks. The five-year-old inside me couldn't have been more comforted unless I also had a handful of balloons.

It was easier to keep the walls up if I didn't talk, and Andrek didn't push. I'd have to talk soon anyway when Viveca found me.

I'd learned something important, I thought, about Viveca. Every time I'd tried to "prepare" myself to talk to her, it went horribly awry, so it was best not to prepare. This way I'd be flexible enough to keep myself steady when she inevitably surprised me. I didn't decide what to tell her about the fleet or Joule or what I'd overheard. All that, I'd figure out after she told me whatever she was bursting to in the sauna.

I was so glad I got a little rest. Now all I needed was a real shower then to lie in some soft, green grass. Once I made it to the courtyard to wait for Viveca, I conked out almost immediately, and I dreamed of home.

Not Faraday's flat or her assassination.

Home.

I was lying on a blanket next to my beautiful big sister. We were cloud watching, but the patch of sky we could see was so tiny and far away, crowded by whispering green trees. A rain cloud had passed below the clearing, allowing us to listen to its patter without getting wet.

My hands were small and fat beside hers as we pointed.

Mom painted while Dad played guitar, and the bubbling creek spilling into the lake in the distance was his drum. The air was linden thick and April wet, and rainbow-colored pebbles dotted the low grass like shining candies.

"I'm hungry," I squeaked.

Faraday's laugh rippled over me. "You're always hungry."

"I'm not!" I argued, tickling her waist with my bare feet. "Can we swim yet?"

"Still too cold," Mom said. "Soon."

"How soon?"

"A month, at least." Dad's fingers thumped the strings in a looping rhythm.

I snuggled into Faraday's side, certain that a month was a lifetime and that I couldn't possibly wait that long. I held my eyes shut for as long as I could when I woke, keeping my breath shallow, savoring the humidity of sleep.

I'd been happy since that afternoon. Many times.

But never like that.

I wondered if there was enough time left to try.

CHAPTER FIFTEEN

MEASURING THE END OF THE WORLD

Viveca breezed into the courtyard alongside a crowd wearing workout clothes and carrying mats. Those exercising set up on one side, where short bushes had begun to outgrow their planters. One had sprouted tiny white flowers.

Viveca went the opposite way, and, after petting a spindly tree's lowest branches, she waved me over. She wore a shiny, silvery blue knee-length dress.

I walked toward her like my boots weighed a hundred pounds. Just because I didn't have a plan didn't mean I was ready to face what she wanted to tell me. No more than I could face what I already knew. Did she know the RC would invade? Was she going to say why she didn't trust Andrek? I could hardly make my body respond with my head this full.

"You slept," she said once I was a few steps away. She sat on the grass and touched the ground in front of her. "That's good. I know how hard it can be after a meltdown."

I sat too, and let her take my hands in hers. There was something eerie about the way she looked at me, as if she were reading me. Could she see the fleet in my face? Could she hear herself pleading with Halle?

She was so still, like statue-still. I wondered if this was

a new mask I hadn't seen yet.

A haunting melody floated toward us, and it took me several full seconds to realize it was music from a tablet. The exercisers had started yoga poses. They'd lit incense too, a musky rose that sent wispy tendrils through the courtyard.

Grass tickled my ankles. It'd be just like me to develop an allergy to the only piece of outside I'd ever enjoy again.

"What did you want to tell me?" I asked. Her hands were cold, and they held mine tight, so I didn't let on that my brain was mush and we only had a few days or weeks left to live.

"Bear with me, all right?" she asked. "Just let me finish before you ask questions."

"Oh," I said, except that wasn't exactly an answer, so I added, "Fine. That's fine. I'll listen." For now, at least. But once I got the chance, I was not going to only ask polite questions.

I needed to know what she knew about Andrek. I hadn't begun to wonder what might be so important for her to share yet. So of course, in the moment before she opened her mouth, my thoughts revved to warp speed, trying to anticipate appropriate reactions for even the wildest possibilities.

I like you.

Easy.

Kiss her. Keep kissing her whenever possible until the final kablooie.

I know your parents cheated to get you here.

Shrug and say, "Who doesn't know that?" and wonder why that mattered anymore.

Including you in the memorial was a bad idea.

Awkward, but probably not wrong. Disagree and press family relationship. Or don't, because we'd both likely be included in the next memorial after the RC swallowed us with its fleet. Either way, I participated. Go me.

I've been sending messages to Earth—

Feign surprise; ask why—

Because (insert her reason).

Try to understand and weigh turning her in versus

minding my own business till the world ended anyway.

That was as far as my imagination got. Warp speed was exhausting.

"I didn't lie to you. I never met Faraday in person," Viveca began, her velvety voice pitched only for my ears. "I did know her though, Lane. She was my mentor, my friend, and she saved my life more times than I can count. When I send you her correspondence, you'll see. That's why I couldn't send it before. Because I wanted to explain first."

Her words ricocheted through my insides like a pinball, setting free a cascade of questions. I clamped my mouth shut, because I'd said I'd wait, but I couldn't control what my face did.

She didn't see me anyway. Her eyes were either closed or staring unfocused at the grass.

Eyes my sister saved.

"I started wrong," she muttered, her fingers tightening over mine. Too tight, like she was measuring my bones. "I have to go back further, or it won't make sense."

"All right," I said then bit my lip, since I was supposed to stay quiet till she finished. Maybe it didn't count if she hadn't properly started.

One of the yoga folks ripped a loud, squelchy fart. Somehow nobody laughed. I guessed they were all very serious about yoga.

I rocked uncomfortably and fixed my gaze on Viveca's nails. She'd cleaned them of polish, but they shined even brighter.

"Should we leave?" she asked. "I thought it would be relaxing here." A new song began with a shrill whistle, and we both winced. "Can I bring you somewhere?"

"Quiet?"

"And private," she promised.

She led me out of the courtyard to the medical department, into a darkened office all the way in the back. Nobody bothered to ask where we were headed.

Her hand in mine—it was different than in the courtyard,

different than catching my hand in her hair. It felt intentional. A togetherness. I ought to be thinking about her and Faraday, lifesaving, but her hand was heaven, and here at the end of the world, a soft, strong, gorgeous hand in mine was enough to hold at one time.

"Sit wherever you want," she said, turning a switch that activated panels of warm golden light around the lower walls of the room.

The office had a meticulously organized desk, two couches, a wall of built-in filing cabinets, and some kind of art sculpture that looked like a bathtub inside a dome of its own.

I walked up to the sculpture and ran my palm over the dome. It was nearly the size of a single bed.

"Beautiful, isn't it? Joule built this for me, but it wouldn't fit in our quarters. Patients love it. Actually, this could be perfect. Do you want to try it? After what I said, I imagine you're rattled. Hang on a moment, and I'll get it ready."

I leaned against the door as she did whatever she was doing. The dome came off and retracted into a clear slice of plastic, like an orange wedge but only the peel. Underneath were two molded tubs, one sitting inside the other at an angle.

The whole contraption rested on a short platform, the top of which looked like the drain on Chef's espresso machine. It was oddly beautiful for plastic, with deep purple to lavender staining in the simulated grain.

"The water beads are sanitized after every use. Go on in. Wait!" She pulled me backward so sharply as I was about to step in that we toppled onto the couch, her leg sliding between mine, her whole body pressed on top of me.

My veins sang with electricity.

Kiss her, my body screamed, but I said nothing and stared into her eyes an inch from my own.

I bit my lip hard. She wanted to talk about my sister, not us. There was no us.

She scrambled to her feet. "Sorry about that. You'll want to take off your jumpsuit and boots. Socks too. And bra, if you want. I'll wait."

I started to ask why, but from this angle I could see for myself. The tub was filled with water beads, like the kind used in stress balls, and it looked so inviting. I undressed quickly, eager to climb in.

She helped me get situated on the smaller bowl. It tilted to provide the perfect backrest. The beads parted easily, slipping around my limbs in the most delicious way. I drew my knees up, and they poked through the beads like icebergs.

Viveca told me to relax while she fetched us drinks. Apparently, she had a lot more to say.

I dipped my hand under the surface and thought a bowl full of bubbles was the best possible place to process the end of the world.

Then she told me her story. Her truth.

Her parents had been obsessed with my sister, turned out. That explained the wallpaper in her quarters. "Dad thought if one kid like Faraday existed, why not two, though he was far more interested in your sister's social reach and influence than her message. If he could recreate that in me, it could change his whole business model. But I was a huge disappointment, though I tested well and made great marks. I don't get along with people. You've seen it. They meet me on paper, and everything's fine, then they meet me in person and call me abrasive and arrogant. Cold. Bitchy. Not worthy of public attention."

I tried not to react and continued weaving my fingers through the cool, viscous beads of sensory bliss. I was glad she didn't stop to ask what I thought of her at first, since I hadn't liked her simply because my parents had. On paper, anyway. Meeting her only worsened her paper impression.

"I did my best to act like her, all warm and friendly. It was so unnatural for me. Fake."

Same, girl, same.

"When I was ten, I realized my mom was faking too. For my dad. He was—" she took a labored breath "—abusive."

An "oh no" squeaked out of me in sympathy. She didn't

complain.

"Verbally and physically. She was Fijian, so she'd lost her family, her whole country. He made sure she had no one but him, and she let him, for my sake. I didn't know what to do, so, like the kid I was, I reached out to my hero. I never expected to hear back."

We were getting to it. I heard it in her voice. It got softer and less formal, with a tremor at the end of the long vowels. I lowered my knees and stretched the length of the tub. Buried legs, buried questions.

"She referred me to a therapist," Viveca said. "*Her* therapist. Do you understand what that meant to me? How special I felt that she cared about me, a strange kid? My mom came along, and eventually we made a plan to leave. We were going to get away and—"

I thought she was choking, but no. Viveca was crying, two great rivers that met at her ocean chin. I didn't know what the right thing to do was.

"You don't have to tell me this," I said, breaking my agreement to keep quiet. "It's not my business." If I'd had any willpower to leave this tub, I might have gone to her. I didn't think she wanted me to though.

"No, Lane! I do. Can you not look at me till I finish? I'm not even halfway through."

"I—Yeah, sorry. I'm listening. Not looking." I forced my gaze to the beads. Clear, grape-sized spheres of perfection. They glowed in the low light.

She took a few moments to collect herself then told me the worst story I'd ever heard. Her dad had discovered their escape plan and "put an end to it."

The abuse escalated. Her nanny got involved somehow. He hurt her too.

Her mom had stopped eating. Viveca kept talking to the therapist secretly, but her mom couldn't, or didn't.

"It's like—" her verbal masks had fallen away "—the more obvious the struggle gets, the less willing people are to examine it, but that's when I have to look the hardest or else

I can't breathe."

I trailed my fingers over the surface, my lips gratefully sealed, because no words of mine were equal, or on the same scale, to the pain she held.

"She overdosed that summer, or that's what the doctors said. I think it was him," Viveca's voice was so quiet I could barely hear it over my own breath. "Your sister, and our therapist, they helped me run away with my nanny. I was only twelve."

My insides twisted into fractals, completely at odds with the glorious slickness of the beads against my skin. The pasty white woman in the pictures was her nanny, because her mom, her real mom, was dead.

"I thought if I ran far enough, he'd eventually leave me alone, but he convinced people I died too. If you're a rich white man, you can make people believe anything. And Faraday eventually gave him a new obsession. Spaceships. His ultimate fantasy, owning the future.

"So, I went on with life, as much as one can on the run. I changed my name, relaxed my hair, graduated high school online, and tried to leave him behind me. The only way I stayed ahead of him was through your sister's contacts. Her fan club as well as her friends."

It was getting hard to think and listen at the same time. I knew parts of her story somehow, like it'd been scribbled in the margins of pages I'd already read.

Viveca wasn't her name. She knew my sister, and they shared a therapist. Her dad was rich, white, into spaceships. But she couldn't have recognized Andrek as an RC soldier; she would have been far away from all that by the time he was drafted. It nagged at me that I still couldn't figure out why she didn't trust him, what she could have possibly seen in him to make her suspicious.

"Dad found me. I don't know how. He sent me a message on a private channel I'd forgotten I still had, telling me not to join the collective, even if they accepted me. I told Faraday it wasn't safe, but she said to come anyway. That it'd be okay, since we were leaving soon, that he wouldn't be able to hurt me again. She couldn't see him anymore, what he really was. What he'll always be."

I shivered even though the tub was pleasantly warm. Her fingers raked over her face in a slow, slow motion. Hair dripped like thick syrup. It was all too much.

"It's my fault, Lane, don't you see? That's why I have to stop him. It wasn't me he wanted. It never was. It's the ships the trust will build, the power he'll own if they're his. He'll do anything to get them, kill anyone. That's why I tried to get people to listen from the moment we got here, to make them see the danger.

"But nobody wants to believe in monsters. I think even Faraday lost sight, at the end. People think they can ignore evil, and it will just go away. Like they can reason with it, buy it off, work things out. But he'll never stop. Never."

I locked eyes with her, a fire building in my brain as the pieces clicked together. These were so close to my words from yesterday.

We were talking about the same monster.

"Your dad," I started, watching her closely for confirmation but not needing it so much as dreading it, "is Brand Masters."

She tore her gaze away, and I felt set adrift.

He's on his way here right now, I wanted to scream, but how did I argue with a girl shedding her most painful history while letting me, the leftover, enjoy her tub? I'd let myself ache over the mere embarrassment of cheating my way into the trust, while she'd been carrying this knowledge that her evil father hunted her across a planet and murdered thousands of people. His business model.

I gripped the tub handles and tried to hoist myself to my feet, but she jumped up to stop me.

"You might as well relax. I mean, please sit. I'm not done yet."

"You get in too, at least," I said.

She didn't take long to think. When she climbed in, she

sat across from me, her long legs making a wall over and around mine.

Now was not the time to notice her skin, her warmth. Her bra straps were wide sapphire ribbons, and her eyes glinted like fire. This was not the right time to feel things.

"He's coming," she said.

That stopped my heart for a beat until I realized she probably didn't mean right now.

"Right now."

Oh. I gulped. Apparently, she did.

"He's not coming here, though. Not yet. I'm sure that's what they're thinking in ops. Attacking isn't his style at first, not for the real prize. He'll go after another base first to chokehold our resources, then a second to damage our relationships with our Earth allies, if the first goes well. He'll want us good and scared and hopeless. Then he'll come. When we've lost any spirit to challenge him."

"How do you know all this?"

She looked away shamefully, then straightened her back. The movement sent beads spilling over my skin, sucking me closer to her.

Don't be the spy, I thought loudly, certain she couldn't be helping the RC. I vouched for her before I knew anything, and I needed that not to backfire.

"I've been monitoring transmissions and skirting the lockdown since we got here."

Dammit, dammit.

"There are at least two other trustees messing with communications from what I can tell, though operations is only looking for one. Nobody here understands what they're up against with Brand. People seriously believe the glitches and false messages are pranks! But it's all related, along with the missing supplies. This is how Brand's insiders operate. We have to outmaneuver him."

"Huh." Of all the things she'd told me, this was the only part that seemed unbelievable.

"Huh what?"

"You think you can outmaneuver your dad and his fleet? Better than Commander Han or President Marshall and all the great minds my sister handpicked? You haven't even been able to hide that you're sending messages to Earth during the communication ban. Joule got hauled in for questioning because you used his tab, right? I vouched for you, but they know!" It came out different than I wanted, but I couldn't unsay it.

The way her eyes heated made me wish I could.

"I'm not being conceited. These are simply facts. I've spent the last ten years learning everything about my dad's strategies, and my whole life learning how to avoid the danger he poses wherever he goes." She tucked her hair behind her ears and studied my face. "Nobody alive knows him better than me."

My brain coughed up "Andrek," but I squashed that down. Besides, Andrek said he barely knew Brand, having only met him a few times.

"If you know all this stuff about him that's the only way to save us, then tell my parents, or Commander Han. They're the ones who—"

"The ones who ignored my petitions about backup security plans, because nobody listens to someone fresh out of grad school. The only way they'll listen to me is if I tell them who I am, and I haven't run this far from my father to claim him now. To give up the whole life I've built.

"And if I tell them what I know without admitting who I am, I'll end up being their top suspect for the missing supplies and glitching systems. All of it. No, I have to find who Brand's contact here is first and expose them without throwing myself in the fire."

I chewed on her words, on her logic, on the way it felt inside my ears and clanging through my head. The puzzle hadn't come apart yet. In fact, it'd grown into a 3D model that was likely to take its first breath soon.

My parents would probably hush me and say I was being dramatic if I brought them this story of hers. They hadn't wanted me to know about the fleet; they'd have been happy sending me off to work and bed, blissfully ignorant. They so much as told me the only way they saw people our age having an impact was if someone older manipulated us.

Trust had to go both ways.

"There's some time left before he'll make his move here. If I can figure out who he's talking to, it could buy the trust a few more weeks. Maybe months, if we're lucky, to figure out better solutions than simply waiting for help from Earth. I've no doubt skipped over key details, and you'll have more questions, but this is what I couldn't risk you finding out the wrong way or thinking I used her memorial to cover it up for the wrong reasons. You deserve to hear it from me."

"But then what?" I blurted, feeling mocked by the now-in-definite stretch to the end of the world. "Assuming we find out who's talking to the RC on our own, what difference will that make? He has a fleet. What do we have, head games and hot lunch?"

"We?" she asked, a smile lurking in the curve of her lips.

I could say no, that I misspoke. I could wrench myself out of this bead palace, march straight to my parents, and leave this whole mess for smarter, older, and stronger people. I could do that easily, and it wouldn't be my fault if the world ended anyway.

But what if I could have a tiny part in saving us? Not just protecting Andrek or Viveca's secrets from each other, but stopping the monster who'd killed my sister?

Fuck, it was all so much bigger than my sister. It was families, countries. And all those smart, old, strong people had let Brand and his ilk get away with his routine, over and over again.

I crossed my heart then snaked through the beads to find her hand. "We."

She grinned. "*We* have the element of surprise and access to everything they know."

Attention: Department Leads

Subject: Meal Delivery

Week Options: Submarine sandwich tray, stir fry platter, margherita pizza.

Please confer with your staff and return department orders by the end of today for the following week of deliveries, specifying condiments, toppings, and number of diners.

Dessert Snickerdoodle cookies

CHAPTER SIXTEEN

JUGGLING SECRETS

My parents sat uncomfortably on the couch the next morning waiting to talk, but they didn't start till Andrek joined us. I couldn't figure out how to act, so I let my face go blank and slumped beside Dad. That did the trick, because he put an arm around me.

"I know, baby," he said. Quiet, gentle. "I wish things were different."

Mom closed her eyes for a long time. "We need to talk about what happens next."

Andrek rested on the arm of the chair, and I sank into Dad's side.

"We're listening," Dad told her.

She stood and paced, her arms stuffed into the pockets of her lab coat. "I need you to go about your routines as normally as possible and return to these quarters the moment your shifts end. Rationing must start today, though it won't be announced yet. You'll need to be ready to go to the subbasement shelter at a moment's notice. And no talking about the fleet with your friends. This is privileged information and must remain so as our investigations into the communications breach continues."

"How long?"

Dad misunderstood me and said, "As long as it takes to find them, honey."

"No, I mean, how long are we supposed to keep things secret? The RC's fleet and all of it?"

"Oh. President Marshall will decide that with ops," he said. "Though I expect it will be within a few days, maybe as early as tonight."

"That's fine for you three, but folks in the kitchen are going to notice rationing, whether anyone tells them or not."

Mom wrapped her arms tightly around her chest and croaked, "Can you please just have a normal day and come straight back?"

"I think the news is going to spread with or without my help."

Andrek met my gaze for the first time all morning with I-need-to-talk-to-you eyes.

I almost smiled, a reflex, until I remembered I couldn't be open with him either. I was holding his secret and Viveca's, and I was all alone with both.

"But I'll do my best," I said, and I meant it. I'd try my best to pretend everything's normal.

Just not for them.

This made breakfast awkward smothered with extra tricky. I took three bites, and each lodged in my throat like tiny rocks.

Mom's Major Mom mouth. *Remember what we agreed.* One rock wiggled its way free. Dad's checked out face. Impotent. Hoping and waiting. The second rock dropped and knocked against the first in my gut.

Andrek pinched me, not hard, but if he kept at the same spot any longer, I might bruise. I wrapped my foot around his leg, pulling it closer, then thwacked his knee twice. *Stop it.*

He kissed my cheek and whispered, "I'm going to tell them about my service. Even if it means I'm in some trouble for a minute. I can tell it's tearing you apart."

"'Kay."

"I know you're mad at me for not speaking up, but," he twisted a curl free from my hairnet, "I don't want to lose you either."

The third rock plunked as Viveca sat on my other side, her jumpsuit tied around her waist, the same way I'd been wearing mine. She rested her uniform—a soft cardigan sweater with reinforced pockets—next to her.

Her lips were black today. A strong look.

The rocks inside me tittered and clacked. I blushed, sandwiched by secrets and beauty.

Space me, this girl. A tiger's eye pendant blinked atop her clavicle, fixed by a delicate black chain, and her shining hair fanned her shoulders. Her bare arm rubbed against mine on the table, and her energy was a whole cup of coffee.

She smiled. I thought it was a "game on" smile.

"Good morning," we said at the same time.

I wore myself out feeling every seam on my jumpsuit, the tips of my hair, the air on my face. How was she going to play this normal morning, she who saw two steps ahead of the rest of the trust? Then, instead of saying something to shake the table's world, she laced her fingers through mine and took a slow sip of her juice.

I swallowed a squeal as Andrek tensed and tried to pull his leg back.

"Good morning," my parents returned, several seconds too late to sound ordinary. They picked at their food, glaring at my hand in hers. If they weren't going to eat, why wouldn't they leave?

Andrek mumbled a good morning too. I wished someone, anyone, would say something less boring, because the rocks had done an impossible thing. They'd grown. I checked my plate, positive that wasn't how soy eggs worked.

"Can I get a minute alone with you before you go to work? It's about the memorial." Viveca's thumb moved over my index finger and sent a shiver of joy down my spine.

"Now works." It was hard to make myself move, but I managed to do it. I quickly kissed Andrek and whispered,

"Tonight."

"Walk with me," I told Viveca.

"Have a good day," Mom called as I walked away, emphasizing *good* to mean "perfectly normal."

"Smoothly done," Viveca said, giving me another shiver. I was not used to compliments that weren't from Andrek.

"I have names from ops' suspect list for you to watch for in the line today, but—"

"I probably won't recognize names," I cut in.

"I thought of that actually, so I have pictures. As well as some questions that might be conversation starters. But be yourself and talk like you usually do at work. If you notice anyone acting peculiar, we can talk about it after lunch. Will you be free after your shift?"

I dumped the rest of my rock-eggs and settled the tray in the sanitizer cart. "My parents ordered me straight back to our quarters. For safety."

"Of course they did."

"I'm not doing that though."

She breathed out a laugh. "I guessed not."

She put her tray on top of mine. I liked the click it made. We slid into seats at an empty table so she could show me the faces and guiding questions. I committed them to memory as best as I could, and we shared the rest of her juice before she left for work.

My job today was to hunt for the spy without drawing attention. Meanwhile, she'd be digging through personnel files and records for proof of foul play that wasn't her own. I adjusted my uniform, slung on an apron, fixed my hairnet in place, and started my shift prep. All the while I practiced the first question, mouthing it to myself as I worked.

What was your favorite holiday growing up?

Viveca thought this would spark some emotional conversation, and I was to watch for anything weird, because people with a secret act all kinds of ways, she'd said. Overly talkative or oddly quiet or sweaty, clumsy, off, anything out of the norm. It didn't seem like enough to me, but she said my "strong intuition" should be plenty to speed our investigation forward.

I was supposed to start the conversation circling the kitchen first, because one of Viveca's names was Ty, and I was supposed to say I was asking "for the memorial," if anyone got at me for being nosy. These supposed-tos lined up nicely with my parents' musts, and holiday talk sparked around the kitchen as soon as I practiced on Stephan, so I was feeling pretty smug about my espionage efforts by the time I carried lunch to the serving line.

Seared butternut squash curry on rice. Snow peas. Pineapple compote with coconut cookies. A bright and happy spread.

Stephan joined me on the line. He'd been stuck prepping lunch deliveries most of the morning.

"Can I get—" he took the tray and an extra cookie and crouched by my feet. "Thanks. I'm starving," he mumbled between bites. He scarfed the whole meal in seconds.

I shielded him from view as I plated more trays, because Chef would flip to see him eating on the line. "No worries. I got you."

Ty was as normal as ever with her one-word answers, so I ticked her off the suspect list and smiled at the first person in line. A doctor, I figured, because of the red Medical emblem on her left shoulder. She wasn't one Viveca told me to watch for, but I might as well get things moving.

"What was your most memorable holiday," I asked her, "when you were growing up?"

She jerked to attention as if caught unaware and stood frozen for a moment, her hands hovering over the edges of the tray she reached for. Her eyes widened then contracted, emotions spilling over her face. It was like watching a train crash in slow motion.

"Why would you—you can't ask someone that!" she said hotly. "My home flooded on Christmas day, if you must know."

"I'm—I'm sorry. I didn't mean to—"

"Thanks a lot." She stormed away with her tray, but not before I saw tears spilling onto her cheeks. She brushed them away with an angry tug of her sleeve.

Stephan cuffed my shoulder and helped the next person. "What was that about?"

"A mistake," I said, trying to shrug it off. I should have stuck with "best." Maybe I'd do better with the next question.

I gave myself a solid minute to let the line move further and hide the crying doctor from easy view. Then I picked a happy looking couple out of uniform. "What's the best thing you've ever tasted?"

"Easy," the first man said. "My mother's paella."

The second man bristled and cut a look at his partner. "Your mother's? Your *mother's*?"

"Well, yeah," mama's boy answered defensively.

"You said mine was your favorite," bristly man whined. "The best meal of your life, remember?"

"Baby, I mean, it's not like I'll ever have my mother's again."

"Or mine! If you hadn't noticed, I don't get to do any cooking anymore."

Their argument trailed off as they walked away, but I was left blinking after them and wondering how I'd failed so badly so fast.

Stephan rolled his eyes. "Maybe you shouldn't talk so much."

I laughed, mostly with embarrassment, and definitely did not talk for several minutes.

When Danny came through the line with her friends, I got to practice on them, to slightly better, if bittersweet, results. The best meal of Danny's life was one I cooked for Faraday's campaign, and the last Danny shared with her mom and brother. Luckily, none of the other faces I was looking for showed up in line after, and once I spotted Viveca I decided to take a quick break.

I dragged her to Chef's office and heaved a sigh of relief nobody was using it. Less lucky, I noticed the mama's boy talking to Chef, who saw me watching.

She rubbed her forehead and waved me on.

I pulled the curtain closed with a huff. "This isn't working."

I spun around and nearly knocked into Viveca. The rocks in my gut rattled like they expected me to tumble them smooth.

She scanned me, locking onto my mouth. I couldn't imagine what she saw there, but she hadn't stepped back to let me further inside.

"I see. Don't sweat it. It's only one prong of Plan A. Anything stand out to you?"

I chewed my lower lip, which she was still staring at. "Only how phenomenally bad that went."

She crossed her arms, a thinking pose. "That's weird, because usually you present rather well. Warm. Friendly."

"I do?"

"How do you not know that? You're very approachable. Anyway, I think you're in your head. How about this." She brought a finger close to my lips, pointing. "Relax. This is only a start, to see if you notice something I don't."

That shriveled me more than I liked. "Oh."

"I said that wrong. Your part in the plan is the most important because people I call to my office come prepared with 'versions' of their truth. You're more likely to see folks how they really are."

"I just relax?"

"Yes," she said. "And be yourself. Stick to food topics, but maybe take things down a notch? Make it less personal?"

I squirmed a little. "Yeah, yeah. I can do that. Thanks for the pep talk." I turned to leave, but she took my arm and slid her fingers between mine again. My head went light and fizzy.

Her smile bloomed. A black rose. "Lane."

"Yeah?"

"Thank you," she said, and brushed that rose between my cheek and my mouth. The room spun or I did. "For believing me."

Maybe I should never kiss her. Our nearness made me feel supercharged. I could power a planet.

"I should go back out. Stephan's got deliveries soon, and I don't want to miss—you know."

"I'll stay close. In case you need me." She whirled past me through the curtain, revealing Chef frowning quizzically at the hole in the line.

I checked the ovens with Chef's attention boring into my back, but she was busy once I returned to my position.

Stephan shot me a curious look but softened when I laid more cookies out. He still acted hungry, so I sent him off to eat again before he had to dash. Deliveries must have been wearing him out, and I wondered why he hadn't asked for more help when he'd taught me his routes through all the weird hidden hallways between departments. I didn't know how he ever came up with it, because he still hadn't been assigned his own tablet. Anyway, I'd had fun learning the secret, windy paths of the trust, even though I'd rather be in the kitchen.

With my courage mustered and the bain-maries freshened, I surveyed the tail end of the lunch line. There were four others that Viveca had me looking for, but I only saw one of them, a guy in his thirties. Thick-jawed and white, not much taller than me. I'd noticed him before, usually at breakfast, because he piled every kind of available cereal into a box and left with it right away. If there weren't at least three kinds available, he went hunting for Chef to complain.

Cereal Box wasn't carrying his box today. He scratched at the back of his neck, his gaze darting to the west hallway. I supposed that was a little weird.

I wouldn't waste my question this time. Keep it about food. Not heavy. I waited till he was one person shy of the counter and asked, "Is there something you'd like us to make next week?"

The person in front of me was twice the height of Cereal Box and had shoulders that wouldn't fit through most doorways without twisting. His watery blue eyes were marred by bloodshot cracks. He was, I realized, the drunkest person I'd ever seen in real life.

"Your tits on a tray will do, sugar," he quipped, sticking his finger into his compote and smearing it on his tongue.

"Ew," was all I managed to say, because Cereal Box squawked and pulled Giant Drunk away from the line.

"Don't talk to her that way!"

"What're you—" a branch-sized white finger poked at Cereal Box's nose "—gonna do, you tiny—"

Cereal Box did some fancy one-two fist work that doubled Giant Drunk in half, but while Cereal Box cradled his knuckles, Giant Drunk snapped a trunk-like arm around his neck.

Shouts from the cafeteria got drowned out by Giant Drunk's unintelligible hollering and Cereal Box's cries. I cast about helplessly, my hands pulled in to cover myself, though the counter separated me from the fray.

All of a sudden, Stephan was there to save me, sliding over the line and bursting the men apart with sharp barks at both. I wouldn't have thought it possible, but Stephan got Drunk Giant kneeling, held by the back of his collar, and Cereal Box by the front of his shirt.

Stephan caught my eye and mouthed, "Go," so I did, backing into Chef's arms, who hustled me to her office with gentle words.

"You are having a real day of it," Chef said, pulling off my hairnet and patting my cheeks. I let her. "One thing after another all shift, then this. How are you? You know that wasn't your fault, right?"

I inched over to Chef's couch and hauled myself onto it. "I'm not so sure about that."

"I am. Boorish drunks and hothead men. Not you." She laughed her baritone laugh, the one even the freezer doors couldn't muffle. "However! You have been stirring the pot on the line today. What's that about? Best tell me so I can get in front of it."

I caught my breath and tried to untangle my stiff limbs. "It's…"

Chef had been so amazing to me. Patient. Kind. She'd let me play at being a dessert chef, though my recipes were amateur hour. Baking 101. She provided her office as a retreat, whether or not I was on shift.

I didn't want to lie to her.

"Oh my, now I've stirred something myself, and you're—"

"It's okay. I should tell you," I said. "It's for the memorial."

"How?" she asked, which was perfectly reasonable to wonder, but my preparation didn't stretch that far.

So maybe I wouldn't lie. How could I not lie? "I'm trying to gather ideas for it, for..." If I said something and *made* it true, then it wouldn't be a lie. "A holiday. A Memorial Day."

Viveca lifted the curtain and swept across the room to me in one step. "I saw."

"Yeah." I said. "I'm all right. I was about to pitch Chef our memorial plan. For a holiday."

Chef glanced between us shiftily. She was too clever not to sense something was up. "Like, a Faraday... day?"

I screeched. "Under no circumstances will we call it that."

"But yes," Viveca slid in. "A holiday, with a better name. And we'll need to build an entire day's menu."

Oh, I saw where she was taking us. I shored up my voice, which was still a tad shaky. "And games and other stuff, but yeah. Food's at the center of any holiday tradition."

"That's true about food." Chef sniffed and tapped her teeth. "But we can't have you disrupting meals like this, with people all in their moods."

An idea flashed. I'd never been great in groups, or timed settings, but maybe there was a different way. "I was going to ask if I could meet with a few people at a time, actually. Not during meals. Maybe after dinner service? That way we could run some tasting trials. Without disruptions."

Chef kept tapping, considering. "A focus group. I could make that work."

Viveca's eyes twinkled. "And could we also get a list of trustees' dietary requirements and restrictions? We don't want to do Faraday an injustice by not thinking things through. Or do anything to mess up your orderly kitchen."

"Little thick there, dear." Chef smoothed her apron. "I'll make those records available. You'll need to double check the pantry first, of course."

"I will," I said. "Thank you!"

Chef shooed us from her office with a wicked grin. "Go on then, you two. Faraday Day."

Viveca and I held hands on our way out of the kitchen and through the cafeteria, our surprise victory flapping like a lightning bug trapped between our palms.

Attention: SECOND SHIFT

Subject: New Evening Delivery Options

Entrees: Crispy tofu and microgreens wrap, four bean burrito

Sides: Tortilla chips and salsa, tangerines

Dessert Lemon cupcakes

CHAPTER SEVENTEEN

WHAT THEY DON'T KNOW

Every time Viveca was right and my parents' crowd was wrong, it gave me chills. It felt like my sister's halo of clarity had passed over to Viveca, and I was the lucky one allowed to bask in that glow all over again.

I'd been on the outside of big decisions and happenings since I could remember. Even before my sister stole the world's heart, my parents' dinner table conversations had become the next semester's coursework for the stringy-haired students who babysat on Saturday nights. Their vacation chats turned into books in the bookstore.

As the listener, and interrupter, of those conversations, I knew my place.

Now, here came Viveca, sharing with me. Being on the inside was exhilarating.

When I found my parents waiting for me again the next day, I was buoyed by Viveca's faith in me. She made sure I knew my help, in both the hunt for the leak and the now-official holiday prep, was invaluable. I practically floated onto a chair.

Andrek plodded in and perched on the chair's arm, looking more run-down than yesterday. He passed me a weak-tea smile and nodded along to my parents' even weaker good morning platitudes.

I tuned them out aside from occasionally ticking off

another "Viveca said so" box. They droned on about necessary decisions, as if they didn't say the same nonsense yesterday, while I ran my fingertips absently over the vial labels in my bubble case.

When Mom finally got to the part where she urged me to come straight to our quarters, I outright refused without feeling the least bit sorry.

"I'm going on with normal life, like you wanted. I've got grief group and work then memorial planning. You know, for your daughter? Who was murdered by the people you think we can hide from?"

Mom gasped, and Dad jumped to her defense. "That's not fair, Lane!"

"Are we only worried about things that are fair now?" I asked. "I thought that was something that died with Faraday."

"You are so out of line, I don't know how to talk to you," Mom said. "But I'll say this. Nobody wants to beg or hide or surrender. Nobody. But unless military aid arrives in time, our only other option is complete isolation in the subbasement. If we run out of food and water, what would you have us do? Die? We're a community, not a suicide cult. We have to be prepared for the worst, even while hoping it never comes."

"But by planning how to surrender, you're psyching yourselves up to do it!"

"That's because supplies keep vanishing!" Mom screamed. "With every crate that gets stolen, surrender becomes more likely!"

I screamed right back. "Why are you yelling at me about it? I'm not the thief!"

Andrek went so tense beside me, I was afraid I might knock him off the chair with a word.

"We understand your anger," my dad said slowly. "We're angry too. None of us wanted things to happen this way."

"Not enough to stop it."

"What do you mean?" Dad pressed.

"You've never been angry enough. That's why Faraday

had to be so bright and cheerful all the time, because it was the only way to make you people listen."

"You people? What *are* you on about?" Mom's face was stone.

I aimed to crack it open.

"We're giving her a holiday, so you know. To honor who she was, what she really wanted for us. Equality, transparency, and all that. She never wanted to be president. She just couldn't trust anyone else to follow through with the promises the collective made in the first place. So even if you give her dreams away to the RC, others can remember. Maybe some of them might be angry enough to protect what matters." The words tripped over themselves on their way out, and I vibrated with the force of them, with how close they were to my true plans.

If they would listen, they'd know everything.

But they wouldn't.

So they didn't.

Dad's cheeks puffed and flattened rapidly. He looked like an owl. "Lane!"

Such a bizarre reversal this morning had brought. Them doing the yelling, while I rejected them.

"That's what you wanted, right, to remind everyone of her? I'm only sorry I wasn't fast enough to make any difference before you agreed to sell us all out."

Mom couldn't look at me anymore. I hoped she felt ashamed. She should have.

She said, "That's never what we meant, and you know—"

I snapped my bubble case closed as loud as I could then talked over her to Andrek. "I have to go. Are you coming with me?"

Andrek trailed after me to breakfast, and I did feel the teensiest bit guilty for putting him in the middle, especially since he had to be with my parents the rest of the day at work.

"You couldn't tell them, I take it?" I asked, once we were far enough down the hallway. I thought I already knew the answer from his mood.

He slumped against the wall, dragging me with him. "I really tried. I started to at least four times, but—" he held me close. I could feel the words swirling inside him, trying to land.

"Too hard?"

"Maybe?" His bangs fell loose. "More like... It's not theirs to know, and it'll only complicate things between us. If I had more time to explain, it wouldn't be so risky, but Brand's in our orbit now. Time's up."

I let my gaze drift with the trustees passing by, wanting to say we had more time. Today was not the end of the dream; it still breathed, and so did we. But I couldn't tell him that, not convincingly, without explaining how I knew.

"Plus," he whispered only to me, "if I don't tell anyone, I might be able to use it to protect us. It's not like I burned bridges with the RC. I just left. I could at least try to keep our family safe."

I saw the delusion of hope pulling over his ice blue eyes. Even if I did tell him, he wouldn't believe me, because his fear erased what he knew about Brand and the RC, convincing him that working with Brand would save him from the truth.

Shaking hands with a monster wouldn't turn the monster into a man.

During grief group after breakfast, we were in a conference room inside the medical department. Dr. Fromme led a discussion about trauma responses—what was normal, what wasn't, and when to be concerned and seek more help. Apparently, my reaction during the moon quake was totally normal, but if it happened again, I might need medicine or some other treatment.

I didn't mention that I relived the day of my sister's death every time I was alone when I fell asleep. I did, however, casually drop to Dr. Fromme that I'd be stopping by her office soon. She must have been very good at her job, because all she did was change the subject while making a note on her tablet.

The idea of taking medicine sat uncomfortably in my head as the others kept talking. There was something itchy about it that nagged at me. It was silly, I told myself, because I wouldn't hesitate to get a cast if I broke a bone or to pop an ibuprofen for a headache. What had happened to my sister, in front of me—why should that affect me any less?

When President Marshall's voice blared from the speakers, it was an accidental victory. I got pulled out of my head so abruptly that I probably looked as surprised as the rest of the group.

The RC had attacked our allies at the Blackstone Base, our most fiercely defended ally on the moon, and more security measures would be implemented at once to ensure our safety. We were advised to pack a crate per person for pickup and storage in case we had to shelter below. Blah blah blah, death, doom, and gloom was what I heard, and I sank into my seat to let everyone else react.

Dr. Fromme looked agitated, her professional reserve of calm pushed to its limit, but she stuck with us. Milo ugly cried, saying they had family on Blackstone, and Cheese held their hand. Danny pulled on her braid and stared wordlessly at the wall. Ty said little, her hands balled into fists atop the table. Ira hugged himself, rocking, mumbling his worries aloud, and because his worries were all of ours—were we next, was the dream over, what could we do, would we have to go back to Earth, on and on. Dr. Fromme gently responded to each question well enough for the rest of us to take some comfort.

I watched, wringing my hands, tracing over Viveca's words for reassurance. I wanted to go to her, right now, to feel like I was doing something, but she'd warned me last night not to. I was to "keep my eyes open" and stay on track, because once the trust all knew the RC was on the moon, the spy might say or do something to draw attention. But as my group's energy built and swayed, I became more certain than ever that none of them was the spy.

It was so easy to see they were innocent that it set off another worm of worry in my thoughts. Was this busy work? My tutors used to do that—when they'd tired of my questions, they'd assign tasks simply meant to occupy my time. While I stayed busy looking at people who couldn't be the spy, what was Viveca doing? She'd told me finding the spy was "Plan A," but why hadn't she said anything about her "Plan B?" Who was she sharing that with, if not me? Halle, for sure, maybe Joule?

Grief group fizzled out, with Milo, Cheese, and Danny following Dr. Fromme out of the conference room, and Ty and me taking our sweet time as we wound through the hallway. A heavy sort of quiet hung around us and everyone we passed, as though we were all afraid we might summon the RC by talking too much. Once we reached the doors to the cafeteria, I lingered while Ty went inside.

I didn't want to be at work. Or in my quarters. Everyone knew the RC was coming, soon-ish if not today, and nobody was going to be acting "normal," so why should I? I'd rather be doing something, anything, to make sure surrender never happened. I felt so discouraged that we hadn't found the spy yet, and I was starting to think we never would. Not unless they walked up and introduced themselves anyway. I had to get Viveca to level with me about the rest of her plans, because spinning my wheels in this search of ours felt worse than useless.

Eventually I mustered the courage to go ask Chef for the day off, and I was shocked when she refused me.

"It isn't a good day for anyone," Chef explained. "But we still need to eat, and I'm counting on you to do your part. We need your sweetness more than ever."

It was pointless to argue with her, because I could see that the kitchen was barely half staffed already. She must have let a lot of people leave after the announcement. Even Stephan had begged off, which I didn't think was in his vocabulary, so I tried to stuff my feelings away and picked up the slack with lunch prep.

I baked cakes—nothing difficult, really, just iced sheet cakes. I'd had elaborate decorations planned when I pitched the idea to Chef, but now that felt wrong. I mixed the icing with navy blue and purple food coloring, leaving the colors swirled and not fully blended. The end results were vaguely space-like squares. I thought they looked sad, but Chef approved them and let me hang up my apron before lunch service began.

"Don't forget to eat," she said, handing me a couple packaged meals. "For you and your lovely friend."

I headed straight to Viveca's office. It wasn't that I didn't trust her all of a sudden. If anything, today's announcement confirmed she was trustworthy three times over.

But seeing Andrek deny what he knew to be true simply because it hurt him too much not to had me scratching at my own brain, looking for curtains that might need to be peeled back. I didn't want to trust Viveca merely because I was afraid of the alternative, of having no one to trust. Or because if she didn't have the answer, there wasn't one.

Too much was riding on finding the saboteur and getting our leaders to go on the offensive for me to leave any question unanswered.

I also wanted to be trusted too. I didn't want to waste precious time flailing around with pointless projects, even if we were headed toward failure and the end of everything no matter what—hell, especially if that was what we were headed for. If these were my last days, I wanted to live them with my eyes wide open, doing things that mattered. I refused to be played or left out anymore.

"I need to know the whole plan, and whatever else you're keeping from me," I announced, bursting into Viveca's office. "I want—"

I broke off when I noticed someone sitting in the bubble tub. President Marshall. She wore a black slip, a matching eye mask, and a mechanical medical bracelet, the kind used for monitoring vitals. She jolted, rising unsteadily and removing her mask.

"Can't I have ten minutes to myself?" she yelled, and Viveca rushed to her side, helping her sit back down. The water beads whirled clockwise, tumbling over her legs. I didn't know the tub could do that.

"I'm so sorry, excuse me! I'm sorry." I backed out of the office and flung myself against the wall outside the door. Once I caught my breath, I slunk down the hall to the waiting room. There were no empty seats, and at least five others standing. Milo was one of them, their eyes red-rimmed and hollow, like the life had been sucked right out.

And it smelled.

Really bad. Like nobody had bothered to shower for days.

I kicked myself for being annoyed with Chef for making me stay at work earlier. I forgave her now, in my head. She must have seen I was okay "enough" to get the trust fed when others weren't. We were all in this mess basket together. I opened my lunch sack and offered it to the people closest to me before handing Milo the extra. The contents disappeared in less than a minute.

The nurse clocked me and waved me closer. "Have you checked in yet? Do you know who you're here to see?"

"Yes, I—" Too many answers crowded my tongue. "You should call Chef to get more lunches delivered. People are hungry. Viveca. President Marshall was with her."

"You can wait here for Dr. Osborne or have us call your quarters when she's free," he said.

"Sorry, I'll—I'll—"

"Lane." Viveca appeared in the waiting room. The only sign that she was flustered was a slight flutter in her fingers atop her tablet. She met my gaze and ticked her head to the side, indicating the outer hallway. Her lips shined like raspberry jelly. To the nurse, she said, "I'm taking thirty."

President Marshall skirted around behind her, pausing only to shake a few hands on her way out of the medical department. She scanned me with recognition and a large helping of annoyance.

"I'm really sorry," I ventured, but she didn't respond. An angry cloud hovered in the air after she left.

Guilt locked my knees in place. Had the president been pushed out of her sensory appointment for me? My cheeks heated, and I couldn't tell if it was from embarrassment or elation that I mattered that much to Viveca. Others might wait hours for her time, but she gave it to me freely.

Viveca stopped to talk to several patients, issuing quick, three-word statements, settling them as she worked across the room. I stammered something else to the nurse about lunch getting sent, then blushed harder when Viveca looped her arm around the crook of my elbow. I told myself that this was what friends did, but it had been a while since I'd had a "just a friend" and this felt like so much more.

Milo quirked a rainbow-jeweled eyebrow at me as we passed them.

Maybe this wasn't how "just friends" walked. I needed to get my head in order and focus on why I came to talk, but it was so hard when her long hair smelled so good and whispered like silk when it swept over my arm.

"Not here," she said quietly. "Too crowded. Everyone's freaking out. Understandably." It wasn't quite a whisper, but it had the same effect on me, the way she leaned lower to speak only to me. It was crowded outside Medical too, as if everyone in the trust had left work to aimlessly wander the halls.

We went to her quarters—they were closest—which put me in the awkward position of choosing whether to follow Viveca to her room or wait for her in the living room with the I-love-Faraday wallpaper. I picked the chair facing away from the collage. Easier to concentrate.

"So I need to know what your real plan is, the other one, because—and I'm sorry I crashed into your session—it's just, in group, when the announcement came, everyone was so surprised and upset. I know I already said Ty can't be the spy, but Danny really can't be, and I don't think I'm going to have any luck watching people in the lunch line. We don't have time to waste on dead ends."

She returned with a hairbrush and stood in her doorway. "Maybe the focus group will be more helpful. Don't you start that tomorrow?"

"Yeah, but..." I'd forgotten the tastings already, and I thought I must have left my bubble case in the kitchen. "President Marshall is your patient. You didn't tell me you're a doctor now! That's so big! Congratulations, seriously. But like, what am *I* going to learn from a few minutes with someone that you won't from an actual session?"

"Maybe nothing. Or everything. We won't know unless we listen." She kicked off her boots. "Can you braid? Would you mind? I have a patient that talks so slow I end up fidgeting with my hair, and then it becomes a whole thing."

I could braid—I'd done Faraday's hair whenever she let me—but that was the opposite of concentrating. "I guess. Sure."

Viveca sat on the carpet and scooted between my legs.

"Thanks," she said, handing me the brush. "And my doctorate just happened. I haven't been able to think about it, so I haven't told anyone yet. Don't sweat it. Are you asking why I don't make appointments with everyone I suspect to be the spy?"

I rolled the brush over her hair pointlessly. There weren't any tangles. "Yeah. Why not do that?"

"I basically have. Not basically. I *have*. At least with everyone it wouldn't draw suspicion to call in. I only gave you half my list."

"Oh." I started the braid high on her crown. She held very still, even when I pulled the strands tight. "Who else is on your list?"

She didn't answer. Her fingers twisted through the carpet like she was mimicking my movements. I wondered if she was ever going to respond. Her neck was tight as a drum. Even her hair seemed to resist me, slipping out of my grasp so I had to braid faster and faster or risk loosing it all.

"Viveca?"

She sighed, her breath catching. "I believe it's best to keep—"

"Why don't you want to tell me?" I tied off the braid with considerably less care than I'd taken so far. "Don't you trust me?"

Viveca pulled the braid and hung her head. With another sigh, she planted her hands on the carpet and turned around, her coal-black lashes making half-moons above her cheeks.

"I do... as much as I can trust anyone," she said, each word a bitter scratch. "You can't understand. After my mom, there was only one person I felt safe sharing everything with, and she—even she..."

"Even she let you down." I knew it was fucked up to think of my sister this way. Severely fucked up. It wasn't like Faraday wanted to be wrong about the RC. She definitely hadn't wanted to die.

But I understood. I felt let down too.

I grabbed the brush again for something to hold. "What about Halle? Or Joule?"

"No, no," she said. "I could, but I don't risk saying more than they need to know."

"I didn't realize it was so hard." I rubbed the brush over my thigh. "And you hardly know me, so of course you wouldn't be ready to..."

She lifted those bottomless brown eyes. "It's not that. If you knew who else I was looking into, you'd probably never talk to me again."

She said that like it was someone I knew. Someone I cared about.

"Is it my parents?" I couldn't let this go, because doubt will creep into my head the moment she was out of sight. I have to know. "Andrek? It's Andrek, isn't it?"

"Please drop it." A single bead of sweat built above her mouth. "I have to get back to the office anyway."

"I'm right, aren't I?" The brush clattered to the floor. "Andrek would never betray the trust. Believe what you want about my parents—I hate them right now—but Andrek has nothing to do with the spy. He's on our side, I swear it."

"Lane." She looked deeply at me, her head shaking. "He has secrets. I don't know what they are, but—"

I put my hands on her shoulders, wishing I could stop her suspicion with my certainty. I was so glad I'd covered for her with my parents now, because she definitely would have pointed right at Andrek. "But I do! I know them, and you don't have to trust him. Trust *me*."

"How can you be sure?" she asked, and it was like she was asking about more than Andrek, about more than right now. She wanted to know how to believe in anyone or anything when monsters were so good at hiding.

"I just am," I answered, but it had me reeling. Being certain about Andrek was one thing, because he was my boyfriend, and I knew his secrets. But I felt certain about Ty, about my whole grief group too. I knew any one of them would help us in a heartbeat. All we'd have to do was ask. "Maybe we should be looking for allies instead of enemies? The spy is what? One person or two, while there are a thousand more trustees who want the same thing as us."

She took my hands from her shoulders and stared up at me, her gaze soft and wet. "You truly are extraordinary."

I knew many things at once. I knew it was the wrong time to catch feelings. We had a trust to save from her father first. And I knew everything was messed up with both our families, even both our boyfriends.

But I also knew her lips were raspberry pink, and her hands rose petal soft, and absolutely nothing I said to myself could stop me from pressing my mouth to hers.

She tasted of sugared oranges, like summer sunshine. A strong, spicy taste that made me feel at once fearless and fierce, wild and weak.

I drew back, astonished by myself, and terrified I'd gone too far. Too fast.

"Viveca," I started, and she smiled wide.

"Verona," she whispered, touching my fingers to her heart. "But please call me V."

And she returned my kiss. Deeply and without a flicker of hesitation.

Verona. *Verona*. Verona. She was breakfast, lunch, and dinner, and I was starving.

It may have been the wrong time, but this was a rocket that had already launched. And I was in it, not strapped tight but set loose and free-floating. Every slip of her tongue and brush of her fingers sent me spinning, weightless.

My tongue parted her lips, and we shared a long, buzzing breath, testing and falling. Our eyes drank in each other's as we moved closer. Somehow I was off the couch, kneeling over her legs, and our hands had found new ways to hold tight—hers on my waist and back, mine on her jaw and neck. Her work sweater pooled around us, and she tugged me down.

Kissing had never felt so much like swimming.

When her tablet sang an alarm, we broke apart. Our fingers tangled in each other's clothes and hair, and we laughed for no reason besides adrenaline. Her braid had fallen out, so I scrambled to find the brush one of us had kicked under the couch. Her masks faded into place, and the mood shifted. We walked arm in arm to the medical department, slackening our pace as we approached.

I wanted to kiss her again already, but I didn't know if that was who we were yet. Or how to ask.

A patient came out of Medical and threw a not-so-subtle look of disapproval at us, muttering something about "not having more time to wait around." V didn't respond, but I cringed and felt guilty all over again for taking her away from work, especially since my reasons unraveled into a make out session. I needed to redeem myself somehow.

Under my breath, I said, "I can't tell you how I know, but Andrek, and my parents, they aren't who you're looking for."

She smoothed her hair once more, tucking it into her sweater, then cupped my cheek gently. "For all our sake, I hope that's true."

And I felt floaty and wonderful for a whole minute until

I realized she'd completely avoided my question about what else she was plotting.

Attention: ALL

Subject: Evening Menu

Entrees: Coconut curry with sweet peas, fried rice

Sides: Steamed edamame, roasted sweet potato, fruit salad

Dessert None

CHAPTER EIGHTEEN

EARNING IT

My family quarters were dark and empty when I bounced in, high from the very public moment with V despite her evasion. It was dark, except for the ambient light that was always on above the lone shelf. Empty, except for Faraday in her urn, sitting under that lone light in silent, shiny judgment.

"Stop staring at me," I told her, and I wandered through our rooms restlessly, alert to the wheezing air filters and the low droning of the generators, letting the automatic lights blink on as I entered each room, then turn off as I left. I hated feeling this useless and stuck, especially when my brain kept repeating that the RC would be here *soon, soon, soon.*

She watched me come and go, the lights blinking over her as steadily as if she were shaking her head.

I hid on the couch from her disapproval for a while, staring up at the ceiling. I shouldn't have kissed V. *Verona.* Not yet.

"I'm sorry," I said, peeking over the back of the couch. "I have the worst timing."

Faraday's urn sat under its light, defying my apology. She must have gotten so bored on that shelf. I brought her to Andrek's room, because at least in here we had the projector. I set it to a panorama of the trust's exterior since she'd never gotten to see it for herself.

"Listen," I started, flopping onto my stomach on Andrek's bed and gazing into the urn as if it were a crystal ball. I was about to launch into an explanation about catching feelings and timing, how she should understand because it had happened to her too once. Maybe more than once. She'd had a whole life away from me that I never saw.

You could look now, she reminded me, and my attention flicked to the open door, to the tablet screen on the living room wall. Viveca had sent me files days ago, and so had Chef. I'd told myself I'd been too busy and overwhelmed. I tried to tell myself that now, but Faraday was humming like she used to when we baked. A silly tune that my mind overlaid the words "Faraday Day" on top of.

"I promise we won't call it that," I told her, but she hummed on, reflecting the lunar landscape coldly. "That's why you're mad at me? Because I'm using your memorial as a cover?"

She stopped her song. *Yes.*

I guessed right.

The unfairness of it all was worse than a slap in the face. There was no point in honoring her if I didn't fight for the dream she'd valued most. Shouldn't that be my priority? Saving the trust from her murderer had to be the best way to keep her memory intact.

In the history of me and my dreams, Faraday argued, *did you ever know me to lie about anything that I cared about?*

"Actually, yeah," I returned immediately. "About mentoring a monster's daughter and playing like you were a one-woman witness protection program!"

My elbows dug into the mattress, sending her rocking. Sibling squabble was in full swing now.

I didn't lie.

"Neither have I!" I yelled.

Except I had. To my parents. To Chef. My parents might literally have been the worst, but Chef had done nothing but offer encouragement and support. No wonder my sister was upset with me. She was fine with me being unambitious and flighty, with me being a goof-off and a slacker, because—no matter what—I was always honest.

That was the me she'd known, the me I was supposed to be.

If I didn't do something to change the course I was on, right now, I'd be lying to a kitchen full of potential spy suspects tomorrow afternoon.

Get to work, dove, Faraday pressed sweetly.

I returned her to the shelf, regret stinging my throat and guilt knocking around my empty stomach. My breath sounded raucous and strange as I opened the comm screen.

Viveca had only sent one message, with the subject line "Memorial Research." The attachment file was a hundred times the size of everything Chef had sent me. She had said it had all of Faraday's correspondence. A veritable treasure trove. What better way to listen to my sister than to read her own words?

I reached for the screen, but I couldn't make myself select the message.

Earn it, the urn said.

"You're not funny," I told it.

Eeeeeearn itttt.

I wanted to open the message. I did. It was right there.

But so was the rest of her, glaring into my back, while the rocks inside me rumbled like my everything was downhill.

I couldn't read any of this here. And if my parents wouldn't help me get my own tablet, then I'd find someone else who would.

It took me forever to find the communications department, which was tucked below the center of the dome, past the cafeteria. It was accessible only through an unmarked side hallway that wound back around the way I had come and dead ended into wide glass doors. I went through these to find a ring of living quarters surrounding a gently sloped spiral walkway leading down into a vast open room. It was easily as big as the cafeteria down there, though the walls had jungle print wallpaper and there were very few tables.

Instead they had bean bag chairs, whiteboards on wheels, long, padded benches, and random color blocked screens. I felt like I'd entered an entirely different world. Even the gravity felt different.

"Oho, Lane!" Milo saw me coming down the slope and beamed. "Meat Team, come meet my friend from therapy."

People emerged from every direction as I reached the bottom floor. A few were little people like Commander Han and Cheese, but they weren't using wheelchairs now. Most were women, I guessed, two with obvious prosthetics. They seemed more relaxed than anyone I'd seen in the trust the last few days.

"Is this the baker?" someone asked.

"Yup, this is Lane." Milo laid an arm over my shoulder. "And you know Cheese, but this is the rest of my family. Roast, Steak, Turkey, Tenders, and Buffet."

I must have been doing something weird with my face, because they all looked like they were about to break into collective laughter. This was a gag. They were messing with me. "Come on."

Milo patted my back. "We know it's weird. When we moved to the moon a decade ago, we were worried we'd miss meat, so we changed our names."

"All except you?"

"Lifelong vegetarian," Milo answered smoothly.

I noticed one white woman at a corner desk ignoring us. She had the only real desk in the room. "Who's that then?"

Milo laughed loudly, and Cheese answered, "That's Karen. She's not with us."

"My name's not Karen," she said, annoyed. "It's Christina."

The team rolled their eyes, and several whispered, "*So Karen.*"

"We don't have much patience for strangers," Cheese explained. "We're enough for each other."

In a weird way, I understood without asking. There was a palpable energy between them all. More than family.

Milo ran a finger over their jeweled eyebrows. "Did you

come to hang out, or..."

I cast around to remember what I came for, but everything about the room, the journey here, and the barrage of meat talk had gotten my brain feeling emptied out. There was so much information everywhere I looked that I could only stand there with my mouth open.

"Got a problem with your tablet or something?" Cheese asked. "That's why most folks swing by."

Milo held out their palm to take my imaginary broken tablet, and it came back to me.

"I don't have one," I admitted, relieved. "I hoped you all might have an extra I could borrow."

Milo, Cheese, and Roast shared a look, and the rest of the team dispersed to whatever they were doing before I arrived. Milo lowered their hand and started shaking a finger, their face morphing from their easy smile into one about to rage.

"Even here," Milo began. "Here! I knew, knew, this would come back around to hurt us all. It's not like we don't have the resources. And then some!"

I shuffled my feet and wondered if I should find a bean bag to plant myself in until they were done. Cheese and Roast mimed behind Milo as they gestured emphatically.

"There's no reason everyone shouldn't have one! And you, Lane, you're this trust go-getter, with your desserts and holiday planning—what, do they expect you to stand in your living room for hours every day?" Milo spun and caught Cheese mid-air-punch.

"This cramp in my hand is really something," Cheese said. "I should—yeah." Cheese darted away from Milo's line of sight with Roast on her heels.

"Aaagh!" Milo roared at their backs but wore a smile when they turned to me. "Save your mocking for people with ridiculous complaints. Like herding cats, I swear."

"Aw," Cheese sang as Roast said, "We strive to be much worse than cats."

I loved this crowd. "So, you do have extra tablets? The standing around my living room part is true, and I hate it."

"Of course you do." Milo shook their head. "Hang on a bit. Joule!"

Joule? This wasn't his department.

"Hey man, do you know Lane? She needs one of those spare tablets, if you haven't taken them all apart."

I squinted past Milo at some ruckus past the bean bags. The forest wall rippled and peeled as Cheese and Roast slipped through. It was a curtain. And there was Joule behind it, in all his gorgeous glory, elbows deep in a crate and surrounded by a landscape of electrical parts. Turkey and Tenders squatted on floor pillows nearby, sorting parts like they were preparing for an epic Lego project.

"Hi!" I said, and Joule looked my way. He stared unblinking for a moment as if the last few minutes were only now catching up to him. That was probably exactly what was happening.

"Oh, hey. Yeah, I know Lane," he said coolly. "But I thought you were avoiding me since our date."

"Y'all had a date?" Milo's face shined with curiosity, and they whispered to me, "You could've mentioned that nugget in group, little red."

I walked closer, trying not to appear too eager or too hesitant. "I'm not avoiding you. I swear! It's just... You know. Stuff's happening."

Joule's brows drew in. "Stuff. Sure."

"So... I am decidedly not walking into young lovers' drama today. Outside my wheelhouse," Milo said, shrugging like they were brushing off our "stuff" with their shoulder. "But get her that tab, will you?"

"No problem," he answered, his eyes still hard set on my forehead, then fluffed the bean bag chair nearest him. "Come on over, if you're not avoiding me, that is. I've got them under here somewhere."

Cheese and the others were gone by the time I slipped past the curtain and flopped into the chair. I thought this room was huge when I mistook the curtains for walls, but now I saw it was even bigger than I'd realized, at least half the size of the dome.

Joule rummaged through crates, mumbling to himself as he named the items he found and eyed me in his periphery.

"I'm not avoiding you," I said, keeping my voice as soft as I could. I'd had no idea he'd been stressed about me. "There's been so much going on with—"

"You've hung out with V every day since." He said it without judgment, but it sliced into me.

"I mean, yeah, I have, but—"

"Did I do something? Was it the g-jumping? I thought we had fun besides your meltdown, except you haven't said a word to me since. I keep looking for you at dinner, but you've been skipping meals all of a sudden, and I worried." He pulled another crate in front of him so forcefully that it tipped over onto his feet. "Is it because Andrek's staying over with me so much? I don't understand what I did to upset you."

Another slice. I hadn't realized Andrek had been staying with him, let alone "so much." I thought he'd been working late when he wasn't home at night.

V's words came to me in a rush: *They'll be lost in each other for weeks, right when I need Joule the most.* Between the RC's fleet, the spy hunt, V opening up, and Faraday's holiday planning, it'd been all I could manage to make it into work with my jumpsuit on correctly.

"I wanted us to be friends. Whatever I did, I'm sorry." He tapped the tips of his fingers with his thumbs, back and forth, his arms hanging stiff by his sides, the spilled crate parts ignored. "You don't have to tell me. You don't owe me anything. I shouldn't have asked."

"Stop a moment and let me think," I said. It came out far more exasperated than I wanted it to, but he'd gone full freight-train forward, and I was still trying to catch up to the platform. "I had no idea you were worried about any of this. The date was awesome, even with, especially with, my meltdown, you know? You haven't done anything wrong! I've been all over the place since, and that's on me, seriously.

I'm trying to do too much and not doing anything well."

I couldn't tell if I was explaining myself right. If I were him and I'd been muddling through everything he just poured out of his head, I'd need to hear a lot more.

He faced me but didn't raise his attention from the floor. "It's not me. It's you."

"Right."

"Because you're busy and stretched too thin."

"Exactly!" He got it. I gave myself a mental high five.

"Oh." He gritted his teeth. Tap, tap, tap, tap.

I thought he'd understood, but he seemed to feel worse. "I want us to be friends too. Honestly. I'm not sure how to fit more in yet."

"Even sex?"

"What?"

"It's just that, if you're very stressed, I could help," he said. "With your projects but also, you know, relief."

My jaw dropped, and my cheeks went chili pepper hot. "I'm not going to use you like a stress ball, Joule."

"I'm saying that would be okay with me, even if we're only friends. Whatever you want."

Words failed me. This must have been the strangest come on in the history of ever. He was so sweet, and I felt rotten. *Tell me what's wrong or take what's wrong out on me, whichever.*

I wasn't crafty enough to lie. The truth was the best plan. As long as I skirted the rim of everyone else's secrets, I could let him in. I wanted to.

"I mean, you could help in other ways, I suppose. I'm swallowed by problems, afraid the trust's about to collapse in a steaming pile of RC smoke. I'm only holding it together by pretending I can save the trust somehow by throwing my sister a holiday." Fuck. I dove right in. "I didn't expect to catch feelings so fast. With V."

"Oh!" He was through with tapping. Instead, he rubbed his square jaw with that mad glint in his eyes that happened before surprises poured out his mouth. "So, if I help you save the trust, we can hang out again?"

I squirmed. That wasn't precisely what I'd meant. "I don't *actually* know how to save the trust."

He drew back. Squinted at my mouth. "That's what people want me around for. Not saving worlds, obviously, but solving sticky, unsolvable problems."

I laughed, as much to break the tension as in response to his shift into troubleshooting mode. "But first I need a tablet so I can work on the memorial."

"Yes. Right. It might take me a while to find it, though." A light blinked on inside him. He grinned and lowered his chiseled face like we were in a soap commercial. The forest-covered curtain shivered, watching. "I actually designed a program for V to keep all her memorial files organized. If you want, I can load that on yours too."

"That would be great, thanks!" I settled into the bean bag chair as he searched for several quiet seconds. He and V were so different, but both were completely disarming in their own ways. I'd never imagined people as accomplished as them would want to be friends with someone like me.

"By the way," Joule said slyly, as if he heard my thoughts, "I notice you're calling her V now."

I didn't answer, because it occurred to me that her nickname meant something important, and I'd missed the significance entirely. She'd told me that he didn't know about her dad or her mission to stop him, but it seemed absurd to me that Joule the genius wouldn't have solved some of her puzzles on his own.

"She kissed you?"

I startled. "I kissed *her*!"

"No judgment. I'm simply letting you know I think it's cool. One step closer to a happy hand."

"Huh?"

"That's what the Meat Team call a romantic family of five," he said, then made a joyful whoop noise and lifted a tablet. "Wait here. I'll be right back."

He danced away, flapping with abandon through the curtain. In his wake, Cheese and Turkey zipped in with more bean bags, and, in seconds, the whole Meat Team had me surrounded. They played at sorting parts, though mostly they chattered to each other about things over my head. They were the least stuffy grownups I'd ever met, so I tried to help. Along with circuit boards, couplings, and alligator clips—the only parts I could name, I found a palm-sized flat device with three terminals.

"What about this one?" I asked. "I don't see any others like it."

"The bipolar junction transmitter! Milo!" Cheese cried, cupping it between her hands like it was too precious to behold. The others gasped and squealed then dragged me and my chair further into the vast room where there was, in fact, a Lego-style construction project. It took up more square footage than my whole family's quarters.

Cheese placed the transmitter thing into a wire cage of some kind, and Roast shushed everyone as he clapped.

The lights dimmed dramatically, and everyone's quiet anticipation sent a shiver up my back.

Milo approached with a switch of some kind that looked like part of a remote-control toy I'd had as a kid. "Let there be life," they said and flipped the switch.

Faint lights, barely more than a candle's dying flicker, trickled and pulsed from one spot to another, and I saw, at last, that their creation was one I should have recognized immediately. It was a map of the moon's human spaces. After months of living here, I'd already forgotten what the models looked like.

Blocky rectangles for the first military bases, trails of short domes for the early research stations built by the former USA, and larger domes for the newer bases, including all four of the domes planned by the trust. Between each major site ran skinny colored lines of power, teaching me more in a glance about shared lunar resources than anything I'd ever learned on Earth.

Milo stood next to my chair and explained in a hushed tone. "Blue's for water, yellow is energy, and red's for fiber optic cables. The big white ones show where we've got tunnels for transportation, though only the ones that blink are finished. When those are completed though, we should be able to travel between stations in under three hours, with the trust at the center, of course."

I felt weirdly emotional seeing it all laid out like this. Not one of these bases would have existed without my sister's gravdrive. It was overwhelming to imagine her second big invention, the trust itself, becoming the pumping heart of a massive lunar city. I supposed it could still be that, even if the RC took the whole moon.

For all their carefree play, the Meat Team was obviously thinking something similar. A dozen or more toy ships encircled one of the rectangular bases. I only recognized one, Guanghan, the Chinese base, because it was the largest and someone had placed a figurine of the moon goddess herself on top of it.

"Which base is that?" I asked, pointing to one that had a pirate flag toothpick stuck to it.

"Blackstone Research Facility," Milo answered, their voice cavernous. "A collaborative station run by Free Brazil and Argentina. They've been doing field tests on a new engine for our ships."

"We haven't heard from them since the invasion," Turkey added sorrowfully, though it earned her a smack from Cheese. "My brother works there."

V had said there were two others transmitting without authorization, and I thought they'd told me their department was one of those. I dismissed the knowledge out of hand. The Meat Team weren't traitors. If they were, the RC's toy ships wouldn't be painted poop brown with "Evil Fuckers" written across the wings.

Still, I couldn't connect their easy banter and carefree smiles with how the rest of the trust had been acting. Like the way I had, like the world was almost over. "But you all seem so..."

Milo barked a hot laugh, and the others followed.

"Well," Cheese said, "it's nothing new, is it? Nowhere is safe forever. At least we're together."

"And you've probably noticed," Turkey interjected, waving her prosthetic arm, "we're disabled. Safety's an illusion. And comfort passes like gas. What good will it do to stress over things we can't control?"

Milo cleared their throat. "We can control only one thing, finding ways to be valuable. Hating who feeds us is nothing new."

"Wait, are we hating our president again? I thought Faraday was supposed to—" Roast started, but Cheese shot him a hard glare, and Roast's attention flicked to me. Realization slumped his shoulders.

I wasn't offended. She was supposed to do a lot of things, Roast. I got it.

"We only *resent* this one so far," Tenders offered. "Bet we'll keep her once she's bought."

Roast laughed from his belly, which was soft and round and poked from his unzipped jumpsuit. "Plenty of time to learn to hate her then, I'll remember now."

I tiptoed toward our own dome, careful not to step on any pieces. The lunar expanse between facilities—though mostly empty—held clusters of odd trash, with labels that read things like iron, precious metals, and regolith. I thought regolith was used for fuel somehow.

Our dome, the main one for the trust, was like the center of a compass, except it was smaller than its southern third arm, Dome 3, which was the only other one I'd visited. Models had never quite clicked in my brain, but staring down at the glittering roof, I was tempted to peek underneath to see if a tinier me was in their comms department. I felt weightless, detached from my skin, when Joule walked up beside me, like I'd been caught in outer space.

"I guess I made more tweaks than I realized. Took longer than expected to load all my updates, but here. I registered it under my discretionary code, except with your login. Should work like a dream." He shoved the tablet forward awkwardly, but softened the move with a proud smile. "Oh, and I also put on my favorite scheduler, for tracking different projects."

"Wow, thank you so much!" I said, taking it from him and sliding it into the front pocket of my jumpsuit. It fit snugly, hand in glove, and it was lighter than I'd guessed it would be.

He went to talk with Milo and the others swarmed around them, pulling up chairs and jumping into a heated discussion. Joule hadn't been kidding when he said his assignment was to be on loan to whoever needed him.

The model was so much more than a toy, no matter how it looked to me. They were problem-solving.

I wandered through the curtain and found another seat where it was quiet to dive into my sister's emails. I opened them, marveling at the ease of using Joule's smart program. On loading, it recognized and organized each correspondence by timeline and parties involved, with sectional tabs for frequently used words to get a summary without delving deeper.

Wonderful technology, but it still didn't do anything to prepare my heart for reading, so I started skimming through other files V had sent, allowing the program to sort as I meandered. I ended up with an array of icons for each concept—memorial research, holiday research, early life, education, public service, publications and documentation, personal correspondence, business correspondence, miscellaneous.

Miscellaneous, which sparked my browsing mood most, had nothing but locked folders inside. Joule, once he had a moment, told me he'd look into it right away.

"I'll ask V, don't bother," I said, worried that I'd set him on a trail of something V didn't want him to see. "Maybe they're supposed to be locked."

He looked incredulous but didn't argue. As he walked away, I was left wishing I could bring our entire unhappy hand into one room and make everyone talk. Together, we made at least half of a Faraday. If we could stop working at cross purposes, the trust might stand a chance.

I started with V, because Andrek was mysteriously hard to track down again. She was in her quarters with Halle, like the first time I'd visited. Except V had a setup similar to Andrek's, with a projector connected to her tab, and the readings she was doing for work were arranged over the ceiling in a grid.

This time I didn't let up until I got the truth about her Plan B.

And, this time, she told it to me straight.

"We're trying to resurrect Faraday's war crimes accord by retracing her steps with its original supporters," V said. "And before you wonder, I'll admit that it's the reason I first thought of planning a memorial, to get access to her files and correspondence."

"I—V, are you for real?"

"Follow my thinking for a moment. Which is more important, throwing a big party for your sister or rescuing her legacy on the moon *and* Earth?"

"Obviously, it's—"

"Tell me something I don't know about the great Faraday Tanner."

If I hadn't been waiting all my life for someone to say exactly these words to me, I'd have been annoyed at her for interrupting, but I knew this answer, even if I didn't know how it connected.

"Her feet stank like raisins."

Halle burst out laughing until V shot her a look, and she clamped her mouth shut and lifted her tablet higher.

"Be serious, Lane."

"I am. They were rank. Sour, sweaty raisins. That's why she wore sandals everywhere, to let them breathe." She'd tried rinses and creams, vitamins and herbal cures, and a full year in special socks that were supposed to rejuvenate her circulation and eliminate the odor. It had all failed her.

Her, the world's sweetheart scientist with the stinkiest feet. "That's my earliest memory. Her stank ass feet. I must've been a toddler, because her feet were all I could see, dangling off the couch in my face. Big girl feet, full adult stink."

"...Okay."

"And that's where it all began," I explained. "Her interest in science. She was teased about it so much in grade school that our parents pulled her out. And in trying to solve the problem of her natural smell, she fell in love with the natural world, with solving problems. That's the part of the story nobody else knows."

"Feet," she repeated quietly.

"You hoped the unknown thing would be some revelation? Nope, just good old-fashioned vanity."

"Vanity."

"Yep." I'd stumped her, which gave me a fizzy sense of pride alongside a gnawing dread for what'd follow when she moved past single word responses. "Why, though? Why did you ask that, and what does that have to do with the war crimes accord?"

She straightened on her bed. Instant poise. She was finally going to let me in deeper. I could hardly breathe through my anticipation.

"Your sister made friends everywhere. Powerful ones. That's who I've been talking to since we got here." V's lips, a shimmery brown today, slid into a smile. "With the accord or something close to it at least, we can do what should have been done years ago to stop the RC. Charge and convict Brand as a war criminal."

I shook my head. "But how? And if that's even possible, why hasn't it happened already?"

Halle leapt off the couch and beamed, tossing her tablet to V. "Finally. Okay. V, you got it?" She waited for V to adjust the screen's view to the wall beside her, replacing her pages of text with a map of Earth's nation states, each color-coded to show which were incorporated, free, RC, or other. "You see how the RC, in red, is all over the map, but it's spotty.

Strategic. V says that's because Brand is making sure to cover himself legally, weakening the strength of any region that can challenge him."

"Alliances have been stretched thin for decades already," V said, clicking her tablet to shift the map slightly, highlighting areas which, I assumed, had some kind of political pact. "Without a strong governing body that's global, like there used to be with the United Nations, there hasn't been a way to address what Brand's doing."

I stared at the map as Halle pointed out several areas with large Xs over them.

"These are states that have already signed on to reinstate a global court and hold him accountable. So far, thirty state leaders have agreed to commit, privately, but we need at least eighteen more to make it concrete. Then we can go public, which means we, the trust, can call for Brand's arrest and send him back to Earth for a trial and sentencing."

"And with him arrested, the RC's reign of terror will stop, so long as we can get enough support from Earth. It's no small task, since we're having to slip messages through coded packages within official communications," V added. "Still, we're close, but I can't get these holdouts to respond. It's like they're mad at me for not being your sister, and nothing I say gets through."

"Sounds like my whole life," I said. "But how is knowing more about Faraday going to help get them to talk? And excuse me, but why would they talk to you?"

"Knowing more might not help, but I'm hoping it will. Logically, it should, because all of the original parties had personal ties to her, close enough that she could call them up if she wanted and not get a runaround." V turned off the map. "She coordinated the whole thing, and she had fifty states ready to sign and move on Brand immediately, but..."

Something in my stomach cracked. "He killed her first."

V hung her head sadly. "And without her keeping everyone talking, it fell to pieces. I've been working with a contact on Earth to patch it together, but—I'm not her. The only reason anyone talks to me at all is because I tell them who I am and why this matters so much to me."

"That doesn't end things right there? That's a huge risk to admit."

"When I explain what he's done to me and my mom, they realize no one is more committed to seeing his downfall than I am. So if there's anything you can think of…" she let the question linger between us.

"Faraday did have a way of making people agree to do impossible, scary things to make her happy, I guess." I said. "And you want to know how she did it."

"Exactly."

I ran my hands through my hair. How many times had I wondered the same thing about my sister? She'd had that magical effect on people all my life, and it was as consistent as it was baffling. I'd always assumed she was made that way. Lucky. Pretty, white, smart, and optimistic. It hadn't hurt that she also talked like a little professor.

My parents didn't have the same effect on people.

I certainly didn't.

If I hadn't made sense of her magic in twenty years, I probably wasn't going to figure it out in the next few minutes. "The others who've agreed already, did you ask them why they decided to?"

Halle belted out a laugh, but V only shook her head.

"I'm not in any position to ask that. These are leaders who called her a 'friend,' and I'm just Brand's kid," V said testily. "A kid who seems to annoy them no matter what I say."

"Why do you say that?" Faraday was actually a kid when she met most of the people who worked with her, not a degreed professional like V.

"Well." She and Halle shared a look. "It's that sometimes, when a state agrees to sign, they always word it like…"

"Weird," Halle tried.

V glared. "Like I'm not the only one they're talking to about signing."

"Okay, yeah, that is weird. What does it mean?"

"Who knows," V said. "But weird or not, if someone else is out there doing the same thing, maybe one of us will get it done."

"But even if it's done, what would that mean? The RC will still be everywhere. Sounds like it'll just make more problems."

Halle choked another laugh when V shot her a stern look. There was more then that they weren't telling me.

"Not if the rest of my plan works out," V answered. "When Brand comes, I'll have one last thing to deal with. But that's it. So long as the accord's formalized by then, we can end the RC for good."

"Do you think…" I hesitated to ask, because I had enough to juggle already, and she was still holding back details, probably the ones I'd needed to know to understand. "Maybe I can help somehow?"

"Like what?" V asked.

"I don't know, but I'm her sister. I'm not famous for anything besides that, but at least people know who I am. Maybe they'll talk to me."

V studied my face, and though I couldn't see what she found there, she said, "Okay. It's worth a try."

I risked one more question, because I knew I wouldn't be able to function unless I knew the truth. "Before, when I asked, when we…"

"Kissed?" she offered, rolling her eyes when Halle snickered.

"Did you let me, because—" Why was this so hard to talk about? "Was that only to distract me? So you wouldn't have to tell me the truth?"

"No." She looked me straight in the face. "I let you because I wanted you to kiss me. And if it didn't happen before I told you, I was afraid it never would."

Attention: Group Therapy Participants

Subject: Meeting Schedule Adjustments

Due to the increase in participants, the following group meetings are rescheduled:

Grief groups will meet MWF evenings after last meal.

General mental health support will meet TRS evenings after last meal.

Daily support will meet in west gym for the first hour of each shift and in the northern courtyard for drop-ins with an available counselor.

All other ongoing support groups will continue as scheduled.

—Medical Department

CHAPTER NINETEEN

FORWARD FOCUS

I was probably overthinking because of what Dr. Fromme had said. Still, as much as I tried, sleep hadn't arrived. Neither did Andrek. Not even for my parents' sendoff before breakfast when they told me that three of our greatest allies on Earth had fallen unexpectedly to the RC.

At work, I stumbled clumsily from one task to the next until Chef sent me to wash up from breakfast with Stephan. The dishwashers were automatic, but Stephan and I scraped and sprayed everything, per Chef's instructions, before loading the machines. I scraped, and he sprayed, and our shift creeped on.

The kitchen whirred with talk of the RC and rumors about the trust's options. Arguments broke out between people I thought were the best of friends. The fights started small. Circumstantial accidents, nothings. Then voices rose, dishes fell, and pots and pans clanged onto the countertops we'd spent months babying. Danny's friends got so heated she ended up hauling one of them out of the cafeteria by his ear.

Nobody was okay. We were all on edge.

I scraped, straining to hear the arguments which spiked in Chef's office every few minutes. The trust's plans hadn't been announced, but everyone knew the RC would be coming for us soon.

Kitchen staff all wanted to know what Chef knew. If we had any allies left on Earth, and if they'd come, and if they didn't, whether the RC would space us or swallow us into itself. Or would we be living with RC troops, serving them food, and cleaning up after them? Would we be replaced by RC staff and sent home? What if we didn't have another home to go back to? They spun around words like siege and subbasement shelter and stored supplies.

And though they didn't outright mention surrender, it was always there behind their questions alongside the basic understanding that even it couldn't guarantee safety, even if it included some form of survival. Surrender. It was such a curious, slippery word. It started out so soft, like a sweet and secret whisper, then it shifted into something ominous and cold. Like murder or cinder, it ended with a threat. I wondered if whoever made up the word in the first place designed it that way on purpose, to make "giving up" sound better. To make it sound like it was some grand and noble choice when it was really a non-choice.

Stephan was the exception on staff. Of everyone, he seemed the least affected by the news about our allies. He kept saying this was how life worked, holding his spray bottle menacingly as he recounted the horrors of his life on Earth, assuring me how much better off we were, no matter what happened next. "There were forty-six of us when we escaped the group home. Twenty-five boys. Twenty-one girls. Fourteen were still in diapers. Diapers, Lane."

I was afraid to interrupt, but terrified he'd continue.

He sprayed. "We lost eight the first week. Radiation sickness. They were so little, too weak to manage the trek through the wastes. The youngest, Katia, was just learning to walk. Her mother Luba, she was only fourteen, wasted away nursing little Katia. They died in their sleep at least. The second week we were caught by—I don't know who. They took—" he choked, emptying his spray bottle onto a helpless handful of silverware. "They stole twelve. Two, right from my arms. They stole them."

My heart broke. His life had been a nightmare, a grim survival story. Like Andrek's, it sounded surreal to me. They lived real lives, while mine was as sheltered as they came. Me and my famous family. We had clean water, good food, cars, and homes. We stayed safe behind our gated walls, protected. Pampered.

"Nine of us made it to the outskirts of Masdar," Stephan continued. "Six girls, two boys, and me. And I'm the only one who made it through selection. The others are still stuck in a tent. Starving, scared. How am I supposed to live with myself?"

He went quiet a while, even made a couple unexpected jokes. The mood lightened by a fraction as I chewed my lip and wracked my brain for words. Anything I had to say would come across as insulting or trivializing. Except he seemed to need me to say something, to have answers, when all I had were my sister's dreams and a head full of secrets and worries.

"It's not your fault, you know. What happened to them," I said. "Or you."

"What I was saying was," he grumbled back, his mood pivoting again, "nothing's guaranteed. Not on Earth, and not on the moon. We can pretend it's different here, but life is struggle. That'll never change."

"What if you came to one of the grief groups?" I asked. "It's been pretty helpful for me."

He stopped spraying to study my face. "Has it, though? You don't look like it's helping much."

"So sweet of you. And that's not why I'm not sleeping. It's the RC stuff. Makes it hard to—" I caught myself before saying more than I should "—plan a holiday."

"I bet."

"You could help with planning, if you want, even if you only want to hang out and watch," I said, though I wasn't sure why I felt so compelled to get him involved. He was a nice guy was all, who deserved to feel something besides buckets full of sadness. All he seemed to do on the moon was work.

"I'm doing a flavor taste later. Focus group kind of thing. Could be fun." I didn't mention that the tasting was only a ruse for me to narrow down suspects, because that wasn't for him to know.

"Yeah, those black circles under your eyes look like lots of fun." Stephan's laugh bounced through the steamy washroom, but his eyebrows swore he wasn't convinced.

"Honestly, help with the menu would mean a lot. I'm in way over my head."

I wondered, not for the first time, how Stephan had landed in food service. He was clever and had a great memory, and he didn't trip over himself with people like I did. Here in the kitchen, he was everywhere Chef pointed him, anticipating where she wanted him to go next.

"I'll think about it, but I don't know." He ducked around the steamer and pushed the last loaded cart toward me. "I doubt it's for me. I've got enough on my plate."

"Like what?"

"Are you asking me because you want to know, or so you can convince me to do something I don't want to?"

I scraped and passed, scraped and passed, chewing on my lip. "Why are you avoiding the question?"

He glanced at me funny. "You tell me why you're doing this. Why are you bothering when everything your sister tried to do is doomed to fail?"

I stared at him. The gravdrive was said to be an impossible invention too, according to the reporters who came to our house after Faraday's viral video. They'd said, "To imagine such a thing working requires a fundamental paradigm shift that no one trained in modern science can fathom."

I remembered because I'd had to have that quote explained to me at least a dozen ways before I could wrap my five-year old head around it. They meant: *We'd worked so hard to wire our brains to think one way that we couldn't understand what was right in front of us.* Or something.

They also said the same things about the trust, about Faraday's goals for it to be an independent refuge for people of all abilities, neurotypes, and skillsets. Whenever she'd been told "You can't," she'd replied with "Watch me."

And maybe they were a little bit right, because not a year into her experiment our independence was trembling like a dry leaf in autumn, but this couldn't be the end of us, or her. Someone could try again. If the trust fell, blown away by the RC hurricane, then I sure as hell wanted to leave some kind of signpost, like the holiday, a reminder to someone else that trying was worth it.

"Because it's still hers," I told Stephan at last. "At first, I wanted to make sure Viveca didn't fuck it up, but now it's different. I guess, if the trust fails, I still want us to remember that she tried. That we all gave our best to try."

He blew out his breath. "That's fair. I get it."

Faraday would've loved him, I thought then. His freckled cheeks and quick smile, the way his dark curls swung when he skipped around the kitchen for Chef.

He took the tray and sprayed it slowly, then rested it in the washer. As he turned back to me, his mouth twisted with concentration. "But why a holiday? Won't that be a sick reminder of her failure year after year?"

I shrugged, scraped, passed. "Maybe." If we were that lucky. "Or maybe it'll make us remember why we believed her dreams were important enough to try in the first place."

As I spoke, my brain lit up with an idea for a holiday name at last, something far more suitable and resonant than Faraday Day. It was so perfect, I shivered as the word sank through me, like I could imagine it being as significant a word as "Christmas" used to be, or "Earth Day."

I wanted to say it aloud, to test it between my tongue and

teeth, but Stephan was the wrong person to share it with.

He stayed pretzel-mouthed until Chef walked over, then he took the empty cart to fetch more dishes.

"You made an excellent argument for the memorial, Lane," Chef said, surprising me into realizing she'd been listening to us. "Don't worry about whether or not other people see your reasons yet. They will in time."

I grinned at her, but I didn't feel so confident anymore. "But what if he's right, and all it does is make people upset? Wouldn't that be worse?"

She *tsked* me. "Scrub that worry from your noggin. Memorials can be an important form of resistance, the way I see it. Daring to be alive and to celebrate that. Oh, and spray that tray again. I see grease on the rim."

"I'll get it done."

Chef looked at me and, for a moment, it was as if she were looking somewhere else. Then her wide, bright smile came up like a sunrise. "I know you will."

Chef offered to let me use the kitchen for my tasting, but if I'd learned anything cooking for my sister's crowds it was that civilians in the kitchen could go wrong real fast. Anyway, we weren't tasting actual food. I gathered my group in the cafeteria, since everyone was at least familiar with that space, even if they weren't comfortable.

Joule and Halle showed up right before I started, saying V had asked them to join in if they had the time. She was trying to get a hold of her contact today, meanwhile, which had me all in my nerves about what I might say that she hadn't already tried. I tried not to let my paranoia drive my reactions, but it snuck up a few times. It was all I could do to keep a straight face while mixing new bubble batches.

There were two potential traitors I was supposed to be watching in particular. A middle-aged white man named George Rhodes who worked in entertainment and Lorelei

Forrester, an upper twenty-something white woman from security.

Otherwise it was me, Joule, Halle, their mutual friend Xiao Li, Danny Hetzel, and, oddly enough, Vice President Rosamund Barre, who V said was on her own list.

After we got about halfway through the whole shebang, Stephan showed up, dragging his feet. I guessed Chef agreed he needed a push to participate in something too.

"All right, everyone, we're nearly done." Public speaking was so not my thing, like, it was light-years from my thing. But I'd seen it all my life coming from voices that sounded a lot like mine, so I pretended as best as I could to keep from freezing. I let my eyes linger on my friends' faces, taking warmth and encouragement from Halle and Stephan, strength and support from Danny and Joule.

"I've got our favorites narrowed down to five taste-courses per meal. Once you've all made the rounds and recorded your initial reactions, we'll have a quick discussion about everyone's final thoughts."

I directed them to queue at the breakfast bubbles first, that way they'd go through the day worth of flavors in the right order. It wasn't totally efficient, and I'd been having them start in different places for the other rounds, but I thought it was important, for this final test, to see how the flavors built through the day.

Joule finished first and came to sit next to me as the others worked their way through. He'd already tasted everything anyway, having been the one to help me mix the vials and print extra bubble machines.

"I can't thank you enough," I told him. "None of this would be possible without your bubble invention."

"I like to help," he said easily. His long legs stretched under the tabletop as he tried to get comfortable.

"You're awesome at it."

We watched the others tasting and tapping into their tablets. I'd been observing Lorelei and George pretty close and had come to a few tentative conclusions.

First, they were both clearly uncomfortable and trying not to show it. So that probably confirmed V's "they've got a secret" theory.

Second, Lorelei did not like being interrupted or hurried, especially by men. After she'd snapped at Stephan, George, and Joule, none of whom were being pushy or anything, I switched up the groups to keep her with Halle, Danny, and Vice President Barre.

Third, George was possibly the most unnoticeable person I'd ever met. Like, if I weren't supposed to pay special attention to him, I'd have forgotten he was here at least twice.

It wasn't that he was quiet. He talked plenty. It was more like nothing he said had any flavor to it, as if he were afraid of saying anything off-putting. He was mild in every way I could see.

"Brand prefers to turn people who aren't confrontational," V had told me. "Loners. Underdogs. The less personal fortitude they show, the better he can mold them. Leaders are only useful to him if he can make them into puppets once he's taken over."

If I were picking Brand's perfect spy, George would top the list. Fourth, and this was not what I was told to watch for, but it was probably my biggest takeaway so far, Halle was an absolute delight to be around. She talked to everyone, whoever was near her, and with her easy manner and warm smile, she kept her group laughing and light-hearted, at least once I got Lorelei away from the guys. I didn't know how she did it, but within moments of meeting George and Lorelei, she came up with inside jokes for both of them.

Vice President Barre, Danny, Halle, and Lorelei finished tasting and sat down the table from me and Joule, chatting as they filled out the questionnaire on their tablets. Halle had the VP cackling about who-knew-what, and even Lorelei chuckled along, wiping her cheeks.

I couldn't hear them well since George and Stephan talked too loudly, but V let me know she'd programmed our tabs to record so long as the questionnaires were open. Sneaky.

Maybe not completely ethical, but still smart. We were going to listen to them tomorrow after her shift, unless her contact responded in time, in which case we'd—I'd—be in little sister mode trying to persuade Earth politicians to rejoin the accord.

"Everyone done?" I asked loudly, pushing to my feet. Should I clap? I'd seen people clap, but it didn't feel natural to me. Regardless, they responded without more prodding.

They scooted down to fill up the seats around Joule and waited for me to lead them. How weird.

"I have a few questions, but mostly I want to hear your thoughts. Does it feel like a holiday menu to you? Special or memorable?"

They chimed in excitedly, talking over each other and making it impossible to hear any one of them. No big deal. V and I could sort it out later, paying extra close attention to George. It was enough for me to know that they were smiling, using broad gestures, laughing a lot.

Positive reactions. What more did I need to hear?

The VP shook my hand enthusiastically, thanking me for allowing her to participate before she left with the rest. Danny hugged me and spun me around, then told me how much she was looking forward to the holiday feast. Even Stephan clapped me on the back and said he was glad he'd come.

Halle stayed behind to help. So did Joule. Together we cleaned up, letting Halle fill us in. She'd learned so much about the others that I might not need to listen to the recordings.

Lorelei had confessed some major drama to her. How she *wasn't* Lorelei Forrester. That was her cousin, who died alongside my sister. Our not-Lorelei was actually Karris Jones, but she'd taken her cousin's place in the launch, using it as her chance to escape the dangers of Earth. Apparently she'd been in panic mode ever since, stuck in a job she never prepared for.

Something about the group, whether Halle's natural charisma or the opportunity to be open with someone who would really listen, got her to open up. Then Halle convinced her to talk to the VP and Danny.

Rosamund took the confession in stride, promising to help Karris get a different position, one she was suited for, and adjust the paperwork so she didn't have to carry the burden of her deception along with grieving her cousin. And Danny promised to smooth things over with Commander Han, because she'd been promoted to Han's personal unit. It would work out for Karris.

It was good, right? One more suspect was eliminated. No thanks to me, other than providing the venue. Still, I'd learned something else that had nothing to do with my sister's holiday.

Getting the right people together could explode secrets into the open to let in healing and change. This was exactly what we needed for our unhappy hand, which was less like a hand than Andrek and V in a thumb war, with the rest of us flailing to support them. I refused to be in the middle of that anymore when we could be so much better.

If it worked for us, maybe it would for the trust too. We all had far too many secrets to suit Faraday's ideals, especially with someone plotting our sabotage.

Attention: ALL

Subject: Privacy Update from Command

Internal communications are now being monitored and recorded for security purposes due to the increase in anonymous postings in the community forums. Please be mindful that words have weight, and divisive messages will be investigated thoroughly in accordance with MCO Ruling 11.3.

Department heads will be reviewing safety procedures with each shift over the next three days.

—Commander Han

CHAPTER TWENTY

GROWING A HAND

Andrek hadn't come home, and he'd missed breakfast again. I could have messaged him, but everything I thought to write felt like nagging. If he wanted me to know what he was doing, he ought to tell me without me needing to ask.

I plunked balls of dough on the floured counter and rolled up my sleeves, annoyance biting at my nerves. Squeeze and pound. I couldn't sort through this mess, and it stirred me up all wrong. Was this what jealousy felt like?

No. I knew jealousy.

I was Faraday fucking Tanner's sister. Jealousy was hot and gnarly like a web of vines growing out of a dark pit. So I wasn't jealous. I was *annoyed*, and it wasn't about them having sleepovers.

"It's totally not that," I mumbled and slammed more dough on the counter. Somehow I'd slipped from being his number one for "always" to not hearing from him all day and going to bed to not-sleep alone at night. I'd become a zero.

Any minute our lives could be overrun with RC soldiers, like Blackstone was *despite* their defenses, and who knew what would happen to us after that. Andrek must have known how stressed I was.

This would change. Today.

Preferably with us still together.

I kneaded, and I stewed another hour. I was all into this dough, pushing and pulling, and squeezing and rolling, and I completely forgot what I was making.

I was pretty sure that people were talking to me, but I was gone.

In. It.

My sister stayed with me, in my head, the whole time. Guiding my fingers and pushing my back, like I was the dough and she was the ghost that drove me as one hundred balls of dough turned into tight wads, sealed and stored in silver bowls. Her whispers to *save the trust* were non-stop and the only other words I could find of hers in my head were snippets from campaign speeches.

It was super unhelpful. I needed her private words in my head now, her jokes and personal stories, things only her real friends would recognize. That was what I was supposed to bring to the accord table, not the stuff everyone else could repeat.

I wished I could climb inside the Meat Team's brains and borrow their calm. Looking lightly at life, able to experience without being swept under, analyzing the worst things imaginable and saying, "Yeah, that sucks a lot, but it's been worse."

I didn't know how to do that. I tried hard, but I still felt it all: My sister was always going to die. Maybe not then or that way, but death was always going to come for her. But because she'd died when and how she had, other things happened differently—the launch, the presidency, my family coming apart at the seams. An infinite number of ripples, but the death *itself* had never been avoidable.

I would die, and so would Andrek, V, my parents, everyone. Even the trust, even the moon and sun and Earth. All temporary. Imagining otherwise wouldn't change the endings.

These thoughts made my head throb, and I felt the surface of my skin touching my clothes, my socks, the hair whispering over the back of my neck, and the tight elastic of my hairnet. Couldn't stop feeling it all. I was too inside me, this machine of flesh and blood and bone that would inevitably also die someday. Having feelings about it didn't change the facts.

Hope was a racket then, only ever for rent.

I'd leveraged all my hope through Faraday though, and she took it all with her.

"What's that?" Stephan lifted several bowls off the counter and stowed them on a cart.

"Nothing," I muttered as I spread out the final seal. "I'm not feeling great."

"Distant? Moody? Disturbed?"

"Wow, Stephan." Any other morning before yesterday, I might have elaborated. Everyone working near us would have chimed in, making up games and keeping the mood moving. We'd have joked about anything at all and ended shiny with tears of laughter. Except, after hearing about his past in horrible detail, I couldn't bring myself to let my sadness out, especially not for it to get turned funny.

"Out with it already." He yanked at his apron which had slipped low over his chest and hung it on a nearby hook. "I can tell something's eating at you. I know you don't want to put bad vibes into the food."

I wiped my hands on my own apron then grabbed a rag to wipe the counter. He was right about not putting my yuck into the food. "Besides the obvious and the RC slowly eating up the moon? My boyfriend's forgotten I exist."

"That all?" His tone was so flippant I drew back. Maybe he was feeling some kind of way about his storytelling yesterday too.

"No, that's *not* all. I'm not sleeping."

"Welcome to the club."

He was definitely not funny today.

I knew I should ask him if he was all right, except I was too deep into feeling hopeless and annoyed about it to worry about him too. I scrubbed the counter harder, but the flour dust wouldn't budge.

"Sorry you're suffering too," I managed. "Thanks so much for your support."

"I just don't think you're the only one wound up. You're definitely not the only one who can't rest. And if your boyfriend's ignoring you, he sucks and doesn't deserve you. End it and spare yourself the drama."

This crimped my already frazzled nerves. "That's not what I want."

I hoped that wasn't what Andrek wanted. He would've said something, wouldn't he? Had he said something, and I'd missed it? An ache to go to him bloomed in my chest. I had a plan to fix things, but whether or not I was successful wasn't up to me. Besides, I still had to get through my shift without letting the despair all the way in.

"Maybe it should be though. If you were my girl, I'd never treat you that way."

"Maybe mind your business!" I dug harder over the counter surface as if adding more pressure would wipe away everything I didn't want to be real.

Stephan put his hand over mine with the rag. "It's clean, Lane."

I stared at the counter, certain there were still specks dusting the surface. "But it's not."

Off work at last, I hurried about the kitchen, gathering ingredients Chef said I could take without denting our week's rations. I'd sent messages to Andrek, Joule, V, and Halle to go to the second dome, on "urgent business."

It was urgent. The RC had swallowed two more of our allies on Earth, Dad had told me. I didn't tell anyone why we needed to meet or who else was coming. Ironic considering what I planned to say.

"We have to talk."

I steeled my voice against the stone-hard look V shot me. She was the least interested in this outing, because even though she hadn't heard from her Earth contact yet, she wanted us to practice what I'd say when she did.

"About secrets," I finished.

She and Halle held hands on the far edge of the table-cloth. Joule was on the other side of V, with Andrek trying not to be tense beside him. Maybe he wasn't tense.

It was probably just me.

We had the second dome, called "The Orchard" in my sister's models, mostly to ourselves. "It's the original dome, donated and planted by a consortium of the other research stations the same time the collective was formed," Joule had said.

Its rows of young trees weren't all so young, and they were heavy with fruit and tall enough to picnic under. The real sun beat down non-stop through the transparent exterior, and if we stayed long enough, we'd be here to watch those panes shutter for the fabricated night.

Joule called it "the turning of the tide," explaining how even trees needed sleep.

It smelled like spring, and the circulated air swam with pollen and insects. Fat, lazy bees buzzed nearby, ignoring us and our sandwiches on their way to richer harvest. If I didn't raise my eyes too far or high, I could imagine we were truly outside, or in some pastoral painting of pre-melt Earth.

"What I mean is this sucks," I said this part fast, because both V and Andrek seemed ready to interrupt. "It sucks when I know what I want to say, but for one reason or another I can't get the words out. Like, they don't work the way they do in my head."

V took the longest breath in history, and Andrek stared out the dome the way he did, but Halle and Joule nodded.

"Spectrum squad." Halle winked.

"But this is different than just that. Harder. Because the

words aren't *mine* to say."

It occurred to me, several hours into this plan, that it could explode in my face. Full failure, total break up, no more boyfriend, no more almost-girlfriend, no new friends.

I could end up locked out of V's confidence, abandoned by Andrek, rejected by Joule and Halle. Just me alone, still not sleeping, and not helping save anyone from a damn thing.

"Food first." I started unpacking our meal. One side benefit of getting the trustees' nutrition records and having my own tablet was that I was able to make each person's perfect sandwich, bulking up or trimming out ingredients according to their recorded preferences. After the focus group, I was also an expert in label-making. I'd brought a case of water tubes, pretzels, popcorn, and leftover pudding cups. The pudding got frozen by accident, which Chef said turned it into something she called a windy frost. I'd have to clean carefully before we left, because two pounds of unexpected waste could tip the ecosystem and I could already see specialized ants creeping toward our blanket.

"They're not my secrets, because they're yours, Andrek." I pinned him with my gaze, catching his attention with the pitch of my voice and giving him a water tube. *I'm talking to you.* Easier when he was close, when I could touch him to say what was underneath.

He rolled his shoulders and drank it one gulp, which I read as *let's hear it then.*

"And yours, V," I continued. "Because I'm tiptoeing around the both of you, and you're being weird about each other, to each other. *At* each other. How can I ever to get to know Joule when y'all do this?"

I went with "weird" since "suspicious" or "flat-out wrong" were both too direct, and both V and Andrek deserved the chance to say, "Fuck this, Lane," and storm away with their secrets intact. If they wanted.

"I don't want this, like this, anymore." I handed a tube to V, who'd gone full guard, and I held my palm out a second too long after she started drinking. "And I think, I mean, I need you to *consider* telling each other what you trusted me with. And Joule and Halle. So things can stop being weird and maybe get a whole lot better for everyone. Before this is all over, or you know, maybe instead of letting our world end, we choose to stop Brand together."

Even the ants paused when I said Brand's name. *We don't want to work for him*, they said. I wondered if they'd heard about the RC's labor camps and forced drafts too.

"Whoa," said Halle.

"Huh," said Joule.

V said nothing, showed nothing, and Andrek's temple and jaw throbbed.

How dare you, his clenched muscles said, but at least he hadn't left. Yet.

I let my hands do what they wanted in my lap and hoped as hard as I could that they both cared enough about me to understand how much I needed this, or at least cared enough about the trust to hear what I was asking.

"This is an end-of-the-world picnic. As in, the trust won't exist much longer unless we save it, and also I will literally burst if I have to keep secrets from either one of you any longer, so please for fucks sake will you—"

"Brand Masters is my dad, and I'll die before I let him take the trust." V pulled her knees tight to her chest. I recognized this pose.

"Finally! Finally, finally, finally!" Joule threw his long arms out over his head, his hands swinging at the wrists. The trees swung with him, caught in his breeze. "I couldn't take it one more minute either, Lane. Thank you, science gods, thank you." He sighed contentedly several times in a row, as though he'd been short of breath for weeks.

I got it. Something rotten that had been rattling in my stomach for days crumbled, and I felt looser and lighter.

Halle danced a circle around the tablecloth. She wasn't forming words exactly, but the noises she made were loud and sounded relieved. After the first round, she stopped to grab a water before continuing.

"Finally," she exclaimed between gulps. "Finally!"

Andrek hadn't moved, not even to get clear of Joule's swinging hands.

"He's your dad," he said, enunciating each word somehow without changing his expression.

"That's what I said." V quirked an eyebrow. "I disowned him and ran away after he killed my mom."

"You..." Andrek rocked in place. "And he..."

I tossed a sandwich to Halle, and Joule stood and took his, I guessed to give me some space to reach both V and Andrek.

"Andrek," I said nice and slow, hoping it'd help him snap out of whatever fog V's confession had slipped him into.

He looked right at me for a moment, and there was so much packed there it sent me reeling. *I was wrong; I'm sorry; I've been a jerk; how you managed not to burst already is basically a miracle.*

I nodded in response, waiting for the words.

"Wow, so, wow. I completely read you wrong," he told V, and one of the other rocks in my stomach burst into powder. "From the first day it was like you were digging for information, and I thought—damn. All wrong. It doesn't matter. I'm sorry, truly. So here goes. I was in the RC. Not by choice. I was drafted. Now you know. That's my secret."

V blanched, her eyes widening. "So, you know then. What it's like, what he's like. What he does to people."

"Yeah." Andrek issued a strangled sort of noise inside that one syllable. "I do."

I gave him a sandwich, letting my fingers linger. When Faraday was alive, and my mom had said some hurtful thing in passing, not thinking about how I'd hear it, I could go to my sister, and she'd understand. I'd never have that again, but somehow I'd given that to V and Andrek. This was winning.

I reminded myself this was what I wanted for all of us. Honesty and openness. I hadn't expected it to sting so much to see them gain what I'd lost for good.

"That's it then," I said, unwrapping the last two meals and passing one to V. "Eat."

Halle and Joule sat, only now we were in a circle. Fruits thudded into the nets tied below the branches. I risked peeking further past the trees and caught the rolling white horizon of the moon outside and the velvety black sky. This time, when that view sent my heart pounding, I didn't flinch. I simply chewed my food and looked.

I'd never be used to this, but it didn't mean I was ready to give up.

"I have to get something off my chest too," Halle said. "And don't you dare lecture me, V, because you got me and Mom tangled up with the accord, and I'm still freaking out. So I've been stealing fertilizer. I'd rather die fighting too."

"You've done what now?" The insides of V's sandwich spilled onto the tablecloth.

"That's incredibly unsafe," Andrek agreed. "Tell me they aren't rigged."

I couldn't help but laugh because they were on the same side.

Joule's face contorted, jaw wide. "Halle. All this time you've had me helping you build bombs?"

"Uh huh. I figured you knew. You never asked."

Joule covered his mouth with both hands, muffling the repeating *I didn't know*s.

"And what did you mean about being tangled up with the accord?" Andrek asked Halle, but looped V into his confused stare. "You don't mean the war crimes accord."

"We do," V said. "But we've hit some snags. My contact went dark."

Andrek rubbed a hand through his hair. "That's too bad. The accord could solve a ton of problems, and not only here on the moon."

"We know," I said, though the news about V's contact had hit me like a brick. I was so hopeful that finally there was something important I'd be able to contribute. Not like, "Lane saves the day!" or anything, but also... maybe that? I knew if Faraday were here, she'd be far more invested in reviving her accord than getting a holiday in her honor.

"We won't give up yet," Halle put in. "Maybe there's some other way to track down your contact? And—" she laughed "—if there is someone else working to get the accord going, they might succeed even if we're stuck."

Andrek met my eyes, and his were butter soft. "I might have some channels to go through. It's worth a shot."

"Okay," V said. "Let's do that then."

"Anyone else? Horrifying secrets? No?" I asked, but the others shook their heads, maybe still stunned by Halle's confession. None of us seemed to want to circle back to it. I sure didn't.

"Then we can talk about what we're doing and work together now, right? We're trying to find the spy, who isn't V or the comm department, but so far, we're not having much luck, or at least I'm not. But maybe you know things we don't, Andrek?"

He did. I saw it in his jaw twitch. "We haven't found the leak either."

"And it's not you," V said, like she was still open to the idea.

"No. I've entertained some ideas if we end up having to surrender, but—" Andrek stopped himself, probably because he'd acknowledged the not-so-secret official surrender policy. "You already know about that too, don't you?"

"I didn't tell!" I threw in, in case that was what he was thinking.

"We all know," V said. "The only thing I didn't know is that you'd worked for my monster father. I wouldn't blame you if you were still in touch with other draftees. I'd think it was stupid and irresponsible, but I'd get it."

"I'm not, though," Andrek cried.

"But what if you were?" I wondered.

Joule let out a long "Ohhhh," as Andrek and V turned to me.

"What do you mean?" they asked in unison. I chalked that up as an end-of-the-world picnic victory.

"What if you play like you want to work with him?" I suggested.

"Viveca would be a better choice for that, I think," Andrek said.

V huffed. "It can't be me, not until I get other things ironed out. But I'll help you do it."

"I suppose that could work. And that might help with your accord too."

"Not my accord," she said. "Hers."

"Ours now, if we pull this off." I meant it. For anything we had to last, everything that had been Faraday's must become ours.

"I don't like it though," V continued. "If we get caught, we'll look more guilty than ever."

"We all will," Andrek agreed.

"Nobody has to like it. Forget like!" I hated it, and I didn't want to show how much. "But we're running out of time! The RC's been at Blackstone for days already. Dad says they'll be lucky to last the night."

Andrek balled up his sandwich paper. "Lane's right. We're out of time."

"Shit," I said, and everyone else's faces echoed it.

V dabbed her mouth. "Honestly, I'd prefer it if we don't try to contact him first, rather we should start with your old squad mates. But we're racing a ticking clock now, so we'll have to be methodical and fast. There's only one other base worth taking before he comes for the trust."

"What about Guanghan?" Joule asked.

"Nobody will mess with Guanghan," V said. "Not unless they want all of China retaliating."

"Let's start now." Andrek retrieved his tablet from my makeshift picnic basket, but then he hesitated. "Except, Lane, can we get a minute to talk? Just us?"

That familiar and so adorable twinkle in his blue eyes almost got me. "Is it about us? Because, if it is, but it's *not* because you want to break up," I choked out the words, my mouth desert dry, "we should include Joule and V."

Andrek's Adam's apple yo-yoed. "You think I want—God, no. That's what you think? Oh, Lane." He patted his chest and reached for me, his thick eyebrows drawn. Pleading.

I fought the urge to crawl over the remaining water tubes and climb in his lap. Sleepy me wanted to. But knowing he didn't want us to split did this weird thing to my chest, all that fear about losing him poofed away. In its place was something else entirely, something hot and whistling that I didn't recognize.

"Good call," V said. Her arms crossed tightly, and there was a hint of this thing inside me resonating in the hard set of her mouth. "Because you two—" she cast a simmering between Andrek and Joule "—need to make up your minds about showing up for us. We get it. New love. High drama. But if we're talking about clean slates and being honest, what's been going on isn't working. And it's made it impossible to concentrate."

Joule frowned. Did he not understand? Andrek hung his head, so I was pretty sure he must.

"You've been sucky boyfriends," Halle explained between bites of sandwich. "Maybe not the absolute worst, but not close to good. Look at poor Lane. It's like she hasn't slept in a week, and V—Sorry, babe, but it's true—You're so high-strung you'll break a bone if you sneeze."

"I'm fine!" V snapped.

"I'm not." I zipped and unzipped the top of my jumpsuit.

"I... I know," Andrek said, feather light.

"And they've both got their own baby love whatever going on too, but look how they're handling themselves," Halle scolded. "Putting the trust first every day like damn goddesses. You boys should take a lesson."

"Is that true? Am I sucky?" Joule's frown had doubled in size. I wouldn't have been surprised if he cried. "I thought I was helping!"

"Helping who? Not me, when you stop honoring our schedule," V said, her masks slipping more every second.

Joule tapped fingers against his thumbs one at a time, and I watched him, rapt by the beautiful rhythm of his stim. I tapped too sometimes, but it wasn't precise or nearly as fun to look at. A feeling I couldn't totally understand tightened inside my stomach. A hollow almost swishy sense that told me if I ever saw Joule cry, I would have to cry too.

Maybe I had been jealous before, but of Andrek, not Joule. I'd had a rough time admitting I liked V at first, and I was doing the same thing with Joule. The feeling in my stomach sat a lot like fear, like I was afraid to let myself like him.

"I'm sorry!" Joule said, and my stomach twisted with certainty. I *did* like him. "I thought when you saw what we've been working on, you'd understand. Tell them, Andrek. It doesn't matter if it's not finished."

"Oh!" Halle squealed. "See, V? I told you it'd be all right. It's another surprise!"

"Tell us what, Andrek?" I couldn't stand being on the outside anymore, and I regretted opening this talk to the group so soon. "You said you don't have more secrets. What kind of surprise makes you skip out on me for days in a row?"

His hands raked over his knees. "Because of your parents, Lane. How am I supposed to tell you anything when half our mornings together get railroaded by you and your parents fighting? They're my bosses, remember. I have to spend the rest of the day with them while you're working and getting a break."

"Yes, but—"

"I know, we're supposed to keep work separate and all, but you don't know what that's like for me. They're hurting too, like you wouldn't believe," Andrek spilled out. "I'm not saying they're right or that I'm taking their side. That's *not* it. But I'm stuck in the middle of the three of you, and I can't make anyone feel better. Not without making it worse for somebody else, so, yeah, I'm sorry I didn't tell you what I've been doing. I thought about how to say this a million times, but could barely face it myself. And it's not an excuse for bailing on you and flaking out. I'm sorry for that."

I opened my mouth, but words didn't come. Andrek wasn't avoiding me, not exactly, and it wasn't only some new relationship honeymoon with Joule either. I hadn't been thinking of his feelings. Definitely not about how awkward that must have been for him, caught between me and my parents. Their pain and mine. Somehow that was worse than me being in denial about my jealousy about him and Joule.

I didn't know how to fix any of this. If it was even possible.

"You still haven't said what the surprise is," Halle chided.

Andrek glanced between Joule and me, the weight on him now clear as day.

My breath tasted rotten, and my cheeks burned. I'd been the sucky one. Selfish and self-absorbed.

Joule pushed to his feet and offered Andrek a hand up. "The most prudent option is to show them. Finished or not. No more secrets."

CHAPTER TWENTY-ONE

MUSHY ALSO

"Sweet girl, I'm sorry I waited so long to tell you." Andrek traced a curling pattern up and down my arm and held me against his chest.

It wasn't like I was starving or anything, but I had missed him.

This. Us.

His skin moving with mine. The easiness of who we were together.

We lay on a mattress, a double, wedged into a tiny room that was more like a cubicle than a proper bedroom. Andrek's surprise—I was still deciding how I felt about it—had been a converted storage room concealed behind the back wall of the kitchen, only accessible through a hidden panel along the side wall behind the pantry. New quarters, ish.

It was about the same size as our family quarters, minus my parents' room, except he'd set it up completely differently to cordon off three minuscule bedrooms, saving the largest space for a living area, which was where we had left the others.

He could have asked for his own quarters, probably should have, but he hadn't wanted my parents asking why he wanted it. So Andrek had designed this for all of us, a world of our own free of prying eyes or a wall comm, and Joule had been helping him commandeer materials and locate other spaces for everything that used to be here.

Short version: Andrek was moving out, from our shared quarters to this forgotten storage closet.

The longer version was a lot more complicated and would take me longer to process than it took for him to come up with.

He hadn't wanted to spring this on anyone, he said, and he'd planned to get all the boxes and extra equipment out before he showed me. The pressure had simply been too much, between the guilt he carried about his connection with the RC, the increased need for secrecy in light of the investigations. He needed to be able to let his guard down somehow after holding that in all day, somewhere he wouldn't be noticed.

"It's not that I want space from you. Not you, or even them exactly." He combed through my hair and planted a kiss on my forehead. "I just can't stay in the middle like I've been, you know? You have every right to be angry at your mom, to feel whatever you need to feel, and I want to always take your side, but you've got to see where that leaves me. I'm still new at this whole 'family' thing, and I can't always be 'on' like everyone needs. There's stuff you don't know about what they're going through too, but it's not my place to defend them, not when you need my support."

I snuggled into his chest, mussing my hair worse but not caring. "What kind of stuff?"

"I *just* said."

"Come on." I pinched his jumpsuit, pulling it into my fist. "If I have to give up sleeping next to you every night, I want to know why."

"First, you don't have to give that up. You can stay here whenever you want. But it's not my place to say."

"Yes, it is! They're basically your parents too, and you know they'll never tell me if something's wrong."

He wrapped his hands around mine. "They're falling apart, Lane. Working non-stop, as you know, but you don't see all of it. Your mom, she's struggling. A lot. She naps in her office sometimes, when it's too much. She's been taking antidepressants, but she hasn't found the right fit yet. They're not working. And your dad is paper-thin, you know? It's so hard seeing them like that, like mushy, scared people, and then to see them screwing up so bad with you."

I studied the ceiling stipple, thinking. Mom was on antidepressants? That actually made me feel better about wanting medicine for sleep. And Andrek said *my* parents were mushy?

Mushy.

"I had no idea."

"Of course not. That's the way they want it. I know you say you can't handle more secrets, but please don't let on that I told you."

"I won't." How would I even bring that up if I wanted to? No way. "But maybe..."

"You can't."

"I'm saying that *maybe* I can cut them a little slack."

"That's my girl."

"But I'm not moving here. Not permanently." I thought of Faraday's urn in the living room and how I liked waking up to her every day, even when it broke my heart. There wasn't a chance my parents were ready to let that go yet either, so while she stayed with them, so would I. "Not yet anyway."

"Oh," he said, barely covering his disappointment. "What about the whole not sleeping thing?"

"I'll take pills. The way I should have been since forever ago. In the meantime—" I freed my hands from his and twisted to face him. "You have nearly a whole week of apologizing to do before I let you go back to saving the world."

"Is that what you think I've been doing?" he asked, smothering a smile.

"Not successfully, no," I answered. "But I do think we're about to change that."

After grief group the next morning, I trailed behind Dr. Fromme, not sure what to say to get the pills I needed for sleep. Medical was swarming with patients when I checked myself in, and far busier than I'd ever seen it. I guessed the whole trust was a bundle of nerves.

An attendant got my name, and I took a seat in the corner. One after another, people approached the desk, then searched for an empty place. They were like me, with some diagnosis they hoped to manage better, or some invisible crisis likely brought on by stress. I sat straighter and met their gaze as they passed.

We were the same, and this was what health looked like. Everyone had their own special suck to manage. I was no different. I was *not* dangerous.

My smile rippled across the waiting room as I caught others' attention. I liked to think it did at least.

A nurse emerged from the psych hall. "Tanner?"

I jumped to my feet.

"Please follow me." She guided me into triage and settled me onto a reclined chair to take my vitals. This part was always the same, on Earth or the moon or anywhere else humans ended up. Blood pressure, temperature, eyes and ears and throat exposed before the medical gaze. Normal. "Any symptoms? New concerns?"

I coughed, but I didn't know why. "I'm having panic attacks."

It was easier than I expected to say aloud. Like breathing. Like saying, "I caught the flu," or "I'm thirsty."

Perfectly normal.

She gasped, not a big gasp, but this sharp intake of breath like she knew she shouldn't react but it was too late already.

"Oh dear," she whispered. "I didn't know. I'm sorry."

Why was she sorry? Was I supposed to comfort her now? Tell her it was okay she didn't know? How could she have?

"I don't wear a special pin to announce it to everyone. So no worries." I didn't want to comfort her or be comforted by her now. I was here for them to tell me what to do, not for sympathy like this. I chewed my lip, watching her, waiting for her to take her polite pain back, so I didn't have to hold it.

Hot potato, lady. Heads up.

She shook her head, just enough. Maybe at herself. "Are you having symptoms right now?" The tablet in her hand angled toward me. Another check box.

"I don't think so, but... I might not know. Is my regular doctor on shift? Dr. Fromme? I'm in one of her groups."

She tapped the screen. "She knows you're here. You'll see her shortly. So, what's happening this morning?"

I pulled my legs to my chest. "I'd rather talk to her."

"Of course, I understand. A few more questions."

I craned my neck to see her screen, but I couldn't make out the words. I'd been in such a good mood before! Lots of boxes left to check. "I'm not hearing voices except the ones I make up. No visions either. But, like, would I even know? My appetite's fucked, and I'm hardly sleeping, but I'm not sure. I'm all dysregulated. I feel... Off. Sad. Distracted. Restless. Lonely when I shouldn't be."

"Have you experienced any—"

"Suicidal thoughts? No."

"That's good, Lane. What about violent thoughts?" She didn't lift her gaze, which I was glad for, because I could tell she was afraid for me even though she tried to hide it.

Hot potato, back in my fumbling hands.

I was afraid too. "Not yet."

"And you're autistic but haven't been on any medications before?"

"Just birth control."

Her finger trembled as she tapped her screen some more. "That's it then." She was all confidence and routine. Now that she'd dumped her pity on me, she was free. "Wait here, and I'll have some lunch brought around. We can't have our dessert cook skipping meals."

"Thanks," I said, though I wasn't sure what for.

She hovered over me when she rose, and I felt like a bug behind glass. "Wait here, please."

"Oh." That was it then. That was the best she had to give. "Thanks," I repeated for no reason. I didn't want to be angry with her, but I couldn't wait for her to leave. When she did, I breathed easier. I had enough feelings to sit in by myself without hers too.

Alone in the room with nothing to do, my senses sharpened, desperate for something to hang onto. The trust was never truly quiet, not with the gravdrive and the air filters and who knew what else running all the time.

Now I heard it all distinctly. Ticking and churning, distant groans, and the yawning silence of space above it all that one forgot to listen for.

In the collective's clinic in Masdar, the quiet had been much louder than this. Busier. Thick with insects and birds and bats. The far-off roar and howl of wind, scattering sand, and the metallic grind of the city industries. The hollow whistle of clay walls and tile rooftops. And always the call of human life, the horde of voices rising like a musical din.

I tried to slip into my last good dream, dragging the memory closer and swimming into its sounds. Though I could name what they should be—the forest full of wildlife, punctuated by fox cries, the stream's song, the lake's bank, my father's copper-wound strings, my mother's precise brush strokes, even my sister's staccato breaths—I couldn't put them back into my ears. I was too far gone.

My tail bone went numb from sitting too long in the chair, so I paced awhile in three short steps like a solo square dance. When the door opened, I came face to face with V, and it was the weirdest reversal of fates, because she was handing *me* a tray of food.

"You did good yesterday. Impressed me."

Her eyes were embers. She had a lot more to say, but

her ice armor was on, and she gripped her tablet like it was trying to jump out of her hands. She leaned the screen so I could read it.

George Rhodes. Our last suspect.

"Wish me luck?" she whispered.

"You won't need it."

The flare of her smile melted me, and I stole a kiss before pushing her out the door.

Dr. Fromme came in right after I finished my lunch and took me to her office. It had softer sofas than my quarters, a fainting couch, a couple desks, and the light shone from lamps instead of overheads or trim lights.

"Have a seat," she said.

"No, thanks. I've been sitting for a while." Pacing felt more like normal walking in here. I passed by a row of shelves and ran my fingertips over the artificial wood grain.

I saw her in my peripheral vision, for the first time noticing her as a regular person instead of just my grief group's wise leader.

She was short like me. Cute. Younger than my mom but older than Faraday had been. Her tight curls were cropped short and chunky, and she didn't have a uniform under her white lab coat. She wore some sort of painted jumpsuit, its pattern like a kaleidoscope. She projected so much Halle energy, I didn't know how I never put together that they were mother and daughter before.

"I didn't expect you on my calendar today," she said. "Couldn't get enough of me, I take it?"

"That's it exactly."

She laughed brightly. Why had I put this off? "So, trouble sleeping still? It's good you came in. I was concerned. And you mentioned panic attacks to the nurse?"

"I keep seeing her on that day, you know? When I try to sleep. It happened during the moon quake too."

"Your sister." It wasn't a question. "How do you feel about that?"

"I feel weird about the whole thing. I was… Embarrassed,

I think? At first, anyway. I thought it would go away on its own. I didn't realize I'd have to, like, live with it."

"The panic attacks, you mean."

"Yeah."

"They might still go away," she said. "On their own."

"I'm afraid they won't."

She leaned forward from her perch atop the fainting couch's spine. "I have something like that too. Panic disorder. Did I not mention it before?"

I stopped in my tracks.

"How does it make you feel to hear that?"

"I don't know. Aren't you supposed to be…?"

"Healthy? Do you think mental health is the absence of abnormality? Nothing funky or atypical happening upstairs?" She rolled her head around which made her curls flop and dance. "I doubt there'd be any practicing therapists if that were the requirement. I like to think of mental health as seeking out and deliberately applying sound mental habits. It doesn't mean there's nothing squirrelly to overcome along the way, or that some mental tangles don't need extra work."

I respected her more the more she talked. "I think I like knowing you have it too. I feel less on display. Like there's hope."

"There's always hope," she said, "if you're willing to fight for it."

I thought of my date with Joule and Andrek, how Joule had launched himself off the steel beams despite how scared he felt. If I could do that, just a little more, I could join in rather than watching others have fun without me, feeling small and far and outside.

"You mean, like, if I want to fly, first I have to jump."

"Precisely. Lane, if you weren't having panic attacks from what we lived through, I'd be surprised. As it is, most of the trustees are riddled with anxiety right now, if not from our lives before, from the RC blowing horns at our gates like we're their personal Jericho."

"I get it," I said, though I didn't actually.

"You little liar!" She clapped her hands like a delighted child, and I thought of Halle again. They had the same playful gestures and happy hair. "I'm saying that it's nothing to be embarrassed about. Even if we weren't living in extraordinary circumstances, some of us are simply wired for extra hurt. The good news is that you've already done the hard part. Coming here for help was the jump. Now let's get you flying!"

I smiled back. "You and Halle are so much alike. I don't know how I missed it. All in my head and stuff."

She nodded in what I took as total understanding. "Let's pull you out of there. I want to start you on a low dose of anti-anxiety pills and see you twice a week for counseling starting tomorrow. It'll be challenging work, but I've seen you in the kitchen. Effort isn't your issue."

I settled on the sofa to see her better. "How do I find out what is?"

Not simply was the answer. Nor quickly.

Three private sessions later, Dr. Fromme and I were still scraping at the surface of my troubles.

I'd complained to V that it seemed like a waste of time, like I ought to be focused on stopping the RC or, at the very least, Faraday's memorial, but she insisted that my mental health mattered whether or not the world ended, and that I'd be no help to anyone unless I was able to sleep enough to think. So I took my pills and showed up twice a week in Dr. Fromme's office.

I should have known from grief group that she wasn't the sort of doctor to send me digging through the past directly. The farthest back we'd discussed was our first day here, drawing a heavy line between before and after, with her reminding me repeatedly that when it came to the grief and trauma of the invasion, I was already well inside my feelings about both the moment I stepped onto the moon.

We returned to that day again and again, each time sorting through another loaded moment.

"Let's rephrase," she told me for probably the tenth time in so many minutes. "Minus judgment."

I picked at a loose thread on the armrest of her couch and tried to figure out another way to say I was too numb to do anything but stay on autopilot. "I guess then... I felt numb and didn't know how to act."

"There you go, yes! We aren't the feelings police, remember. Emotions aren't good or bad, even when they summon positive or negative connotations. Keep going. When you say 'numb,' what do you mean?"

"Not feeling anything—Wait," I caught myself in the lie. "No, I was feeling a lot. Too much. I had this lump in my throat that made it hard to breathe. Moving was hard too, like my body didn't want to do what I told it to. I knew the moment we were having was supposed to be this wonderful thing, historic and important, so I was trying to pay attention instead."

"Instead of...?"

"Experiencing. Like, if I paid enough attention, I could hold it for later, to feel the specialness then."

"This is an example of what we've been talking about. Dissociating. It's your brain's way of protecting you, of maintaining a sense of control when you think you don't have any." She scratched on her tablet then folded her hands over the screen. "But you aren't a camera, Lane. No matter how much you want to save a moment for later, once it's gone, it's gone. We can try to relive those dissociated moments, but the truth is you were there then, and what you felt then will always be part of the memory."

I'd worked the thread free and wrapped it around my finger. Her eyes on me burned. I understood what she meant, that I couldn't revisit memories the way I wanted to, stripped of how I'd felt inside them, but it seemed like I should be able to, at least certain ones.

"Let's shift forward to today. Can you think of anything

happening in your life today that you're avoiding feeling?"

I glanced up from the string, ready to say "Joule," but she shook her head, trapping his name in my mouth. What kind of wizardry had she learned in therapy school to dredge this out of me when I hadn't even realized I'd been circling it?

Even thinking his name brought up a torrent of feelings I'd not let myself name. Guilt, shame, confusion, fear, and—most of all—desire. Could she see all that on my face?

"Don't tell me yet," she said with the barest hint of a smile. "I want you to sit with it and explain why first. Why are you avoiding it?"

"Because I didn't expect it." His feelings about me still didn't make sense. If V and Andrek were Joule's types, how did I fit in? "I'm not convinced I deserve it, so I don't want to accept it and end up disappointed."

Dr. Fromme's expressions moved from delight and surprise to sympathy. "Now I'm incredibly curious, but keep going if you can. Why don't you think you deserve to have and feel this thing?"

I stared at her, unseeing, as my response churned unhappily in my stomach. I didn't deserve Joule's affection because he was too good for me.

Because I'm broken.

I'm too broken for anything that easy and good. Joule wasn't damaged like Andrek and V were, like I was, and unlike them I wasn't brilliant or talented enough to earn his attention. So his sweet advances and amazingly thoughtful gifts—I'd been acting like I was oblivious rather than admitting that I liked him too.

"I see we've reached a sore spot," Dr. Fromme said quietly, resuming her notetaking. "How about this—instead of pushing this train of thought more today, how about you try a little experiment? Sometime today, allow yourself ten minutes to feel whatever comes up, no matter what that is, inside that moment. During this experiment, there is no before or after, just you feeling the emotions within your body in that present moment. Can you try that?"

I nodded and chanced meeting her eyes just as her lips spread into that Halle-like smile her voice had been promising.

"Good! Let me know how it goes? I believe you'll find the more you practice allowing yourself such moments, the more control you'll have over how your emotions affect you. Feelings are so important, but they're only part of the machine that's you. When you give them their due, they can stop trying to run your whole show."

Despite what she'd said, I spent the rest of the session not fully listening. I'd made up my mind to do her experiment, but I wanted to do it when I was with Joule to see what I might feel about him, or for him, without half my brain playing denial games.

He'd be in our makeshift headquarters after dinner, but so would everyone else. Better if I could find him on his own, and if it were just the two of us. A few quick messages let me know he was in the greenhouse lab and "would welcome company."

The entertainment department was hosting some kind of event in the main hallway, so I decided to use the back route to the lab, since it was clear across the middle of the dome. I knew from experience that if I ventured through the kitchen, I'd get lured into some task or another, even if it wasn't my shift.

I rounded the corner before the junction next to Andrek's-slash-our new headquarters and bumped into Stephan, scattering the contents of his cart across the floor.

"Whoa!"

"Shit, my bad! Sorry, sorry!" I ran after the line of water tubes rolling precariously close to our secret entrance. I spoke loudly and made as much noise as I could justify while putting them back on the cart to warn anyone who might be inside that I had company. "I didn't know you were working today."

"Technically I'm not. Ty wasn't feeling great." His voice edged toward suspicion. "What are *you* doing back here?"

"Looking for Ty," I lied automatically, not knowing why I felt like I ought to but trusting the instinct. "Or whoever's delivering. I wanted to grab a couple dinners to go."

"Help yourself," he said, stepping clear of the cart for me to rummage through the mess. "Got a hot date? Guess you and your guy worked things out."

"Oh yeah, we did. Everything's good."

"Awesome. I'm glad to hear it," he said, and he sounded so genuine that I felt awful for lying before. And I'd have to lie again if he asked *how* we worked things out, because I couldn't say the truth.

It sucked, honestly. Stephan was my favorite work partner, and he was always so real with me. Plus he'd helped with the holiday tasting when I knew he hadn't wanted to.

"Thanks," I said and gave him a quick side hug to console myself for not being a better friend while subtly nudging him and the cart further from our headquarters. "Seriously, thanks. I've got to run though. See you later!"

I raced away before he could reply, grateful to shift my attention to the guy I needed to be thinking about instead.

Joule.

I found him crawling on all fours between the vertical garden towers in the lab, his face basically brushing the concrete floor. I said his name, and he sprang upright, a beatific smile stretched ear to ear.

"Look!" He held out his hand to show me a ridged black beetle prancing over his pink palm. When I grimaced, he covered it quickly. "Not a bug person? That's okay. I think I found the last one who got loose. The labs mostly rely on bugbots, but there's no replacing the real thing sometimes."

He prattled for the next fifteen minutes about the wonders of ground beetles for compost and pollination, and though I had zero interest in bugs outside of pictures of butterflies, I loved listening to him talk about his special interests. He had so many to my spare handful, and he entertained my unclever questions without batting his thick eyelashes at them.

I came to realize that listening to him talk about anything at all might actually be one of my special interests. We were halfway through our dinner burritos in the lab's lounge before he finished and asked why I'd come looking for him.

"I don't even remember now," I said with a laugh, then felt my face start to burn as the reason returned to my mind. "I just wanted to hang out with you."

The way he bit his lip and looked away sent a shiver up my neck. Dr. Fromme had told me to "just sit" with my feelings, so I tried to do exactly that, sensing heat in the way it pulsed over my skin. When he looked back toward me, his dark brown eyes colliding with mine, it was like being punched in the chest.

"Just you and me." Joule put his arm around my shoulders and pulled me a few inches closer. "Cool."

"I think so."

Under the weight and warmth of him, my mind started to race. At first I fought it, but then I got to thinking that my mind counted as part of my body, so I let the thoughts run as we snuggled.

We were alone in the lounge, the lab staff away doing whatever their jobs were, and the couch we were on was perfect for cuddling. I liked that we weren't in a place where it was safe to discuss RC stuff or secret plans, because it meant we could just "be" for a while without anything too heavy.

He felt different than Andrek—bigger and stronger, like a whole man. Not that Andrek wasn't a whole man, but his build was much slighter.

In Joule's arms, I felt different too. Aside from the familiar pangs of attraction, the magnetic urge to trace my fingertips over his wrist or to test exactly how sharp his jawline was, he emanated this cozy sense that sapped all that urgency, folding me into relaxation. I wondered what it would be like to fall asleep being held by him. I doubted I'd need pills if that ever happened.

"I worried you'd be mad at me," he said, his voice breezing over my head. "For helping Andrek move out. I should have known you're way too cool for that."

A laugh burst out of me. "I'm totally not, but I can't blame you for Andrek's choices. I was mad at him for weeks because I missed him and felt left out is all. I never thought about what he was going through."

"Still." He brushed my hair back and rested his chin on my head. "I never want to make you mad. Let's not be the kind of friends who wait to share things till it's too late."

"Okay," I said, and I pivoted so I could see him better then surprised us both by planting a kiss on his broad cheek. "But I don't want to be *just* friends."

He gaped at me, letting his attention dance over my face. Curious and hopeful. Yearning.

"You mean…" he whispered, and I gave him a decisive nod. I watched his expressions change, too many and too fast to interpret, enjoying the way he made no effort to hide his reactions. After a full minute of him processing and me grinning back at him, he scooped me up into his arms and carried me out of the lounge.

I laughed again and pounded lightly on his chest. "Where are you taking me? What in the world, Joule!"

"I don't know yet. Everywhere probably," he said happily.

"I still want to go slow, I think."

He slackened his pace. "As you wish."

"Not walking slow!" I was giggling like a kid and couldn't stop. I didn't want to. He kept on holding me tight, my legs swinging uselessly over his forearms.

"Soooo slooooow," he said, nuzzling my neck as he inched over the threshold of the lab.

Maybe this wasn't what Dr. Fromme had meant, but that didn't matter anymore. For once I wasn't letting my self-doubt be in charge. Now that I knew it could feel this good, I might have to do it more often.

Attention: ALL

Subject: Memorial Announcement

Set your calendars for the first weekend of June for the inaugural memorial holiday as we celebrate the life of our founder Faraday Tanner and all who helped Lunar Trust One become a reality.

Shift supervisors will distribute holiday hours so that everyone can participate. Expect feasts, contests, performances, presentations, and extensive decorations throughout common areas. Volunteers welcomed!

—President Marshall

CHAPTER TWENTY-TWO

SURPRISE

My fingers flew over the Playbox controller, smashing buttons in familiar patterns. I'd missed this so much. An airy space in my chest filled with glittery excitement as I played. I was speed. I was luck. I wasn't a stressed-out girl living in a bubble that was about to surrender-slash-pop.

My scores were trash, but I didn't care. All I needed was this moment, freed from the real world of responsibility and heartaches, where I could let my body respond as it wanted, and my mind was honed in on a single purpose. Play.

It wouldn't last long. It never did. Everything that wasn't "right now" may as well not exist, which, in a weird way, made right now that much more real. I wanted to hold onto it all, this right now, but I was afraid of gripping it too tightly.

If the past few weeks had taught me anything, it was that holding my breath and waiting for the other shoe to drop was agonizing. Better to enjoy each moment on its own, to let the past be past and the future come on its own time.

One month ago today—that was how long it had been

since the RC had landed on the moon. We worked, ate, showered, exercised, visited with friends and family. We had meals and dates and sleepovers. Plants had to be watered, washrooms had to be cleaned, and the ordinariness of our routines nearly camouflaged the impending doom.

But there doom sat, floating at the edges of every conversation, simmering with buttery tension. We went through the motions aware that any moment might be the one that ended our shared dream, and we fell asleep—if we could sleep—only to face the same dread when we woke.

People in my lunch line tended to look exhausted, and that was only the people who still showed up for meals, instead of waiting for Stephan to make a delivery round. Nobody finished their food, no matter what we served.

Halle sat next to me, playing a farming game on her tablet while Andrek and V hammered out a new series of messages to send to Earth. Since V's contact had gone dark, Andrek's old squad mates had become our only hope for reaching out to Faraday's former friends. V was a mess about it, because we'd not been able to nudge the accord's progress, and we could get caught breaking the communication ban any day. It seemed we were further away from making the accord happen than when she'd told me about it.

Joule had just left for his shift, though he'd put up a whiteboard to clarify our schedules for next week, adjusting for my new official "bedtime." Which was something I had to have now. At least everyone was supportive about it.

It had taken several terribly bad prescriptions before finding a good fit last week, so I was rested for the first time in ages. With that came a whole rainbow of thoughts and feelings I didn't know how to balance yet, because I was too busy figuring out what they were.

"Message away," Andrek announced, his voice heavy. "Now we wait."

"Again," V added with a sigh.

A shuffling noise behind the whiteboard pulled my attention.

"Does nobody else hear that? Really?" I asked for the third day in a row, but apparently no one did.

I paused my game and lowered the controller. Andrek's eyes were brittle and cold, same as V's. Getting hold of his squad mates had been easy, but moving up through the chain of command to reach those closer to Brand had proved harder than any of us expected. And pandering to Brand's labyrinth of yes-men had taken a huge toll on both Andrek and V. It was weird too, because it didn't seem like anyone working with Brand could stand him, but they all had to act like they did, policing everyone around them to do the same.

The air, which wasn't all that pleasant to begin with, curdled. It was like, by contacting another of Brand's underlings, we'd invited him inside, and now he and his infamous sneer stood here in our living room.

There was only one fool-proof way to shift the mood, so I turned off my game and set the projector back to its usual screen: a sprawling chart that showed every minute detail of our plans for the first lunar memorial. Though our planning had had to take a backseat to the accord and searching for the spy, it was still the thing that had originally brought us together, and the one thing we had to look forward to not sucking.

My sister's energy booted out Brand's like she'd knocked him away with the swing of her hip. Ra ra, no room for monsters.

V brightened, going to the wall at once to study some unmade decision, no doubt. There weren't many left, but even one was too much for her. Halle glanced over, just for a moment, to check that "Memorial Mountain" was still listed on potential ideas for future years. It was, for her sake, but far, far in a future we weren't sure would exist.

"All right, I'm off then. Break's over." Andrek stretched. "Should I tell your parents you'll bring dinner?"

Office picnics had become a regular thing, more out of necessity than desire. My parents wanted to make sure I was eating, which was annoying but fair. I was still angry at them for a hundred reasons, but that wasn't one. Between eating more and sleeping better, I felt less cloudy all over, like I was a stream refilled with water instead of mud.

"Yeah, thanks," I told Andrek, and he came to kiss me on his way out. His eyes were bloodshot and sunken. Not from lack of rest, I didn't think; he got plenty of that. It was the stress of waiting in constant terror. "Pace yourself, okay?"

"Always, princess," he whispered into my hair. "You too. I'll let you all know the moment I hear anything back."

Once he had gone, I settled on the floor to watch V think. She paced in front of the projection and muttered loose strands of whatever she was calculating in her head while her fingers twisted through her hair. I knew she was mulling over the accord and not the memorial still, but she reminded me so much of my sister in moments like this, when she was lost inside a puzzle. It made my heart swell till it was so big in my chest, so exposed and thinly stretched like a balloon, that I had to measure my breaths in the careful in-for-three and out-for-five rhythm Dr. Fromme had taught me.

Our biggest remaining decision, likely the one V was unable to chew on now, may have been the most important one of all: who would emcee. They'd be the voice who set the tone for every other year, their words recited again and again, on top of being the mouthpiece for our message now to the trust and whatever supporters we had left on Earth.

I'd narrowed the applicants down to three trustees. Two professionals from the entertainment department and one amateur comedian-slash-defunct environmental science professor from sanitation. Each were high-energy funny and smart, charismatic, and convincingly solemn when necessary. I couldn't possibly choose between them, and V had grown increasingly frustrated with my indecisiveness.

I'd thought the "when" would be the hardest choice. It couldn't be her birthday, which was my major argument. Nor the day she'd died. For weeks we considered the day she released her first video, but ultimately decided it was too close to two other religious holidays.

We eventually settled on June 5, which was less than one week away.

"Should I play the auditions again?"

V stalled with the energy of a snapped rubber band returning to its normal shape. "Hang on a moment."

I sat on my hands to hold my questions, knowing she'd only speak once she'd found her words.

I'd been playing an RPG Halle sent me, where I was this hero warrior leading my party through battles all over a sprawling empire. In it, I was the one everyone in the game turned to for decisions. That was not my real life, and, frankly, that was for the best. V let me contribute, even veto sometimes, but she was the brains here, the one with vision. There was nothing wrong with being the NPC at her side.

Getting closer to V had been such a bumpy road so far. I wasn't complaining, but it was tricky to know where I stood. It felt stupid to ask with everything going on. We'd kissed a few more times, and we held hands a lot, but she was hot and cold with me. Not brittle, ice-queen cold, anymore, but not yet comfortably "warm." She'd been thrilled that Joule and I decided to date.

"I actually like them all," V said finally. "I don't want to pick only one."

"Does that mean it's time for me?" Halle withdrew a die from her chest pocket. She always had one on her. She said it was easier to leave decisions to chance than to worry over each one.

V frowned and spun to the screen. "I don't think that's right either."

I freed my hands and shook them a bit to get the blood flowing. "What if we don't pick? Why not use all three?"

"If only it were so easy," V said, her eyes glazing over as the "other" topic loomed between us.

"Let's make it that easy," I offered, perking up as the idea sank in. "They could riff off each other, take turns and stuff. It could actually solve a few issues with the schedule, if it's

244   JR CREADEN

not just one person."

V made a noise that meant she was considering it. I was convinced she'd come around to agreeing. She'd have had a quicker counterpoint otherwise.

"Meanwhile, is anyone hungry?" I asked. We'd gotten into the habit of eating here. Most people weren't using the cafeteria much anymore, whether because they had "too much work to do" or because they were avoiding the security patrols clogging the hallways, I didn't know.

I retrieved three sack lunches and passed them out. Sacks—what half our menu was reduced to these days, for convenience and portability. Today there were cupcakes, though I was only making dessert twice a week lately since I'd been running deliveries with Stephan so much.

The shuffling noise came from behind the wall again.

"Do you hear it now?" I asked.

"I heard something!" Halle said around a mouthful of burrito.

V swallowed fast, cocking her head to the side to listen. We passed a beat, quiet. "I don't hear—"

"Shh!" Halle said and mouthed, "Listen."

A scraping sound came from behind us on the couch.

Concussive thumps. Footfalls.

The wall panel popped some wholly unnatural way, and I jumped up, pulling V and Halle along with me. Just in time.

Three security guards pushed the panel open, spilling its broken parts and insulation all over our abandoned seats. They wore lightweight armored suits, fit for emergency space procedures. Boots to helmets white.

Halle shrieked once then clamped her mouth shut hard, her peachy cheeks mottling. V stiffened into her full mask, arms tight at her sides. The guards clocked us, unsure who to zero in on as dangerous. Me, ghost-white and gripping the other two by their arms; my friends, wide-eyed but hard-jawed.

One clicked open their visor. It rose ridiculously slowly, revealing suspicious gray eyes and pale white skin. Only then did I notice the long blonde braid snaking out the back of the helmet.

"Danny?" I said.

"You three alone here?" she asked, ignoring me calling her name.

"Yes," I answered, instinctively stepping between her and my friends. I wasn't expecting violence—the guards were trustees, same as us—but she recognized what I'd done almost before I realized I'd done it.

Danny relaxed and moved back. "We didn't know there was anyone here. It's supposed to be a closet, not..." She glanced around, taking in our couch and projector, our spilled lunches fallen onto a rug. *Nobody puts a rug in a closet,* her face said. "Whose quarters are these?"

"Well," I started awkwardly.

That was a complicated question. No one's. Andrek's. Sometimes mine. Joule, V, and Halle all used it too, but like me they returned to their own rooms more often than not. I decided she probably only wanted surface facts, not the deep-down story behind it.

"My boyfriend's. He's an assistant to my parents in Planning, the Tanners, you know?"

"He at work? Who else has access to this space?" one of the other guards asked.

"Why?" V countered. "Is something wrong?"

"Besides y'all storming into our living room?" Halle added.

Danny jerked her head, meeting my stare with a weary, almost sad, expression. "You three need to come with me."

"Why?" V asked again, her pitch rising.

They urged us out the hole they'd made in the wall, revealing a hidey-place I knew nothing about. It wasn't a large space, probably only big enough for one person to stretch their arms out and touch each wall, but inside...

Inside was a hoard of supplies. I saw crates of various sizes, with labels like "H2O" and "Pantry" and "First Aid," scrawled in an almost illegible script.

The missing supplies, right here in our secret head-quarters.

"To be questioned and charged," Danny answered gravely. "For crimes against the trust."

Faraday had expressed a lot of opinions about security on the trust, and I vaguely recalled a number of heated talks with my parents and the board. It would start at the breakfast table, follow us through the hallways into the collective's foyer, and spill out of the conference rooms hours later.

She never wanted a police force, that was what I remembered most. Something about armed forces turning violence inward. Part of her presidential campaign had been about resisting the urge to have a fully surveilled settlement, which is why security cameras were only in high-profile areas like the labs and the unpopulated domes.

In the end, security came to mean emergency first-re-sponders—not cops, but defenders. I wondered if she ever imagined they'd end up patrolling daily and busting through walls.

Probably not. She probably never imagined the RC would follow us to the moon either. Or that there'd be an RC mole, or maybe two, making trouble. I didn't have the first clue how she'd be responding to all this.

The lead guard brought us to Commander Han's office and left us there. I guessed they had to get back and help their partners gather the stash they found. While we waited, V whispered instructions in a too-calm voice.

"We haven't done anything wrong," she reassured us, "so there's nothing to be afraid of. Tell them it's not ours, and we don't know whose it was. Someone's obviously setting us up. Our best course now is cooperation in figuring out who, because that's Brand's insider."

I heard her, and I knew her advice was sound, but I couldn't help but sweat waiting. What if the guards looked at the tabs they confiscated and read the messages we'd written to the RC? What if they noticed the notes we'd made about our hunt for the spy? There were so many things that could make us look more suspicious than a stash of water tubes and towels.

A flash of Commander Han finding out all our secrets filled my mind, plus Andrek's and V's and everything we'd tried doing to thwart the RC.

My parents and Dr. Fromme filed into the office first, accosting us.

"What's going on?" asked my dad.

He was quickly interrupted by my mom, frantic and accusing: "What did you do?"

"Are you okay?" This from Dr. Fromme to Halle, then V. "Do you need your inhaler?"

The device passed from her hands to her daughters' pocket. Then Joule and Andrek got marched in, guards glued to their sides. Only then did Commander Han join us, driving her chair into the center of our crowd and directing us to gather in front of her.

"Thank you all for coming in so quickly," Han said, as if we'd been politely invited for tea instead of having been dragged in like criminals. "It seems these young people have gotten mixed up in rather serious matters involving a hoard of missing supplies. I need to speak with them urgently."

"We don't know anything about what was behind that wall," I blurted.

"We really don't," Andrek agreed, his voice reedy with tension. "And I'm the one who commandeered the closet for personal use. No one else was involved, so you can let them go."

"On the contrary, at least these four others were involved," Han said. "You weren't living there alone."

"Why didn't you ask for new quarters?" My mother rounded on Andrek.

"If we'd known from the start, we could have helped," my dad insisted.

"I just—I'm sorry." Andrek's face turned a disturbing shade of hot pink. "I didn't want to seem ungrateful. But it's more than that? You're my only family. So long as I didn't officially take new quarters, then I haven't left. Not really. And you all could grieve without—well, without dealing with my stuff too."

"All of that is beside the point and can be dealt with privately later. Please excuse us for now." Han gestured to the guards who, politely but firmly, escorted my parents and Dr. Fromme back out of her office. "Now then. You five. You must admit how suspicious this seems."

"Was it all of the supplies that are missing?" Andrek asked. "Is there any evidence we put it there?"

"No, and curiously no," Han answered. "It's only about half of what's been reported missing, and it seems the crates have been wiped of fingerprints. Therefore, we must go on the facts we do have. You five are complicit in sabotaging the trust. Whether through theft and hoarding or something more sinister."

"It wasn't us!" I cried, but I doubted she cared what I had to say. "We would never steal from the trust!"

"So you've said, but the facts remain in contradiction, where they'll be until we uncover the truth. I understand at least three of you are aware that we have a major ongoing security problem involving hacked communications, deliberate mishandling of trust resources and equipment, as well as outright sabotage that amounts to treason. Since you seem so close, I wager all of you know. So what am I to make of what's been found in your possession?"

Halle puffed on her inhaler, as the rest of us stood in uneasy silence.

"How did you come upon this discovery?" Joule wondered aloud. "It seems reckless to go around busting through random walls."

"Nothing random about it," Han said. "We received an anonymous tip."

"Then we're exactly where we were before finding

anything." Andrek shook his head. "You still have missing supplies and a traitor to find."

"Unless the answers are right in front of me."

"That wouldn't make any sense though," V countered, her gaze fixed on a point below Han's wheels. "If we took those supplies, we certainly wouldn't have tipped you off. So whoever told you must be the one responsible for the theft. Why else would they stay anonymous? It's obvious the real saboteur is framing us."

"That's one possibility, but one which doesn't absolve any of you of appropriating community space for private use, which is also theft." Han rolled her chair back an inch, jarring V's attention as the two locked eyes. Surely the commander must see V was right.

"*Empty* community space," Andrek said, breaking the look between them. "I know it wasn't exactly 'right,' but I don't see how it's theft. As for the supplies, another possibility is that the supplies were already there before us and have nothing to do with us at all."

"Say that's true," Han said. "Say that the stolen goods were hidden before you came upon the space and claimed it. What would the thief benefit from by revealing its location? They must have intended the goods to serve some purpose, presumably not simply to return them intact. The more interesting question, to me, is why you would jump to the conclusion that you're being framed. What would be gained by that, unless you have some leverage over the saboteur you're not telling me about."

"How could we?" Joule asked. "If we knew that, wouldn't we also know who it is setting us up to take the fall for them?"

"My thought precisely," Han said, not missing a beat. "Which is why this requires further investigation before any charges are formalized. This matter is far from resolved."

V lifted her chin. "Are you releasing us then?"

"Not quite." Han pinned each of us with another hard look. She wasn't convinced we were innocent, but she wasn't convinced we weren't either. "But I'm not holding you here for the moment. Obviously, you won't be able to use that closet for private quarters anymore. Whatever your reasons, whatever the truth is behind the supplies and the discovery of you five abusing unmonitored spaces, you've exposed a critical weakness in trust security. For that I'm grateful. For now I'll waive immediate consequences while we investigate further, provided that you and your friends don't cause more trouble or go looking for another clubhouse. Leave this to us."

"We will," Andrek lied, and the rest of us chimed in our agreement. I stared at my feet instead of meeting anyone's gaze, my whole body hot with embarrassment, terror, and anger at whomever had put us in this position.

"I suggest you take my warning seriously lest more trouble find you," Han reiterated, signaling a guard to open her office door.

"So we can go?" I asked through my clenched jaw.

Commander Han exhaled heavily. "I don't think any of you realize how damning this is, or how dangerous. I may have other questions, so respond promptly if I message you. I'll be assigning each of you a guard." Seeing us bristle, she added, "For your own safety. They'll maintain a respectful distance unless more evidence against you comes to light. You must understand the position you're in. If we come to learn you five had nothing to do with the theft, there will still be consequences for your misuse of other property. Regardless, whoever reported you didn't give up these supplies haphazardly. It was a calculated move, though to what end, I can't conclude yet. Return to your normal routines, but be vigilant."

CHAPTER TWENTY-THREE

GUARDED

We trudged silently through the hallways with Halle's mom, my parents, and a knot of guards trailing after us. The guards let us collect the most portable of our belongings from our half-demolished living room, but then we were left trying to figure out where to take it all. I didn't know whether to be relieved or furious or scared, so I tried to feel nothing. And all the while, my parents' disappointed and confused stares followed my every move.

Finally Dr. Fromme convinced them to walk with her to Medical, and I could take a full breath without them dissecting me.

We stayed quiet for a very long time. Joule and Andrek left wordlessly to return to work, their guards splitting off from ours, and we stayed quiet as we lugged Andrek's things to his old room and dumped them unceremoniously on his bed. We stayed quiet even as we sat awkwardly on the couch in my quarters, Faraday's urn shining on the shelf behind us.

The quiet became comforting, like a heavy blanket over sore muscles. Inside it we could stretch and at least pretend to relax. Every once in a while, we heard our posted guards outside the door, though we couldn't hear what they said.

Not so thin as the walls, those doors.

"What do we do now?" Halle whispered, breaking the silence and, apparently, V's intense concentration on the wall comm.

V put a finger over her lips, then led us into my bedroom. "I don't think they can hear us, but... Best to be certain."

"Then what do we *do*?" Halle asked again, sounding desperate. She was still a bit green.

"I'm processing," V said. "I don't know what to make of it yet."

"Other than 'everything is bad'?" I flopped onto my bed as Halle groaned and curled up beside me, tucking herself under my arm. "Someone stashed a bunch of stolen supplies right next to us then tried to frame us for it, and now we've got guards watching us for who-knows-how-long while we're—"

"I don't need you to replay details, Lane. I need to think." V wrung her hands and set into pacing in a tiny circle at the end of my bed. Her stims grew bigger as she walked.

I wanted to snap at her, because I needed to process too, except I had to do it out loud, but she looked so ruffled. I decided this wasn't the best time to argue about whose sensory accommodations got met first. "In the meantime, we've got to find another place to work from, because it can't be here or either of your quarters. And Joule's is too crowded. I could ask Chef if we could use one of her extra offices, I guess?"

"That might work for the memorial, but what about after?" Halle asked. "We can't talk freely about Brand with Chef and a bunch of guards right there, can we?"

"I don't know, I don't know," I said, wishing there were something, anything, I could do or say to make any of us feel better. "I want to go backwards and—"

Halle placed a warm hand on my cheek. "V." Halle went to her, careful not to cross into her circle. "V, you're crying."

"Am I?" Tears streamed silently down her lovely face, soaking her tank top. V didn't notice, or, if she did, she didn't react.

"Yeah, baby." Halle reached for me, and together we helped V to bed.

V wiped at her face, looking surprised when her hands came away wet. Her tears continued to fall steadily like rain.

I missed the rain. And I missed knowing what to do, though I didn't know if I ever had.

Halle held V as I sat by, helpless. "Is it the guards? Because I'll go right back to Han and tell her you can't have—"

"No, no, I mean, yes, maybe, but..." V grabbed my hand and squeezed, sending a shock wave through my chest. I squeezed back with my whole heart. "It's all too much. The surprise of it, then the guards, the questioning. The still not knowing who. Or why. It's got to be the spy—who else? But that means they're onto us. Which either means we were getting too close to them or—or my father is ready to make his move."

"What can I do?" Worry left lumps in my throat because I knew anything she needed would be more than I could give her. "Do you want me to get Joule?"

V's tears multiplied. Became a monsoon. She collapsed onto Halle's chest as if her bones were liquified too. Halle smoothed her hair, but that didn't slow the storm.

I ducked out of the bedroom to message Joule. He read it right away but didn't answer as fast. I watched the screen, not wanting to interrupt the cryfest without something helpful to say. Anyway, it was Halle and Joule she needed now.

A guard knocked on the door. I was sure it was a guard because no one else tap-tap-tapped that loud and insistently.

I palmed the latch, expecting Joule on the other side, but instead it was Commander Han. She drove inside with an air of importance and parked, not by the couch, but in front of my sister's urn on the shelf.

One guard blocked the hatch like he expected me to try to run, and three more streamed around him. They opened every door and brought Halle and V to the living room couch before taking positions way too closely behind each of us.

I recognized Danny at once this time, but she looked straight through me, her mouth fixed in a blank expression. I couldn't get mad at her, not really. She was treating us exactly how I'd hope our enemies would be treated.

"We need to talk," Han said, staring intensely at Faraday's urn. She waited for Halle and V, still sniffling, to sit, then she drove around the couch to face us all, including what remained of my sister and the hovering guards. "It seems your group has been much *busier* than you let on."

I froze, but it was too late. My face had confirmed whatever Han thought she knew.

The energy in the room shifted like someone turned on a heat lamp.

"We can explain," V said, her masks fighting to fold into place but not quite fitting. Her mascara smeared messily over her cheeks. "It's all a—"

Han lifted a calloused finger and the guards moved in unison, clasping hands behind their backs. It wasn't an especially threatening movement, but it felt menacing nonetheless. "You've been accessing personnel records by some ungodly means I haven't figured out."

V said nothing this time, and neither did I, not even with my face. My breath had gone hot in my mouth, hot and so thick it was basically chewy. Halle stared resolutely at the floor.

"You've also been using similar illicit means to break the communication blockade, sending encoded messages to both our allies and enemies on Earth." Han used precise diction, spitting words like spears.

I felt our hopes crashing through the floor, all the way into the cold white rock deep below. We were exposed, found out, over. There was no hiding anymore.

I tried again to get Danny to look back at me, to give some indication that we were okay, because we were still friends, right? She couldn't believe this was the whole story. All those hours we'd spent together grieving—she *had* to know how much the trust mattered to me, for my sister's legacy if nothing else.

Danny's stare, cold and gleaming, didn't shift from her commander. I guessed that meant her loyalty to the trust ranked well above our friendship. And wasn't that just as it ought to be?

"From what I can tell, this has been happening since the day we arrived," Han continued.

V tensed, stirring herself straighter but still not managing to hide the fear in her eyes. "No, that's not—"

"Don't lie!" Han shook her head, her voice a terrible, hissed whisper. "I did not come here to be lied to. I came to make sure I pieced things together correctly, and I see that I have. And one other thing..."

My heart twisted. This was it, the end.

All our plans, our hopes, my sister's dreams...

Here was where they died.

"I take full responsibility, Commander," V started again.

Brave V, dear V. So noble too, to try to spare me and Halle.

"Whatever punishment due is mine alone to take," V said.

"Punishment, ah. I was getting there."

"You've got it all upside down. It's not what you think at all!" I couldn't hold the words in; they were too heavy, too true. I had to make her understand before she delivered consequences. "We're *trying* to save the trust! That's all any of us have ever done!"

"Oh, poor misguided youth." Han frowned grimly, pinning me with her rock-hard stare as Danny grabbed me by the shoulders and forced me back into my seat before I even realized I'd tried to stand.

"Hold your excuses for when they might matter," Han said. "At your trials. Until that time, you'll not be permitted to speak to each other outside of memorial planning, for which I will set the schedule and select supervisors for. That holiday may be the only thing keeping the trust together at this point, or I'd pull you from that too. Whatever else you three have been plotting on your own, whatever your motives, it ends now."

"Lane? You awake?"

I snapped to alertness at Andrek's voice, but my meds made it impossible for my body to respond with the same speed. My eyelids weighed as much as bags of flour, and I blinked blearily into the dark of my room.

Two welcome blurry figures took form, framed by a skinny line of light shining from the doorway.

Andrek and Joule.

I tried and failed to push myself off my pillow, mumbling weakly. "How?"

In a beat, they crossed the room and Joule lifted me into his arms, and the three of us huddled together on my bed. Andrek held my hands and pressed them to his heart.

"We only have a minute," Andrek whispered. "The guards are in the hallway waiting, but they let us come in to get some things."

"V," I managed, clawing uselessly at my foggy brain and mushy mouth.

"She's all right," Joule said, then lowered his voice when Andrek hushed him. "I rigged her home comm a while back so we could talk privately. She's worried, of course."

"I'm not," Andrek put in. "Han's a hard case, but she's a genius. There's no way she blames you for conspiring against the trust. She knows your family too well to believe that."

"But she said—" I choked on the words, and Joule held me tighter.

"We'll figure this out."

"One way or another," Andrek agreed, kissing and returning my hands. "Get some rest if you can, and try not to stress too much. I'm going to bunk with Joule for now, but I'll find you tomorrow. I love you."

"Love you," I repeated.

"Good night." Joule tucked me back into bed and the two of them vanished into the sliver of light.

Sleep claimed me before I could think through anything the guys had said, then I floated through dreams full of memories.

I was in a stroller, and my parents were nearby, locked by a chain to a door and surrounded by handwritten posters. They were facing off with some enemy of theirs.

Mom's chest heaved as she glowered at men in black suits. My dad looked twice the size he should have been. My parents and their friends—the last holdouts against the Royal Corps. The district government had already fallen, turning over control to the RC, but the university where my parents worked wouldn't surrender without a fight.

This was their final stand.

I remembered being hungry, wanting my lunch and a cuddle-nap with my stuffed cat. Faraday hummed some cartoon theme song I loved at the time, keeping me as calm as she could, but I was inconsolable, banging a sippy cup against the tray on my chair.

The suits were surrounded too by local police and private guards whose guns pointed at my parents' knees. This was before Faraday invented the gravdrive.

Mom's arm extended, beckoning me, and I fell forward several years.

My lungs cramped like I'd run for too long uphill. I pumped my arms against damp mountain air, racing to the porch where my parents waved and cameras blinked like out-of-season fireflies.

This was the first day news vans rolled up our drive. A train of them, winding like a lazy snake over the hills. My sister's sudden stardom, which launched a movement and thrust my parents into the scientific spotlight, was actually going to change the world. Her ideas were going to become reality.

We were leaving the wet, wild Pacific Northwest for a sandy corporate republic off the Persian Gulf, and then for Masdar City. As far as the moon for a six-year-old.

I followed her over tidy sidewalks that hugged graceful clay-colored buildings, through science departments, round and round her project boards and the kitchen island. I never left her side unless forced to for tutoring or sleep.

She was my North Star, the free world's champion but my own personal big sister.

I walked the tile hallways of the top floor of the collective with a tote bag bumping into my side. It was my sixteenth birthday, and I had just returned from a weekend working in the diner. Zara's spicy chicken wraps competed with the dusty scent of hopeful applicants who queued outside the doorways. I saw a boy with the bluest eyes, as blue as the seas used to be.

The door behind me opened and closed. Clipped voices bounced raucously through the heavy air and nervous racket of stretched packing tape and rolling wheels.

Everything moved but me.

I was in Faraday's room, gripping loose pages from the bottom of her filing cabinet. Sketched in careful blue ink over smudged crayon doodles.

Memory overlapped with memory. These were my doodles, my shaking forms. Atop them or beneath them, Faraday had brainstormed her first design for her "dream station."

I wasn't ready to leave.

Not without my sister.

Attention: ALL

Subject: Evening Menu

Entrees: Spaghetti with marinara, tofu-pesto meatballs

Sides: Ciabatta and olives, microgreens salad

Dessert Cannoli

CHAPTER TWENTY-FOUR

PLANS WITHIN PLANS

"Formal charges aren't set," my dad told me the next morning. "But the ones ops floated are treason, felony theft, conspiracy to commit theft, withholding evidence, felony hacking, and—" he gulped "—espionage."

Mom couldn't look at me, let alone talk. Neither of them seemed like they'd rested.

"Who gets which charges and to what degree also isn't set yet, but as you three are the first crime ring of lunar citizens, it's difficult to predict much about what your trials will be like, or the range of sentencing you might face."

I waited for him to continue.

"For certain, capital punishment's off the table. Our constitution makes that clear. As is isolated confinement. That's all I can say for now. Catherine?"

Mom was still speechless. And since I was trying to practice what Dr. Fromme said in group last time, about only assigning emotional meaning to our own known reactions, I didn't try to figure out what was on Mom's mind.

I knew my own mind. And my feelings. I was a dense, frozen droplet of fear.

But maybe that was what the moon was too, and it managed to find its orbit and participate and inspire dreams of life.

I didn't exactly shove my fear from my attention, as much

as I moved my thoughts to what was further out.

That took a while because I was afraid of so many things. The RC. Brand Masters himself. Failing my sister. Proving my mother right. Disappointing my father.

Losing Andrek or anyone else ever again.

Hurting V or Joule.

I had this slim layer of wishes way past all that, and I held onto it and breathed deep through my feet, reaching for that far away warmth and light. No matter how distant, it was real.

More than anything, I wished for a chance to turn all this around somehow. It had to be possible, had to be, because for all that Commander Han had accused us of, and for all we were facing, she had not said "the five of you."

Three, not five.

There was still a chance.

"Can I go to work now?" I asked.

Dad grimaced, the lower half of his face wrinkling into stubble. "You have memorial planning first, Han said. She'll inform Chef Maria. It seems you're the only one permitted to continue work shifts."

First? "Did she say where?"

"In comms," he said.

I thought I said, "Great, thanks," but who knew? I was throwing all in with my wish and the prize it had already granted.

This wouldn't be where our mission ended. It was where a slim wish went to get super-powered by the Meat Team.

A wish put us on this rock after all. And Milo and their crew, even Commander Han herself, were the ones my sister handpicked to carry out that wish. Maybe they didn't trust me yet, but I was choosing to trust them.

It was what my sister had done.

Maybe it was reckless, but I marched that wish four steps ahead of my security detail all the way to comms, where my guard posted beside the door and handed me my tablet.

But still, I wasn't my sister. Nobody had elected me

president or signed on to trust me with their lives. So before I barreled ahead with my wish, I needed to check in with my four fellow conspirators, each of whom happened to be looking pretty defeated as they greeted me with loose hugs at the bottom of the ramp.

"Cheer up!" I told them, putting on my most natural smile. "I know it doesn't feel like it, but this is the best thing that could have happened, and the best place for us to be." When nobody responded, aside from rolling their eyes or looking away, I pushed on. "We all trusted Faraday, right? Can you trust me now?"

V's attention snapped to me, and I wondered if she understood what I meant. She must have noticed the bad math already. Andrek and Joule nodded, and Halle only shrugged, but I'd take it.

"I don't think transparency will work this time," V said.

"I'm almost positive it will." Then I added, "but I won't go through with it if you say not to."

"What are you planning to do?" Halle asked.

"She wants to tell them." V gestured to Milo's crew.

"Oh!" Halle's eyes widened. "Ohhhhh!"

I looked between V and Andrek, who had the most at risk if I was wrong, waiting for some kind of answer. "Are we all in?"

Andrek sighed but nodded again, this time with more certainty, and V, however reluctantly, did too. Then, with their approval driving me forward, I walked right over to Milo, with Cheese at their side, and I spilled.

Every detail.

No matter how minor it seemed or whether it was supposed to be a secret.

I admitted to all the things we'd been accused of and more—from Halle's stash of explosives to Joule's reconfiguring of our tablets. But I was most careful to explain *why* we'd done it, and why we couldn't stop yet.

Not yet.

"Except when we couldn't find the spy," I said, rushing

my words to be sure I got through everything, "we tried to talk to people Andrek knew from his time in the RC, trying to find out what they could tell us to help us revive the war crimes accord. All we've found out so far is that the spy was a second wave applicant and works first shift. Oh, and they're white. But the trust is next after Mirage, and we have to get that accord signed before it's too late for it to help. If our president surrenders first, the accord won't apply to us even if we want it to."

I stared at my boots and Milo's, worried that if I looked up at anyone's faces even for a moment, I might lose my nerve. "You knew my sister before me. You believed in her, in this trust. You've got to know what it means to me. You have to know I'll never betray it. None of us would! It's all I have left of her, and she was my whole world. You followed her all the way here, so you must understand. Everything we've done has been to save us from the RC before they do here what they've done everywhere else. And maybe with your help, if you'll help us, we can move all our plans a lot farther."

I finally raised my gaze, and I held my wish as tightly as I could manage and begged reality to keep bending our way.

Milo snorted.

So did Cheese.

Soon the entire comms department had surrounded us, all wild with laughter.

"Stop it," I demanded. "I'm not joking!"

"We know," Milo said. "Why do you think you're here?"

"What?" It was what I wanted to hear, but was I really hearing it, or was I so far gone in my head that I was imagining words in their mouth?

"That's why you're here, Ms. Tanner," someone said from behind the curtain separating this side of the room from the lunar model.

Turkey pulled the curtain back, and I peered behind Milo and Cheese to see who had spoken.

It was freaking Han. On a freaking bean bag.

She'd heard every word I said.

Why had no one mentioned she was here? Why didn't *anyone* shut me up?

"Y-yes, Commander?" I squeaked.

"You sound a lot like her once you let yourself get going," Han said. "And while I appreciate your rather specific confession and for catching us up on all your schemes together, we have work to do and no more time to waste."

"We do?" Andrek managed weakly.

"Prime ministers to convince and armies to infiltrate, as you said. So far as ops is concerned, you three are valuable assets now under the mentorship of my best intelligence team."

"But... But they're the comms department!" Joule exclaimed, obviously stuck on this single point rather than how miraculous it was that my gamble hadn't backfired.

"Same thing," Milo told him.

Han narrowed her gaze on Andrek and V, both of whom still had worry etched across their faces. "Just so you kids know, the only thing Lane said that's news to me is about the explosives. That's quite unexpected. The rest I've known all along."

"If you already knew, then..." V's face changed at least three times as she processed Han's revelations. "Then yesterday at Lane's—that whole tirade at us was a performance! You think one of your guards is a spy."

"I know one of them is, just not which one yet. I would apologize for scaring you, though I believe you all understand I did what was necessary for the sake of us all, playing whatever role I must." Han didn't sound apologetic, but I didn't see why she should. She was doing her job better than any of us had expected. Just like Danny last night, her priorities were exactly in the right place.

"But the fact that you five trusted each other with your histories, and that you worked through them—that stands out to me most," Han went on. "I now understand why Faraday urged me to approve Andrek and Viveca's selections despite your pasts, and why she believed you both belonged here in our trust, perhaps because of your pasts. None of us would ever have gotten this far without knowing when to hide information and when to be transparent."

She patted her bean bag, settling into it deeper. "Sit close to me. I want you all near enough to join these calls if it comes to it. Unlike you, I *don't* need help cutting through low level diplomatic channels, but there's no telling how fast we'll need to adapt our persuasion tactics once we begin."

"No, wait!" Halle gasped. "It was you the others were talking to!"

Han chuckled lightly. "Not only me, but Marshall and Barre. In fact, Viveca's 'contact' is my niece. I honestly thought you would have guessed that. Her name is Han, after all."

"It's a common name," V said defensively, but then she laughed too, her voice cracking with relief. "It didn't ever occur to me we were being watched *and* encouraged all the while."

"Welcome to Faraday's trust at last," Han said. "That's how we operate."

Five calls later, my throat was raw from speaking. I hadn't expected any of the state leaders to want to talk to me, of all people, but it seemed mine was the voice they wanted to hear. Not because I had answers or any power, but because I sounded the most like my sister. Because I was the closest human connection to the dream she'd sold them. So I kept telling the truth, no matter what I was asked.

"My parents? Dad's looking pretty ragged lately. I think he's trying so hard to hold my mom together that he's not taking care of himself. And if you knew my mom, you know how she is. Worried and trying to fix everything that's broken," I told the president of Free France. "And we've got my sister's remains in an urn. It's purple, did you know that?

And a sphere, of course. Her favorite shape."

This president spoke English fluently, so we didn't have to wait for a translator.

"What about you?" the president asked. "Tell me about your life there."

"I'm just a lunch lady. But I've been helping plan a memorial for my sister, to celebrate her life and vision for humanity, not only those of us who made it to the moon."

"My grandmother was a lunch lady at my university. A fierce matriarch she was, besides being a terrific cook. I would love to hear more about the memorial. Perhaps some other time. You sound so tired. How are you, aside from work?"

I breathed out a half-laugh, and I heard the weariness in the noise. "It's been hard," I admitted, not bothering to hide the feelings swelling in my chest and leaking through my words. "I'm so scared, you know? We all are all the time now. I've been trying to grieve and doing therapy for my panic attacks, from when I saw Faraday killed. But it's kind of impossible to move past trauma that's going to repeat itself any day. Like, how can anyone move on when the pain's promising to get worse?"

"Oh, you poor dear," she said, and maybe it was only her politician voice, but she sounded genuine.

Commander Han took over. "That's why we're reaching out to you again personally, Madame President. We understand why you had to pull support from the accord, but that was months ago and under different circumstances. Can we count on you? Will you help us stop the RC's terror and hold Brand Masters to account?"

"I..." the president's transmission muffled for a few seconds while all of us in comms waited in silent hope. "Yes. Free France will sign. And do let me know if there's more we can do to encourage the others to return."

Halle whooped, and Cheese joined her in a dance. The rest of us though, we kept breathing deeply. Carefully. We had a lot more calls to make.

Attention: ALL

Subject: Evening Menu

Entrees: Black beans and yellow rice, moussaka, stir-fried noodles

Sides: Squash casserole, stewed legumes, coleslaw

Dessert None

CHAPTER TWENTY-FIVE

CHANGE OF PLANS

Unfortunately, we weren't able to get the last heads of state on the line before I had to leave for work, so I recorded a few messages with Roast's help in case they needed them while I was gone. Han said I was the only one still working, because the kitchen staff was stretched too thin to spare me. That reasoning seemed thin to me, but I decided to let it go, especially since I didn't want to miss more time in the kitchen.

I fixed my hairnet in place and made for the winding ramp up to the main floor, no longer caring that a guard waited for me at the top. "I'm off, folks. Don't save the world without me."

"Wouldn't dream of it," Andrek called and blew me a kiss.

Chef had me scheduled for memorial prep except for when I served lunch, and the kitchen buzzed with excitement. She called a quick meeting to announce what I was doing to the rest of the staff.

"I want you all to mark these moments," she told us, "and lend your support however you're able. This holiday isn't only about looking back at Faraday's life, but also marching forward with the dreams she shared with us. When faced with danger and terrible uncertainties, we must rise to the challenge with hope and strength. This is what makes us Lunar, and what makes being Lunar something worth striving to be. When we remember Faraday and all those we lost beside her, we will celebrate what they believed in, what we still believe in. And, Lane, we owe you our thanks for the reminder."

"Preach!" Ty hollered, digging an elbow into my side with a smile.

"We are Lunar!" someone from the prep crew chimed in, and most of the staff repeated it back.

The grill cooks clapped, and I blushed as others dipped their heads at me in a sort of bow. I'd never be comfortable being the center of attention, but this wasn't so bad. Everyone wore smiles, whether wistful or broad.

Except Stephan. He had his hands twisted in his apron strings, his curly head drooped low. As I watched him, he glanced my way with bloodshot eyes, and I wondered if he was okay. He'd been much less cheerful the last few weeks. Maybe Chef's speech had him thinking about his siblings? I resolved to check in on him later once I took a break.

"All right, you rascals," Chef said, laughing. "Back to work. Line service in forty minutes."

The kitchen continued to buzz as I gathered and sorted ingredients for the holiday meals. The actual memorial was only one day, but our celebration would last two. Six meals for two days plus four desserts. Everyone wanted to know what I'd decided to make, and nearly all of them had thoughts on how to tweak the recipes further.

I tried to be grateful and accept the advice, but with some saying, "more spices" and others saying "fewer spices" or "*different* spices," it was impossible to apply it all. I ended up babbling and dropping things until Chef saw me struggling to keep the peace, and she sent me to the private dining room I'd used for the tasting sessions.

It felt weird working alone, but I didn't mind it once I got my head in the right zone. I pounded and shaped dough, humming tunes I didn't know the words for but I remembered Khalid singing to my sister. Faraday would have loved my menu, more so that I was making it all myself. I lost myself a while imagining how proud she'd be. The table-tops swiftly filled with soaked beans, batches of dough, piles of spice blends, and cut vegetables and fruits, ready for freezing or storage.

I loaded what was ready onto carts and separated the rest to finish tomorrow or the shift after. If I kept going at this rate, I'd be done much earlier than expected. My arms and back ached in a good way when I bothered to look at the time, realizing I was hours past the end of my shift and had dozens of missed messages.

Andrek found me as I pulled the last unloaded cart from the freezer and wrestled it into place along the wall. "There you are!"

"Hi! Sorry! I got caught up." I spun around to hug him, but the cloudy look on his face stopped me halfway. I dropped my arms. "What's wrong? Something happen with the other calls?"

"Why does something have to be wrong for me to come looking for my girl?" He circled my waist and rested his chin on my head to nuzzle.

"Andrek." I wasn't fooled. Tension radiated off him like fumes. Maybe I should have read my messages before cleaning up.

"I don't want you to worry, all right?" He held me tighter, and I let him. My mind raced through everything that could have possibly gone wrong in the short hours I was happy and not watching. His breath hitched against me like it caught in the zipper of his throat. "I'm going to be busy doing something for Han for a few days is all. Away. I needed you to know."

"Away?" I wiggled free of him, craning to see his eyes and what he hid there, but he turned away from me. "Going on a trip to the beach on your private space yacht, are you?"

"Lane, I... This thing I'm doing for Han, whatever happens or comes out or whatever, you know me. You know us. I need you to remember that, okay? No matter what."

"Us? What are you talking about?" My hands beat against

my thighs as I searched the slant of his shoulders and the invisible weight bearing down there. For some reason I thought of noodles squeezed too thin and tomatoes fuzzy with mold. The single step between us lengthened, and it was all I could do to hold still, to hold on.

Andrek's tablet chirped a message alert, then another as he reached for it, then twice more. Our guards, who stood far back by the serving line, didn't acknowledge us. I guessed being Han's assets had perks.

"I wish I could explain better, but I've got to go. Now. I love you, Lane. No matter what." His hand went to his heart, and he started for the exit.

"Andrek." I forced myself to move, to chase after him, but my feet moved so slow, and my lungs strained inside my ribs. "You can't say things like that and run off alone. Andrek, wait!"

He stutter-stepped, like his legs were arguing with each other, and stopped. Turned. The whites of his eyes were red, and tears lined his thick lashes. I watched the muscles in his jaw clicking as he fought some war inside I didn't understand.

"I won't be alone," he whispered. "Everything's going to turn out fine. The accord's in motion, so all you need to do now is keep going with the memorial."

I couldn't believe this was happening. Where could he go? He couldn't go anywhere, not without me! What did "no matter what" mean? We were stupid to trust Han, to think she'd treat us or him any better than my parents or Brand would. If I hadn't been sent away to cook for the memorial, then I would know what was happening already. I could have stopped it. Was that the real reason I was the only one still working? Han trusted the others with her plans, but not me?

I wanted to grab him and kiss him and make him stay. Anything to stop him from the thing that had him scared and worried. Worried about us. But I couldn't will myself to move closer. He was already far away in his mind, far enough that actually touching him might break reality.

"I hate this!" I waved my hands uselessly in the air at the whatever-was-going-on.

"Me too."

I stayed in the kitchen, just standing there, a long time after Andrek passed through the cafeteria doors. The image of him shrinking as he walked farther and farther replayed in my head. Each iteration made me angrier than the last, until I was bursting with it, explosive.

At the start I was only angry at him. He should have sought me out earlier, told me everything. He had to have known what it would mean to leave me with this muddy confusion and loneliness gnawing at my insides. He knew, but he'd done it anyway. I didn't care that he was doing something for Han, for the trust. I was the trust too!

My anger spread to Commander Han next. She was taking advantage of Andrek, of his loyalty and his history; she must be. She was moving him like a pawn into Brand's line of fire somehow, no matter how much I needed him and how important he was to my family. Didn't that make her like Brand? I wished I'd never said a word to her, that we'd denied everything she said she knew and sent her rolling back to operations empty-handed.

V should have known this would happen. How could someone be so smart, so educated in the machinery of power not see that the moment we let Han in we'd be nothing but extras in our own play? Why hadn't she stopped me? I'd have listened to her. I was furious with V for being weak, for having feelings and crying when we needed her to stay the Strong One and keep us safe.

And that thought made me mad at Halle, for being so stinking cute but not better at consoling V when she was supposed to. At Joule for hoarding so much of my boyfriend's attention that Andrek could do this to me, leaving me in the dark. At my parents, for everything, for driving a wedge between me and Andrek, for treating me like a child but also never treating me like an actual child who was a real person and not just a problem to solve. At Faraday, most of all, for dying and creating this whole mess in the first place.

I stood there, seething at everyone and everything, so long that I lost the feeling in my legs, so long that I wasn't Lane anymore. I was a meat sack of anger and misery and frustration. Eventually a sanitation crew came in, shocking me into myself, and I stalked to my quarters and lay on Andrek's bed, contemplating how much I hated him for agreeing to leave me.

Attention: ALL

Subject: Earth Weather Update

With great sorrow, we share the latest developments of this year's hurricane season: five islands lost in the South Pacific and Indian Ocean; 4 million casualties; 19+ million displaced souls. For more details, please refer to the attached documentation.

—President Marshall

CHAPTER TWENTY-SIX

THE ACTUAL END OF THE WORLD

I dipped out for work early, to miss my parents and their demands, and went straight to the private dining room, avoiding the rest of the staff. Chef was off today, but I expected she'd pop in around lunchtime like usual. I silenced notifications on my tablet so I could concentrate. I didn't want to hear anyone's excuses about Andrek or their updates about plans they were making without me.

It was probably for the best. I needed to stick to what I knew.

Mix the spices. Season with care. Shape the dough and bake it just underdone so nothing got ruined in the reheating.

Nobody needed my questions forcing them three steps backward to explain things to me. And if they did explain—V's method of plunging past all pleasantries or Joule's zillion words a minute, all details weighted equally—what was I going to add besides my worry? What had I ever added? And why did I let myself care so much? It wasn't like they sat around wondering what I thought about them, twisting themselves into knots about being enough, doing enough. They were always enough for each other, while I wasn't even enough for myself.

Stop.

Faraday's voice.

Fantastic. This was happening again.

"What do you want from me?" I yelled. "I'm sleeping now, going to group, and I mostly remember to eat. I'm doing your stupid holiday and everything, so you can leave me alone!"

"I said stop and let me pass."

That was not my sister, and it was not in my head.

It was my mom. What was she doing here?

"I don't care if the room is closed," she said. "I need to see my daughter right now."

I ran to the door and opened it to find my mother pushing past someone with a cart loaded with reserve water crates from the back-storage freezer. Three tablets bulged out of their back pocket. Curious.

"What's going on?" I asked her, but I peered beyond her to see who the runner was.

As their cart collided with the door to the eastern hallway, a hairnet dropped on the ground behind them. Dark curls caught the light as he turned the corner.

Stephan.

"Why haven't you answered your tablet?" Mom looked me over, but for what I didn't know. Her hair was a wreck, grizzled gray strands pointing all directions like they were static charged.

"I've been busy working. Where's Dad?" Why wasn't he with her? And why would Stephan be carting water crates around?

I didn't think he ever got a tablet assigned either, let alone three.

"You missed dinner too," she said and sent her gaze roaming over the tables behind me, stacked high with bain-maries ready for the freezer. I registered what she meant, that I'd been in this room hours longer than I realized. Again.

My shoulder twitched in a half-shrug. "I'm fine here. I'll be finished soon."

"Someone else can do that, Lane." She touched my back, catching me as I tried to turn away. I didn't like the look of her, the storm brewing. "Come home."

"I can't leave things like this. Nothing's labeled. No one else will know what needs to be done with it," I said, but my mind flicked again to Stephan, my thoughts speeding forward. No way he'd suddenly get issued three tablets. Why would anyone need three?

And there was no reason to be lugging the reserve water anywhere, because the whole back freezer was on a lift that went straight down.

Unless he wasn't taking them to the subbasement.

Unless he was stealing them, because *he* was the white, first shift, second wave trustee guy who'd also been sabotaging systems. Probably using those hidden routes through the trust he showed me.

I'd thought he was my friend.

I didn't want to believe this.

But I did.

Because even if he'd played like my friend, Stephan was a brother for real. With his family suffering a world away that he would do anything for. All he had here was work—no friends, no hobbies, nothing.

How could I not have seen it before? He'd been in front of me the whole time.

"They'll manage fine," Mom said, startling me from my thoughts enough to make me wonder how long I'd been staring at the door. "Can you please come home so we can talk?"

"I don't think I can," I told her. "I have to talk to Han right now. I think… I think I know who the leak is. Brand's spy."

"Home first," Mom insisted, and the tone of her voice left no room for argument. "Message her on the way."

I had to quicken my steps to keep up with her, but I managed to type "Stephan from the kitchen is the spy," before reaching the hallway.

Where it was strangely empty. No guards, not even mine anymore, though Mom was just talking to him. Nor the knots of off-shift trustees who tended to mill outside the washrooms and rec areas.

A heaviness moved between Mom and I, but no matter how many questions I asked or how hard I pressed about Stephan being the spy, she didn't answer until we were in our living room. At that point, Han sent me, "I'm on it. Thx."

Mom palmed the door locked and stood with her back turned for a full minute before she heaved a sigh and faced me. "It doesn't matter now. The RC. They're at the shipyard. I need you to promise me you won't leave here until I say it's clear. Keep these doors locked and stay inside."

I shivered, though the temperature was the same as ever. "Mom, I—"

"It can't be like before when..." She stopped herself from saying it, but I knew what she meant. Like Faraday's campaign when I'd snuck out of the collective repeatedly. Like the night she'd died, when I was supposed to be snuggled in our flat, watching my sister accept the election results from a screen. "Promise me, Lane. You'll stay here, no matter what."

Those words again. They stung extra coming from her, though I didn't know why.

"I can't stay," I said. "There's no bathroom!"

"I've got all that covered. Water tubes, protein bars—I know you hate them but they're necessary—dried fruit. You won't like using it, but I've got a bin for waste. Whatever you need, actually need, you'll find packed in the crate stored under my bed. Sanitowels, the works. Rest, play games, do whatever you want, but stay inside. Safe. If we're lucky, this will be over in a matter of hours, days at the most, but you're set up for weeks if need be. Be smart, Lane, and do what I tell you."

I followed her to her bedroom as she talked. She unloaded the crate onto her bed and sorted the packaged meals like a robot while my thoughts whirled a tornado inside me, muddying my capacity to listen.

"Why did you bring this stuff here?" I asked, because what she said didn't make sense. "What about the subbasement? Is that where everyone's gone? That's where we're supposed to be safe, you said. We can wait the RC out there."

She touched me, which I wasn't expecting, and I nearly jerked away out of surprise. Both her hands on my upper shoulders. "There was an incident. Right before I came to get you. We won't be able to unseal the subbasement until it's resolved, so none of the supplies we set aside are accessible."

"So, we can't—was anyone—what kind of—"

"We didn't lose anyone," she told me, holding me still. "But now you *have* to stay here."

"What about you?" I knew full well that I was ignoring other important matters. That the lockdown scheme had failed the very moment we needed it. That she wanted me to barricade myself in our quarters for the unforeseen future. That she still hadn't told me where Dad was.

Mom wrapped her arms around me, close this time, and she felt so much smaller than I remembered her being. Breakable. "I have to go deal with the fallout. I'll be back as soon as I can."

"But what about the peace accord? Can't that help us? Andrek said it was handled!"

"I'm sure I don't know why you're bringing that up now, but please, for once in your life, just—" She released me and shook her head. More white hairs sprang free. "I can't lose another daughter. Keep your tablet near you, but don't watch the feed, okay? And lock the door behind me. Double check it, to make sure. I love you, baby."

Then, like Andrek, she was gone.

I left the door open a while, watching as she broke into a run halfway down the hall.

I locked the hatch door and double checked it, the way she wanted, but I also turned on the home comm and cranked up the volume as I skimmed through my missed messages, waiting and hoping to hear more from Han about Stephan.

The screen lit with an image of President Marshall, a handful of security officers and operations assistants, my father, Andrek, Joule, and Joule's supervisor, all boarding the underground tram.

Andrek had said he wouldn't be alone. No wonder Han wanted to keep me busy, because she was planning to send half my family into the fray.

"The RC has graciously offered to host diplomatic negotiations on their ship, which is where the president and her envoy are heading now," said a husky feminine voice. "Our hopes travel with her and her team that the parties reach a swift and peaceful resolution. We will report all updates as we receive them."

I returned, stunned, to my parents' room and surveyed the piles upon piles of foodstuffs and whatnots. Stephan may have started the stealing and hoarding, but it obviously hadn't stopped with him.

How long had Mom been gathering these things? Did Dad know? Did he help her?

I couldn't believe the RC was here. Really here. In the trust.

I *could*, but it was happening so much differently than I'd imagined, even with V's warnings.

There weren't soldiers swooping down from the sky like last time.

No explosions. No gunfire.

No one screaming and running for their lives.

This was like... when I'd been young and neighbors would pop by for cake and coffee, gently rapping on the back door and leaving their muddy shoes on the stoop. One moment they'd be outside and the next they weren't.

Only I knew the RC wouldn't leave as politely as neighbors, no matter how quietly they arrived.

I couldn't say this was worse, because the last invasion I'd lived through had been a massacre. A nightmare.

This was scarier somehow. Sneakier.

Like it was business as usual, minimum ruffled feathers.

This was how our freedom ended, surrender served on a silver platter, delivered with smiles and apologies for the inconvenience of coming all the way here.

Thank you, sir, we are so pleased to be of service. This thing we built with our sweat and tears, take it. Really, it's no trouble for us to let your spy sabotage our peaceful community. We don't mind in the slightest. We hope we'll be happy and safe being your dutiful servants. Do whatever you like with us.

You think you deserve it, so of course you should have it.

You want it, so it's yours.

We are yours. Everything is yours. The Earth, the moon, the vastness of space.

Take it all.

And me, the youngest, the least of us—my task was to hide, to survive, and to keep my dang mouth shut.

I *wouldn't*.

I *couldn't*.

I already knew how much survival weighed when everything beautiful was murdered.

I swiped at the piles, my arms crashing like bulldozers, sending the collection scattering to the floor. Then I kicked the bed for good measure.

I didn't lock the door behind me when I left.

I didn't even bother to see if it closed.

CHAPTER TWENTY-SEVEN

LIVE TURKEY, DEAD SHIP

I had to stop in the kitchen first, real fast, because I couldn't stand the thought of all my hard work sitting out and going to waste. Maybe it was wishful thinking, but the more I believed there might still be a holiday, the less terrified I was about the RC.

I answered a call I thought was from Milo, but it was actually Cheese and Turkey.

"Why aren't you here yet? We're all in comms," Cheese said.

"I'll be there soon," I told them. "Right after I get all this food put away."

"You're still in the kitchen?" Turkey asked. "Could you grab us some popcorn?"

I laughed awkwardly. "No promises. Hey, why aren't we going to the subbasement? My mom said there was an incident, but that's all I know."

"Lane!" Cheese yelled. "It's so bad!"

"Two water reservoirs got damaged," Turkey said.

"That's six hundred thousand gallons," Cheese explained.

"Spilling out all over the shelter," Turkey finished.

I paused, looking around the freezer as I unloaded, trying to remember if I'd seen the reservoirs in person.

"That's fixable, right? The reservoirs are frozen, so it should all be ice."

"Would've been, yeah. Except the gravdrives got off cycle," Cheese said gravely.

"Meaning they all got turned on at once," Turkey clarified. "Didn't you feel it today? The weight?"

"Anyway, that created a lot of heat," Cheese continued, "so the whole shelter and our siege storage are flooded, almost two meters deep. And we can't access any of the supplies until we find a way to reclaim the water."

"Not to mention those reservoirs are what fed the plumbing. So, like, we're all going to smell extremely bad."

"That's hardly the worst part. The worst part is the RC's here, and we're sitting ducks."

"Oh my god!" I shook my head in disbelief. "What are we going to do? My mom tried to get me to lock myself in our quarters."

"That's what most folks are doing," Turkey said. "But you, grab some popcorn and head down here with us. We'll fill you in."

"Wait! Did Han tell you I found the spy? It's my—it's Stephan Novak. I caught him stealing water a little while ago. I think the RC might be using his family to pressure him."

"He's been a busy boy today," Cheese said. "But yeah, we know. Han's coming by later. She'll deal with him."

"On my way then." I took one last sweep through to make sure I hadn't missed anything, then I raced down to comms.

V and Halle were there with Milo's whole crowd. A cheer erupted when I got spotted on the ramp, and I tossed a sealed bag of popcorn to Turkey. Everyone was smiling except for V, whose arms were crossed tightly.

She cut me off at the landing and scowled, gold painted nails tapping impatiently. "It's about time you showed. Halle and I were starting to think you let your parents lock you away for good. I assume you haven't read our messages."

"Ha!" It was so close to the truth, it hurt more than the face she made. I covered with something else almost true.

"Yeah, no," I said. "Stephan's the spy!"

"Han told us. She's got him under watch for now, so he won't get away with any more sabotage. And you're terrified and simmering toward a meltdown."

I lost my cool. My face certainly must have, because her chin dimpled and that quiver of her lips happened, things I wouldn't have noticed if I weren't hoping for them. If I weren't wearing the same. It was like rocks blocked my lungs from taking a full breath. "Can we skip the part where we're mad at each other for no reason? Just today?"

"What I mean is that I'm scared too. Halle and Milo and their crew are acting like it's a series finale night, so I'm glad you're here. I wanted you here." V rolled her shoulders and took my hand.

"It's starting!" Halle called. "Come on!"

The back wall lit, not quite like Andrek's projector did, but with an array of pictures—no, videos. Six of them, surveilling various places in the trust, including the second and third domes, affectionately labeled "The Orchard" and "Shipssssss."

"What's going on?" I asked V, not whispering but feeling like I ought to be. "What is all this?"

She frowned hard at the screens. "Plan F? Or maybe it should be Plan H for horrid?"

"What were C through E?"

"Wait for allies, hunker down, or feign surrender," she said. "I suppose this could technically be E, with an asterisk."

"What's the asterisk for?" I pressed.

"We're about to watch it."

Turkey dashed in front of the wall, arms outstretched, casting a tall shadow as she bowed. "Ladies and gents, enbies and bents, may I have your attention, please?"

"Freebird!" Cheese yelled and Milo whistled.

Halle burst into applause, and I joined in hesitantly as I fell onto a bean bag. V shot me a look of disapproval.

Turkey laughed then pointed a laser to the video in the far-left corner. "Eleven brave volunteers traverse the tunnel toward the airlock which leads to the hangar bay. They do not all know precisely what they've volunteered for, alas, but let's assume they're brave in other ways."

I saw the presidential envoy, clad in thick white space suits. Andrek was sandwiched between my dad and Joule, guessing by their gaits.

"Next we have the RC delegation in red and black space gear, led by none other than Brand Masters, the Big Bad himself, who exits his armored yacht to greet our intrepid heroes. Let's count his minions, shall we?" Turkey moved the laser point to one soldier at a time. "One, two, three, four. Okay, fuck that, I think there are well over a hundred. So much for a peaceful negotiation, this is a pageant of menace. Why so many to walk down a ramp? Some could've been tidying up or brewing coffee or something."

"The two groups are going to meet in the hangar, then they think they'll be boarding the RC ship," V whispered. "That's not what's going to happen though."

V's hand tightened in mine, and my breath hitched as we stared. Halle jittered on the other side of V, enough to cause her seat to make soft poofing noises like the world's fluffiest drum. We watched as our tiny delegation approached Brand's forces.

Turkey shifted the pointer to the lower row of videos, skipping the last one on the top where I assumed the first two met. I recognized the other two domes' interiors, and an exterior camera somehow captured both from above. It was easy to tell the two apart, because the shipyard dome was open, like a wedge plucked out of an orange. They'd tapped into a satellite for this, I realized.

"What we're waiting to see here is key. The third act turn, as some might call it," Turkey explained.

Steak sucked his teeth and spilled a handful of popcorn. "They'd be wrong though, that would've been sometime this afternoon during the flooding, this is well into—"

"As I was saying...We are waiting to see—" She circled the orchard dome video with the laser, "—nightfall come early. And also," she repeated the motion around the ship-yard's video, "for the seal to seal, the shuttering to shut. And here it goes…"

The trees in the orchard rose like bleachers then started to rotate out of sight. Opaque metal slid into place where the tree sections had been, locking into a smooth floor. The orchard dome had shuttered tight.

"To protect the plants and the dome itself," V whispered.

"That's one," Milo said, their voice breathy as they spoke into a short-wave radio tablet.

"Charges are set," answered a man's voice. "Ready."

I flinched at the word "charges." There was no way any-one messaged me details about all this. It would have been too risky. This was all too risky, but the only thing I could do was watch.

The shipyard dome closed unbearably slowly. We might as well have been watching grass grow. I swore I saw stars twinkling over the horizon. My gaze kept flicking up to the top right corner video, willing the president's envoy to never arrive, to stop and turn back.

Come back, Dad. Andrek. Joule.

What if Brand takes you aboard and you're gone forever?

Are we a trust without our president?

"Shipyard dome has closed," Turkey said. "Call it."

"Brace yourself," V told me. "This will look worse than it is."

Milo held the radio close to their mouth. "And two. Blue-bird, go."

"Now the moment comes, and my heart—I almost can't take it!" Turkey palmed her chest and heaved a sigh. "I hope this goes as planned. Our heroes, here they are now, face to face at last with the corporate king, the spoiler of sustainability, and what will they do? Our valiant presi-dent—aw—she extends her hand. And Brand? He is, literally, folks, lifting his wrist to her. Does he think she'll kiss it? I can't with this guy."

Turkey had a momentary tantrum with the laser pointer

then cleared her throat. "Wait for it..."

Brand's soldiers filed near their ship, taking position on either side of the ramp to wait for the others to pass inside.

V had shut her eyes, but Halle's were as wide as they'd ever been.

"What are the charges for?" I asked at the same moment I got the answer.

What else could they be for? Charges light explosions. Just like this.

There was no sound.

Not from the videos, and not from the others in the room.

There was only light, white and blinding, popping across the top right first and spreading across both rows. For moments too long, that was all I could see, and I was frozen with fear, with loss, with anger. I screamed. I couldn't tell anymore; I couldn't do anything but stare and stare and wait for the light to dim and return my family to me.

Turkey and Milo joined hands with the rest of their department, forming a ring. They started humming something, out of sync and off key.

There was static. It grew over all six videos then resolved screen by screen into something worse than the light.

The shipyard dome appeared to be all right, if singed black.

The underground tunnel, the one our envoy took, however, had collapsed. All the camera showed was rubble and dust.

As the RC's ship came into view, I ran to the wall, searching for my father, my boyfriends. They couldn't be gone. That couldn't have been the plan. The ship itself looked destroyed, the back half of it careening into the black through a gaping hole in the hangar roof. I saw figures floating near the floor, twisted into unnatural poses.

All the bodies I saw wore black and red. I craned my head to search for specks of white, but they were gone.

Gone.

"Where'd they go? Where are they?" I cried and found I

was also crying real tears. They rolled off me in rivers and soaked into my shirt. "Where the hell did they go?"

Halle appeared at my side and wrapped her arms around me. "It's going to be all right."

"How can you say that? They just—they're dead!" I tore myself away from her only to find myself wrapped up again, this time by V.

I didn't want a damn hug. I wanted the dying to stop. I wanted my sister.

"Shh, shh," V said. "They'll be fine. They were ready, Lane. Their suits were armored, equipped with gravdrives. Andrek knew what to do. Any minute now we'll see them. It's going to be all right."

"That's right, folks," Turkey interjected, sliding in front of the wall. She shooed us out of her way. "The fireworks portion of this show is complete. Any second now we'll see our wayward warriors, wounded but not wrecked. Ah, here they come!"

I saw figures hobbling into view in the lower left corner. Black and red, white and red. They limped or dragged each other over the slick metal. Some pulled off helmets as they collapsed onto the floor of the orchard dome.

"My, my, my!" Turkey strutted and gestured wildly. "Didn't we promise you romance? Drama? Foes facing off against uncertain odds? No one can say these players haven't delivered."

"See? They made it," Halle said, though her voice trembled so much it told me she hadn't been sure they would either.

I spotted Joule and Andrek, holding each other, forehead against forehead. My dad too. He was tending to the president, and his hair was a wreck. One of her aides had her pulled onto their lap, and another was tying something around her thigh.

Trust security officers circled nervously as Brand stalked toward them, hands clasped loosely behind his back. He seemed unscathed.

His eyes found the camera, and he turned to holler at his soldiers.

The unthinkable happened.

More unthinkable than this whole year, than anything I'd ever imagined.

An RC soldier slung his shouldered weapon forward. Pointed to the ground and barked something at Andrek and Joule.

Joule rose first, offering a hand to Andrek.

Andrek stood on his own, swatting Joule's arm out of his way. The way he moved—stilted and off-balance—I knew something had happened to his prosthesis. He turned his back on Joule and reached for the soldier who surrendered his weapon.

To my Andrek.

He limped several steps away, approaching the trust security guards as one stepped forward, their long blonde braid hanging from beneath her helmet.

Danny? No, I couldn't believe it.

But there she was, accepting the weapon from Andrek. She pulled the strap around her neck and looked up, straight at the camera.

Then the rifle was in both her hands, the barrel reflecting in her helmet as she aimed.

The image went black.

CHAPTER TWENTY-EIGHT

NO MATTER WHAT VIOLENCE

No matter what, Andrek had said.

No matter what. No matter what. No matter what. No matter what. No matter what. No matter what. No matter what. No matter what. No matter what. No matter what.

But *Danny*? Sweet, agreeable, helpful, *loyal* Danny?

"We expected this," V told me.

Milo agreed. "It had to be done."

"Sometimes violence is the only way," Cheese added. "You know it's true."

I heard them talking, explaining, filling the air with noise. Every precaution taken, they said. All contingencies prepared for. We used what we had. Any later would have been too late. Any sooner would have been too soon. The president would recover, they were sure of it. They were also certain that Brand wouldn't kill the others, that they'd be his hostages as he and the trust attempted to sort out what had happened and who had done it. At least we finally knew who the other spy was, the leak, the mole, the traitor, and it made all kinds of sense, didn't it? As a security officer, trusted by Commander Han so much she was sent to protect the Vice President, Danny would've had far more access and influence than poor Stephan.

But in my head, nothing they said added up.

They couldn't *know*. They'd planned, expected, hoped. Just like they'd planned on having us take shelter in the subbasement and expected help to arrive in time. No one had ever suspected Danny. If they had, she'd have been stopped long ago, maybe even long enough ago to have made a difference.

I hoped too. I hoped that wasn't the last time I'd see Andrek and Dad's faces. Or Joule's. I hoped what I saw didn't mean what I thought it did. Because if any of my fears proved true, then I would never be okay again, not for a second let alone a lifetime. Because if I was wrong to trust Stephan *and* Danny, what else was I wrong about?

Who else?

"Here we go," Turkey said, and the six videos merged into one.

No. No more.

I couldn't bear it anymore.

I also couldn't look away. I didn't dare.

The woman who'd announced earlier, what felt like years ago, took over the screen. She was larger than life, the bust of her as tall as two people end to end, her deep brown skin lit up with lavender light. "Fellow trustees, I have Vice President Barre standing by with updates on the situation with President Marshall's envoy. Vice President?"

The image shifted to Barre, who saluted in lieu of smiling and tucked her hair behind her ears. "The president and her entourage are safe for the time being, and they're recuperating in Dome 2 until we can arrange repairs to the tunnels and ferry them here for medical treatment. In the meantime, we ask that all trustees stay in their quarters when not working. New washroom schedules will be sent following this announcement. We appreciate your cooperation as we resolve this situation."

"Situation?" Cheese exploded. "Washroom schedules?

They're literally trying to brush this invasion away like it's a technicality!"

"You should be glad someone came up with a plumbing work around," Turkey said mildly. "You haven't known stink until you've known recycled air stink without regular showers."

Milo stared at the ceiling as if searching for words.

"We knew they'd do this," V said. "Let's not waste our emotions on met expectations."

"What she said," Turkey agreed. "Oh! I've got an extra camera hidden. I doubt the RC's spotted it yet. We can watch while we wait for official news." She switched to the split screens, but the orchard dome's square remained blank. I tried to will it to life, so I could see what was happening.

"What kind of sick joke is this? These are restricted security feeds!"

My mom. She stepped off the ramp with the expression of a woman who'd seen far more than she could handle.

"That we installed," Cheese said.

"And you let just anyone watch this gross display of violence? Did you enjoy seeing my daughter's heart break?"

"That wasn't real, Mom," I argued, though saying it aloud did nothing to erase what I felt. What we'd all seen. Even if Andrek's ruse was true, that still left Danny's betrayal. "Why are you here?"

"I came looking for you! I went back to our quarters to be with you when... You can't possibly imagine what went through my mind when you weren't there. The way you left everything. And with your father—" She clutched her chest and made a gargled noise. She shook like her bones were gelatin. "I'm calling Barre now and—"

"That won't be necessary." Han and a contingent of security came around the last curve of the ramp.

"Commander, you're just in time!" Mom fumbled with her tablet, squinting at the screen. She trembled and seemed like she was having trouble breathing. "I'm getting Barre on the line and together we can sort out how to recover negotiations. I can't—I can't—"

"I'm sorry, Dr. Tanner. I really am." Han gestured to a guard, who slid a needle into Mom's neck.

Another guard caught her as she slumped.

"Mom!" I yelled.

Turkey and Steak rushed over to help, and Cheese tossed them a bean bag. They lowered her onto it as I reached her side with V.

V checked Mom's pulse, counting quietly. She smoothed hair from Mom's face. "She's sedated, Lane, but her breathing is steady. I think she was having a panic attack before."

"Did you have to do that?" I demanded of Han, surprised by the intensity of my rising anger. "If you'd given us another minute, we could've talked her down!"

"We didn't have another minute," Han said gravely. "We can't risk her telling anyone what she saw, or heard, when she comes to. I'll send a medic as soon as I leave."

"Is it time to suspend transmissions?" Milo asked.

"Almost. Masters will hijack the main channel any moment now. Get ready to move to short wave on my call."

Milo's crew moved as one unit, pulling their tabs into laps and tapping out commands.

Han caught my gaze as I looked up from my mother's too-pale face. *I'm sorry*, Han's expression said, while her mouth said, "I'm afraid you'll think many actions we take in the days to come are distasteful and difficult. I hoped to spare you as much worry as I could by keeping you busy. You've been through so much already. But you need to prepare yourself and steel your heart as much as you can."

She turned her chair to face the whole department. "The RC has, essentially, taken our people hostage and will use them as leverage for their own ends. This revelation about Danny Hetzel is quite alarming. I knew it had to be someone close to me, but I never would have expected it to be her. Luckily, I had the foresight to keep the bulk of our plans under wraps, but even still, we must anticipate she knows about Andrek's duplicity and a great deal more that disadvantages our position. Trust that if violence weren't necessary, we wouldn't consider it, let alone decide on it."

I thought of the explosion that had destroyed the RC ship, spaced a bunch of RC soldiers, and wounded the president. How that had felt. My dad as a hostage. Andrek and Joule, hostages or traitors or spies, whichever. They were under Brand's control regardless. How it felt to see my mom, despite all our disagreements, knocked out.

I hated every single thing about this. "What kind of choices am I supposed to prepare for next? If your secret plans fail, what then?"

"Are we going to have a problem, Lane?"

I tried not to notice her closest guard step forward. Alert.

"I don't know how to prepare without knowing what for. More bombs? What?"

"Is this about your boyfriends? Or your friend Danny?" Han asked. "Because we can discuss Andrek's decision if you want, but that was his to make, and I, for one, am grateful for his sacrifice."

"Sacrifice?" I should have calmed down. I shouldn't have been yelling at Han, but my self-control had evaporated, and my insides felt like they'd melted into goo. "Is that what I should prepare for?"

"Lane understands, Commander," V said, and Halle slipped an arm around me, coaxing me into backing away. "She's just upset. She'll come around."

Han's expression didn't change, but something in the air around her did and her guard relaxed. "I hope so, because I need the three of you on board tomorrow. Meet me in the kitchen as soon as you're ready and calm, so we can discuss what's to be done about these spies."

Attention: ALL

Subject: MCO Relocation

MCO operations in Masdar have been forced to relocate due to intragovernmental pressures amid the recent influx of refugees seeking asylum within the collective. Temporary accommodations have been made, but a permanent residence for our Earth-bound operations has yet to be designated.

CHAPTER TWENTY-NINE

GOOD COOKIES, BAD BARS

Unspeakably horrible things happened in the kitchen overnight. I was grateful none of my coworkers were here to see me deliberately dosing food. Would they hate me for this? Blame me? Would anyone let me back in a kitchen again?

I did what I was told I must, trusting there was no other way.

Hairnet tight, gloves secure. Measure and pour. No tasting, not today.

Stir and shape. Bake and cool. This was what I could do for my sister's dream, and those of us still clinging to it.

Then I thought of Stephan and felt queasy. He didn't know he was caught yet, but this might prove to be the worst day of his already awful life.

Brand's voice blared from the intercom, and it set my nerves on fire.

V, who'd watched me work in silence for hours, inhaled as if the air itself had filled with poison. That wasn't far from true.

"I thought we had an agreement. In exchange for my protection and extensive resources, I was going to allow this social experiment to continue uninterrupted. I'm a benevolent ruler, a loving father, but like a father I cannot ignore willful disobedience. I cannot allow defiance to go unpunished."

He talked and talked.

I worked, wrapping each sticky portion into colorful waxed papers. I couldn't block him out, but I could do this, one sorry snack at a time.

"Your leaders promised me a peaceful transition. That was a lie, whether of ignorance or duplicity, and it makes what must be done next messy and uncomfortable. It's a shame. I was looking forward to us all being friends. One big family reunited."

V slammed her fists onto the counter. It was the first time I'd seen her react to Brand all night. She closed up instantly, smoothing her face the way I was smoothing wrinkles in the wax paper.

"Are you finished?" she asked.

I stacked the wrapped protein bars, willing them to be something else. Anything else. "I hate this."

"I know," she said. "If it's any consolation, so do I."

Brand was still talking, but we were acting like he wasn't. It didn't matter what he said now. He was playing a game with his words, but we were the ones controlling the board. He was just too arrogant to notice.

Halle walked up to us. I hadn't even noticed her entering the kitchen.

"Han's waiting for us," she said quietly, attempting a smile. "Are we ready to go?"

Something in her face—no, something missing in her face. Her sweetness.

What we'd seen had spoiled all of us.

Then I got an idea.

I'd give them a choice. It was the right thing, the human thing, to do.

The trustee hostages would recognize me, and they'd know to choose dessert over the nasty protein bars. They'd pick dessert, and they'd be fine.

Eventually, they might even forgive me for what I almost

did to them.

Some of Brand's soldiers might opt for dessert too, but there would be enough of us to overpower them. There had to be.

"I'll need fifteen more minutes. Twenty max," I answered as I dashed to the freezer, pausing only to set the oven temperature. "Do you want to help, Halle? We're baking cookies."

We rode in a Rolar, a fancy solar-powered rover that was part awesome and part death trap and our only alternative to the tram. It was supposed to fit six, which sounded like it'd be roomy for four, but it was a terrible lie. Each seat was hard molded metal, and mine squeezed my thighs like it was designed for people half my size.

Halle drove. She was the only one of us certified in heavy machinery.

V sat next to her in the front. I was in the backseat with Stephan and crates of medical supplies and water tubes, plus the food crates. He'd asked a lot of questions when we set off—why Halle and V were here, what the trust's plan was aside from delivering lunch, did we know anything about the bombs in the hangar—but V shut off her helmet's speaker, and eventually Stephan stopped asking.

I was glad my own helmet blocked my view of his face. I didn't think I could stand to look at him yet. I couldn't help but think of the hole he'd dug for himself, placing his family above all of ours. It was deeper than he could climb out of alone, but he was alone. So alone, there was nothing left of him to fear.

We'd spent so much energy trying to find the spy, but for all the trouble they had caused, Stephan was a used tissue now, an afterthought, and he didn't even know it. And Danny—whatever Brand held over her must be just as pitiful. Her mother and brother had been lost and probably dead from the attack that killed Faraday, but even if one had survived, they were collective folks, committed to our cause. How could they ever forgive her?

Han's plan to deal with Stephan and Danny seemed more than fair to me, though I dreaded seeing it unfold. I wanted to hate them, but how could I? What wouldn't I have done for my own sister? What wouldn't she have done for me? Even for her memory, I had taken risk after risk.

This ride should have been amazing, like these seats ought to have been roomy. Instead it was a pensive, miserable agony. When we hit a natural ramp with enough speed, we coasted over craters like we were flying. I was too worried to be afraid, and too in my head with doubt to properly worry.

Every second was so dangerous, and anything could happen.

We could still be riding to our deaths.

I imagined Andrek was here in the Rolar with us, and Joule too. Imaginary Andrek gripped my gloved hand in his while Joule regaled us with disturbing details, like *"A speck of dust could puncture our Rolar's hood and rip a suit open or pierce our brains. We wouldn't know it was happening before the air outside leeched in and froze us."* Just for instance.

My mom had been extremely upset to hear Han's plan for us when I checked in on her, back before we started this hellishly beautiful drive of doom. Chef had come to wish us luck, and Milo and Cheese, and their *we're-all-Lunar*s, but the phrase had a new meaning now that I was out here in the black. Now it meant "Do the thing you do; we need you," and I believed it from my whole pounding heart to the tips of my hair.

Dr. Fromme had invited V and me in for a hug with her and Halle. Then Han told us how long we'd have to wait to leave as she checked my tablet and secured it within my suit.

Nobody said goodbye.

It was such a long ride. The sky was so close, spotted with diamonds, as we rolled and bounced over white ridges. We made clouds of dust each time we landed, and I panicked every time, because I couldn't see much of anything out the front window.

I was probably the youngest person in history to experience this. The four of us definitely were. I put a hand on Halle's and V's shoulders, though I couldn't really feel them through the padded suit and gloves.

The orchard dome loomed into view through the clouds of dust.

The approach seemed to take an eternity. The fate of the trust rode along in silence, but I still heard my mom's argument with Commander Han in the room next door ringing in my ears:

"She's my daughter, Han," Mom had said, her voice wrenched with emotion, her fears weighing down each word. "Barely more than a kid! I don't care how much they know or what they've gotten mixed up in. You can't send the youngest of us into known danger."

Han, implacable. Steel. "Danger there, here. They're hardly innocents anymore, not after the lives they've had."

"Not my Lane! She's—"

"You don't honestly think she's untouched by the traumas she's witnessed. You can't do the job you do and believe that."

"I did the best I could to protect her."

"And now I must do the same for all of us. Lane has a vital role to play, one I don't believe anyone else could fill. People know her, and her food. That's critical. And Masters asked for Viveca, your daughter's girlfriend, specifically. Would you rather I send her in alone? Because if I send her with security, he won't let them so much as exit the Rolar."

"Of course not! But you have to know the risk you're taking."

"Believe me, I know. And so do they."

We knew all right. I hoped that mattered.

Attention: ALL

Subject: EMERGENCY PROCEDURE CODE RED

COLONY SECURITY HAS BEEN BREACHED. Hazard gear highly encouraged. Proceed to home quarters immediately for facility reset. Failure to comply could result in severe injury or death.

CHAPTER THIRTY

WHERE GRASS SHOULD GROW

I knew Brand by his voice first, that whine of his couched inside bravado.

He was unabashedly loud, and sharp, as only a cishet man could be. He had the presidential envoy separated, minus Andrek, all lined up to face him.

Guards patrolled the line, weapons ready, though they outnumbered our people ten to one. I tried to keep my gaze low or on Brand, while he pretended he didn't see us, but there was no way he didn't, no way he hadn't heard the honking sound the airlock made when we entered. No way he hadn't noticed the hollow clanking of our boots on the metal floor.

I hated him.

I hated him so much it turned my stomach to have my eardrums touched by his vibrations.

I was going to be sick.

Brand Masters, in the flesh, had all of V's physical poise but none of her grace. None of her beauty. He had a broad but underweight build, a domineering stare beneath thick black hair speckled with gray.

He was shorter than his presence felt, his leathery face creased with lines that snaked like dry riverbeds. Really, he made no sense in person—how sure he was of himself and his greatness—when he was only a little man. A sour-mouthed, red-cheeked, piss of a man who spat when he talked and gestured like he never learned what hands were for.

That hair though. I hated him extra for wearing V's hair. Her monster father.

My sister's murderer.

I couldn't get my helmet off fast enough to take a proper breath, but I managed not to vomit. The noise I made drew his attention.

"Verona, my dear," Brand said, claiming V immediately. "How wonderful it is to see you alive."

V removed her helmet but didn't answer. She looked past him to President Marshall. "I need to assess the wounded and begin treatment for radiation burns. We've brought refreshments. Enough for everyone."

"So cold still. All business. As you were then." Brand acted amused, but I didn't buy it. He was annoyed. He wanted her to pretend this was a happy reunion. Still, he motioned to a soldier who came forward to check our gear. I wondered if they expected more bombs.

As the soldier opened the crate Stephan and I carried and fished around inside, Stephan flinched. He'd been watching Brand like he anticipated something. The soldier waved us on without finding my tablet.

"This must be your paramour, eh? Halle Fromme?" Brand trained his eye on Halle dismissively, then me. "Plus the lesser Tanner girl. Lane the lunch lady. I've heard a surprising amount about you."

Icicles speared through my chest. Whether it was Stephan or Danny telling him about me, Brand would have all sorts of personal information.

I clamped my teeth shut and dropped my gaze, willing him to move on.

I was nothing, no one, I let my posture say.

My eyes shot to Andrek, because of course I knew exactly where he was, in the void I'd deliberately not looked toward, and I knew that he was still armed, still blood-spattered, and still watching me. I wished I could say it was easy to tell if we were still us, but beside Stephan and Danny's betrayals, those promises seemed too far in the past, not in his ice blue stare.

Brand opened his arms wide. Welcoming. "Come here, my boy. Let me thank you for your tireless efforts on my behalf."

Stephan dropped his side of the crate and stepped toward Brand. It seemed like the man was going to hug him, but then he ended up extending his hand at the last moment.

Stephan didn't take it. I got a little thrill from the refusal, as if it were proof of Stephan's humanity, his *him*ness despite his treachery.

"Where are my siblings? Were they... on your ship?"

This nearly ruined me. Stephan had honestly believed Brand would reunite him with his family. That was unbearably sad.

"Of course not!" Brand said. "I wasn't going to bring children on a military mission. Join the others. You'll see them soon enough."

V looped her arm through mine and Halle's and led us to the line of hostages. "Wait for the signal," she whispered. "We need to be ready the moment Han connects you." She knelt to treat the first in the line, a presidential aide.

I dragged the cart further along, grateful for the nudge into action, until Halle picked up the other side. She and I offered cookies or protein bars to the trustees—they accepted the cookies eagerly after a wink from me. Joule held my hand when I passed him, and so did my dad who whispered, "Please be careful," under his breath.

Halle talked softly to each trustee, instructing them to put their helmets on as soon as possible.

"Take heart," Halle told them. "Help is coming."

I hadn't seen Danny among the other trust guards, though I'd looked for her. Maybe Brand had made her change uniforms to match his other followers.

Soon enough, we'd finished with the hostages, and we

gave the crate to a soldier to pass what was left to their fellows.

So much for choice. No cookies remained for the RC.

All around, helmets slid open.

Mouths bit.

Chewed. Swallowed.

I imagined I could hear each morsel grinding between teeth and tongues, slipping down throats into eager intestines.

How much longer would it take? At triple the dosage I normally used for sleep, it should be kicking in any minute.

From the corner of my vision, I noticed Andrek pocketing his meal without opening it. A shiver of relief crawled up my spine.

Brand unwrapped a protein bar but hesitated to eat, used it to gesture instead. "Verona, Verona, Verona," he chanted as he strutted around her.

She was with President Marshall at the far end of the hostage line, pulling her eyelids open and checking for whatever people check for in the semi-conscious.

"You know how I feel about being ignored," he warned.

V stiffened and leaned away from the president. She moved to the next in line, repeating her procedures. She tested for fever and concussion, examined exposed skin for burns.

Brand hovered behind her and finally took a bite.

Crumbs fell onto the top of her head.

Halle nudged me with an elbow. We put our helmets on, securing them to our suits. Most of the trustees had done the same, but Brand wasn't watching them.

"Look at me, child," Brand demanded, and his oily tenor rippled with menace. "I said look at me!"

V turned, her face a blank canvas, then she went on to the final hostage, her gaze sweeping discreetly over me.

I craned my hearing for the message from Han, but my tablet was still quiet inside my suit. Nothing yet. I shook my helmeted head.

"You have some nerve," Brand sputtered, spit flying. "After everything I've done for you, to build us a legacy, to shield you from charlatans who want to use you up for their own ends. You treat me like this, as an enemy. I am your *father*, and I will not be denied!"

He reached for her, his hand like a claw, and I screamed her name.

She whipped around, and, in a blur of motion, she was on her feet. Whatever nonchalance Brand had lost in his annoyance, she had absorbed. She grew taller and stronger as he shriveled.

"What have *you* ever been denied?"

"Everything!" he yelled. "I wouldn't have had anything if I hadn't taken it for myself."

V stowed her tools in the medical bag carefully and scooped her helmet off the ground. "Like my mother, you mean." Her tone was calm but brittle. If she was afraid, and I was sure she was, she'd buried that fear beneath layers of righteous anger.

"No, she—I made her my wife. I gave her the world, like I plan to give you!"

V walked past him like he was nothing and joined me and Halle. "We're done here," she said, taking off toward the airlock. I was in awe of her strength, not letting his twisty words under her skin.

"I didn't say you could leave."

Soldiers stepped into our path and pulled us apart, holding me and Halle tightly but not laying a finger on V.

My gaze roamed to Andrek, though I didn't know what I expected from him at this point. One friend against a hundred enemies might as well have been zero.

V sighed. "Are we your hostages now too?"

"I'm not through talking to you," Brand said. He tried to collect his bravado, but it failed to snap fully into place. "Why do you hate me so much? All I've ever done is love you."

"You've never loved anyone but yourself," V spouted. "Love isn't control. It isn't violent or cruel. It doesn't demand anything in return, let alone try to steal affection."

I heard her words plainly, but they became something else in my head. This was what Faraday meant when she'd complained about our parents. They weren't anywhere near as horrible as Brand, but they sure were demanding. And controlling. That was why it was so hard to believe they loved me, while I could believe and *feel* it from my friends, our happy hand. They didn't ask me to be anyone but me.

"You're on thin ice, Verona."

"I don't care what you think."

"But you care what *they* think?" Brand pointed at me and Halle, and the soldiers pushed us to our knees.

When my joints met metal, I tried not to cry out. The tablet dug into my ribs, but I didn't dare draw attention by adjusting it. At least the helmet hid my tears. V had a job to do, and I didn't want to make it any harder.

Brand strutted closer to V and spun her around, forcing her to look at us being small and helpless. "This one, the doctor's kid, who plays in the dirt. And that one, a damn lunch lady. *They* matter to you? I understood the boyfriend, but these two... They're beneath you!"

"You're wrong." V straightened her shoulders and glared at Brand, unwavering. "They are *not* beneath me. They're beside me."

"I'm the only one beside you!" He shook her as though trying to force her to relent, to see the truth of their connection. "You're always making me chase you, but I know. I know that's your game. There's nowhere left to run, and we can be a family again."

She didn't wrench herself free of his grasp. She barely reacted to him, even as he shook her harder and harder. Again, she looked my way, but I couldn't give her what she wanted yet, even though she'd just given me the whole world, defending me and Halle. Saying we were her equals, that *I* was her equal. Brand was an absolute tool not to notice what love looked like when he was standing right in front of it.

Hold on, V. Just a little longer.

"I didn't raise an ungrateful brat. That was always my money in your pocket as you charged around the world, and you kept taking it. Knowing I could follow every dime straight to you."

Brand went on and on, loving the sound of his voice apparently. I was grateful for that, if only because my tablet was still silent.

Han will come through, I told myself. Our allies had rallied and were going as fast as they could. *It should be any minute now.*

Sweat rolled down my face, fogging my vision through the helmet.

"And that hero of yours, that hippie freak with all her utopian horseshit. She brainwashed you. You *needed* her out of your way to come into your own. I did that for you!" His voice hardened. Iced over. My sister's corpse was a present to his daughter, frozen there in his mind. He understood nothing. "You wouldn't be here if I hadn't paid for your tutors, your degrees, your whole life. Trace the money, baby, like I know you have. So you know how much I love you. How much you need me."

V was shaking on her own now, trembling all over. And when her face turned to me, it killed me that I still couldn't give her the signal. It didn't matter how wrong he was. The words still hurt. I understood her masks better than I ever imagined I could, because it was all right there in front of me. Her desperation to please, to be loved and accepted, to be seen. She was just as insecure as me inside.

But then my tablet vibrated inside my suit, and I nearly screeched. Somehow I stopped myself and scratched at my chest, activating the live call.

Han's voice whispered through, so low no one else noticed. "Wrap it up," she said. "Call's connecting in less than a minute. Milo's got it ready to link into the PA."

V saw me almost freak out and graced me with a tiny nod of her chin.

This was what love looked like. Partnership. Trust.

"I'm here now, baby. For you." Brand brushed a lock of hair from V's cheek.

He was not wearing gloves, I realized with a start. That would go badly for him.

"I want to give you everything you want."

V steadied, mostly. She croaked a little, asking, "Even if I want everything?"

"Especially then," he said with a laugh. "That's how I know you're mine."

A beat passed between them, and I ached to see it. She searched his face openly, hungry to find anything human there but finding only the monster she knew. A tear fell, rolling down her cheek.

"Okay," she said finally. "Dad."

He dropped his hands. His eyes blazed. "Okay?"

"No!" Halle cried, struggling against her soldier's grip. In response, the soldier knocked her unconscious with an abrupt shake that smacked Halle's head inside the helmet.

I was so upset already, seeing V reduced to this charade, that I was numb. She was V, the unbreakable, though I was watching some part of her break with each refusal. At least Halle didn't have to witness it anymore.

This has to happen, I reminded myself. V could do this, and not only because she'd spent two decades exhausting herself to prove she was exceptional.

Because she was. Exceptional.

But, like my sister, V saw what was exceptional about everyone, and she didn't try to stand alone. And unlike my sister, V was getting a second wind.

V looked right at us, through us, but spoke to Brand. He didn't know how many ears listened through my tablet. It must have been in the hundreds by now.

"I'm your daughter. Your heir and legacy. I won't run anymore. Is that what you want to hear?"

I hated this moment for her almost as much as I relished it. *Get him, V. Hook him in his own trap.*

"Of course, it is," Brand said. "Finally!" He hugged her to

his chest, not seeming to care that her arms hung limp at her sides, the helmet dangling. "Of course! Soldiers, stand down a minute and come meet my daughter. She'll be in charge one day."

"I think there's someone else they'd rather hear from," I said, my voice croaking as the soldier holding me tightened their grip.

From within my suit, a child's voice came clearly, then it reverberated through the PA speakers.

"Stephan? Are you there? I can't hear you!"

Stephan, who'd been loitering between Brand and the soldiers, sprang to motion, running to me and yelling. "It's me! Oh my god, I can hear you! Lane, tell her I can hear her!"

"He's listening," I said loudly, then heard my words clip through the PA. "We all are."

"Stephan, the French lady rescued us from the camp! You said the RC would help us, but they lied! But we're all here now. We're going to be okay. They're bringing us food and new clothes too."

I spoke into the tablet, "We're so glad you're safe. And together. It means everything to your brother." Stephan was at my side now, but he couldn't seem to make himself respond, so I explained for the sake of the rest of Brand's soldiers. "Brand promised Stephan his siblings would be safe and cared for. Instead he dumped them in one of his hundreds of labor camps where they're basically starving. How many of you got the same promise for your families?"

"Is that true?" the soldier behind me yelled, their voice breaking.

"Stop this circus act," Brand screamed.

"And Danny, wherever you are," I continued, shrugging off the soldier's grip without resistance. "We have a message from your brother. Go ahead and play it, Cheese."

"Whatever Masters promised you, he lied, Danielle. He's kept me as a prisoner all these months just for leverage over you. I had to—He made me bury Mom in a mass grave."

The soldier behind me dropped to their knees and moaned

so terribly I knew it had to be Danny. Brand was yelling too, but I couldn't make out his words over her sobs.

All the trustee hostages had their helmets on. So did Andrek, but V's dangled uselessly in her gloved hand.

Brand had his arm around her neck, as though he was clinging to the moment when she'd called him "Dad."

"The signatures are in and finalized, and the Free States Accord has ratified the renewal of the United Nations, with full authority to press charges for crimes against humanity," another voice announced through the speakers. The French president. "We've liberated eleven camps today, but this is only the beginning. RC soldiers, if you hear me, your families are now under our protection. If you surrender peacefully, your charges will be much less severe. It is time to choose sides."

The soldier holding Halle stumbled, tilting like they were about to fall.

Then another soldier did fall, sprawling woozily in front of my dad and the president.

"What did you do?" Brand screamed as he clutched V's neck. "Soldiers! Kill them now. Kill them all."

The soldiers still on their feet raised their weapons sluggishly, but their attention was clearly torn between Danny and Stephan's anguish and Brand's rage.

V twisted away from Brand, but he lunged for her, knocking her helmet far across the dome floor.

Then Andrek saluted the remaining camera.

Attention: ALL

Subject: Emergency Procedures

Thank you for your support as we address the ongoing situation in the orchard dome. Until further notice, please refrain from speculation regarding these events, as we will continue to post updates here for all.

—Vice President Barre

CHAPTER THIRTY-ONE

IN HER HANDS

Darkness descended.

My mind skipped, remembering deep in my bones what could happen in the dark.

What dust hid. How fast death appeared. How even survival stung.

A noise unlike any other enveloped us, the murmured whisper of space pressed close to the eardrum.

Han had reset the power. She was here, at last.

A blip only, but the systems couldn't restart all at once.

They cycled up, warming.

Help had come.

Joule and I collided in the dark in our race toward V.

"Don't you dare," she yelled as we both set about removing our helmets to give to her.

"You'll die!" I yelled back, pushing my gloved fingers uselessly at the locking gear on my collar.

"We have less than a minute before the gravdrives shut down, and half that before you freeze to death," Joule argued, using way too many words for how little time we had to act.

"Both of you, move!" came another voice, followed by a heavy shove that sent Joule and me sliding backward over the floor.

In the seconds it took me to recover my footing, the soldier who'd pushed us had removed their helmet, freeing a long, thick braid that tumbled down their back.

Danny! She strapped her helmet over V's head and pushed her face close to the visor.

"Tell my brother I'm sorry," Danny choked. "Tell him—tell him I said to get his ass up here where he belongs."

Emergency lights blinked red, and I caught sight of Brand a few feet away. He screamed as he scrambled to put on his own helmet. Just in time, but it was too late for gloves.

A full minute was more than enough to freeze an appendage. Or two.

The power stayed off for at least that, during which a million things happened.

The gravdrives weakened, first as a hiccup that hopped me upward, then faster as the tug of gravity overpowered the devices' effects.

I was loosed into the air like a flung balloon. We all were.

Some of us kept our wits while most of the soldiers slid into sleep, their motions blurred by the drugs I'd dissolved into their food, exacerbated by the sudden change in pressure.

The hostages took the opportunity of weightlessness to swim further from the soldiers.

Han's security team barreled through the airlock, dozens of them, wearing magnetic boots and armed with electric net cannons. They scooped up the drowsy soldiers in short order, before the repowered gravdrives sent everyone careening back to the metal floor. By the time the lights came back on, Brand was alone, in agony and white-handed, with only one person left at his side.

Andrek, with an RC weapon trained at Brand's forehead.

Han marched over, unfazed by Brand's screaming. "Brand Masters, you are under arrest for war crimes against the free citizens of the Lunar Collective, among many others, in accordance with the Faraday Peace Act of 2056. Do not resist."

"No! That's not a thing—You can't do this to me!" He cast

about feebly, searching for his human shields. "We have an agreement! We—"

Han rattled on, ignoring him. "You have the right to remain silent. Anything you say can and will be used against you in a court of law. You have the right to obtain counsel."

"Verona! Verona, help me!"

And though she did so with a grimace, V put a hand on his back in a gesture of support.

Han cleared her throat, speaking very carefully. "If you would like to assign a power-of-attorney to manage your affairs while you obtain legal counsel, you may name them now."

Brand fumbled on the ground, then tried to get to his feet but couldn't. His face was ashen with pain and shock through the visor. V helped him stand. "Verona Masters—she—I name my daughter."

V took a sharp breath. "I need a second, for it to count for the RC's board."

"Seconded," Andrek said immediately.

"Does everyone mark that?" V asked.

The remaining RC soldiers who could speak mumbled weak assent from beneath the net cannons.

"Commander Han," V said, "if you would be so kind, please release my troops so they can answer me properly." Han must have known this was coming, because her guards released the cannons at once. "As your commander," V went on, "I order your peaceful cooperation. Offer no more resistance to the lunar guards, and I will dissolve your contracts and see you returned safely to your families. Salute if you agree."

Their movements may have been sluggish, but one after another they saluted, standing taller than before.

"Wait..." Brand's face fell even further. He glared at his daughter miserably. "You! Did you just steal the RC? Was this your plan all along?"

V smiled, and it was like a rose blooming.

She didn't answer him. She didn't have to ever again.

"Let's clean this mess up. We've got a while before the others wake," Han said to her guards, who unceremoniously cuffed Brand's ankles and dragged him toward the airlock. Then she drove to where Danny's corpse had fallen and touched the woman's shoulder.

I couldn't hear what she said, but, to me, it looked like forgiveness.

Andrek rushed to me and Joule, while V shook Halle awake. We threw off our helmets and dissolved into a group hug. It was a weepy, wiped out, and wild group hug, full of too-bright laughter and jumbles of words. At least until my dad tapped my shoulder, and we broke apart.

President Marshall hung onto Dad's side.

"Lane, were you part of this? This coup to arrest Masters and take control of the RC?" Dad meant *Were you sneaking around for months behind our backs and under our noses*?

"More or less," I admitted.

"She was, sir," V added, slipping her hand into mine. This time, despite the glove, I felt her squeeze. "We couldn't have done it without her."

"And you, Andrek?" Dad stammered, and now I felt a little guilty, because what he meant was *Were you lying to us all this time*?

"What you need to understand," I said, hoping my brain would catch up with my mouth by the time the next words fell out, "is that we're all Lunar now, and we owe it to each other to stop monsters from getting into our home. We did exactly what we had to do."

"But the RC—" the president started, sounding almost as baffled as Brand had a moment before. "What happens to them? A whole empire won't evaporate on a word."

"It will on mine, because it now belongs to me," V said confidently. "He was too paranoid to appoint a second-in-command, so there won't be anyone to challenge my position. And I have no doubt that once the rest of his soldiers find out the extent of my father's atrocities, particularly against them, they'll be more than willing to help dissolve any holdouts. Then we can let the incorporated states vote to restructure independently."

"Freedom will flow to the people," Halle put in. "Like it should."

"And we can finally build some damn spaceships!" Joule added happily.

Andrek beamed so hard that he looked like he might burst. We all looked like that, really. He wrapped an arm around V and me, pulling us close. "Who needs an empire anyway, when we've got the moon?"

Attention: ALL

Subject: Evening Menu

Entrees: Tofu or black bean burger with caramelized onion

Sides: Fried potatoes and pickles, tomato salad

Dessert Frozen yogurt with fresh strawberry compote

CHAPTER THIRTY-TWO

HONOR AND HOPE

The night before the holiday weekend began, I skipped sleep. The entertainment department hardly needed my help, especially with V micromanaging them, so I spent all night checking the precise order that dishes needed to be defrosted and cooked. Then I zoned out starting fresh prep and tweaking toppings. After that, while I was confident I'd already done this part, I double checked Chef's notes about allergies and sensitivities to make sure I hadn't overlooked any known triggers that could ruin someone's experience.

I hadn't missed anything, and it felt like winning. I didn't know how Chef dealt with making all these decisions for us every single day, but so far I could manage it well enough too, at least in the short term. I let the feeling fill me up, warming me from the outside like toasted bread.

I was Lane, lunar lunch lady and meeter of needs, body and soul.

Ten minutes before breakfast service started, Halle dragged me away from my tablet to walk through the hallways with her and V. "Entertainment's done way more than y'all asked, and you've got to see this for yourself."

The theme I'd proposed, which V agreed suited perfectly, was "From Earth to space." I figured there'd be Earth areas and spacey areas, and some creative range in between.

Instead, entertainment had staged progressive decorations all through the trust, changing throughout the day in every department, main corridor, and bathrooms.

My senses were overloaded the moment I stepped out of the kitchen, so it took me a minute to break down what I saw.

The cafeteria was Earth, like a sunny meadow. My boots scuffed over a narrow strip of grassy turf, and the tables were arranged in a giant arc around the serving line, with extra tables nearby for our buffet style breakfast. A short stage at the center of the room had been made to look like a rock outcropping, speckled with bright moss.

Somehow the light was altered too, pinker, warmer. By the doors, massive tree branch forms drooped from the ceiling, hung with ferns and baskets stuffed with gift bags. Halle and I both took one on our way out—mine held a fidget fish and hers a stuffed cat.

In the hallway, ribbons strung with live flowering plants wove overhead and along the walls, and there were long strips of molded surfaces. I loved what they'd done even more than I'd hated the blank walls before.

"Touch it!" Halle urged. "This one's rough rock and grainy wood, but there's sand and grass and pebbles—it's kind of addictive."

We met V outside a lift to the subbasement. A group of several dozen people with instruments crowded around her as she gave the bands their final schedules. Despite my excitement, my spirits sank thinking of the subbasement underwater, and what that would mean for weeks' worth of meals.

"Joule has a surprise for us," V said. "He's been helping the reclamation crew."

That tracked for me without asking more. He would be the one to turn a flood into a present. Inside the elevator had been made up like a submarine, and when the doors opened, instead of the catastrophe I expected it looked like a calm lakeside. Or at least so long as I didn't stare too hard at the workers still ferrying supply crates out of the water.

"Did I get pretty close?" Joule asked, sliding over the water's surface in a crudely printed canoe. "To your family's old place?"

I picked up a shiny pebble and ran my thumb over its smooth sides, and a bugbot, the kind used in the garden labs, landed on my hand. Even it was decorated, its tiny wings fitted to appear like a butterfly's.

"Pretty darn close," I told him. "I love it."

Joule smiled so wide I could've counted his teeth. "It can't last all weekend, because we've got to get this water back into the recycling system as quick as possible. But while it does, we might as well enjoy it."

My tab vibrated an alarm, telling me I needed to hurry to the kitchen, but I gave all three hugs and cheek kisses before I dashed away.

I oversaw my staff volunteers through every step, watching the grills and ovens, ensuring each item that reached the buffet platters looked and tasted perfect. Live music filtered into the kitchen, and some early risers stood near the serving line to watch people work, but I was too deep in the zone to pay much attention.

It was nothing like before, when the staff treated every idea I'd had like a debate point. No one questioned me or my recipes, not even the schedule. We just worked, side by side, totally committed.

At last, as we laid out the buffet, I let myself take a breath and admire my handiwork. I had served a mildly sweet, lemony bread, shaped into spheres, green tea lattes, raspberry jelly donuts, saffron scrambled tofu, and tempeh sausage.

The cake bread recipe had been one of the first things Faraday taught me to bake on my own. Otherwise there was a mix of our usual fare, from rice with raisins to fried potatoes and plantains.

"Impressive work, sous-chef Lane," Chef told me as she scanned the buffet.

"It really came together." My mind was on the platters, searching for anything that might tumble and fall, but I felt her looking at me.

"Still so modest," she said, patting my back.

All the department heads came to shake my hand before getting into line.

"Outstanding," they said, along with, "Incredible," and, "Such a tremendous achievement." And everyone, even the president on her crutches, came by to thank me—thank *me*!—for pushing forward with the holiday despite all we'd just been through.

"We all did this together," I reminded them, finally understanding what my sister used to say about her own notoriety. How it had never been only her work or ideas, but folks always forgot that and heaped praise on her.

It was ironic that the holiday meant to honor her would be what brought me the closest to finally seeing her through her own eyes. Fitting.

Once the cafeteria had filled with trustees and most were seated with their first plate, I got in the buffet line to make my own. Andrek and Joule tagged along, both having already eaten, then showed me to a reserved table. V stood off the stage, where a science fair of sorts was going on, and beyond that trustees were taking advantage of the cleared floor to dance. I realized then that music and people weren't the only noises I heard, but also wind interspersed with the light drizzle of rain.

My ears and eyes and stomach got so full, I was almost late starting lunch. For that meal, I kept things light and snackable, but filling enough to serve dinner late. Faraday had liked to serve dinner an hour past sunset, that way she could watch the colors change through the windows while we worked, and I tried to hold that timing.

My next round of volunteers helped me heat up everything I'd made ahead of time, mashups of street foods from places that didn't exist anymore, alongside an array of breads, crisps, and dips, with fresh fruits from the garden.

While carrying out dishes to the buffet though, I got sort of lightheaded, and V convinced me to sneak off for a short nap. Seeing as the talent contest would start on stage any minute, and there was no telling how much commotion that would end up being, I took her advice.

"Sweetheart, please wake up. I know you're exhausted, and you can rest more soon. But wake up now. You don't want to miss this. I can't let you miss it."

Mom sat on my bed, a note in her voice I'd never heard before.

"You've been asleep for over five hours, Lane, please." No, I *had* heard it before, just never to me. For me. "I'm so sorry. And I have so much to tell you, but later. Whenever you want. Now, let's get you a quick shower and you can make it before dinner. Your dinner. Oh, Lane! Please wake up?"

I let her tug my blanket lower. "My dinner?"

"Yes!"

I bolted upright. Smelled myself and gagged. "Shower, okay. And crap! I missed lunch. I'm missing everything!"

"Not yet," she promised, grabbing clothes as she pulled me out the door.

The last few days had been so chaotic. Remnants of memories swam back to me, out of order. I walked over empty water tubes and snacks, atop mine and Andrek's castoff clothes.

When we'd returned back to the main dome, Mom had still been in Medical, and that was where Dad ended up too, so Andrek and Joule, Halle and V had all crashed in our quarters until yesterday, and I had never gotten around to cleaning up.

"So, the lunch?" I started, clawing my way to the present. I was in the final rinse of my shower, and Mom handed me lotion and a towel the moment the mist ended. Words were going to be hard for a while. I hoped she remembered to bear with me. "Did...it?"

She laughed. Lightly. It sounded like she'd finally gotten

some sleep too. "It's been the most wonderful day, Lane. I'll tell you while you dress." She laid out clothes, and I worked on not slipping over the floor.

"The food. Lane. *Lane.* What you made. It's been such an experience. The way your dishes honored the lands we lost in the melt while also celebrating the ways people, and cuisines, joined each other after... Everyone is so moved. This is a tremendous accomplishment. You should feel proud. *I* am so proud."

That note was pride. In me! And she wasn't yelling or yell-whispering even, not about me lying to her or sneaking around, not about outright defying her demands to stay home, locked up tight. We were past all that somehow.

Mom talked while I dried and dressed. She told me how worried everyone had been when I didn't wake up in time to oversee lunch, but V had shared my notes, and trustees from all the departments had pitched in. How Mom, and Dad, apparently, got roped in to represent me.

"Except we couldn't. Not really. All we could do is marvel at what you created. This entire day has been the most beautiful and bittersweet celebration. Not only for Faraday, but for everyone we've lost. For all of us who survived. I should never have doubted your talents. Never." She picked up a comb and worked it through my curls. "Your dad's holding our table with your friends, and—Oh my, Lane!"

Our eyes met in the mirror, and her smile was electric. Catching.

"You look stunning," Mom said. "Absolutely beautiful."

I beamed at her as I adjusted the collar of my dress. V picked this out for me ages ago, but I'd never gotten around to trying it on. The navy neckline plunged low, and it was shorter than anything I'd have chosen for myself. The separate collar was stiff and structured, like a halo around my shoulders.

For the first time in my life, I *felt* like I looked like Faraday's sister.

"I'm ready," I told her, accepting a kiss on my cheek before leading the way to the cafeteria.

The trust had never looked so lunar. Extraterrestrial even.

Colored orbs swam over the floor like a lava lamp, but otherwise it was dim and transformed by tablecloths and gently twinkling centerpieces. A rainbow of plants hung from the walls like latticework, and the stage was full of dancers.

My dad was at the table in front of the stage. Milo and crew were with him, along with my friends. Except I couldn't call them only friends anymore. They were my fellow conspirators, my second family. My happy hand.

Joule spotted me first. "Lane's back!"

Andrek jumped up. Whistled.

Halle charged over and pulled me into a seat next to V, who kissed me and whispered, "Good morning, sleepyhead," without a hint of sarcasm.

Our emcees took the stage, shooing the dancers out of their way as they announced the meal. I'd made most of it, but visitors from Guanghan and Blackstone had brought a few other delicacies—alcohol and moon cakes. The lights darkened further, enough that the floral centerpieces glowed, and the emcees led us in reciting the lunar vow once again. This time, I didn't miss a single beat.

Then Vice President Barre had the microphone, and she called for a moment of silence before her speech. "I want to thank everyone, and I mean everyone, for making our first Dreamtide celebration possible," she said, earning a round of applause. "From one child's invention and invitation to dream, we came together and built a community, one that I believe will serve as a beacon for generations to come.

"Let us never forget the brave souls who inspired us on this journey, and let us never forget their sacrifices. But most of all let us remember their hopefulness to imagine a better future, and their audacity to challenge us to see it through. Faraday showed us the path, but her legacy lives on in those of us walking upon it. Happy Dreamtide to us all!"

More clapping followed, and President Marshall gestured

pointedly until V and I took a bow on stage, letting everyone whoop about their gratitude and approval.

The holiday was everything I'd wanted it to be. Moreover, it was everything my sister's memory deserved, and a tribute to all we'd done with her dream so far.

My face hurt from smiling.

Attention: ALL

Subject: Personal Quarters

Please submit requests for new quarters arrangements within the next two weeks, understanding that there are limited appointments for single and family dwellings. Reassignments will be announced at the end of the month, with a week to appeal decisions.

—Dr. Tanner, Planning

CHAPTER THIRTY-THREE

SOON TO BLOOM

When I wandered into the living room a week later, I expected it to be empty, but Dad was sitting at the little table. He watched me intently as I entered, and a moment's panic seized me.

"What's wrong?" I asked. "Are you sick? Did something happen?"

"I'm fine, honey. Don't stress about me." Dad's worry lines deepened as he shifted in the chair. "Why don't you join me?"

On the table beside him, Faraday's urn was propped atop a too-familiar bundle of red fabric. Her wedding dress.

I thought it was gone forever, just like her.

I squeezed my eyes shut as though that could stall the chasm breaking open in my chest, but memory painted my eyelids with sandy landscapes and skyscrapers. No, no, no. I turned to check the calendar on the home comm like I cared. This was what normal looked like, checking news.

The screen format had been updated, with a brand new discussion forum and daily updates for every department. President Marshall had made a full recovery and commended Commander Han for her foresight and valor. V's progress with dismantling the RC had a section of its own too, noting that there would be six separate elections happening on

Earth today, and that two newly independent states had chosen to repurpose their armies toward sustainable infrastructure, rebuilding what the RC had destroyed.

Meanwhile, Brand was back on Earth for his trial. Stephan was there too, ready to testify against him. One monster down, a million more to go.

I noticed there was faux meatloaf for lunch and shepherd's pie for dinner, neither of which I was cooking. No dessert tonight.

This was Day 336 for the trust. But on Earth, it was June 12.

Faraday's birthday.

How could I have forgotten?

I spun to my dad. "How'd her dress get here?"

"Honey..." Dad's voice was wet gravel, too thick and heavy to handle. "Is there anything I can do?"

"No." A log of emotions dammed my throat, and I couldn't—I couldn't anything, but somehow I wound up in my room, busying myself with the most mundane tasks. Dry washing with a sanitowel. Dressing, not thinking. Clean shirt and pants, no uniform. Trying not to remember how Faraday had twirled in that dress. How she'd kissed my cheek and promised I'd be home before lockdown. I laced my boots extra tight.

Just a day, a normal day. I couldn't let a single feeling squirm its way out. This was our new world, far away from the pains of the past. We'd mourned and medicated, or at least I had. Still, every step back to the living room added another pound to my dam.

The rumpled dress, outrageously red, screamed from its too-close-to-her-urn seat. It wasn't the shock of new crimson satin, nor the candied velvet so popular in the corporate states. Her red was smoked paprika and roasted chili, one shade shy of sunrise, and rose petal soft.

It wasn't fair. Even in death, she kept the liveliest colors.

"I'm here if you need me," Dad said.

I dropped into a chair next to him, silent. If I said

anything, I'd crack wide open. My insides would run and drip like egg yolk.

"Your mother, she couldn't—She needs to work to keep her head. You know." His hands wiped at the table like he was petting it. He went on and on, and I tuned him out. The carpet swam into focus, cold folds of gray. Industrial ripples.

At some point, he took my hand, and I let him, though my eyes stayed locked on her urn, on the fabric's reflection, my dad's and mine, in the cool light from the tablet screen.

She was glaring bright, and we were too small, sucked inside. She was more real than ever, and we were faded distortions.

Last year purple streamers had hung all across the front of her fiancés' diner. Khalid and Zara had shut down the whole block, letting buildings full of people spill into the road. I'd ended the evening with my first hangover. My sister had held my hair and sung me to sleep in her softest booth.

"I'll make it up to you next year," she'd said.

Promises. Once so easy.

Dove... I heard her so clearly, but it couldn't be her. It couldn't.

I missed her so much.

The dam hadn't burst, but it leaked through my pores.

"What can I do? Can I—" Dad wrapped bear-like arms around me. "I love you, I love you. I understand," he murmured while his tears rained onto my head.

Faraday's urn, that ridiculous purple sphere, rocked on the table. She'd be twenty-eight today.

I couldn't leave her here anymore. Not in this boring room, not for another day.

I owed her. We all did. We always would.

When Dad released me, I swaddled her urn with the wedding dress, folding her inside. He didn't ask, my good dad, not even when I walked out the door with her. Somehow I knew it would be the last time I called those quarters home, because with her truly gone, I didn't need to live with my parents anymore. Then I carried my sister all the way to the courtyard and slipped inside as someone left.

The courtyard had changed.

Flowers grew where there had only been grass, and potted trees polka dotted up the walls. I wasn't the first to bring an urn or keepsake. Dozens of such mementos circled the largest tree.

It was a cherry, soon to bloom.

I set Faraday carefully next to a ceramic Buddha and whispered, "Happy birthday," but that broke the dam and there was no going back. I surrendered, spilling out a raw torrent of words and ugly sobs.

"Look at that lovely moon, you said. That's where we belong. But it's your stupid birthday, and you're still gone. And I miss you! I'll never stop missing you."

I beat the ground, bruising the tender green stalks, weeping onto the dirt, and wishing the pain would go away. I wasn't surprised when I thought of Danny's ashes and Stephan testifying back on Earth, where the rest of my sister would remain, though instead of anger at them and all the trouble they'd caused, I only felt worse, missing them too.

"Lane?" Someone who looked like a finger-painting of Andrek put a hand on my shoulder. His smoky scent crashed through my fog.

It *was* Andrek. With Joule, V, and Halle trailing after.

My lips trembled too much to know if my smile worked.

They squatted close by on the grass. Andrek's arm pressed around me, and I let my tears flow until I ran dry. My whole body felt liquefied, afloat.

"Happy birthday," Joule said softly, not to me, but to Faraday. "I brought you a present." He dug a food container from his pocket. Inside was a breakfast muffin he'd stuck an electric candle into. The faux flame shivered as he placed it next to her urn.

V placed a hand on my back. "Sing with us, Lane."

They were so sweet and good, but I didn't want to sing. I tried to say so, but only a strangled hiccup escaped.

Halle grinned. "No worries. We'll sing for you."

And they did. It was horrible and off-key and nauseating to hear, but I was so grateful, so spent, that I gurgled a laugh.

I opened my mouth to choke out a thank you, but that wasn't what came out. "You lot are the absolute worst."

"We know!" Andrek and Joule said together.

"Isn't it great? We should never start a band!" Joule added, which set Halle off into giggle fits.

V slipped her hand into mine and looked like she wanted to kiss me, even with my face all wet. "We love you too."

And though I felt a hundred things at once, the bad exactly as bad as the good was good, I managed to stay in the moment, letting all of it wash over me.

Maybe the pain would never go away, and it would smack me sideways every now and then like it had today. But even if the hole grief left never shrank, I was still growing, and that left more than enough space for a whole lot of life.

ACKNOWLEDGMENTS

I especially want to say thank you to my publisher Patricia Veldstra; I wished for a partner like you, and you exceeded my dreams. Your integrity and expertise continue to impress and inspire me. Thank you to my editors, Chris Barcellona and Zanne Klingenberg, for seeing all this story could be and catching my messes, and my many authenticity readers for your diligence and wisdom, as well as We Need Diverse Books, A Novel Mind, Printrun Podcast, and Writing the Other for your excellent guidance and impact on my craft. And thank you Andy Ra for your incredible work turning my vision into a masterpiece.

Most of all I want to thank my beloved partner Derek for holding me together when I fall to pieces and loving every layer of me we discover—without you, I would have no words, and the universe would be much too small. Thank you to our wildly brilliant children for tolerating my brain fogs and story rants, for teaching me how to be a better parent and person, and for believing this story and I needed to be shared. To my dear grandmother Sylvia, thank you for all the books and for sticking around to see me succeed.

Thank you to my amazing readers, critique partners, and support community. There are so many of you I've come to rely on, especially Karen Jialu Bao, Kayla Whaley, Katie Spina, Margie Fuston, Liselle Sambury, AJ Super, Nia Davenport, Diana Pinguicha, Sally Pla, Tina Chan, Madeline Dyer, Jessica Corra, Kaye Watts, Ty Schalter, Jessie Devine, Xiran Jay Zhao, Latasha Holliman, Sarah Porter, Blu McCormick, Stephanie Crane, Jeni Chappelle, and Patrick Hopkins—without your timely cheerleading, sage advice, and steady friendship, I wouldn't be half the writer I am today. And thank you to the authors whose words rooted in my heart: Tom Robbins, Octavia Butler, NK Jemisin, Neal Shusterman, Rivers Solomon, and CS Friedman.

ABOUT THE AUTHOR

JR Creaden (they/them) writes hopepunk speculative fiction for children and adults from an artistic paradise disguised as a suburban house. If spotted in the wild, they're likely singing sincerely to the sky or nearby trees. Please help them find their flip flops.